Finding Danyaal

Zia Ahmad

INDUS VALLEY PRESS

Copyright © 2023 Zia Ahmad

Published by Indus Valley Press
Book design by Zia Ahmad
Cover design and imaging by Zia Ahmad
Copy editing by Kathleen Wilson

Printed in the United States of America

ISBN Paperback:978-0-9847561-2-4

ISBN Digital:978-0-9847561-3-1

ALSO BY ZIA AHMAD

The One Hundred

This book is dedicated to my late husband, Scott—my *noor*—forever in my heart, and anyone facing persecution for choosing whom they love.

"It is against this God who kills that we are fighting and resisting."—Alexia Salvador

PROLOGUE

October 19, 2014

When the call ended with an abrupt click Rami, left shaken, pushed the phone away from his ear and stared at it for a while. It wasn't until the next-door neighbor's dog startled him with a bark that Rami realized how quiet the room had become. The conversation played in his head. All it took was the mention of a name, which triggered a deluge of memories to wash over him like the torrents of an enraged river.

"The name Danyaal rings a bell?" a voice on the other end of the line had said.

Rami lowered himself onto a chair before a mirror and glanced at his reflection. Someone whistled in the empty Chicago street that night. A child started crying somewhere. Inside, the air was still.

He remembered once, as a young boy, watching a group of boys engaged in a heated game of soccer. While trying to snatch the ball away from the opposing player and running toward the goalkeeper, one of the boys slammed head-on into Rami. The impact knocked Rami to the ground. Coiled in a fetal position, he lay there, gasping for air, as the other boys with concerned looks crowded around him. Rami could hear their muted voices urging him to breathe.

Now, decades later, he again found himself fighting to let air in and out of his lungs. Blood pulsated in his temples. His past, sunken deep in the ocean of his memories and the one he believed long gone, had resurfaced from the briny depths.

Rami's mind raced back to the conversation he'd just had and the chilling message it had delivered.

I have Danyaal. Be smart. Follow the instructions if you want to see him again, the jarring voice said over the static phone line. *The time has come to face your sins, to take care of the unfinished business between us.* Rami closed his eyes, remembering.

The events from that terrifying day, over twenty-six years ago, flashed before his eyes: the tears, the fear, the betrayal.

There was another voice Rami had recognized over the phone. It was Danyaal, his once lover.

"Rami? You remember me?" He recalled the voice saying shakily.

"It's me. Danyaal."

Rami opened his eyes and reached for the dresser's top drawer beneath the mirror. He retrieved a photograph and stared at it for a full minute. It was the photo of him with his parents and siblings that used to sit on the shoulder-height china cabinet in the living room of his childhood home in Lahore. The one of Papa, Rami's father, and his mother, Amma, standing on each side of his sisters Saifa and Narin, and Rami in front with his brother Jalil. Rami ran his finger over the image of his younger self, buoyantly posing for the camera. He thought of the many years that had stood between then and now like an immovable object and thought of the past that had come calling—thought of this only chance at redemption.

Part One

Rami and Danyaal

ONE

Seven-year-old Rami heard the word *hijra* for the first time one warm afternoon in late June 1977.

He remembered feeling anxious that day to get to the veranda on the second floor of the house where he had been born in December 1969 to mimic the dance moves from a Hindi film he'd just seen. It was shortly after a disagreement between his parents that resulted in a couple of porcelain dinner plates smashing against the floor. And a familiar sinking feeling churned in the pit of Rami's stomach. That lingering feeling of apprehension, ambiguity, and fragility in the quiet air that usually followed the cessation of Papa's and Amma's loud voices.

Rami tiptoed his way up the stairs. Like many times before, he ensured no one was watching. With a sense of assurance that he had the tune from the film etched in his memory, Rami made his way to the open veranda, looked around, and cleared his throat. He stood in the middle, surrounded by daylight receding from the adjacent walls.

Rami placed his hands on his sides. He took a deep breath and shook his hips slightly to the right. That was when a familiar voice called his name as though through gritted teeth. He barely had time to react before a hand reached from behind and grabbed him by the ear. Rami winced in pain. He turned and came face to face with the piercing stare of Mullah Hafiz.

"Explain yourself!" Mullah jerked the boy closer and whipped his oiled cane in the air.

Mullah Hafiz, a small, roundish man with a gray beard that hid his Adam's apple, came to the house three days a week to tutor Rami and Jalil in religion. He would lecture the boys on the five pillars of Islam—*shahada, namaz, roza, zakat,* and *hajj*—and tell them about the differences between *halal* and *haram,* between what's permissible and what's forbidden. Drinking alcohol, gambling, masturbating, eating the flesh of swine—and singing—were all *haram,* and the list went on. He called them grave sins. Those engaged in these *haram* things would answer to God on *Qayamat*—Judgment Day—he said.

"This is my reward for teaching the word of Allah, you little *hijra?*" A gust of Mullah's breath slammed against

Rami's cheek. "This is how you repay me? By dancing like a girl?"

Mullah squeezed Rami's ear between his thumb and the index finger and said that singing or playing musical instruments were tools of *Shaytan*, Satan. He told Rami they offered no spiritual benefit and instead promoted idle talk, *haram* speech, and falsehood. "There's no decency in oscillating hips this way, especially for boys," he added, scowling at Rami.

"Do *tauba* … repent."

Rami lowered his head and mumbled something.

"Louder!"

"I repent," Rami said, reluctantly.

Rami did not know at the time the meaning of *hijra*—a pejorative term used to address the marginalized transgender community in Pakistan. Nor did he understand why a seemingly innocent act of dancing would unleash such rage in someone. He did understand, however, that the way Mullah Aziz had uttered the word that it was a slur—something unwanted, loathsome, despised.

Later, when Papa heard about the incident from Amma, he laughed wryly. "Such dual standards of that bearded hypocrite," he said. "I saw him entering the cinema the other day to see a racy English film."

Amma slapped her cheek in disbelief. "You mean Mullah Hafiz?"

"Of course, him. Who else?" Papa barked a bitter laughter.

"But everyone in the neighborhood has such respect for him."

"There you have it. There's your card-carrying, self-righteous, hypocritical donkey," Papa said. He wasn't holding back his aversion for Mullah. "Now, what's for dinner?"

When Papa was washing his hands to sit down to eat, Rami saw him shaking his head in dismay. "If there's a God, I'd think he'd have better things to worry about than people singing or eating pork," Rami heard him say.

That turned into an argument between his parents. Rami feared Papa would abandon dinner and come after Amma. But he didn't. In Rami's conscious memory, he not once had seen Papa raise a hand against Amma.

But he had heard, from Amma and Saifa, that things weren't always amicable between his parents, especially after Narin, the second daughter in the family, was born.

When Amma was pregnant with Saifa, they told Rami that Daadi, his grandmother, traveled on an overnight train from Karachi to Lahore a few weeks before the due date. Every morning, she would reach over and run her arthritic hands over Amma's round stomach, gently stroking its firmness. She would then bend and, like a skilled jeweler assessing the worth of a precious stone, survey the shape of her daughter-in-law's pregnant belly. Rami listened to Amma describing how Daadi would raise herself by placing a hand on her hip, the deep lines on her face stretched by her smile. "It appears the first child will be a boy!" Daadi would squeal and nod her head joyously at Papa while offering *mubarak*. Congratulations. Rami pictured the day when Amma, drained of energy and propped on both elbows, gave birth to Saifa. Amma said their heads tilted in wonder when they saw a girl emerge from the womb instead of a boy. Why did Daadi's prediction not come true? Did she neglect to perform *Nazar Utar* with salt and mustard seed? Did she not cast off the evil eye?

"Eight years later, when I was expecting Narin," Amma told Rami one day while slicing onions for dinner, "your Daadi returned, but she didn't caress my belly like before. She didn't labor over the stove to cook *haldi ka* halva." Rami remembered the deliciously nutritious dessert made with turmeric and semolina.

Saifa entered the kitchen and joined her mother in preparing food. While kneading the dough, she said she remembered the night Narin was born. Saifa described how she had stood by Amma's side and wiped her forehead with a wet cotton cloth. She told Rami Amma's hair had been entwined with sweat and drops of moisture clung to the edge of her curled upper lip. And when Narin came out, Saifa said, a hush fell over the room. Eyes lowered under the weight of disappointment. They called off the celebration for the arrival of the expected male heir to carry the family name.

"If they'd had their way, they would've left Narin tied to me with the umbilical cord," Amma said sharply over the sizzling noise of the vegetable meeting hot oil as she tossed the chopped onions into a shallow pan.

For the next several years, until Jalil was born, Rami learned on that day that Papa's mood shifted.

"More evident when a letter would arrive from Karachi." Amma snickered while stirring the gravy. She said that even mundane arguments between her and her husband resulted in her being slapped, her hair pulled, or even being kicked by Papa.

"He made amends sometimes by offering half-hearted apologies, your Papa." Amma gave Rami a thin smile. "Other times, he didn't even bother," she said.

"I'm sorry, Amma."

WHILE RAMI also listened to the tales of his parents having been bright-eyed newlyweds once, he couldn't shake off memories of frequent arguments erupting between them. It appeared as though there was always a trigger that would ignite their disputes: an unsatisfactory meal not cooked to Papa's liking, a critique from his grandmother whispered into Papa's incensed ear regarding Amma's domestic abilities, or simply a disagreement about a television show at dinner time.

And with every quarrel, every plate smashed against the wall, every exchange of hostile glances between Amma and Papa, that sinking feeling rushed through Rami's stomach.

He felt it the first time a blood-curdling scream tore through one late-summer night. Earlier in the afternoon, the sky had transformed into a shade of iron gray. Soon, after a loud crackle of lightning, it poured with sheets of rain and doused six-year-old Rami's hope of sleeping on the rooftop under the starry sky. Heavy-lidded, he could hear the faint sound of crickets chirping in the moonlit night after the rain had ceased.

In the middle of that night, while Rami and his siblings slept in the back room and Amma and Papa were on separate beds in the front, with ample distance between them, a scream shattered the silence. Rami was jolted from his deep slumber. It bore such pain, such anguish, that it sent shivers down his spine. Rami lay awake at first, clutching his blanket in fistfuls until he heard it again.

Then, there was a sound of heavy-footed feet dragging against the floor. It appeared to be headed toward where that unnerving shriek had come from. Rami's sisters and brother jumped from their beds. One of them hurriedly got up and closed the door.

"Be quick," Jalil grunted. "We know what's about to take place out there."

Saifa gave him a stricken look, "Shut your mouth!"

"'Shut your mouth,'" Jalil mimicked her in a whining voice and tossed the blanket to the side. "You just wait. One day, you'd wake up and find me gone from this hell hole!" he spat.

Rami tugged at Narin's sleeve. "What's going on?" he said sluggishly.

Narin pulled him closer. "Cover your ears, Rami," her voice was kind. Then she placed Rami's hands over the boy's ears. "Don't pay attention. Go back to sleep."

"This boy." Jalil gave Rami an anguished look. "Imagine what it'd do to him hearing his parents squabble like this," he said. "Just imagine." Jalil shook his head.

Rami noticed he was trembling. He listened to what his sister had said. Covered his ears, squinted his eyes, and turned the loud voices of his parents quarreling into muffled sounds.

It was Amma who had let out that cry, and it was Papa's heavy steps that had walked toward her.

"What in God's name has possessed you, woman?" Rami heard Papa grumble.

He wondered if it was true. It did sound as though a *jinn* had entered Amma's body: the way she made that frightening sound—slow at first—then raising it gradually to the highest pitch she could muster.

Rami learned later that Papa, a tall, silver-haired man with a timid demeanor and despite his better judgment, had made a significant financial decision without conferring with Amma. Papa had decided to utilize the family's savings and invest in a precarious scheme that offered quick riches. He had dipped into the money Amma had been saving over the years to provide dowries for her daughters' future weddings. And Amma had discovered what her husband had been up to.

"You go on and bury those girls!" Amma wailed. Rami could hear her behind closed doors, even with cupped ears.

From the window to the right he saw the light come on at the house next door.

"Stop making a scene; you'll wake up the neighbors," Papa's voice lowered an octave.

"Let them listen!" Amma went on.

"I'm warning you, woman."

"Let. Them. Listen."

"I swear to God—"

"You robbed my daughters of their futures."

"Stop!"

"You think suitors will come through these doors without a dowry? They're as good as dead. Go ahead and get rid of this burden."

And it was at that moment that Rami felt his heart drop, felt a knot tightening in his stomach. He hunched over and prayed for that sinking feeling to go away.

Papa grunted something back, then started blubbering himself.

The morning after sunrise, Rami was sitting in the kitchen eating breakfast with his siblings when he caught Papa looking over and giving his children a slow, burdened smile. "Don't pay attention to what your mother says," he muttered, sounding defeated. "Saifa and Narin, you hear me? Don't listen to her."

RAMI HAD little knowledge of how Papa, who had Kashmiri blood in him, had ended up marrying a traditional woman like Rami's mother from Delhi, India. Especially at a time—and in a part of the world—where maintaining family ties through arranged marriages was an obvious choice. Rami knew, through Amma, that his parents were born in British India before the partition of the subcontinent into India and Pakistan in 1947. They were both Sunni Muslims. But besides those similarities, Amma and Papa had little else in common.

Rami always wondered if Amma thought Papa was cheating on her with the neighbor's wife, who lived a few houses down the street. And why wouldn't she? With Papa's striking Indian-Aryan looks: fair complexion, slanted nose, hazel-gold eyes, it was no surprise it quickened the hearts of women in the neighborhood. Who could blame them for stopping whatever they were doing and sticking their heads out the windows to catch a glimpse of Papa's alluring face?

Rami remembered Amma, a simple God-loving housewife with long, coal-black hair, a near-perfect round face, and a broad nose above a pouty upper lip, used to stand at the doorway with him next to her and watch her husband leave for work. He knew it was not only to keep the impish smiles of those women in check but also to ensure there weren't any suggestive nods by Papa had he met their gazes. And on mornings when Amma couldn't get away from her household duties, she delegated the task to the young boy.

"It's not that I don't trust him," Amma said one morning upon Rami dutifully reporting back to his mother. "I just don't want your Papa bothered by these unscrupulous women."

"What's unscrupulous, Amma?" Rami looked at her and blinked.

Amma lifted Rami's chin with a finger. "You're young, my boy, to fret about that," she said. "May you never suffer the pain of rejection and heartache."

Rami wondered what Amma felt when she saw the neighboring housewives gawking admiringly at Papa's radiant face, some even lost in reveries of infidelity. Did she feel envious of the unwanted temptation her husband stirred? Did she feel inferior in comparison whenever she walked the streets next to him? Or did she resent him for putting her in that gratuitous position, even detesting him a little for it?

And their respective appearances were not the only differences between Rami's parents. Although not educated in a traditional sense, Amma was acutely aware of the solemn responsibility of praying five times a day, the virtue of obtaining self-discipline through fasting, and the value of giving through *zakat*. She ensured that her children received proper religious education.

Papa's aloofness toward religion, on the other hand, was no secret to anyone. While he never interfered with Amma's ways of ensuring her children did not stray, he would smile demurely when asked to attend the Friday prayer.

"What's the point of reading sections from a book written in a language I'm unable to understand?" Papa had once jerked his head to the left dismissively and said. Rami recalled that his father preferred reading *The Reader's Digest* over the Quran.

One day, Rami walked into the living room carrying a tray filled with teacups for Papa's visiting friends, only to find they had left abruptly.

"They didn't have the stomach to hear what I had to say," Papa grabbed a cup from Rami and took a sip of tea. "They didn't have the *dil*." "The heart."

Rami set the tray on the table and sat across from his father. "Six million Jews died in the Holocaust, and look at Israel is now." Papa waved a hand. "What do we do? Pull each other's legs and drag us down, caught in a net of jealousy. What do Arabs do? Nothing. Nothing but get fat on oil money." He snickered. "From the reactions on their faces, they seemed bothered hearing that." Papa laughed.

Unencumbered by the ire of his colleagues having accused him of being pro-Yehudi, Papa looked at Rami. "Learn this now, my son," he said, "fantasies of moral and religious superiority lead to detrimental consequences for any nation. Remember that, Rami."

Papa was a man whose lifestyle and mindset reflected the Indian subcontinent's colonial past. The British influence had left him keen to look and act modern. Rami's father belonged to the class of Indians who migrated to Pakistan after the 1947 partition, which others often mockingly referred to as *Gora Sahib* or White Master. It was a class that had Indian in their blood but English in morals and values. Rami remembered one of Papa's friends addressing him that way once instead of the usual Sharif *sahib*.

"You can tell a gentleman by his shoes, children," he used to wag his finger at Rami and Jalil whenever they made faces over polishing shoes for school the next day. "Now be good boys and shine these shoes like the boot-polish *wala* at the train station."

"Yes, Papa," they would mumble and lower their heads. It'd usually be shortly before Amma would say something curtly to Papa from the other room, to which he would return an even more curt retort.

One day, while they were arguing, Rami inserted a cassette tape into the tape recorder, raised the volume, and started humming—cutting the sharp voices from the adjacent room. He kept singing to the metaphor-filled poetry and *ghazals* of Ahmed Faraz, Mohsin Naqvi, and Faiz Ahmed Faiz long after the A-side of the cassette had ended.

A WEEK later at school, when Rami's Urdu teacher, Miss Kiran, asked students if they wanted to play *Naghmabazi* or the singing competition, Rami—sitting in the back row— gingerly raised his hand. Miss Kiran was a woman of diminutive stature and a sharp voice. From time to time, if there were a few minutes left before the school-closing bell, she would push back the reading glasses sliding down her beaky nose, gather students with outstretched arms, and moderate a singing match. Essentially, one team would select a theme ranging from love to heartbreak to seasons. A young singer from that team would then perform a song related to the chosen subject. The opposing team had thirty seconds to think of another piece on the same topic. If it failed, the first team would move to the next round with a new song and a fresh theme.

Rami stood before the class at his turn that day and sang a recently-learned song—a piece about longing for spring to return. When he finished, silence enshrouded the room for a handful of seconds before a flurry of high-pitched cheering, clapping, and patting ensued. Many, including Miss Kiran, congratulated Rami on such a performance.

From that day forward, everyone wanted Rami on his team because not only could he come up with songs in an instant, but he could also carry a tune. He would walk up sprightly to the front of the class and warble Noor Jihan, Benjamin Sisters, and Alamgir songs in classical Raga melody.

It was through music that Rami escaped the troubles in his family, that and mimicking dance moves when no one was watching. Once, he stood in the class and sang for half an hour, winning the competition. When Rami told Jalil about it later, Jalil snickered. "Great. Go on and be a Mirasi! What do I care?" His words stung Rami long after he had left the room. The way he associated his little brother in a demeaning manner with the term as less reputable. The word meant inheritance, usually associated with a hereditary group of singers from the Indian subcontinent.

Rami later read that these inheritors of such rich culture were once part of the elite families and that their presence had adorned the courts of the Mughal rulers, the *darbars*. These followers of Amir Khusrow, the subcontinent's most celebrated Sufi musician, succumbed over time to the strict *fatwas* from religious scholars. The resulting socioeconomic turmoil reduced the once-respected title, *Mirasi*, to a *gali*. A slur. Now, the group shied away from its own identity, shied away for fear of people calling them Mirasis.

But Papa never called Rami a Mirasi. He sat the boy on his lap and clapped when Rami sang. Time passed, and despite pleas from Amma, Papa forbade Mullah Hafiz to come to the house after that incident. Rami went on singing, kept mimicking the dance moves without anyone's glaring eyes staring at him, unaware it was only a tiny glimpse into his tumultuous past. He had yet to confront the inner demons that would take root and live inside him for a long while.

Two

One of Rami's earliest memories was the sound of the squeaky brakes on Papa's powder blue Vespa scooter. At deepening dusk, its rustic coil springs would creak, bouncing on the uneven brick pavement as the vehicle turned the tight corner into the mouth of the narrow street leading to the house, and Papa returned home.

There were days, certain ones, when Rami paid particular attention to that high-pitched sound. On these days, Papa had promised to take him to the cinema to see a film. And these were the days when Rami found himself eagerly awaiting the familiar sound of Papa's scooter, ears perked up at any noise resembling it.

Rami would typically begin the morning feeling sprightly after Papa had left and anticipate the film he'd get to see later. He ran around the veranda and imagined the story in his head. He expected action in the middle of a twisted plot and added the sound effects from the side of his mouth: *pew-*

pew-pew for the hero punching the villain, *rat-a-rat-rat* for the machine gun fire, *cluck-cluck-cluck* of a tongue for a horse galloping in a Western flick.

And then, as the day progressed, Rami's excitement-filled heart would make room for nervousness to sneak in. Anxiety set in mid-afternoon. He would fret that a work commitment might have prevented Papa from delivering on his promise. More time would pass, and he would begin pacing between rooms. He'd thrust his head in and out of the kitchen window, look down at the street below, and long to catch a glimpse of the powder blue Vespa.

And at the first sign of the lengthening shadows, Rami took the stairs down, gaze darting back to the front of the street with a dread-filled heart, until Papa's familiar face appeared.

Rami loved going to the movies. He would stand at the cinema entrance with an awe-stricken look and stare at the life-size canvas posters showcasing emotion-filled faces of movie stars painted in provocative colors of amber, blue, and orange. He marveled at the boisterous crowd lined outside the ticket booth window, eager to snatch a pair of tickets to watch its favorite actors in action.

"Rami, you're coming?" Papa would turn around and call out.

"I'm coming!"

"We're going to be late."

"Coming, Papa."

Rami would step inside and take in the smoky aroma lingering in the air, mingled with the irresistible scent of food.

He fondly remembered the marble stairs past the entrance of the Capri Cinema, one of his favorites, aesthetically decorated with a densely-padded, blue-colored stair runner. Dozens of twinkling lights coiled around the cylindrical pillars and elegantly furnished the long walkway. His head would turn while walking past the walls lined with posters of upcoming films encased in glass displays. Inside the hall, Rami walked through the door and was greeted by a large silver screen. The hall was a multi-story structure with a foyer and an upper balcony. A pair of tall, velvet curtains draped the sides of the screen.

Rami went with his father to see American war movies like *Guns of Navarone*, *Kelly's Heroes*, and *Where Eagles Dare*. He'd also seen timeless Hong Kong classics like *Enter the Dragon* and *The Game of Death*.

Rami would sit in front of the massive screen, mesmerized by the cinematic storytelling, compelling drama, and exhilarating action that unfolded before his eyes. Despite being unable to comprehend the English language in which many of these films were produced or dubbed, he was entranced by the sheer spectacle and artistry on display.

But the truth was, his passion for this art form didn't fully emerge until Rami went to see *Kramer vs. Kramer* shortly after his tenth birthday. It was a crisp December evening in 1979 when Papa took him to the Regal Cinema to see the film. To get ready for a six o'clock showing that evening, Rami wore a sleeveless yellow sweater on top of a button-down, floral-patterned shirt and a pair of blue bell bottoms. He remembered cruising on his father's Vespa and hearing Papa brief him on the upcoming movie they would watch together. Papa explained that the film was a poignant portrayal of familial relationships, much like the ones commonly depicted in Hindi cinema.

Rami ran his fingers through fluttering hair in the wind and nodded. He pretended to display enthusiasm for Papa's words, but, in reality, he didn't care. His excitement lay in the prospect of entering the cinema hall, a mere few minutes away.

Shortly after they arrived and had taken their seats, the velvet curtains parted, and the screen was revealed. The lights dimmed moments later. Rami sank deeper into the chair, his heart somersaulting in anticipation. He heard Papa saying he was going out for a smoke. Rami knew his father to be a recreational smoker who smoked maybe one pack of cigarettes throughout the year, if at all. Rami nodded smilingly.

A minute or two after Papa had left, he heard the distinct sound of the movie projector come on. A speck-filled fluorescent light began casting on the silver screen, and preshow entertainment began to play.

Rami had turned his head to the side and was looking for Papa when a trailer for a film, *Cabaret*, came on. His eyes returned to the screen and he saw an image of a woman with a set of deep eyes and a smiling face. She wore a black top suit, a bowler hat, and a pair of fishnet stockings, standing on a burlesque stage. Some in the audience whistled. The music started playing. At first, sitting in the dark, Rami just stared at the screen. Then, he noticed his legs had begun to move with the danceable beats; his arms and shoulders shook involuntarily with the rhythm.

Enthralled, he blinked—and blinked again. He didn't know what to think. What was it he was watching? Rami had seen actors in Hindi movies adorned in colorful costumes perform sizzling dances, but nothing had caught his attention like this. Never before had he seen anything quite this dazzling: the glamourous setting, the lively singing, the exotic dancing. For the first time in his life, Rami willed himself to be lost in a dream where he was on the stage with that woman on the screen. During a couple of compressed minutes, while the trailer played, Rami took it all in and let his heart fall in love with the flamboyant character played by Liza Minelli. It wasn't until Papa's hand tapped his shaking shoulders that Rami realized the preview was over.

"Rami?" Papa said smilingly, holding a box of pastries. "The film is starting, son."

Rami looked at him, inhaled the smell of tobacco filling the air between them, and forced himself to stop moving to the music still playing in his head. Papa reached from across the seat and flung his arms around him. He remarked that he'd remembered the film for which the trailer had just ended initially released in 1972. "This must be the re-release," he speculated, offering Rami a pastry.

The Pakistan Film Censor Board, closely watched by the conservative administration of President Zia Ul Haq, prohibited the re-opening of the movie *Cabaret* in the country that year, despite it being distributed seven years ago under the liberal leadership of Zulfiqar Ali Bhutto. But it didn't matter to Rami. Witnessing all he had was enough to pique his vivid imagination.

THE HOUSE Rami grew up was in a congested neighborhood called Ram Gali in Old Lahore, also known as the Walled City. Papa once told him that before the 1947 partition, several of the city's *mohallas*, or residential localities including Ram Gali, had large Hindu and Sikh populations. Papa also told his son that night a tale of a Hindu jeweler who'd owned the house before Rami's grandfather had taken possession from the departing British rulers. Rami later learned it had been part of his grandfather's resettlement from Delhi to Lahore during one of the bloodiest mass migrations in human history. Shortly after the subcontinent split, millions of Muslims trudged west toward Pakistan. And just as many Hindus and Sikhs started traveling in the other direction.

The night before fleeing the horrifying outbreak of sectarian violence on both sides of the border, Papa said, the jeweler allegedly buried gold, silver, and ruby in the walls, turning the house into a treasure hunt.

"What happened to the jeweler?" Rami, dreamy-eyed, asked.

"It's getting late."

"Papa." He tugged at his father's sleeve.

"Hmm," Papa let out a soft grunt.

"Tell me."

"Well, no one saw him again. Rumor has it the jeweler took the next train out of Lahore and traveled to Amritsar," Papa told the boy. "Now, close your eyes."

Rami dreamt that night of running around the house and treasure-hunting. In his dream, he examined every nook and cranny; he knocked and prodded against the walls built nearly a century ago.

The house was a multistory structure. Across from the front of the house was a brick wall that ran parallel and ended right at the footsteps of the arched wooden doors. After withstanding countless seasons, the doors' aged timber had started to show signs of splits and cracks. The darkened wood still bore remnants of hand-carved florets and sparrows, relics of the artistry of a woodcarver. There were two cast-iron door knocks for visitors. The doors opened to a steep flight of stairs, which Rami had scaled up and down growing up. The staircase ascended to the landing on the first floor, then proceeded to the second floor leading to an open veranda, and finally reached the rooftop. There Rami's family had spent bright winter days basking in the sun and warm summer nights sleeping under the stars.

On the main floor was the kitchen. Two odd-shaped bedrooms and a narrow hallway were on the left, all divided by a Formica partitioned wall painted green. The hall extended inward from the kitchen to the living room.

The living room was sparsely decorated with four rattan-seating chairs around a coffee table. To the right, a row of comfortable chenille cushions adorned a long bench pressed against the smooth surface of the Formica wall. A television set in a mahogany console stood diagonally across from a shoulder-height china cabinet.

Lined neatly on top of the cabinet were framed black-and-white family pictures. In a wrinkled photo of Rami's grandfather, standing next to a British captain, he is receiving an honorary award. Here was a picture of Rami's parents with their young-looking faces, dressed sharply and posing sideways, gazing into space like newlyweds in love. And there was a photograph of the entire family, all standing: Papa and Amma on the sides, Saifa and Narin in the middle, and Jalil at the front with Rami. In the photo Rami's left arm is resting on his hip, with a mischievous smile on his face. His parents are intently looking at the camera; Saifa appears confused, her mouth slightly open as if muttering something under her breath; Narin is smiling.

And Jalil … Jalil is standing inches away from Rami, stern-faced, throwing his brother a sidelong glare.

Narin had playfully suggested Rami pose like this.

"You wouldn't stop talking about her," she had whispered in Rami's ear seconds before the photographer took the photo, "why not pose like her? Like the actress in the movie commercial."

Rami had turned to look into Narin's smiling eyes.

"In truth?"

Narin nodded.

"What about Jalil?"

"You ignore him." Placing her hands on Rami's shoulders, Narin had said. "You do what your heart tells you."

Rami turned his head to the camera, grinningly and imagining he was on a burlesque stage.

ONE MORNING early that following year in 1980, at the onset of spring, Rami played sick. He faked a cough, sniffled a little, and excused himself from attending school. Then, later in the afternoon, after making sure it was just he and

Amma in the house, with siblings at schools and Papa at work, Rami tiptoed his way up to the veranda. He peeped from behind the kitchen door and watched his mother going to lie down for a nap. Before winding up the twisted staircase, he had remembered to grab Papa's bowler hat and Narin's red *dupatta*, a rectangular swath of cloth made of see-through cotton.

It was the beginning of the *Basant* season. With vibrant-colored kites painting the sky, it was a festival of kites and a celebration of the upcoming spring. *Basant* drew hordes of people across the city to gather on rooftops and engage in kite-flying competitions. Kites of various shapes and sizes would flutter across, glide up and down, and engage in intense duels of cutting each other with glass-laced strings. Deep-throated triumphant roars would fill the air whenever its opponent successfully cut down a kite.

Rami felt a lingering chill from the departing winter. He paused momentarily at the last step of the staircase and listened to the stillness around him. He hugged his arms against the cold. Ill-fitted dressed only in knickers and a T-shirt, he took note of the morning sunshine conceding to the afternoon shadows.

He walked into the room to his right and stood before a rectangular mirror that Narin would sometimes use to apply makeup. Looking at his reflection, he put on the bowler hat and noticed that it was bigger than his head, having slid halfway down to his forehead. He tied the *dupatta* around his waist over the knickers. Moments later, he stepped toward the veranda and closed his eyes. He took a deep breath, placed his left leg forward, and felt his calf muscles flexing seconds before spinning in a revolving twirl. Through the eyes of his imagination, he immersed himself in a daydream, embodying the gazelle-eyed actor performing across the veranda that had been transformed into a film set. Adrenaline rushed through his veins; his limbs floated in rhythm to the music playing in his head.

Life is ... chum
Come to the ...

With each stride, each twist of his bare feet, the music inside him got louder until it rose to his lips and spilled over as a hum. He glided with each leap, heavily breathing and singing, feeling as free as a bird, unburdened, soaring through the open sky. The concept of time eluded him; he flew across the veranda. His eyelids flickered; his mouth repeated the handful of song lyrics he could remember. He was no longer feeling cold. A bead of sweat dripped down his forehead and into the neck opening of the T-shirt onto the chest.

Then, suddenly, Rami bumped into someone.

"*Wah, wah!* Bravo!" a voice said tantalizingly. "Such performance!"

Rami bounced back from the impact, stumbled. His eyes sprang open. His heart jumped when he saw Jalil standing before him with his arms crossed on his chest. Jalil was with two other boys his same age that Rami had seen before walking around the neighborhood. The portly-looking boy was Amjad with a round belly and a pair of deep-set, button-shaped eyes. The other boy, Khalid, had droopy shoulders and a narrow freckled face. In Khalid's hand, Rami noticed a stack of thin paper kites of various colors, unaware they had decided to skip *madrasa*, an educational institute that teaches mainly Islamic subjects, and spend the afternoon flying kites on the rooftop.

The music in Rami's head and the humming on his lips came to a screeching halt. The stillness around the veranda had returned, broken only by the faint cawing of a pair of crows—that and the wheezing sound of Rami's panting. His knees felt weak. His startled gaze skipped from Amjad to Khalid to Jalil. He stepped back.

A strained grin smeared across Jalil's face. "Everyone, this is my brother, Rami," he announced crossly.

Someone shouted *Bo Kata*, a victory cry over cutting a kite. A dog had begun howling somewhere.

"Tell everyone what you were doing," Jalil said. He rubbed his chin with his thumb and index finger, head tilted. "Go on."

"I—" Rami began but couldn't complete the sentence.

"'I ... I,'" Jalil mimicked him in a whining voice. "You have no shame left, do you, you little rat?" he spat, his scrutinizing glare settling on Rami's face. "What were you doing scurrying around like a rodent?"

Rami's weary eyes met Jalil's. He lowered his gaze.

Khalid shifted on his feet nervously. "Come on, Jalil," he said. "He's just a boy having a little fun."

"That's an interesting outfit," Jalil said, laughing bitterly and referring to the oversized bowler hat tilted on Rami's head and the red *dupatta* wrapped around his waist.

A palpable stillness pervaded the veranda as if even the air was holding its breath. Some time passed.

"Such a treat! Double the fun. We spend an afternoon flying kites *and* get a glimpse of how my little brother likes to dress up as these days." Jalil snickered.

How long had they been standing there watching me? Rami's head started to spin. He felt his skin shrinking. He wished to run downstairs, slide under the blanket, and draw it over his head. He wished he could escape the weight of those eyes pressing down on him.

Instead, Rami stood there. Frozen.

"Well. Here, then," Jalil was saying. "Shouldn't we all be entertained?" He threw his friends an affirming look; his arms remained crossed on his chest.

Amjad blinked his eyes nervously.

Jalil then tipped his chin at Rami. "Dance for us."

Stunned, Rami gave Jalil a bewildered look. Had his ears heard correctly? Was Jalil asking him to perform in front of everyone?

"Go on. Impress us with some moves. You clearly know how to dress like a clown. Now be a good boy. Entertain us and we'll clap. Come on now. Show us how good you are."

Rami could feel his face burning, earlobes on fire with embarrassment. Jalil was turning red too, he noticed, but with rising anger and with a look of disgust on his face.

"You've made your point, Jalil," Khalid said quickly. "Now come on."

"Dance. For us."

Rami caught Amjad and Khalid exchanging uncomfortable glances.

His legs started to shake. "Stop it, Jalil, I am—"

He was trying to steady himself when Jalil uncrossed his arms and jabbed his finger into Rami's chest, just below the left shoulder joint, which sent him to the floor.

"Aren't you listening?" Jalil barked.

The bowler hat fell off Rami's head and wheeled away.

Khalid moved forward. "You're wasting time, my friend," he said. "We need to get up to the roof, Jalil; otherwise, there won't be many kites left to fly."

Jalil stood there awhile and stared at Rami with an unblinking gaze. Rami felt the coldness of the concrete seeping into his back. His ears rang, pulse fluttered. Through teary-eyed vision, he propped on his elbows and saw Jalil leaning over and wagging his finger. He was saying something in a muted tone through gritted teeth; flecks of saliva flew from his mouth and landed on Rami's face. Rami blinked. He wondered what Jalil was saying because he hadn't heard him. His stare was focused on another flock of birds in the sky, beyond Jalil's towering profile, soaring through the sky in an upside-down V formation. He especially took notice of the last lagging bird in the V formation. It tirelessly flapped its wings to keep up with the others in the flock and barely made the right tip. Rami wished he was that bird, clumsy but able to fly away—away from here—somewhere with no acute memories, no shame, no fear. A place where no one tormented or ridiculed him for embracing what brought him joy.

Out of the corner of his eye, Rami saw Jalil's friends grabbing him by the elbows and lugging him away. He listened to Jalil's harsh voice gradually receding. Rami forced himself to lie on the gray concrete for a few minutes and waited until they were gone. Then he did what he'd wished for earlier. He propelled himself to his feet and staggered downstairs. Amma was still napping. Rami climbed into his bed, slid under the covers, and pulled it above his eyes and over his shaking body.

Then he cried.

Rami cried tears of anger, grief—and shame. But mostly, he cried tears of disillusionment. How foolish of him to dream this way, to imagine he could have any other life than the life he was born into. What was he thinking?

And how—how in coming years, when a boy named Danyaal would enter his life, Rami would try to convince himself that he hadn't drawn comparisons between his way of life with that of the boy, hadn't noticed the stark disparities in their upbringing, hadn't felt a pang of jealousy strike his chest.

No. Not at all.

THREE

Videogame arcades started appearing in neighborhoods across Lahore by the early 1980s. When one opened near Rami's school, it quickly became his favorite hangout—a dark room crowded with others, where he could stand before a glowing screen and toggle joysticks for hours away from Jalil's accusing stare or Amma's wailing.

It was perfect.

One day, after whiling away the afternoon at the arcade, Rami—walking home with other boys—noticed something odd. A disconnect when others were laughingly discussing female anatomy, and Rami—on the other hand—half listening, found his gaze rested on one of the slender boys walking before him.

Then, a week later, during school recess in sixth grade in 1982, Rami's head turned while walking past a boy sitting on the concrete steps of an arched entryway. His name was Abid. Rami had seen him engaging in sports activities within the school premises before. Abid was about his age. His long hair parted in the middle and dropped to his low-set ears. Rami found his square jaws and large eyes, below the canopy of a pair of bushy eyebrows, quite appealing.

But what got Rami fixated on him that afternoon were not his facial features. It was the outline of the bulge bursting through the inseam of his trousers. Badly distracted, with a fluttering pulse, Rami failed to notice what was ahead and collided with another boy standing a few feet away. Nasir, one of the boys with whom Rami walked to school, laughed and with an arched eyebrow, asked inquisitively what Rami was looking at.

"Nothing," Rami said quickly, startled by the impact and flustered for being caught staring between Abid's spread legs.

"Really?" Nasir's curiosity lingered.

"I said it was nothing!"

"Hmm," Nasir's eyes continued to wonder. He followed Rami around. His eyebrows moved up and down rapidly with a smirk. The leering, the elbowing whenever Rami walked past him, continued all day.

It went on like this for a while. Rami's curious eyes would throw secret glances at a boy before quickly flying away, fighting the urge to return. He would then come home, toss the bag in a corner, and sequester himself in a room. Emotionally drained, he would rock back and forth with knees drawn to his chest and wonder what was happening. Why would the sight of a boy send his heart racing? Why were things different for him? Why didn't he laugh just as hard as his mates at racy female jokes? When no answers came to these questions, he'd mutter a verse from the

Quran—usually the one Mullah Hafiz had made him memorize in Arabic without translating the words.

In school, Rami also learned the meaning of the slang *thuka*. Faggot. Then he realized it was *he* they were referring to when his classmates laughingly told homophobic jokes. And, if caught, he could become the target of those jokes— or worse yet—ostracized. With this more rocking back and forth followed, more verses were recited, more asking for mercy through labored breaths ensued.

'*Do tauba!*' Rami recalled Mullah Hafiz's stony eyes looking down at him.

Unable to peel his stare away from other boys— especially after the incident with Abid—Rami thought it wise to suppress these urges, best to elude them, like dodging Mullah's oiled cane.

ONE EVENING, just before nearly finished daylight, Rami, then thirteen, walked down a quiet, tree-lined street with a friend after spending an afternoon at the video arcade. His friend, Rayan, was lanky, with thin limbs, oblique eyes, and large ears. He had a strange laugh, stopping and starting with pauses in between. To a stranger, it would sound like he was having a bad spell of hiccups. Halfway down the street, Rayan flipped open the top of a cigarette pack and eyed Rami.

"Took it this morning from my father's coat," he said laughingly as he slid out the middle cigarette just an inch and brought it closer to Rami.

Rami took the pack and noticed an image of a sailor in the middle.

"If he noticed it missing, he'd think it slipped out of his pocket." Rayan winked. "Wanna try it?"

After a moment of hesitation, Rami agreed to smoke for the first time. He took the cigarette and pressed it between his lips. Rayan fetched a lighter and rubbed its wheel to ignite. Rami stooped forward and hovered the cigarette's tip over the flame for a couple of seconds until it turned amber. It flickered with the burning tobacco eating away the paper. Rami sucked hard on it. A swirling cloud of noxious smoke covered Rami's face. His eyes burned akin to soapy water getting into them. Rami's lungs revolted against the unknown chemicals. He hunched over, coughing, and fought to draw air.

Rayan patted Rami's hunched back. "There now, Rami. There. There." He was again laughing that strange laugh. After a while, after a few more throat-ripping coughs, Rami began to smoke casually, like Rayan, who clearly had smoked a few of these before.

As they resumed walking, approaching the end of the street to turn the corner and break off from each other to go their separate ways, someone screamed.

Rami and Rayan stopped and traded puzzled looks before sprinting toward the piercing scream. They crossed a fence, jumped over a puddle of water, and quickly turned into another street a couple of blocks down. Rami saw Abdul, accompanied by three other boys, walking in his direction. Abdul lived a few streets from Rami's house and was the son of Mullah Hafiz. They were in the same school. But Rami remembered Abdul had stopped attending after the fifth grade. The lore was that Abdul was being home-schooled to become a *hafez*—the one who memorizes the Quran by heart.

Rami noticed a disgusted look sweeping across Abdul's sweaty face seeing Rami approaching. He knew Mullah Hafiz had told Abdul what'd happened a few years back. He was certain Mullah had described in detail to his son, even exaggerated how he, Rami, had been the reason he lost his job. Rami also remembered Abdul storming out of the class once after watching him engage in an intense battle of *Naghmabazi*.

When Abdul was still in school, he would chase after Rami, tease him, call him names like *bacha jamoora*, a slang term used for street urchins who entertained the crowd for a handful of coins.

"Hey, *bacha jamoora*, what song will you sing for us, *bacha jamoora*?" Abdul would mock Rami by covering his left ear with one hand and stretching his right arm at an angle, mimicking a singer belting a classical Raga tune.

Rami had seen Abdul at the video arcade earlier. But he had not found him there when he departed with Rayan. Rami didn't recognize the two boys with him. And he wasn't sure about the third one, the gaunt-looking boy Abdul was dragging from the collar.

"What's going on?" Rayan said pantingly as he approached Abdul.

Abdul was a couple of years older than Rami. He had a thick belly, broad shoulders, a face with deep black eyes, and a pointy nose. His hands were massive for a boy his age. Rami noticed Abdul's jet-black hair, combed back tightly and glistening with a heavy coating of Brylcreem.

"Well," Abdul started, "you won't believe what I caught this *harami*, this bastard, doing."

Rami looked closer at the grim-looking boy slumped in Abdul's grip. He then realized he had seen him before at the arcade. He was quiet and usually alone. Rami recalled him mostly walking around from game to game. He would stand behind a cluster of other boys clapping and cheering at the game player's skills. Sometimes others shoved him, and the boy would stumble farther back. He would then move to another machine and watch the next player engage in the nail-biting game of battling flies falling from the sky. Again, the boy would stand there and mainly observe.

"What're you talking about? Who's he? What has he done?" Rayan peppered Abdul with questions.

Instead of answering, Abdul twisted the boy's left arm behind his back. "You're one of those, aren't you? Aren't you, you little *harami*?" he gritted his teeth. The boy yelped in pain. His eyes turned glossy with tears pooling around the pupils.

"Abdul, please."

"I caught him in the act, you know? He likes touching other boys!" Abdul exclaimed. His right eyebrow raised above his accusing eye and pierced into the boy's face. Rami could see the expression of revulsion twisting the contours of Abdul's face.

Rayan's smile broadened. "Well, well ..."

The unforgiving look on Abdul's face was undeniable. "This filthy rat tried to slide his hands under my pants at the arcade."

Rayan gasped and offered the boy a rueful look.

Rami would later learn that, albeit the boy brushing his fingers against Abdul's arm and smiling at him, it was—in fact—Abdul who had lured the boy. When the arcade manager found Abdul towering over the boy in the bathroom stall, Abdul fled and placed the blame on the boy for being lewd.

"We can't allow his kind to corrupt other boys. He must pay for what he's done," Abdul was saying. It terrified Rami to see the savagery in his eyes. "The question is how. How do we teach him a lesson, boys?" Abdul said with a malicious grin.

Rayan grabbed his chin with his thumb and index finger. "Good question," he said and faked a concerned look.

Laughter erupted.

"Wait. I got an idea!" Abdul flinched as if a light bulb had flickered to life above his head. "Give me your cigarette," he said to Rayan. Rami saw a wave of fear pass through the boy's face.

"No!" the boy screamed. "Let me go!" He tried to break free.

Abdul brought the amber of the cigarette closer to the boy's face. "Hold him tight," he said in an icy voice. "Every time you look in the mirror, the scar on your face from the burned skin will be a constant reminder of the sin you've committed." His upper lip curled into a sneer. "A symbol of atonement when asking God for forgiveness."

Suddenly, Rami felt his stomach turning; his hands shook with anxiety. He grimaced internally at what they were planning to do to that boy. He wondered if they could see the apprehension oozing through his pores like the beads of sweat gathering on his forehead. Rami felt sorry for the boy. He appeared as harmless as he had at the arcade. An urge to rescue him from Abdul and the other attackers grew in Rami.

He had seen Abdul terrorize other boys in the neighborhood. Not to mention Rami's own experience with him. Abdul spared Rami any physical harm because Jalil went to the same mosque where Mullah Hafiz led prayers, and he knew Rami was Jalil's younger brother.

The tension in the air had become as taut as the cables stretched between the poles above Rami's head.

Abdul took a puff. The cigarette sparkled—brightened and dimmed—before he blew the smoke into the boy's face.

"I got a better idea," Rami broached Abdul with his heart pounding in his chest. He couldn't believe he was stepping in to put an end to a notorious bully's behavior. He kept his tone flat, tried desperately to hide the trembling in his voice. Rami flicked the unfinished cigarette to the ground and calmly crushed it under the sole of his left shoe.

Abdul shifted his gaze to Rami. "You? *You*, of all people, have a better idea?" A chortle burst through his nose, sounding as if he had snorted. "Like what? You'll torture him with your lame singing, *bacha jamoora*?"

Rami grimaced internally again and allowed a few seconds for Abdul's insult to pass. He then cleared his throat. "I suggest the punishment should be more severe. The scar from a cigarette burn will heal eventually." He winked at Abdul. "Let's have a bit more fun with him," he said.

With his eyes locked on Rami's face, Abdul opened his mouth to say something, then closed it as if reconsidering his words.

"You know, maybe you are on to something," he finally said. "Suit yourself. Show us what you got." He winked back.

"What's on your mind, Rami?" Others leaned forward; their curious voices buzzed in a low murmur.

"Hand him to me," Rami beckoned with his right hand's index and middle fingers and said. "I'll teach him a lesson." Rayan shoved the boy toward Rami, nearly knocking him to the ground. Rami slid his hands under the boy's armpits and stopped him from falling. He pulled him up.

Abdul stomped with delirious joy and clapped. He stood inches from Rami, his gleaming eyes filled with excitement as if he eagerly anticipated the spectacle of a cockfight. "Such fun!" he squealed.

The problem, of course, was how to discretely indicate to the boy to start running without alarming others. With his petite physique, Rami figured the boy could take off like a speeding train and disappear quickly. Abdul would probably chase him but soon lose interest, he thought. Rami grabbed the boy by the collar and brought him closer. His intense stare locked into the boy's amber-colored eyes. They had only this one chance to make it work. Rami hoped the boy would decipher the unspoken cue and grasp the intended message.

Looking straight at him, making the tiniest motion with the tip of his chin, the irises in Rami's eyes made a barely noticeable twitch to the right, signaling the boy to run in that direction. It worked. The boy's wide-eyed, pleading-for-mercy facial expression softened. They had understood each other. Rami raised his hand as if to slap the boy in the face and loosened his grip. The boy jerked Rami's hand away and dashed in the other direction.

From the corner of his eye, Rami saw their pupils widen, mouths open in disbelief. Their blood-curdling screams filled the air—and Abdul, Rayan, and the other two ran after the boy.

Rami's heart fell. He was wrong. The boy couldn't run fast enough. Within seconds, like bloodthirsty hyenas, all four caught up to him. Rami ran toward them. With the boy back in Abdul's grip, he turned and gave Rami a cutting look.

"I ... I should've known better than to trust you!" he bellowed through labored breaths.

"He slipped away." Rami faked an uneasy smile. "I'll take care of this *harami* now," he said.

Abdul's face twisted once more with frown lines appearing. "He escapes again," he lurched toward Rami with a clenched fist, "and I'm coming after..." he trailed off and bent over to regain his ragged breathing.

Rami took the boy from the others and threw him against an adjacent wall. The boy's back slammed against the crumbling bricks, chipping away some mortar. Rami's right forearm squeezed the boy's barely visible Adam's apple; their eyes locked again.

Rami could feel the boy's look boring deep into his face, as though trying to read something, as though wondering why Rami had let him go in the first place. He was observing

Rami, but not through the eyes of a stranger. Rami shuddered. He had a distinct suspicion that the boy was looking into his soul, forming some opinion. Rami blinked, hesitated for a moment.

It was like a window had opened, and the boy had peered inside, uninvited, and had seen all that was there to see, all that Rami had been hiding from everyone else. As if holding a book in his hand, the boy glanced through the passages of Rami's life—recognizing him—acknowledging him.

Rami felt exposed. The muscles in the boy's face had relaxed. He didn't seem scared anymore.

Their lips remained still, but they were communicating, once again, through their eyes. The boy's voice echoed in Rami's head. It said he understood what he saw peeking inside and that he and Rami were bound together by the same struggle in life.

Bound together?

The boy said to Rami, pityingly, that he empathized with what it was like to be in hiding, to keep these sorts of things a secret.

With a forlorn expression, Rami conveyed that choking him was not what he wished for. The boy blinked and told him it was okay. Rami could hit him—it was okay. It was better he took the beating from Rami than Abdul, who'd bludgeon him to near death.

Rami's brows curved upwards in a slant and conveyed a morose, apologizing expression. The boy blinked again and gave Rami a slow nod.

Reluctantly, Rami clenched his fist and raised his arm. But that was the limit of its range and capability. His limb remained suspended in the air. He sensed the collective eyes of Abdul, Rayan, and the others, eagerly watching him: wide with anticipation first but then narrowing with a scowl spreading across their faces. Rami's forearm released the pressure on the boy's neck. He couldn't do it. He couldn't hit the boy. Rami heard a grumble behind him. He stepped back. Next, he knew, a pair of hands grabbed him by the elbows and shoved him to the ground.

"It was a mistake to let you take charge." Abdul shot Rami a contemptuous look before hurling a punch at the boy's face. The skin around the boy's left cheekbone turned red with the impact.

"Please don't do this!" Rami exclaimed. His knees stung from the fall.

"What's the matter? I'm only having a little *fun* with him." Abdul snickered. "Isn't that what you'd wanted?"

"Abdul, stop it."

"And if I don't?"

Rami's eyes drifted down.

"What're you going to do to make me?"

The silence around them grew with the encroaching darkness.

"You can go now," Abdul's icy voice entered Rami's ears moments later. "Go on and play with a doll or something? Like a girl."

Rami rose to his feet sluggishly, his face cringed with pain. He threw the boy a hollow look. Abdul landed another blow to the boy's face.

His skin must feel the warmth of the blood trickling down his nose; the thought ran through Rami's mind.

Oddly enough, the boy hadn't flinched. His expressionless eyes bounced from Abdul to Rami.

Rami stood there a while longer, knowing he had a choice to lunge and separate Abdul from the boy, intervene, tell Abdul to stop this nonsense. He also had the option to stand up to these bullies for real this time. Stand up for the boy whose misguided, innocent gesture had brought him such emotional and physical pain.

Or he could walk away from this and run.

And that's what Rami did. He ran.

He ran while telling himself that he had tried. *That boy shouldn't have touched Abdul that way*; Rami justified his gutlessness by condemning the boy. *And, in the end, wasn't he just a stranger? There wasn't much else he could have done*; he forced himself to believe that. He tried, desperately, to shrug off the real reason—that he was afraid. Afraid that his secrets could be exposed, the ones that the boy could see so clearly. Also scared of what they would do to him if Abdul and the others found out.

Halfway up the street, Rami came across a dumpster on the side and hurriedly crouched behind it. He turned, and, teary-eyed, peeked around the corner.

Another punch to his stomach, and Rami saw the boy bend—still no sign of a struggle—not even a groan.

That look of resignation on the boy's face would haunt Rami for years.

Like being inside the ring of a boxing match, Abdul held the boy. With his right arm on his back, he pressed forcibly against him. And with his left hand shaped into a fist, Rami watched Abdul pummel the boy's lower abdomen near the bladder. With each blow, the boy's body lurched a little.

Rami stopped watching, turned, leaned against the dumpster, and slid down to the ground with his legs splayed before him.

He closed his eyes.

Later, Rami came to doubt that any prayers could make him feel differently. He came to disbelieve that regular penance would change anything. He was convinced he would have to continue living like this, in hiding. Forever.

But he was desperate to get away from things so gloomy around him. He wanted movement, some action, which would take his mind off his closeted life. Quite frankly, Rami was ready for anything.

Four

Aside from the grim reality of his surroundings, there was another world Rami took notice of, a world unconfined beyond the streets where he grew up, beyond Lahore, beyond Pakistan even. In that world, the first internet domain was registered in 1985; an actor named Rock Hudson had died, succumbing to AIDS in October of that same year. And months later, the Challenger space shuttle disaster occurred in the United States of America in March of 1986.

Closer to home, Rami heard the news of a nearly decade-long war ending. The martial law instituted by Zia-Ul-Haq, decried by many as curbing democracy, was lifted. Zia-Ul-Haq had been a significant player in the Soviet War in Afghanistan. His systematic efforts against the Soviet Union's occupation, rigorously supported by the United States, would result in the Soviet withdrawal from Afghanistan a few years later.

Rami saw news headlines describing the impact of the war in the form of a refugee crisis. Millions of Afghanis were crossing the border, he caught a reporter saying on television, after fleeing their war-torn homeland and hoping to seek asylum in the neighboring country. Rami also read an article about the conflict and how it had resulted in an influx of heroin and weapons smuggled into Pakistan, another unintended consequence of the war that would change the lives of many.

Including Rami's.

For many in the country, it was a time to feel a revitalized sense of vigor and enthusiasm. The awareness of a progressive and modern world had been sweeping across the nation. Rami heard people around him speak of new ideas, art, and technology.

The younger generation of students stepping into academia felt the same adrenaline. Raised under the shadow of authoritarian rule and the constant threat of martial law, the sentiment was strong to look for a new ideology and to challenge the status quo.

The Pakistan Peoples Party, touted as a progressive political organization, was regaining popularity in the country around the same time. It had the strong support of the National Student Federation, a prominent liberal student union in colleges and universities nationwide. NSF was pro-democracy in sharp contrast with its conservative rival, the Muslim Student Federation. It organized rallies across cities and demanded Zia-Ul-Haq step down for taking over the government through a military coup in 1977. Newly enrolled college students were the prime candidates for NSF recruits to participate in PPP's political activities.

On the first day in April of 1986, a Friday, Rami remembered feeling nervous about entering college after completing matric, his ten years of pre-college education. Pakistan's education system at that time followed the British model, where high school ended after grade ten and intermediate college began at grade eleven.

The college he had joined, Forman Christian College, stood on one hundred acres of land along the picturesque banks of the Lahore Canal. An American Presbyterian missionary, Charles Foreman, had founded the college in 1864. Its architecture was reminiscent of Indo-gothic and colonial construction—a mixture of Victorian British and Mughal dynasties.

Rami was exiting the Registration Office with his class assignment sheet when two boys wearing NSF badges greeted him by the stairs with warm smiles. There were several others like them scattered across the lawn, talking smoothly to unsuspecting new students, Rami noticed.

One of the two boys had tousled hair, a pair of deep black eyes, and stubble running along his curved cheekbones. Wearing a blue shirt and fitted black pants, he impressively revealed his thick chest under the shirt that had a couple of buttons opened down from the collar. He introduced himself as Qasim.

The other boy was taller than his companion, a bit goofy-looking, with curly hair and a broad nose. Rami couldn't help but notice a few extra pounds concealed under his loose outfit. "This is Raheem," Qasim introduced him. "We're also students at this college."

"*Salaam* and welcome, brother!" Raheem said enthusiastically and shook Rami's hand with both of his.

Qasim handed Rami a pamphlet. "We're seeking ambitious and passionate students like you," he said in a masculine voice.

Rami glanced at the brochure before returning his gaze.

"Also, students with specific talents," Raheem quickly added.

Rami blinked. "Talent?"

"You know, things you might be good at," Raheem said. Qasim nodded in agreement.

"You have any talents, Rami? Did I say your name right?"

Rami hesitated for a moment. "Well, I like singing."

"*Mashallah!*" "God willed!" Raheem offered high-pitched praise. "So, you sing those gloriously harmonic *Hamd*? Or perhaps *Naa't*?" he said with a wide smile. Asked if Rami sang religious chants praising God or Prophet Muhammad.

Rami cleared his throat. "Mostly film songs and poetry through *ghazals*, actually," he said.

"Oh. Well, so just singing then."

Rami couldn't help but sense disappointment in Raheem's lowered voice. He gave a slow nod, thinking of the countless times he had practiced songs from legendary singers like Mehdi Hassan and Kishore Kumar, wondering why he was suddenly feeling embarrassed in front of these strangers.

"We need singers for our rallies to boost the morale," Raheem said. Rami caught him eyeing Qasim warily. "We could use you."

"What rallies?"

Qasim stepped forward and stood beside Rami. He pointed toward a white tent where several shapes were huddled together. Rami fought the urge to stare at his sculpted physique.

"You see that crowd of people? Go there. There is a group of NSF members who would be happy to answer all your questions," Qasim said gently.

Rami followed Qasim's advice and began moving forward. It was when—halfway toward the white tent—that his eyes fell on a tall, curly-haired boy with green eyes walking past him.

FIVE

The following Monday, Rami was sitting in the college canteen, closer to the kitchen, when he saw him again: the curly-haired boy he'd noticed a couple of days ago.

The canteen was a spacious hall boasting a high ceiling and wide aisles for walking, separated by square wooden tables, plastic chairs sporting shiny chrome legs, and a few benches scattered across. To the left, the west wall had tall rectangular windows overlooking the college grounds. The right wall was bathed in a warm glow of natural light.

Rami noticed the receding rays of the late afternoon sun shining through the dusty windows. Like some celestial deity descending from heaven, they spilled over the black-and-white checkered floor before him.

The canteen bustled with loud chatter. Huddled students filled most tables. At times, their voices rose over each other as they expressed themselves with fervor. Rami could smell the aroma of freshly baked naan, barbequed meat, and buttery patties permeating the air.

Looking past the table in front of him, where a group of students was busy discussing a cliffhanger episode of a television show, Rami glanced at the entrance and saw the boy standing at the door looking in nervously.

The boy's sunlit profile hovered against the peeping slivers of the sunlight, eclipsing it. It created a striking contrast between the illuminated areas and the shadows playing across his face. Clasping a stack of books against his chest, he stepped forward. The light shifted and brought his previously obscured features into view.

Rami saw him lingering by the doorway for a while and took in the uneasy look in the boy's eyes, an image that would remain etched in Rami's memory forever. The boy's face glowed in the flickering light that filtered through the windows from the low-hanging foliage of the salt cedar trees outside. It washed over his glossy skin, accentuating his looks, a look that—Rami thought—could only be from another world: translucent skin tone, sparkling green eyes, broad nose ... rosy lips.

Rami took note of the button-down checkered shirt, ink-blue jeans, and a pair of brown Converse shoes he was wearing. The boy readjusted the slumping set of books against his chest and strolled past Rami toward the kitchen. Rami snapped his ears to the sound of the boy's voice ordering food.

"Two beef patties and a bottle of 7 Up, please."

The boy was digging through his pocket to fish out some cash when a sheet of paper slipped through and twirled down the floor next to Rami's feet. Rami glanced slyly and recognized what it was. It was the class assignment sheet all new students received upon registering for their courses. A nerve-wracking yet enticing opportunity had presented for Rami to approach the boy.

The boy hadn't noticed his assignment sheet lying on the floor. Rami leaned over and picked up the paper. He had already peered at the top section of the document where the boy's name was printed.

Rami got up, cleared his throat. "*Salaam*" was the first word he uttered to the boy. He spoke loudly, inches from the boy's left ear, to cut through the reverberating noise bouncing off the canteen's vaulted ceiling.

Startled, the boy turned and faced Rami, nearly dropping the food tray.

"Danyaal?"

The boy blinked. "Do we know each other?"

"You dropped this," Rami said and met Danyaal's puzzled stare.

Danyaal's eyes flitted from Rami's face to the paper stuck between his thumb and index finger.

"Don't lose it."

Danyaal nodded.

A few seconds passed. They stood there in uncomfortable silence. Danyaal held the food tray in one hand and balanced the books with the other. From the confused look on Danyaal's face, Rami could tell he was contemplating how to take the sheet back from Rami without a free arm.

"There." Rami folded the document in half and slid it inside the cracked edge of one of Danyaal's books.

"It's kind of you," Danyaal's lips moved. He offered a polite tip of his head.

And then he smiled, and Rami saw, for the first time, the distinct crevices etched on Danyaal's cheeks.

Danyaal's luminous eyes were the next thing Rami noticed; they seemed to draw all the light in the room toward them. Danyaal blinked, and, at that moment, Rami saw them vanish behind the shields of his eyelashes. When they re-emerged, Rami found his reflection in the green depths of Danyaal's irises.

He caught Danyaal's gaze searching the crowded hall for an empty table.

"Join me," Rami offered. He pulled out a chair for him and smiled at Danyaal's curious gaze now lingering on his face.

"I'm Rami." He extended his arm after they had taken their seats.

"—I'm Danyaal."

Their first touch, the hand Danyaal offered to shake, had soft skin. Rami felt a sense of self-assurance in Danyaal's demeanor, the way he shook Rami's hand with a warm embrace, squeezing it with just the proper pressure.

"I looked at your name on the course sheet." The corner of Rami's lower lip creased in a smile. "I know," he said.

He reminded Danyaal that he had called him by his name.

"Of course." Danyaal blushed.

They sat across from each other at the table. Between them, the sweating green bottle of 7 Up rested in the middle, and the food tray was on Danyaal's side.

Danyaal rolled up his sleeves, unbuttoned the top of his shirt, and gave Rami a look.

Rami's pulse quickened.

"This weather," Danyaal fanned his face with one hand and said. "Only spring and so warm already." He then leaned forward and clutched the bottle with the other hand.

Before Rami could say anything, Danyaal pulled the bottle to his mouth and started drinking.

Rami watched the subtle up and down movement of Danyaal's Adam's apple beneath the smooth surface of his skin; his head pulled back, the bottle placed against his seemingly parched lips as Danyaal downed the ice-cold beverage.

"Nice shirt," Danyaal said in a complimentary voice after setting the bottle back on the table. Rami noticed his lips were glistening from the condensation gathered around his mouth from drinking. "I like it."

Rami noticed Danyaal's unblinking gaze had settled on him.

He's observing me; Rami's heart jumped.

He tore his gaze away. He surprised himself for behaving that way. Rami wasn't accustomed to having a boy throw him a compliment like that, especially not for an old, black-and-red floral-patterned shirt.

"You do?"

Danyaal placed his elbows upright on the table and cupped his face in the palms of his hands. Nodded. "Looks good on you." He offered Rami an approving smile. "Suits the amber of your eyes," he said.

Feeling bashful suddenly, Rami muttered a quick *thanks* and looked down at his feet.

No one had flattered him like this, not any of his male friends, anyway. Their idea of a compliment, whenever Rami tried on a dress he thought he looked good in, was to tease him—elbow him—laugh mischievously, and ask if Rami was pretending to look like Waheed Murad, a Pakistani film actor famous for his flamboyant costumes and charming expressions.

He sat across from Danyaal and felt his cheeks burning.

And then there was another emotion that came over him in Danyaal's company, foreign to Rami. He sensed an air of serenity swirling around him, almost euphoric-like, something he hadn't encountered before.

After the introduction and talking loudly to make sure they heard each other, Danyaal and Rami began conversing in a calm and composed tone, asking questions, learning they were nearly the same age, discovering they lived in the same neighborhood—just on the opposite ends—and found it to be a surprising coincidence that they were both left-handed. There was no need to holler at each other from across the table anymore.

That day—their first day together—they told jokes, laughed at times for no reason, and stole glances at each other from time to time.

Danyaal, exuding an air of quiet reserve at times, tall with striking looks, and well-mannered, reflected the embodiment of a happy household. A loving home.

More than what Rami could say about the family to which he belonged.

SIX

Rami was lumbering along the college lawn when he saw Danyaal next. A stack of flattened cardboard was clumsily shoved under his left armpit while his right hand clutched a handful of wooden poles. It was late in the day, and the afternoon shadows had lengthened. As a recruit, he had received the assignment of making banners for the upcoming march, which had been organized to welcome the return of Benazir Bhutto—the exiled daughter of the former Prime Minister, Zulfikar-Ali-Bhutto—and the future female Prime Minister of Pakistan.

Danyaal was coming out of a class. They saw each other. Waved.

"What's all this?" Danyaal approached Rami. Rami noticed Danyaal's hair glistening in the sunlight. A whiff of its scent filled his senses.

He adjusted the slipping cardboard, flashed a thin smile, and invited Danyaal to tea.

Danyaal responded in the affirmative and even lent a hand by taking the poles from Rami. They trotted past the lawn toward the canteen, which was nearly empty. Rami found a table near where they had sat a week or so ago. When he returned holding two cups, he saw Danyaal's eyes under the canopy of his shapely eyebrows, staring at the random words sprawled across the square tabletop, which had been scribbled by students who'd occupied it before them.

"What do you think this is?" Rami pointed at a seemingly mindless drawing after handing Danyaal the tea.

Danyaal leaned forward and ran the pad of his index finger over the nearly faded image. "Looks to be the shape of a heart with an arrow piercing through it."

"One of those." Rami chuckled.

"Sadly, yes," Danyaal sighed. "Another love story between a boy and a girl that ends in tragedy." He made a face.

"It's not like we don't see enough of these melodramatic tales of star-crossed lovers, separated by the tragic turn of events in Hindi movies," Rami taunted.

"Sometimes," Danyaal muttered. "Sometimes, I wish there were other love stories, too."

Rami looked at him.

"Tales of love not just between a boy and a girl. You know?"

Rami's eyes drifted down, and he stared at the steaming cup briefly before blowing into it and taking a sip. They sat in a thick shroud of silence for a while.

"I would love to hear about your new adventure," Danyaal said finally.

Rami curled his fingers around the cup, took a deep breath, and told Danyaal about joining the NSF, something he hadn't mentioned before, and his task: making banners for the upcoming rally.

"Didn't realize you were interested in politics," Danyaal sounded impressed.

"Something different," Rami shrugged. "Something new."

Danyaal smiled encouragingly. "New college life, new experiences. I get it."

"You know about student politics?" Rami said and noticed a look of confusion cross Danyaal's face.

"I mean, are you familiar with NSF and its affiliation with PPP?" he said, sensing the teasing curiosity in his voice, pondering what had prompted it. He hoped Danyaal would take his tantalizing tone as playful inquisitiveness.

Danyaal rested his intertwined fingers on the table. Sitting to the right of Rami, his left leg crossed over the right at the knee, and the left foot swung casually by the ankle like a pendulum of a hand-wound clock. "Well," he started—

Then he got busy telling Rami how, during the 1977 military coup, Zia-Ul-Haq overthrew Benazir's father's government and put her and her mother under house arrest. When, in 1979, the Supreme Court controversially tried and hanged Zulfikar-Ali-Bhutto, he said, she carried on her father's legacy to lead the movement to restore democracy. And how all of this had resulted in a love-hate, on-again-off-again relationship between the NSF and the PPP in the past.

Next, Rami knew, Danyaal went on about Benazir and her mother going into exile and leaving Lahore for London, England.

Rami was stunned. He listened, and when Danyaal finished, he opened his mouth to say something, closed it. Opened it again.

"I'm sorry. I—" was all he could manage, impressed with Danyaal's knowledge and feeling stupid at the same time for having made assumptions about him.

Danyaal smiled. "My father is an editor at *The Pakistan Times*," he said. "Our dinner table on many nights is like a newsroom. It buzzes with news from around the world." He chuckled. Then he leaned forward as though sharing a secret with Rami. "I've no choice but to catch up on boring history lessons."

Rami thought about the nights at his home when Amma would put a fresh meal before Papa. She would sit across from him and watch his facial expression while he ate. Rami knew she agonized over the consistency of the curry: did it taste all right? Was there enough salt? Could there be too much chili? And how her hopes of receiving praise for her cooking would be doused, with a slow gathering of moisture around the corners of her eyes, when Papa would push the plate away after two bites, his nose turned up in distaste.

"Rami?" Danyaal reached across and squeezed Rami's forearm with his hand.

"Sorry," Rami said and looked the other way.

Danyaal leaned on his crossed elbows and glanced at him intently before asking if Rami had any ideas for designing the banners. Rami informed him that he had received multiple suggestions from fellow students. One idea had been to make a sign that read *Welcome Home, Benazir, Daughter of Pakistan!*

"All good ideas. But ..." Danyaal said, his fingers drumming the tabletop. Rami could tell his mind was contemplating something.

"But what?"

"Something is missing," Danyaal muttered under his breath.

He then reached over and grabbed a thin cardboard from the stack. He fetched a pencil from his bag and began sketching something.

"What're you doing?"

"One second, please." Danyaal continued.

Several minutes later, Danyaal finished and flipped the cardboard toward Rami.

It was a sketch of two arms raised in a distinct 'V' formation, and both hands' index and middle fingers made a gesture of triumph.

"This might be better."

Rami glanced at the drawing. It was brilliant, he thought.

"You like it?"

"It's perfect!" Rami's face beamed with joy.

Danyaal's lips stretched into a smile.

"Rami?"

"Yes, Danyaal."

"I'm glad to see your face brighten like this," Danyaal said. He then placed his hand on Rami's.

The flesh of Danyaal's palm pressed against the back of Rami's hand—against the fluttering pulse beneath the skin—and set Rami's heart racing. With this, the warmth emanating from Danyaal's skin aroused Rami's sense of touch with an intense awareness of intimacy coursing through his body.

The tips of Danyaal's fingers subtly traced the bumps on his knuckles, raising the hair on Rami's arm. Rami felt his ears turning warm.

He slowly slid his hand out from under Danyaal's.

No words passed between them; they sat in silence for a dozen or so heartbeats.

"I'm going to the march," Rami said after allowing the rapid fluttering of his pulse to subside, his voice still smoky.

"You want to come?"

"Me?"

Rami met Danyaal's puzzled stare. "Why not!"

"I suppose I could …"

"There'll be a large crowd, lots of activity."

"You're trying to recruit me or something?" A smile swept across Danyaal's face.

"No. Of course not," Rami chortled.

"Think about it?"

"I'll think about it," Danyaal said.

Rami began to say something but stopped. Through the corner of his eye, beyond the tall, rectangular window, he caught sight of a few NSF recruits approaching. He recognized them. They were new like him; some had even introduced themselves the day he joined the student union. Among them was Bilal. Rami had collaborated and teamed up with him to participate in the march. Bilal sauntered toward the canteen and waved.

An uneasy feeling washed over Rami. He hurriedly began gathering the stack of cardboard and the wooden poles. The chair legs dragged against the floor; Rami rose from his seat, sensing Danyaal's confused gaze shifting from the collected supplies in Rami's hands to his face.

"Is something wrong?"

"No."

"What happened, Rami?"

"Nothing."

"Something I said?" Danyaal sounded baffled.

"I've got to go," Rami said timidly and began to walk away.

"But ... wait!"

Rami whirled around and arched his left hand around the corner of his mouth. "Join me at the march!" he exclaimed, turned, and exited the canteen before Bilal and the others could find him sitting alone with Danyaal.

SEVEN

The march took place on May 15, 1986. Already that morning temperatures were on the rise. The mercury was predicted to climb to a sweltering high of thirty-eight degrees Celsius by the afternoon. The smog-filled sunlight merged with exhaust fumes from the congested morning traffic and cast a smudged orange tint across the horizon. The accumulated dew from earlier lingered on the verdant foliage of a shrub outside Rami's house before fizzling away.

Rami left home on his motorcycle, a used Honda CD-70 Papa had bought him, and soon felt his shirt dampening and clinging to his back. He rode through busy streets and noticed the trees still in the warm air. Even in the shadows, the heat had persisted.

He left the motorcycle at the college and made his way to the march with Bilal. Upon arrival at the gathering grounds, Rami climbed on top of the knee-high concrete base of a streetlamp and wiped the drops of sweat gathered on his forehead with the back of his sleeve. He held the pole taped to the banner with the victory arms Danyaal had designed in one hand, arched his other hand above his eyebrows, and searched sanguinely for Danyaal's face in the crowd. But he didn't find him.

When Rami saw Danyaal in passing at the college a few days earlier, they chatted for a while. He recalled shifting on his feet, standing before the curly-haired boy, hands shoved in his pants pockets, eyes flicking sheepishly from side to side. Danyaal didn't mention Rami's abrupt departure from the canteen the other day, and Rami pretended it hadn't happened. But he wondered if Danyaal knew.

Did Danyaal know that Rami was concerned about being seen in the company of a boy such as himself? Concerned that the collective eyes of many would shift to them, lips would stop midsentence, stares would narrow with keen interest if people saw them *together*? And before they would know it, with a whisper here and a quip there, they would become gossip material.

Rami also wondered if Danyaal could tell that he, Rami, was fretting internally that others could label them in a certain way through each other's company. And that it was less cumbersome to be with Danyaal in a crowd than just the two of them being spotted. Hence the reason he'd invited Danyaal to the march.

Rami felt a tug on his leg. His eyes drifted downward. It was Bilal. "We need to go," he said to Rami. "You're looking for someone?"

Rami glanced at his black Casio watch and realized it was almost time to move. He skimmed the crowd ahead with hopes of seeing Danyaal approaching in the distance and jumped off the base.

"No one," Rami said with a faint smile. "Let's go."

They had gathered at Lawrence Road, one of the main multi-lane avenues in the city. It ran along the Lahore Zoo and the Jinnah Garden. The road lay before Rami like a vast, black, and infinite stream of paved asphalt. He watched the crowd pouring in from every direction. Feet crushed gravel sidewalks with a loud crunching before stepping onto the heat-soaked tar-paving. Rami had never witnessed anything like this. He found himself amazed at the jubilant sea of people rubbing shoulders, chanting, and singing.

The PPP flag fluttered above his head, and the procession marched toward the airport. Many expected a glimpse of Benazir Bhutto. Rami noticed the onlookers had begun gathering on the sidewalks on both sides. They cheered on the marchers with friendly smiles and words of encouragement. A few marching waved back and reciprocated with polite nods. With wonder, Rami glanced ahead and saw a band in a gold-and-scarlet uniform. He could hear their bagpipes and drums playing.

Several minutes into the march Rami felt a tap on his shoulder. While chatting with someone from his group, he turned. It was Bilal. Bilal nudged Rami with his elbow and pointed at a hand jumping up and down behind the human chain of spectators standing in the front row.

"Someone's trying to gain your attention," he said.

Rami's gaze followed Bilal's subtle gesture. He squinted his eyes under the arched eyebrows and realized it was

Danyaal's hand waving behind the hordes of heads. His half-face disappeared and reappeared with each jump.

"Looks familiar," Bilal was saying. "Isn't he the boy I saw at the college with—?"

Rami quickly interrupted him. "Go ahead without me, won't you?" He handed the banner to another boy to his right—the one he was speaking with earlier—and hurried over in Danyaal's direction.

"Danyaal!" Rami shouted his name through the cupped mouth.

"Over here!" The hand jumped again. Rami lurched to grab it. Missed.

He waited a few seconds. Danyaal's hand and eyes resurfaced above heads. Rami made another attempt and clamped on Danyaal's fingers this time. With a firm grip, his hand pierced through the mass of squirming bodies, latched on to Danyaal's raised hand, and squeezed him out of the crowd like a newborn emerging from a womb.

"You're here!" Rami exclaimed joyously. "I didn't think I would see you."

Danyaal stumbled a bit. He held Rami's hand to steady himself and took a deep breath. "Yet here I am," he finally said. "I thought I wouldn't find you in this immense crowd."

Rami caught him looking around.

"God," Danyaal mumbled. The sound of marchers shouting slogans was deafening.

Rami fixed his eyes at Danyaal and mouthed, "I'm glad you came." Danyaal read his lips. He smiled.

Rami's gaze then skimmed nervously over the adjacent area. The group of students he was with, including Bilal, had walked on.

"Follow me." With a quick hand-waving motion, he beckoned Danyaal to join the march.

They dove into the sea of people. For the next several minutes, they attempted to inch forward with the boisterous crowd moving along the route, but, like being caught in a riptide, the unrelenting waves of masses kept them from moving ahead.

Another hour passed and they were still lagging at the back, way behind the crowds of people. Rami heard someone shout a rumor that Benazir had arrived and that her convoy had already left the airport. The air burst into heaves of disappointing sighs. Packed like sardines, they took tiny steps; their arms bumped with passing shoulders on each side.

By now, the hour had approached high noon, and the sun was beating with unrelenting brutality. The muggy heat pressed on them. Sweat was trickling down Rami's neck like molten lava. He looked around and saw signs of exhaustion appearing on many faces. He then glanced at Danyaal. Danyaal's skin glistened like the condensation on an ice-cold glass of water.

Rami pressed into Danyaal's arm. "You're all right?" he said, noticing the fatigued look on Danyaal's face. Danyaal nodded.

It was becoming unbearable with each passing minute. One could barely move an inch in the crowd.

"This is hopeless." Rami finally heaved a sigh of impatience. "We should head back," he said.

"Sure?"

"We'll never get past these many people ahead of us."

Danyaal shook his head in agreement. "I also heard someone saying Benazir had already left the airport," he said.

"God knows," Rami muttered. He was suddenly feeling withdrawn. He stopped and turned to face Danyaal, hands on his hips. "Let's go."

"Where to next?"

Rami let Danyaal know that his motorcycle had been parked at the college.

"Back to the college."

"Maybe find lunch on the way?" Danyaal suggested. "Have you eaten anything?"

Danyaal's question made Rami acutely aware of his gnawing hunger pangs.

They began plodding in the opposite direction of the procession and, just as Rami turned the corner onto Jail Road, a smell of something acrid like burning rubber, flooded his nostrils. Danyaal, who was following close behind, also wrinkled his nose. "You smell that?" he said. "What is it?"

Unsure, Rami shook his head. His unblinking eyes stared at the cloud of black smoke rising from something lying on the road. Moved a few feet farther, and it became clear it was a tire ablaze. Rami also noticed a few shapes huddled beyond the swirling smoke, their silhouettes thrown against the smoldering fire. He could hear their spiraling chants:

"Zia is America's pet! He's a dog!"

One emerged from around the dancing flames. He pressed a loudspeaker to his mouth and shouted into it, *"Freedom from the Western world's puppet! Freedom from America!"*

The others around him pumped fists in the air and screamed something similar. Alarmed, Rami and Danyaal stopped in their tracks. With the large fire burning in the middle of the road and a protesting mob gathered around it, there was little room to bypass without being noticed.

"What's going on, Rami?"

Rami grabbed Danyaal's hand into his. "Don't pay attention to them," he muttered. "Keep moving."

Someone from the group of insurgents shuffled through a backpack and fetched an American flag. He unfolded it. Another joined and held each end of the red, white, and blue fabric. A third protestor, dressed in a black T-shirt and slacks, fished a box of matches from his back pocket.

He grabbed the wooden stick of the match firmly between his index finger and thumb and dragged the matchhead along the red striker. In no time, the matchstick flickered into a flame. He brought it closer to the bottom edge of the flag. The fabric wrinkled around the flame; it recoiled as if it could sense being set on fire.

Mortified, Rami stood with Danyaal a few yards away, feet numb, and watched the flames lick through the delicate cotton fast. The smoke began to rise. The flag tore from the middle; its charred remains swirled to the ground. The chants intensified.

Rami told Danyaal to keep his head down and start moving ... keep moving.

"They won't bother us if we don't look," he was saying in a panicked voice, his eyes lowered, his heart convulsing in his chest. "Ignore what they're doing. Stay close. We'll be ..." Rami stopped talking. He noticed he was no longer holding Danyaal's hand. He turned.

Danyaal stood a few feet behind, motionless, stunned by what was happening before him. Rami could sense the fear in Danyaal through his widened, green eyes; they carried a look of terror. He scuttled back and gripped Danyaal's shaking hand.

"Danyaal, let's go," he hissed. "We need to leave. Now."

But Danyaal didn't move. Rami followed his gaze that darted from the charred flag to the angry crowd stomping around it.

Rami shook Danyaal's shoulder—violently almost— "Danyaal!"

Danyaal flinched. It was as though he'd awakened from a dream.

"Are you listening?"

"Hey, *firangi!*" someone shouted from across before Danyaal could say anything.

'*Firangi?*'

Rami's attention shifted from Danyaal to where the voice had come from. It was the man—in black—who had set the flag on fire; his eyes settled on Danyaal.

"What are you doing here, *firangi?*" he said to Danyaal smug-facedly.

Rami's puzzled eyes bounced back to Danyaal. He could see the water pooling in Danyaal's eyes. There was something about that pain-stricken expression on his face that Rami couldn't bear. He dropped his gaze.

"Hey! Look at me when I'm talking to you! Yes, you. White face," the man shouted again. A lit cigarette dangled from the side of his mouth and moved up and down when he spoke.

Rami raised his head and attempted to offer Danyaal a broken smile, while desperately trying to hide his fears. He gulped saliva down his dry throat.

"I'm not a *firangi*," Danyaal's voice choked when he spoke of the word that could be described in many ways: a white person, a foreigner. Privileged.

"*Sala angrez*, you a spy?" the man verbally assaulted him by calling him *angrez*, a slang used to describe English men from the British colonial era. Others joined. "Not one of us. Tell us, who sent you, *firangi*?"

The man who'd shouted first now had a rock in his hand; his eyes crinkled against the cigarette smoke. He tossed the rock a few times before stretching his arm like a baseball pitcher and hurling it toward Danyaal. The rock shot in the air with great speed and landed near Danyaal's feet.

Rami lifted Danyaal's chin with his curled finger and met his weary eyes. "Danyaal, look at me," he said in a pleading voice. "This isn't us. You hear me? This could be a ploy from MSF to disrupt the rally. It just wants to stir some trouble. Look at me."

Things were taking a turn for the worse. Rami heard spiraling voices. He turned and saw Bilal and the others approaching. He could tell they were gearing up to confront the flag-burning mob.

Danyaal wiped the tears from his eyes with the back of his hand. Rami told him the gathering had intended to hold a peaceful procession, not to protest against anyone.

Next, Rami knew, Danyaal reached over and threw his arms around him in a tight clasp. His chest pressed against Rami's, his arms slung over Rami's shoulders. At first, feeling apprehensive, Rami let his body hang loose in

Danyaal's embrace. Then, his arms moved and curled around Danyaal. Rami reciprocated. He felt the wetness of Danyaal's right cheek resting on his shoulder. He heard Danyaal choking between jagged breaths and held his body, jerking with shuddering sobs.

"I'm not a *firangi*, Rami," Danyaal repeated, this time as a whisper in Rami's ear.

"I believe you," Rami said in a muted, consoling tone. "It's all right; I believe you."

Within seconds, Rami felt heads begin to turn around them, gazes begin to lock. Before long, there was a buzz of rising murmurs. Rami could feel the blinking eyes upon them, watching.

He quickly separated himself from Danyaal and clutched him by the shoulders. "How good are you at running?"

"What?"

"Can you run? Fast?"

"I guess," Danyaal muttered in a puzzled voice.

From the corner of his eye, Rami saw the group of insurgents closing in on them. More rocks were bouncing in their hands.

"Run! Now!" Rami cried out.

And without wasting another second, he dashed in the opposite direction, away from the fast-approaching rioters. Danyaal followed close behind. Their feet barely kissed the asphalt; their heads bobbed side-to-side with each footfall. Many walking the rally cursed at the reckless behavior of the two obstacles-flinging boys who nearly collided with them. Rami caught a glimpse of Danyaal's windblown hair whipping back and forth as he rounded tight corners. Up ahead, he saw the banner with victory hands lying on the side of the road, ripped through the middle.

THEY GALLOPED, crushing through thick air, zigzagging through the other marchers who had spilled over from Lawrence Road. Rami and Danyaal bolted down the city streets: a sharp left onto the Mozang Road, a quick right to Shadman Avenue, and a hop into a tucked away alley before breaking into another crowded road bustling with colorful buses and lorries. For a while they kept running without looking back. They didn't know where they were or where they were headed. They just kept running.

At long last, they slowed their pace and jogged before coming to a stop. Rami spotted a willow tree to his right and gasped as he lurched to wrap his hands around its trunk. Danyaal was leaning over and panting also. A few minutes passed between them in silence, save for their ragged breathing.

Once the pounding of his heartbeat subsided, Rami regained composure and realized they were on Shah Jamal Road. Danyaal stood a few feet ahead, his back toward Rami. He appeared to be reading a worn-out metal sign of a local bus route.

"Danyaal," Rami called out.

"Yes, Rami."

Rami meant to ask if he felt all right after enduring the trauma of the hostile mob almost pelting him with stones.

Wanted to mention that it felt good when Danyaal dropped in his arms, when their bodies pressed against each other and hugged for the first time, albeit briefly.

"What're you looking for?" Rami walked up to Danyaal, placed his hand on his shoulder, and said instead.

"A way to get home."

"I know where we are," Rami said. "I can take you."

Danyaal turned his head toward Rami. Despite the experience he'd just had, there was an air of contentment surrounding him.

"We're not far from the college," Rami continued. "Let me give you a ride home."

He could tell Danyaal was considering this. They stood in silence under the willow tree, the same tree to which Rami had glued himself minutes ago. Then, instead of saying anything, Danyaal took a position to Rami's right. Their shoulders touched; Danyaal put his left foot out as if ready to stroll.

"Okay," he said smilingly.

Rami smiled back and tipped his chin.

They resumed moving. Rami turned the corner toward Lahore Canal, and a warm, gentle breeze greeted him. It blew against his face and carried a poignant smell of salt as though sweeping through a shoreline. It reminded Rami of his past visits to see relatives in Karachi with his family. And how they would take him to picnics at Hawksbay Beach by the Arabian Sea and how his hair would blow against the cool breeze drifting across the shore. He then noticed a strand of Danyaal's hair rumpled by the salty wind. Rami loved watching his curls bounce as Danyaal walked.

THE CANAL, bound by roads on each side, was part of a one-of-a-kind linear park that served as one of Lahore's longest urban green belts, also a favorite recreational destination for many.

Danyaal grabbed two kabab rolls from a street vendor on the side of the road.

"We can eat by the canal," he spoke for the first time since they'd begun walking. Despite wanting to say something, looking for a way to empathize with Danyaal and curse those protestors for calling him names, Rami had refrained from disturbing the quietude they were sharing.

"You read my mind."

Once at the canal, they found a patch of shade under an old ailanthus tree. Locals called it the Tree of Heaven.

"This is a good spot," Danyaal said.

Rami nodded. He slid his feet from his shoes, felt the soft blades of grass caressing his toes, and let gravity pull him down. He slumped to the ground and gazed at Danyaal standing beside him, eclipsing the sun.

Rami watched Danyaal unbutton his shirt and hold it open. Danyaal stood there with his head tilted back, his face pointed toward the sky, his eyes closed. The front of his shirt fluttered with the wind rushing through it. It swept across his body as if licking away the salty sweat clinging to his torso.

Rami took a sharp breath and stared at Danyaal's broad chest swelling and shrinking with each lungful of air.

Suddenly, he felt the urge to touch Danyaal.

In Pakistan two boys, or men, holding each other was a culturally acceptable norm. It was customary for people of the same sex to show affection and camaraderie by holding hands or walking side-by-side with arms curled around each other's necks without any sexual connotation.

But that rousing desire inside Rami was not to be mistaken for platonic affection.

With the quickening of his heart—and blood gushing through pulsating veins—Rami wanted to reach over and touch Danyaal's glistening skin. He pictured Danyaal lying next to him and the tip of Rami's fingers running over the curves of Danyaal's torso. He imagined Danyaal's warm body quivering to Rami's touch. But with the contact of their flesh, it would clench, cascading an ice-cold sensation down Rami's core. The inner layers of his skin tingled with a longing he had never felt before.

Rami found himself aroused.

Danyaal opened his eyes. And before he could lower his head, Rami raised his knees and hurriedly pressed his erection between his thighs. Danyaal dropped to the grass and lay next to him. Their fingers brushed against each other. Danyaal's breathing had a soft, rhythmic motion to it. Rami let out an unnoticeable puff of air from his mouth and looked the other way.

He had to.

Because, wasn't it against *fitrat*, the natural order of things, to feel this way toward other boys, toward Danyaal?

He recalled once in the fifth grade when the *Islamyat* teacher had found him with another boy in a classroom during recess, while the other students were out playing. The religious studies teacher grabbed Rami by the ear and dragged him from behind the desk. The other boy pulled up his trousers and hurriedly left the room.

"It'll produce nothing but absolute evil!" the teacher bellowed.

"Hold out your hand."

Rami remembered the teacher had said that these *corrupt* and *impure* thoughts of harboring such desires toward other boys would make Rami commit grave sins.

"This is no good! No good for a boy to act this way!" his wispy beard shook when he spoke.

The memory of the teacher's screeching voice and the accusing finger wagging before his face flashed through Rami's mind.

He heard Danyaal saying something.

"What?"

Danyaal said he would offer *Nazar Utar* if he knew what Rami was thinking. Like the idiom saying, 'A penny for your thoughts.'

"It's nothing." Rami took the kabab roll from Danyaal. Lied.

"You've been quiet."

"It's been a long day," he sighed.

"A tiring day," Danyaal added.

Rami took a bite.

"You want to know what I'm thinking?" Danyaal asked.

Rami turned his face to look at him, his temples working.

Danyaal paused for a second. "I'm thinking I like lying here, on this soft grass next to you," he said.

Rami only looked at him. He felt Danyaal's fingers fumbling for his and noticed he hadn't pulled his hand away.

"I like this."

"This?"

"Spending time with you."

"Even after today?"

"Even after today," Danyaal chortled softly. "Besides, it wasn't your fault."

Some time passed. They took small bites from the kabab rolls.

"Danyaal—" Rami then said.

"Yes?"

"I want to say something."

"What is it?"

Rami gathered his courage. He couldn't hold it in any longer. "I'm sorry for walking away from you the other day at the canteen," words rolled off his tongue.

"You don't have to—"

"It's just that … just that," Rami trailed off.

They lay in an uneasy silence for a while. A patch of puffy clouds floated by above.

"You know, Rami, when I was in high school at St. Anthony," Danyaal began, "I had a friend, my only friend. His name was Naveed. We both bonded quickly because others labeled us as outcasts. Naveed used to stutter; I was known for being the shy, quiet kid.

"Anyway, we were best friends from the fifth to the eighth grade. Then, at the beginning of the seventh grade, a group of senior students began picking on us. They would harass us during recess, between classes, or whenever possible. They would shove us into lockers and intentionally bump into us in the hallways. They'd walk behind me every so often, grin, and imitate my walk. The teasing, the name-calling, and the mimicking of Naveed's stutter by those boys continued for months. I complained to one of my teachers and even took it to the headmaster once, but they laughed it off. They called it part of the growing-up experience. One day, I found Naveed in the hallway surrounded by that same group of tormentors." Danyaal paused to take a deep breath.

"They were verbally abusing him, pushing him around, talking over him when he struggled to complete a sentence, asking why he hung out with me, the boy who talked differently, walked differently—appeared differently from the others. After they left I approached Naveed, who was in tears. We held each other for a long while, you know?"

The image of the boy from the video arcade, the one Rami had abandoned, the one Abdul and his band of friends had assaulted, raced through Rami's mind.

"The next day, when I saw Naveed at recess, he was kind—yet distant. Then he said it'd be better if we stopped spending time together," Danyaal went on. "I had become a liability and a burden to him. He said the only way the other boys would leave him alone would be if he severed ties with me." Danyaal sighed, "So he did."

"I'm sorry," Rami said.

"The point of telling you this story is that I understood then why Naveed ended his friendship with me the same way I realize now why you had to leave me that day at the canteen abruptly."

Stunned, Rami felt he had been slapped.

Danyaal knew, he thought.

Danyaal knew Rami left because he felt embarrassed to be seen with him.

'*He knows deep down you're a coward,*' a voice in Rami's head snickered. Rami's contrite gaze met Danyaal's burdened eyes. "You don't have to explain anything," Danyaal said with a thin smile. "I understand."

Danyaal's saying that made Rami sad. Sad to sense the tone of resignation in his voice, for who he was, the way he had accepted the consequence of being different from others: solitude.

Rami felt like telling Danyaal that he also had a way of dealing with these types of things and that he chose avoidance over submission. He wanted to share with Danyaal how he longed to be open about his feelings. But the thought of being labeled *differently* made him cringe internally. He wished to tell Danyaal that a boy, Nasir, had also bullied him in school.

But he didn't.

Instead, Rami envied Danyaal. To have the courage to be open and honest about the past, his life, he envied him. And for that, he figured Danyaal was a better person for being sincere. Rami knew that his furtive truth, on the other hand, was buried deep inside his soul to dig up to the surface that easily.

A drop of water landed on Rami's cheek. Far on the horizon, he saw black clouds starting to move across the sky. He could smell the scent of rain beginning to infuse the dense air around him. A flock of birds took flight. It formed a black silhouette against an already leaden sky, and, sensing the upcoming storm, fled. In the stillness around them, before the downpour, came a faint rumble of thunder followed by a flash of lightning.

"Storm's coming" was all Rami could manage to say. "We should go, Danyaal."

They jumped up and rushed to make their way toward the college, a couple of blocks away now, to get to the parked motorcycle.

Another crackle in the sky.

"Hop on!" Rami cried out. He kickstarted the bike.

By now, heavy raindrops had started to splatter on their heads like an army descending from the sky in an aerial assault and defeating them in their escape plan. Danyaal quickly mounted the vehicle behind Rami. The rear wheel spun. Rami geared the bike in motion, loose mud stirred.

The motorcycle began to roll. Rami twisted the handlebar grip toward him to rev up the throttle. It gained speed. The rain slapped his face cruelly as he rode through streets against side winds. The bike bounced over puddles of water amid rapidly cooling temperatures. Rami's eyes made a desperate attempt to remain open against the sheets of downpour.

He tasted the raindrops on the edge of his upper lip before they leaked into his mouth. Water seeped through Rami's already-drenched clothes. The wind had shifted direction. It brought cooler air from the north, a much-needed reprieve from the sweltering heat earlier in the day.

Soaked, they rode past barefoot children getting wet. Rami saw them cheering and jumping up and down in the puddles. Some even waved at the two teenagers speeding past them on a motorcycle. Men sat on the wooden benches of outdoor teahouses and smoked hookahs while listening to the rain dripping from the edges of the canopies.

Rami felt Danyaal's chest pressed against his back, sensed his arms snaked around Rami's torso. He noticed Danyaal's fingers had interlocked on his belly. Danyaal's chin was resting on Rami's left shoulder. The warmth of their merged bodies helped ward off the chill in the wind and the raised goosebumps on Rami's arms.

Rami wished for the rain to keep falling, the shivering cold to keep creeping under his shirt, and for Danyaal's body to keep sharing its heat. He longed for these bending streets with steep turns to go on longer.

He didn't know what he was feeling, but he wished for it not to end.

They were two wet, sticky bodies—a real mess—by the time the wheels of Rami's motorcycle came to a crawl in front of Danyaal's house. They sat on the idling bike outside the front gate for a while. Danyaal kept his arms wrapped around Rami's waist, chin on his shoulder, teeth chattering in the cold. Rami came to believe that, just like him, Danyaal was also not wanting to separate from the warmth and from the day they'd had together. With only the sound of the motorcycle engine puttering around them, Rami and Danyaal merely sat there long after the rain had gone.

It was the awakening of Rami's yearning to be with someone. In his heart, he held fast to the belief that having found Danyaal would unlock the door to joy and happiness. He really did believe—until the demons in him stirred one day.

EIGHT

I have an idea," said Danyaal one midsummer day. It was a Wednesday, and two days later—on a Friday—Rami went to the Lahore Canal Lighting Festival with him.

Rami had finished a lecture and was coming out of the Liberal Arts building when Danyaal approached him in the hallway.

They made their way to the redbrick walkway fringed with sweet-scented shrubs, where Rami and Danyaal would often mill around the crowd of students on sunny afternoons. They ambled along the narrow path lined with palm trees. Rami enjoyed listening to the rustling sound of the palmate-shaped leaves gently fanning in the breeze.

He had remained vigilant. He couldn't help but feel pangs of apprehension whenever he caught a classmate casting a sidelong glance in his direction when walking next to Danyaal. He would still drop his head and hurry past someone who'd spot and wave at them. But despite the nervousness of being in Danyaal's company, Rami had committed to not be *another* Naveed to him. They often arranged to meet at the college during breaks between their lectures or crossing paths when switching between classes.

Every so often, Rami would see Danyaal halfway between the multi-story Science Department and the high-domed Liberal Arts building where Danyaal studied I. Com—or Intermediate of Commerce.

It was like stars had aligned and filled Rami with immense joy. This was the happiest he had felt in all his sixteen years.

With time, Rami would have ample occasion to look back and recall the morning fog of early spring, the late summer's monsoons, the scent of burning coal in the still autumn air, and the moonlit wintry chill he would share with Danyaal—the memories of which would live in him forever. He would grow into adulthood and nostalgically allow his olfactory senses to evoke memories of bygone seasons. He would long to inhale the sweet scent of cotton on Danyaal's shirt like a washed piece of laundry just off the clothesline.

During the early summer of 1986, Rami's days were bright under the sky's brilliant blue, nights infused with the intoxicating scent of jasmine. It was the immense feeling of euphoric restlessness, the novelty of which was exhilarating to him: sudden outbursts of laughter, sprightliness, and a sense of fulfillment—like a balloon blowing up in his chest, ready to float him away. There was an air of contentment in those days that he'd never felt before.

Rami strolled past the walkway with Danyaal and found a black, backless bench just to the right of the Department of History building. A gust of breeze blew and rustled the branches of a nearby tree.

Seated across from Danyaal, he recalled when they would skip the canteen and find one of the lawn benches under the Clock Tower for lunch. After college, Rami often rode the streets of Lahore with Danyaal. They would park the bike by a street vendor and stuff their mouths snacking on *samosas*, or they would sit at the riverbank of Ravi, no words passing between them, feet dangling above the water.

Also, when Rami watched Danyaal tear up watching a film and when the demons living in his head reared their ugly heads—Rami recalled that also.

"FOR SOMETHING fun for us to do this week," Danyaal was saying now, "I have a plan."

The past few days, ever since what had happened at the cinema when they saw their first film together, Danyaal had been coming up with ideas for them to do activities together.

"How about a picnic at the canal?"

Rami looked at him. "We've been to the canal several times," he said.

"This time, it's different," Danyaal explained with a twinkle in his eyes.

Rami blinked, said nothing.

Danyaal made the sound of a drumroll before creating a dramatic pause. "You're ready?"

Rami tilted his head and gave him a *seriously?* look.

"The Canal Lighting Festival is this Friday!" Danyaal sat facing Rami with a cheery expression; arms extended, fingers splayed like a magician putting on a dazzling show for a captivated audience.

With this, Rami stirred in his seat. He noticed Danyaal had sensed the shift in the atmosphere, too.

"The lighting festival?" He hated the way the excitement dissipated from Danyaal's face.

"You're not impressed," Danyaal said in a lowered voice.

TWO WEEKS before this conversation, they had gone to see their first film together.

It had also happened on a Wednesday. When Danyaal suggested a movie he hadn't heard of before, Rami asked about it. Danyaal said *Pretty in Pink* was a romantic drama where a girl had to choose between her childhood friend and a wealthy playboy.

"It's about friends like us, Rami," Danyaal had said. "Just like us."

Depending on its popularity, a movie usually played for several weeks at movie theaters across Lahore.

Rami picked up Danyaal from his house for a five o'clock showing that afternoon.

When they arrived at the Alfalah Cinema, it was half empty. The film had been playing for a while, Danyaal clarified. Rami selected the middle row from the auditorium-style seating toward the center. Meanwhile,

Danyaal grabbed two bottles of Coca-Cola from a vendor hawking snacks up and down the aisles.

They were a few minutes into the trailers for the upcoming attractions when Rami saw a head a few rows ahead turn toward them. Then, the profile of a boy with a confident smile came into clear view. The boy rose from his seat and headed in their direction. He had a strong jawline, ruffled black hair, and piercing hazel eyes. He wore fitted black jeans, a purple shirt, and a gold necklace that hung from his long neck.

"I thought it might be you." The boy ascended the stairs; his eyes settled on Danyaal. "How are you?" he said.

Rami caught the puzzled look in Danyaal's eyes that lingered on the boy's face for a while before registering a flash of recognition.

"I'm good. Sonam, right? Sonam Ahuja?"

Sonam nodded. "You look good!" His bright stare was settled on Danyaal.

Danyaal muttered a quick thanks.

"We graduated from St. Anthony the same year," Sonam said. He was toying with the leather bracelet hanging loosely from his left wrist. "Too bad we didn't get to know each other back then. I wish we had," the smile on Sonam's face creased the corner of his mouth.

Rami couldn't help but sense a suggestive, unscrupulous smirk playing on the curves of Sonam's large upper lip.

"I guess so," said Danyaal.

"Why don't we hang out sometime and catch up?"

Danyaal gave Sonam a slow nod.

Was that a pang of jealousy that just stung Rami's chest?

Rami thought of Amma standing in the doorway of the house, warding off the impish smiles of neighboring housewives aimed at Papa. And for the first time, he comprehended the complexity of emotions she must have felt.

"Who's this with you?" Sonam shot a sideways glance at Rami.

And Rami felt surprised at the way his insecurities got unleashed, how they washed over him, swept him up, and tossed him upside down. He felt his hands sweating, felt his skin shrinking. Suddenly, he had this urge to hug his arms against Sonam's curious stare and vanish.

"Rami and I are collegemates at F.C. College," Danyaal introduced him.

"Nice to meet you," Sonam said. Rami returned the gesture with a close-lipped, half-hearted smile.

"Well, enjoy the film. I've heard it's a good one," Sonam said and turned to go back to his seat.

Danyaal waved and remarked what a nice coincidence it had been reconnecting with Sonam. He then turned his head toward Rami.

"Are you all right?" Danyaal asked.

Rami grunted something and kept his eyes on the screen. The lights dimmed shortly after. The film *began*:

The not-so-popular teenage girl's best friend is secretly in love with her. Then, a rich teenager joins the school and asks the girl out. The girl says yes. Her friend is heartbroken to see her go out with another boy. The girl and the rich boy feel out of place due to their social differences. Ultimately, her best friend relents. He sacrifices his love for her and lets her and the wealthy teenager be together.

However, an altered version of the movie played in Rami's head:

The teenager Rami lurks around, masked behind his secrets, and is furtively attracted to his best friend, Danyaal. Then, someone named Sonam comes out of nowhere and asks Danyaal out. Rami, incensed with jealousy, feels pushed to the side. The social differences between Danyaal and Rami are too vast to reconcile. And then, Danyaal breaks his heart by choosing Sonam over him.

'Of course, he brought you to this film to prove that someone good-looking, better suited like Sonam, might be waiting for him,' a voice whispered tauntingly in Rami's head. He felt his demons, anger and jealousy stir.

'It's only a matter of time until Danyaal finds another companion,' their voices echoed again. *'And why would he be with the likes of you? Has he met your dysfunctional family? Does he know the things you have done?'* Their voices laughed sardonically.

Sitting in the dark next to Danyaal, Rami's eyes were settled on the screen, but these fiends that lurked beneath the surface and appeared whenever he was struck with anxiety had kidnapped his mind. He could feel his insecurities crawling under the skin. They rose in his chest like undead spirits; their throat-ripping screams slammed against the insides of his skull. His heart fluttered, his breathing grown ragged; Rami was aware of the beads of sweat erupting across his forehead. He wanted to withdraw. Wanted to walk away. But he stayed, sulking.

When the film ended, Rami rolled his head to the side and saw Danyaal sniffling and dabbing at his eyes. As they exited the cinema, Sonam approached Danyaal from behind, and they went on about how touched they were by the film.

Rami heaved a sigh and kept walking ahead of them with long strides.

Behind him, he could hear Danyaal continuing how he loved the characters and the undertones of so many emotional messages. Sonam agreed with him. Then he called out a goodbye.

"Bye, Rami."

But Rami didn't turn or wave back at Sonam. He kept stomping forward.

They approached the back of the cinema where the motorcycle was parked.

"Rami, please. Let me catch up to you." Danyaal hurriedly walked behind Rami. "Don't walk so fast. What did you think of the film? Such a powerful story with a message, na?" he said.

Rami stopped. Turned.

"What message?" he said sharply. The moon hung just above Danyaal's head. "What powerful story?"

His reaction startled Danyaal.

"I ... I thought the characters' commitment toward each other ..." Danyaal's voice faded. He hesitated a moment. "You didn't like it?"

Rami said nothing.

"Tell me, please. What did you think of the movie?"

Rami swung his right leg over the motorcycle and took it off its sidestand. "Well, I thought it was stupid. I didn't see the point of it," he said and inserted the key into the ignition.

What happened next should have been the end of what existed between Rami and Danyaal; Rami would reminisce later. Looking back at it, he'd be sure that if it were someone other than Danyaal, they would have disappeared from his life, even if Rami were the only person left on the face of the earth.

"I'm sorry," Danyaal's voice carried a morose tone, "I'm sorry you didn't enjoy it."

"Whatever," Rami said, "get on. It's getting late."

But Danyaal continued to stand across from him with his fingers shoved into the front pockets of his jeans. He paused briefly before mentioning that Sonam had felt the same about the story.

"I agree with him. I found the film to be about friendship and devotion."

Rami kick-started the motorcycle and let it idle. He twisted the throttle and threw Danyaal a glaring look. "You should've come with Sonam, then. He's so smart and knows all about these things!" Words came out more curtly than he had intended.

"But I wanted to watch it with you." Danyaal returned Rami's stare.

Rami knew he should have stopped; he knew he should have apologized. But he didn't. He went on.

"And what about you crying in the end?" he said.

"What?"

"Toward the end of the film. I couldn't stand to see you cry like that."

Undoubtedly, Rami's mouth had forgotten when to shut up.

"Cry like what?"

Rami crossed his arms. "Like a girl, Danyaal. I saw you cry like a girl."

In his head—Jealousy clapped—fear whistled, insecurity rolled around exultantly. They cheered how quickly Rami had succumbed to their conniving ploy to reveal himself to Danyaal.

The moon was now hiding behind Danyaal, making a halo around his head. Rami couldn't tell the difference between its color and the shade of pale on Danyaal's face. They both seemed bone colored.

"I ... I was ... It was just so," Danyaal broke off.

"You're getting on or not?"

A few awkward moments passed between them before Rami spoke again.

"We're supposed to be tough and resilient, us boys. Shedding tears for boys is a sign of weakness. Did you know that, Danyaal? They say that a boy crying means he can't face the world on his own. Did you know that?" Rami's voice grew over the hum of the idling engine. Then he felt the sting from the disappointing look passing through Danyaal's eyes.

He didn't explain who "they" were, and Danyaal didn't seem interested in finding out. Instead, he stood across from Rami and stared at him for a while. Then he removed his fingers from the front pockets of his jeans and got on the motorcycle behind Rami.

"You're right. It's late."

They spoke of not much else after that. Rami rode the motorcycle under the pulsating gleam of streetlights. The flickering neon signs on the closed shops were zipping by; the pale moon hung behind them. Danyaal sat behind Rami, silent. Rami's mind was forlorn, drained with mental exhaustion. The voices in his head had gone quiet. They'd done their job. And Rami wanted nothing more than to get home, bury his ashamed face in a pillow, and melt away.

THE FOLLOWING day, Rami found Danyaal sitting cross-legged on the grass under the shade of a willow tree at the college. It was an overcast afternoon. The white clouds from earlier in the morning had turned gray. Rami started walking toward Danyaal, stopped, took a few steps back, and peered from the side of a tree. Aware of his behavior from the previous night, he paced back and forth and contemplated how to approach Danyaal.

Danyaal caught him lurking. His lips stretched into a smile. "Come sit with me, Rami," he said and patted the green patch to his side.

Rami traipsed forward. He lowered himself to the warm grass next to Danyaal and returned the smile shamefacedly.

"Danyaal ... I'm," he began. "About last night ..."

Danyaal squeezed Rami's hand and stopped him midsentence. "You don't have to say anything," he said. A team of cricket players donned in white uniforms carrying protective gear trotted past them.

"There're things," Rami resumed after the players had left, save for the small cloud of dust behind their feet, "you know, there are things no one knows about me."

"There are things many don't know about me either."

"It's hard to explain," Rami said. He kept his gaze low. "These things from my past … sometimes make me act this way." He felt his cheeks flush against Danyaal's unwavering stare.

"We all have things we're not proud of, Rami," Danyaal said. "We all have secrets. Some, like specks of dust, we can brush aside; others, like a stubborn stain on a piece of fabric, stay with us forever."

Rami lifted his head and met Danyaal's gaze.

"Secrets?"

"Things we keep from others. Things we're not proud of. Things we might be too embarrassed to share with anyone."

Rami flinched internally. *Is Danyaal like that boy from a few years back who could look through me and see things, uninvited?* He looked at Danyaal's face intently. They sat there. Two boys under the willow tree, amid the occasional roars of the cricket players' cheers bursting in the air. Rami searched Danyaal's face for a while. What he found in it was sheer sincerity. There wasn't another implication lurking underneath. Rami nodded.

"I'll understand if you'd want not to see me anymore," he said. He dreaded Danyaal would agree.

"You're not listening. You see, everyone has memories from their past—some good—some bad. We can't change what's already happened. But we can try to control the future through our actions. I don't want to look back years from now and wonder what could've been," Danyaal said. Paused. "I don't want us to stop seeing each other over one thing, Rami. I hope you want the same."

'*More than anything*,' Rami wanted to scream. "Yes," he said instead, in a low voice.

"Perhaps one day you'll tell me what's troubling you."

"You wouldn't understand if I did."

"How do you know that?"

"I know," Rami said.

Danyaal curled his arms around Rami's shoulder, "If you say so," he said smilingly, the dimples in his cheeks deepened. "I trust you."

He said it with such sincerity, such conviction; Rami could tell he had meant it. Danyaal was one of those people who placed their trust in others unconditionally and meant what they said. Rami felt a phony in front of him.

"YOU DON'T want to go to the lighting festival?" Danyaal, sitting on the bench across from Rami, said wistfully.

Twice a year, the Lahore Canal came to life at dusk. Thousands of tiny lights looped around the willow and ailanthus trees lined along the banks. Families, groups, and city-sponsored organizations all came together and took part in the cheerful festival.

Local artists designed with utmost care large, life-size lanterns in the shapes of butterflies, ducks, and grasshoppers. Decorated with candles and oil lamps, the lanterns would then be lowered into the canal's calm waters and set to sail along the curvy banks. The city descended at the festival and watched in excitement the eye-catching display. The crowd on each side of the canal would cheer and clap while the participants boasted about their works of art.

"That's not a good idea," Rami said.

"Why not?"

Rami shifted on the bench and gave Danyaal a strained smile.

He couldn't bring himself to confide in Danyaal that the conceited behavior he had witnessed in him two weeks prior—when he'd accused him of crying like a girl—had stemmed from the same lighting festival he had attended over seven years ago.

Rami, struggling internally, held back disclosing it to Danyaal for several reasons. Perhaps because he was embarrassed, afraid Danyaal would reject him if the truth were revealed. Or maybe there was a sense of vulnerability due to his origin, where he'd come from—unable to see that the systematic chain of events in his formative years, created by others, was responsible for his behavior, not him—the boy without fully developed consciousness.

Rami coughed. "You know," he said after clearing his throat, "it would be crowded with people. Maybe we can find another activity."

Danyaal's hand slid across the bench and closed over Rami's. "I understand if you don't want to go."

"I'm sorry."

Danyaal then asked if he wanted to stop at the fruit *chaat* stand after class for a snack. Rami said he couldn't.

He always had some excuse on Wednesday afternoons.

LATER, AFTER parting from Danyaal, Rami went to see Daadi. She wasn't his actual grandmother. It was a name given to her by the boys in the neighborhood for her old age. He had heard she was an excellent cook in her day, which was apparent by the tasty sweets she would make for the neighboring children despite having no vision left. Daadi was a tubby woman who huffed around the house. She would lean on a cane with a pained expression, mainly when lowering herself to sit down.

"If it weren't for the love of music coursing through my blood, my child," she would run her hand on Rami's face to feel his eyes, his nose, his lips, her sightless eyes wandering into space, "this old age would've washed me away a long time ago."

Daadi lived in a tiny shack of a house in Bhati Gate with her son, Masood. The house's red-colored facade and black gate stood out from other one-story dwellings on the street.

Masood, her son, was a thirty-five-year-old man with shoulder-length hair thinning at the scalp. He had a pencil-thin mustache and dark, almost mocha-colored skin. They made their living through singing at weddings and private parties.

Masood answered the door. "Come on. Come inside," he said smilingly.

"Who is it?" It was Daadi's voice calling from the adjacent room.

"Rami."

"Put the water in the kettle for tea, son," she said.

"We'll have tea after Rami's lesson, Ma," Masood said over his shoulder as he closed the door behind Rami.

Rami crossed the small veranda and entered the living room, clean yet stark, with a single bed for Daadi and a mattress on the floor for Masood. There was a tattered rug in the center of the cement floor with frayed edges, two chairs, and a small wooden table with a tabla set atop. A patchwork tapestry of a young woman playing sitar hung on one of the walls. Rami always wondered if it was Daadi at a young age. Across the living room was a doorway that led to a bathroom, a cramped kitchen, and a nook where Daadi prayed *namaz.*

"*Salaam*, Daadi," Rami said when he saw her entering the room with Masood escorting her through the door. As usual, Daadi ran her hand over his head and asked if he'd been practicing. Rami said he had.

"Good. Let's begin, then," she said. Masood lifted the tabla and hauled them to the bed where Daadi was sitting. He grabbed a *chimta*, a percussion instrument made of a long, flat piece of iron pointed at both ends and folded over in the middle.

Daadi's hands, covered in a thin layer of skin with protruding blue veins, gently ran over the taut membrane of one tabla. The heels of her hands stroked the bass instrument; her fingers drummed the playing surface as though saying hello to a long-time friend.

"We'll continue with the raga scales lessons," she told Rami. "Last week, we learned *Alap*. Let's continue with that and learn the *Bandish* scale." She referred to the opening section of Indian classical performance, the prelude, followed by the second, structured composition accompanied by a musical instrument.

This was Rami's weekly routine. He came to see Daadi and Masood every Wednesday. He would receive lessons in musical scales and vocal training in exchange for a modest fee, which he budgeted from his pocket money.

And it was yet another secret Rami hadn't shared with anyone. Concerned about the social stigma attached to associating with Mirasis, he had kept his visits to Daadi to himself. No one was aware of his whereabouts between four and five o'clock on Wednesday afternoons, when he would arrive at her house and take voice lessons for an hour, then help Masood clean the dishes after tea before leaving.

That afternoon, after kissing Daadi on the hand and saying *salaam* to Masood, Rami exited the house and walked for a while to get to the parked motorcycle a few streets over, a precaution he took. On the way there, he noticed the daylight reflected from the sidewalks. He turned the corner onto a narrow brick-paved street, where the motorcycle was, and took note of the dirt on the vehicle in the fading glow of fast-approaching dusk. He was mentally reminding himself to take it for a wash when a familiar voice from behind made him jump. "So, this is where you disappear to every week."

Rami turned and came face to face with Jalil's stony eyes staring at him.

Rami stood there, dumbfounded, wondering how Jalil had found him.

"Explain yourself." Jalil's one eyebrow raised; his tapered cheekbones moved while chewing on a piece of gum.

Rami had always envied his brother for being taller than he. At twenty-four, Jalil stood an inch or two over six feet, while Rami's growth had stopped a few inches shorter. Jalil had a head full of black hair and a full mustache covering the top border of his upper lip. His right eyebrow split in the middle from a noticeable scar sustained during a childhood injury before Rami was born. The furrow line between Jalil's eyebrows gave his downturned, black eyes a perpetual grim look.

"What are you doing in this neighborhood?"

"Mind your own business, Jalil."

Jalil crossed his arms.

"Visiting a friend, okay!" Rami said testily.

"I don't believe you."

"I told you," Rami said. "Now, will you please step aside?"

"Don't think I'm stupid. I saw you come out of that house. I know who lives there." Jalil ignored the curt tone in Rami's voice and continued.

Rami flinched.

"I'd told you to stay away from these people. But you don't listen. You want to be labeled a Mirasi and dance on the streets?" Jalil spat. "Is that how you plan on tarnishing the family name?" he scowled, adding to the list of things he had previously accused Rami of.

"Who gave you the right to follow me around?" Rami shot back.

Jalil laughed. "You're such an idiot. I saw your motorcycle parked in the middle of an unknown street with you nowhere in sight. I walked around looking for you and caught you sneaking out of *that* house," Jalil winced with such distaste at the mention of the house; it was as though he had caught Rami stepping into a pile of feces. He spat the gum on the sidewalk. "Everyone knows a couple of low-caste Mirasis live there," he flicked his thumb over his shoulder.

"These people are musicians with knowledge for their profession," Rami threw Jalil a sidelong glare. "Not something I'd expect you to grasp."

"*Musicians*," Jalil jeered. "Playing at weddings for a few rupees doesn't make one a respected musician."

Rami hopped on the motorcycle. "Think whatever you want," he said. He didn't see the point in arguing with him anymore. "I'm leaving."

The banter between the two brothers continued long after they got home. Jalil kept following Rami around the house, kept taunting him. Finally, Rami shut himself into a room and locked the door behind him in order to drown Jalil's shrill voice from the other side.

THE NEXT day, when he saw Danyaal at the college, Rami asked if he still wanted to go to the Canal Lighting Festival.

Danyaal lifted his head from the book he was reading. "I thought you didn't want to go," he said. They were sitting on the lawn across from the Liberal Arts building.

"I've changed my mind."

Danyaal asked if something had happened. "Is everything all right?"

With this, Rami's chest inflated and deflated between breaths for the next few minutes as he sulkily recounted his encounter with Jalil.

"I don't want to be home tomorrow and have to face him," he said after finishing.

"Right, especially after the Friday prayer," Danyaal nodded.

"I'd rather be at the festival with you."

"And what's this singing business about?" Danyaal gave Rami a friendly shove.

"I was going to tell you," Rami muttered.

"Well, now you must sing me a song," Danyaal crossed his arms and tipped his chin.

Rami blinked. "Now?"

"Why not!" Danyaal said. Rami saw the corners of Danyaal's mouth stretching in a mischievous smile.

"Shut up." Rami shook his head in mock disbelief.

Danyaal laughed.

"Are we going to the lighting festival?"

Danyaal arched his left arm outward and extended his elbow, a gesture for Rami to sling his arm around it. "Yes, we are. Let's have a picnic at the canal, dear Rami."

NINE

After arriving at the canal, they found an area along a steep bend under a flowering tree. Rami enjoyed the occasional gust of breeze sweeping over his perspiring skin. The sweet scent of summer grass in the air filled his nostrils. It was early, and the neighboring area hadn't begun to fill in for the festival. At a distance, someone played tabla-infused Hindi music. A street vendor had been busy fanning skewers of lamb and beef sizzling over a make-shift charcoal grill. He must have been expecting a large crowd later. Up ahead, a group of men was busy putting the finishing touches on a lantern shaped like a dove. Rami could hear their occasional high-pitched chatter and spiraling laughter.

Danyaal removed a blanket from a brown-colored backpack and spread it along the base of the tree trunk. He sat beside Rami on the bank's edge, their jeans cuffed above the ankles, feet dangling, toes occasionally dipping into the water.

They ate sandwiches, made small talk, and asked each other how their studies were progressing. Rami threw a pebble in the water, watched it ripple their reflections, and told Danyaal he'd been struggling in mathematics.

"Look, Rami! *Bulbuls*!" Danyaal pointed his finger at a pair of red-whiskered nightingales that had fluttered in and were now perched on a low-hanging branch above their heads. Soon after, the air filled with their loud crescendo singing. Danyaal was busy saying something about the history of the Lahore Canal that the Mughals had built long before the British Empire took over the subcontinent in 1861. And that it stretched sixty kilometers along the waterway. The canal was over 1.5 meters deep; Rami heard him describe it while biting an apple.

But, in reality, what Rami heard mostly was the muted tone of Danyaal's voice. He'd stopped paying attention to the words coming out of Danyaal's mouth in the middle of his talking. Rami's wandering gaze was settled on another lantern being lowered into the water.

He couldn't tell how much time had lapsed before his stare shifted from the lantern to Danyaal. Neither he nor the *bulbuls* were making any sounds, he noticed. The birds had flown away, and Danyaal's intent stare was fixed on him.

"Rami." Danyaal snapped his fingers before Rami's eyes.

"Hmm ..." Rami let out a soft grunt.

"You're making a face."

"I am not."

"You've been staring off into space like ruminating on something."

Rami sensed Danyaal's eyes lingering over his face. "It's nothing," he said. He lowered his head and absently plucked grass from the ground.

"That's not the face of *nothing*," Danyaal drew closer. Persisted.

Rami gave Danyaal a side look and kept his head down.

"You're thinking of something, aren't you?"

"Danyaal, please—" Rami pulled some more grass blades.

"Did something happen?" Danyaal pressed.

"Years ago."

"Rami—"

Rami lifted his head.

"You can tell me."

"It's a long story."

"We have lots of time," Danyaal said.

The corner of Rami's eyes cringed nervously. "I am a little embarrassed."

"Nothing you say will make me think any less of you." Danyaal insisted.

Rami considered this. Then he eventually pulled himself up, leaned against the tree trunk, and, with a sense of unease, shared the account of that day, eight years ago, for the first time with another person.

IT HAD happened around his ninth birthday, Rami told Danyaal. It was a sunny November day in 1978. The brisk air rustling through the leaves hinted at the upcoming change in the season. Days were shorter; afternoon shadows had begun growing longer. Rami sat on the rooftop of his house with Amma, Narin, and a couple of visiting neighbors, enjoying the warm feeling of the sun on the back of his neck. Amma had applied a large amount of hair oil to Narin's hair, which glistened like ebony silk in the sunlight.

Narin, eighteen then, was the girl other females in the neighborhood loved to hate. Her liquid brown eyes on a face with symmetrical cheekbones and long hair snaking down the waist of her willowy figure were often coveted by the young women in the nearby houses.

Unlike Saifa, who was shy and quiet, Narin was the life of the party. Her quick wit, jokes, and ability to mimic celebrity accents were infamously popular.

Do the pouty lips of Noor Jehan, Narin, you know ... when she comes on the television and sings! Someone would nudge Narin and suggest gleamingly. After a moment of bashfulness, Narin would clear her throat and do a mock celebrity impression. The room would burst into laughter. Some held their stomachs before rolling off their chairs.

Bibi Jaan, Amma's friend and neighbor, along with her daughter, Salma, had come by for a visit that day. She was a woman with a creased forehead, hooded eyes, and grizzled hair that limply framed her aging face. They lived in the house closest to Rami's—so close that the two houses' back walls were separated only by a few inches. One could lean over the living room window and kiss the other person standing in the other house. Both households comfortably exchanged provisions such as cups of sugar, flour, or milk by simply stooping over the window ledges and stretching an arm. Bibi Jaan was the first to know whenever an abrupt burst of shouts would come from her neighbor's house: an argument between Rami's sisters, his parents bickering over the house finances, or Rami and Jalil tearing after each other around the house. Bibi Jaan would come over the following day with a woebegone look, and Amma would confide in her about her ungrateful husband.

So, he thinks these dinners cook themselves? Bibi Jaan would adjust the shawl on her head. Amma would dab at her eyes.

He said this, he actually said this ... I swear.

You just wait until your sons are grown and strong. There, there now.

Rami liked Salma. She had an oval face, unblemished skin, and close-set sparkling hazel eyes. Salma always let her curly hair hang loose on her shoulder. Rami was amazed at the number of dolls Salma had. When she came to visit, she brought a different one each time. He looked forward to seeing her, knowing they'd play together. He read her stories from the books he had collected: Arzang, the Superman, *Naag,* a king cobra who could adopt human form after living ninety-nine years. And sometimes Tarzan chronicles. Rami fictionalized the stories for Salma since he hadn't learned to read many Urdu words at the time. Afterward, they'd play with Salma's doll over a tea party.

"Guess what's coming up soon, Rami?" Narin's voice entered Rami's ears. He looked up from playing Ludo, a board game of racing the tokens from start to finish.

"Your birthday!" Narin said excitingly. "What do you say we make a lantern?" She was sitting with Bibi Jaan;

they were knitting sweaters. "The Canal Lighting Festival will be around the same time this year as your birthday."

It was a family annual tradition for Papa to take everyone to Lahore Canal for the lighting festival. Amma would pack a tiffin, a multi-stack lunch box, with various food items and spread a blanket by the canal amid the hordes of people milling about. And at dusk, they sat on the throw, snacked on *samosas* and *pakoras*, and cheered the shimmering lanterns floating by.

"A birthday present for you," Narin continued.

"In truth?" Rami's face perked up. He and Salma were sitting cross-legged across from each other on the *charpoy*, or traditional woven bed. Rami hurriedly abandoned Salma and the game and ran barefoot toward Narin.

"Why not!" Narin said smilingly. "I've got a home economics project to prepare. This could be it."

Everyone clapped.

With renewed excitement, Rami ran in circles around Narin. "It'll be the most beautiful lantern in the canal!"

Narin pulled the young boy closer and tousled his hair. "Think of a design."

"A lotus flower," Rami said with the innocent nod of an eight-year-old, "I want it to be a flower."

"*Mashallah*. A flower of beauty and eternity," Narin said thoughtfully. Rami was unaware of the symbolic significance of the lotus flower at the time. He had only seen it inside one of the pages of a *Reader's Digest* Papa kept.

He had shown the picture to Salma also.

"It's beautiful!" Salma exclaimed from across the way.

"And the color?" Narin ran her fingers through the hair draping Rami's forehead. "What would be the color of this flower?"

Rami told Narin he wanted each petal painted in a distinct color. "Red, orange, yellow, green, blue, and purple."

He named all colors in one breath, the same hues he'd seen in the image inside the magazine. Salma nodded in agreement. They eyed each other. Rami raised his shoulders closer to his ears. They both giggled.

EVERYONE WAS in favor of the idea. Almost everyone. When Jalil, sixteen then, learned about Rami's birthday plan later that day, he threw Rami a glaring look and left, slamming the door behind him. A teenager, Jalil had turned into a broad-shouldered, long-faced boy with oily skin and a pimpled nose. He also decided that traditional schooling was not for him. One morning, Jalil announced he was quitting school. It was shortly after the exam results had come out, and everyone learned he had failed an entire school year. Despite Papa and Amma trying all parenting techniques: anger, threats, pleading—Jalil didn't repeat grade eight that he had flunked. He pulled out of school and stopped taking the Quran lessons from Saifa. Jalil said he preferred going to the *madrasa* and studying religion through Mullah Hafiz.

Later that night, Jalil came up to Rami before dinner.

"A flower?" He placed his hands on his hips and wrinkled his nose like he had smelled the rotting carcass of a rodent.

Rami cringed.

"Why?" He raised his split eyebrow and leaned forward. "Why a flower? Would it have killed you to think of something more … boy-like … more manly? How about a horse or something, huh? Real men ride horses," he said. His scrutinizing eyes remained on his brother's face.

Rami backpedaled and ran away from Jalil. The baggy, mustard-colored knickers on Rami's bony hips flapped; he took panicked breaths as he scampered in and out of different rooms.

"Let the child be!" Amma called out irritatingly from the kitchen. She was preparing dinner. "You're frightening your brother."

A few weeks prior, Jalil had spotted Rami and Salma playing on the veranda and had thrown stricken looks their way. Rami had finished narrating another Tarzan story and was watching Salma comb her doll's hair when Jalil came up behind him. His hands slid under the boy's armpits and hauled him away. Salma shrieked and hurried down to her mother.

Jalil took Rami to the adjacent room, shook his shoulders, and asked why he couldn't go out and play with other boys.

Now, Jalil finally ambushed Rami. "I don't know why I'm surprised," Jalil said through gritted teeth. "That's what you get for playing with girls and their dolls instead of boys. *A flower.*"

Rami struggled to escape Jalil's reach. "Leave me alone!" He flailed his arms aimlessly.

Jalil grabbed him by the wrist and jerked him closer. "Listen, boy. I hope there's still a chance for you to grow up and be a man one day." Sarcasm dripped from his contorted face. "If we'd wanted another girl in the family, we would've prayed to God for one!" he spat before shoving Rami away.

"Of all the brothers I could've had, I got stuck with this clumsy little excuse for a boy." Rami heard Jalil's insult behind him.

He wiped the snot and tears from his face and forgot about it by the time the family sat for dinner. But, when he was older, Rami realized that that moment and that night—with Jalil's words—had begun to shape the person he would ultimately become.

RAMI PAUSED. He and Danyaal sat in silence for a while, and some time passed. Then Danyaal pressed the hand with which he was holding Rami's.

"What happened next?" he murmured.

THE EVENING before his birthday, Rami resumed; he and Narin were busy applying the final touches to the lantern when Papa summoned everyone into the living room.

He revealed how the eight-foot-tall lotus flower, made of Plaster of Paris, would make its way to Lahore Canal. With the help of a couple of his friends, Rami heard him say, Jalil would carry the lantern down to Mohammad Khan's green-colored Suzuki pickup. They would lift the flower and put it in the tarpaulin-covered cab of the vehicle. Mohammed Khan was Bibi Jaan's husband. Salma's father. He was a bulky, middle-aged man with neatly combed hair that parted from his left. He used to let Rami crawl into his lap, fingers laced around the young boy's belly, and read him stories in a nasal voice.

Jalil would ride in the pickup and bring the lantern to the canal; Papa went on. The rest of them, along with Mohammad Khan and his family, would secure an area for the picnic and wait for him to arrive.

That night, the excitement stole sleep from Rami. He stayed up dreaming with open eyes, the rainbow-colored flower lit against the fading blue of the encroaching dusk. He pictured it glowing under the sky, smudged with pink brushstrokes, and drifting proudly among other lanterns. He imagined everyone gawking with awe-stricken sparkles in their eyes at the beauty of the artisanship, the detail, and the attention put into constructing such an exquisite piece of work. Rami buried his face into the pillow and squealed in glee.

But things didn't go as planned.

SITTING IN the kitchen for breakfast the following morning, Rami saw Jalil come and sit across from him. Jalil stirred the metal spoon into the teacup filled with Kashmiri tea. Rami breathed in the sweet aroma of cardamom wafting from the swirling steam.

"So, then," Jalil started, "you want to be a man, and I'll help you become one. Consider this my gift to you for your birthday."

Rami stopped eating. He dropped the bite of *paratha*, the flaky flatbread he was about to put in his mouth, back on the plate. Internally, he frowned. Wondered if he had, perhaps with a slip of the tongue, sought Jalil's mentorship.

He hadn't.

"I understand you're confused," Jalil said in a composed tone. "You've been spending much time with your sisters and that girlfriend of yours. What's her name? Salma, right? Well, that can't be good."

Rami raised his buttocks an inch over Jalil's shoulder and glanced at Amma, who was busy flipping *paratha* dough back and forth in her hand. Good thing she was nearby, he thought. He suspected he might be running toward her shortly, screaming for help.

Jalil crossed his arms over his chest. "Being your brother, I'll tell you, but just this once. Pay attention."

Rami looked at him, blinked.

"Listen carefully. And don't interrupt while I'm talking," Jalil went on.

Rami's mouth opened. Closed—opened again—eyes drew blank stares.

"Being older than you," Jalil said, his large hand draped over Rami's, covering it entirely, "I have wisdom. It's time to prepare you for knowing right from wrong and what's in your best interest."

He then leaned on his elbow an inch or two from Rami's face. "We're boys, you and me, you see? Soon to be men." A gust of his breath struck Rami's cheeks. "We must emerge powerful, striving for strength, not weakness. Mullah Hafiz has taught well. Society expects us to withstand pain and yet keep our heads high. We don't cry." Jalil wiggled his finger before Rami's eyes.

"Pay attention. Boys don't cry. You hear me?" he said.

Jalil then reverted his attention to the metal spoon and began stirring the tea again. He lifted the cup, took a sip.

"Boys don't play with dolls." He backslapped his other hand dismissively in the air. He was communicating with his mouth and with his hand equally.

"We do manly things, not some namby-pamby thing like painting a flower made out of plaster, *phhht*," his lips fluttered, making a facetious sound. "It's for girls, you know; it's their role to do these things. Not us. Not boys."

Jalil continued and added that such activities would make Rami weak. He warned sternly that if Rami didn't stop, he could soon be tempted to think of *haram* things, and the *sazaa*, or punishment for such acts of sins, would be beating, or worse yet, denunciation from the family. Rami could be thrown out of the house, he said.

"You understand me?" Jalil patted Rami's back.

"I don't ..." Rami began but trailed off.

"'I don't,'" Jalil mimicked him in a whining voice. "Didn't I tell you to pay attention?"

Rami watched Jalil. He watched his brother go on and say things he didn't understand at the time.

No one knew about the day Rami had been at a wedding three months before and had found himself staring at Auntie Jamila's—one of Amma's friends—son. He recalled steeling himself and waiting for the swelling in his knickers to subside before steadily making his way to the dinner hall.

He wondered how Jalil would react if he found out that those *namby-pamby* tendencies he mentioned went beyond painting a flower or playing with Salma. Way beyond.

The thought made him recoil internally. Rami placed his free hand on the fork lying on the side of the table and hid it under his palm.

Jalil finally rose from his seat to leave.

"Always remember," he turned and threw Rami a sharp look. "Boys, don't cry." He winked at him and left the kitchen.

LATER IN the afternoon, Rami went with his family and sat on the soft, blue-green grass under a willow tree a few feet away from the canal. Amma took out her red-and-gold chenille quilt, which her mother had made for her, and spread it on the ground. Rami returned smiles, let hands tousle his hair, and expressed gratitude to anyone who wished him a happy birthday. He watched a flock of sparrows dart from one tree to another and chirp an evening song. Bibi Jaan was sitting at the quilt's edge. She kept her attention on the rosary beads she was twirling. Far in the distance, the enchanting sound of *azan*, the call for prayer, echoed on the horizon. Rami followed the gathering crowd with his eyes, ate *koftas*—meatballs, some cake; and waited for the lantern to arrive.

All the while, his eyes kept wandering over to the road behind him, imagining that one of the vehicles in the traffic would be the green pickup. He pictured it pulling over and Jalil jumping out, perhaps in a sour mood but obliging. He'd then fetch the lantern from the back of the pickup and transport it to lower it into the canal; Rami's mind wandered.

Papa caught Rami's nervous eyes flicking from side to side. He pulled him closer and flung his right arm around his son. "Your brother knows better. He'll be here soon," he said. But the anxiety was quickly setting in on Rami's face.

He had begun to worry that darkness would fall before Jalil would show up when he heard the honking sound of a fast-approaching vehicle. Rami sprang up and squinted at the headlights beaming against his face. He saw Jalil in the passenger seat. He was leaning over to the driver's side. The vehicle got closer, and Rami noticed Jalil's right arm reaching across to the steering wheel, hand pressing on the horn, blaring it.

The driver, one of Jalil's friends, pulled over to the gravel curbside along the canal. A cloud of dust arose. Rami ran toward the vehicle. His eyes searched for the flower, except it wasn't there. He felt a knot tightening in his stomach. Two faces appeared. Two boys about Jalil's age Rami hadn't seen before. One had a broad forehead, thin eyebrows, and bamboo-leaf-shaped eyes; the other was lanky-looking with an arched nose, pale eyes, and a round face. They both had squiggly, thin beards. They peered from behind the tarp where the lantern was supposed to be. Jalil slid out of the vehicle and flashed a grin. He stood there for a second, swayed on his feet as though he would tumble, but then grabbed the vehicle's door and steadied himself. Rami's eyes darted back and skimmed over the back of the pickup again. He was right; his eyes hadn't betrayed him. The lantern was missing. Jalil took uneven steps and started walking toward his family. From the corner of his eye, Rami saw Mohammed Khan rushing over to Papa and muttering something in his ear.

"Jalil!" Papa's voice thundered. His face flushed red, fists clenched. Jalil moved closer, and everyone saw his eyes. They were red.

Bibi Jaan started twirling the rosary beads at an accelerated pace. She rocked back and forth and muttered a verse under her breath. Maybe she was trying to ward off the *jinn* she assumed had possessed Jalil, Rami thought.

"Where's Rami's lantern?" Papa snapped. "Where is it?"

Jalil shrugged. "I don't know," he said with slurred words. His eyelids tremored. He swayed on his feet again, smirked.

Papa lunged at him, knocking over a food plate. "Answer me! What have you done with this boy's gift?"

Mohammed Khan quickly moved in behind Papa and held him by the elbows. Jalil's entourage, the boys who had accompanied him in the pickup, walked over and stood beside Jalil. It was as though they were readying to protect him from his father in case the situation escalated.

"*Bas!*" Enough! Jalil waved a dismissive hand before Papa.

Stunned, incensed, feeling reduced—all these emotions swept across Papa's face in the handful of seconds that elapsed. Papa stepped back. One of his sons had suddenly outgrown him.

"Ask yourself!" Jalil spat. "Instead of yelling at me, ask yourself. Am I the only one in this family with the stomach to do the right thing?"

Salma had walked over to Rami. She grabbed Rami's hand. "What's going on?" she said shakily.

Bibi Jaan beckoned her to return to her.

"This boy ..." Jalil turned his head toward Rami. Rami retreated behind Papa.

"Can't you see the harm you're all doing to him?" His upper lip curled into a sneer. It tilted the faded scar on his right eyebrow. "What's the sense of encouraging him to paint flowers, run around and sing? Where is the benefit in any of it? He'll learn nothing of value from this."

No one said anything. Everyone stood silently around Rami—oblivious to the cheery crowd nearby—too numb to move, too numb to speak.

Jalil then staggered toward his mother and cupped his palms around her shoulders. "Look at me, Amma," he said.

Amma slapped her hands on his chest. "What's gotten into you, Jalil?"

"God has given you two sons. *Two sons*, Amma," Jalil spoke to her in a bristly voice. "You understand, don't you? You get that, right?"

In the distance, between pauses, one could hear Bibi Jaan's intensified panicked prayers.

"All I want is for Rami to become a man one day. Do you see that? Unless you prefer, we tie *ghungroos* to his ankles and watch him dance around the neighborhood." Jalil shook his left hand before Amma by placing the index finger and the thumb together, mimicking an anklet with small metallic bells strung together. "Is that what you want?"

Amma squeezed the inner corner of her eyes with her fingers. Tears leaked down her cheeks.

"Amma, look at me," Jalil said.

She did.

"Or have the heart to sharpen one of your knives." Jalil kept one hand on her right shoulder. "Sharpen it and do the honorable thing. Spare yourself the shame one of your offspring may bring on you. Shield yourself from the day you won't be able to walk with your head held high."

Papa sulked in Mohammed Khan's grip. He struggled to break free and charge toward Jalil. One of Jalil's companions, the boy with the narrow-shaped eyes, stepped forward and revealed the holstered gun underneath his shirt. It became clear who was in charge of the situation.

Rami saw Amma slap her forehead with the palm of her hand. She shook her head in dismay. "Come to your senses, Jalil," she wailed. "Stop this madness!"

Earlier, Mohammed Khan had whispered in Papa's ears that Jalil might have been under the influence of some substance. He was right. Jalil had smoked *ganja*, a form of cannabis, before coming over. And, in his inebriated state, Rami later learned—encouraged by Mullah Hafiz—Jalil and the boys knocked the lantern off the speeding vehicle while chanting and comparing it to idol worshiping.

Humiliated, Rami stood there. His body shook; his pulse fluttered. But no tear escaped Rami's eyes.

He remembered what Jalil had said about crying. Despite being traumatized—despite feeling crushed for losing the lantern—despite having been chastened in front of a crowd of onlookers, no sigh, not even a whimper escaped his lips.

In front of him: a food plate turned upside-down, a father agonizing in the grip of his friend, frightened—near tears—girls huddled together, and a sobbing mother. Rami's body shook from the rippling effects of what had just happened. But he didn't cry.

His senses dulled as if submerged underwater; Rami heard Papa's muffled voice calling his name. He was asking something. Instead of responding, Rami doubled over and dropped to the ground. Retched.

A GUST of wind blew. Rami took a deep breath and inhaled the scent of summer grass. Something tickled Rami's hand. It was a hair on Danyaal's arm. Rami looked up and returned Danyaal's solemn stare.

"Oh, Rami."

Rami noticed Danyaal had held onto his hand tightly while he spoke. He felt a sense of comfort and solace in the warmth of Danyaal's touch, a reminder of the power of human connection. Amid the hordes of people, he longed to run his finger over the thickness of Danyaal's lips. Rami fought the urge to reach over and kiss him.

Someone cheered at the sight of the first lantern floating by. Another in the swiftly gathering crowd clapped.

Rami heard Danyaal whisper his name.

"What?"

"I'm sorry I asked you to come."

"I'm glad we did."

"Rami?"

"What is it?"

"Did you ever try making another lantern?"

Rami shook his head no.

Danyaal grew quiet for a dozen or so heartbeats.

"Rami?"

"Yes?"

"You want to make a paper ship and set it to sail along the other lanterns?"

Rami's eyes met Danyaal's stare and caught a smile playing on Danyaal's lips. "It won't be as grand as others, but it will be uniquely ours," Danyaal said.

Rami's face brightened. It was one of the things he loved about Danyaal. He possessed the talent for saying the perfect thing at the perfect moment. He gave him a nod.

DANYAAL QUICKLY reached into the backpack and fished for a red-colored, two-ply paper napkin. He folded it in half along its short side. Rami watched Danyaal's fingers, like a skilled artisan, move flawlessly: folding down the top corners of the napkin, lining the bottom against both sides, making the triangle into a square, firmly folding up the bottom flaps and pulling out the triangles on the side of the square.

"There," Danyaal said a few minutes later after pressing against the final crease along the edges, after lining it neatly. "Our red paper ship."

Rami felt his eyes moistening. "Danyaal."

"Wait, there's more."

Danyaal went back to the backpack and fetched two tea-light candles. He placed them on each side of the seam running down the ship's middle.

"Now it's ready."

They got on their knees and placed their palms on the grass. Danyaal gently dropped the ship into the canal and asked Rami to hold it. He then struck a match and lit the candles.

Around them, the evening shadows had grown duskier in the encroaching darkness. Night had fallen, and with it came the welcoming coolness in the air. In the reflection of the water, Rami could see the candlelight flickering against their faces. And in that same reflection, he saw Danyaal's eyes settled on his.

It was the look of a companion, asking him to let go, encouraging Rami to shed the demons of his past. And now, the eyes said, Rami had a friend in whom he could always confide.

Always.

A faint breeze stroked against the canal's surface and ruffled its stillness. Danyaal nodded, and Rami let the paper ship go. They sat back down on the grass, knees drawn to their chests, shoulders touching. Rami watched it sail briefly before flipping over and sinking. After nearly eight years, his wish to float his lantern in the canal had come true—because of the person sitting next to him—this boy he'd only known for a short while. Up above, the moon was cowering behind the puffy clouds. Rami cocooned himself in Danyaal's protective presence. He heard Danyaal hum a poem by the legendary poet Faiz Ahmad Faiz.

"Sing with me," Danyaal whispered to Rami.

Rami began:

Gar mujhe is ka yakeen ho, mere hamdam, mere dost …

If I could believe, for one second, my friend, my confidante,
that my words, my songs, could wither away
that weariness in your heart, that sadness in your eyes, that
pain in your chest
If I could believe it …
I would sing and sing for you; I would knit new songs for
you
I would sit by your side forever and ever

TEN

July 22, 1986, was the day of many 'firsts' for Rami: The first time he visited Danyaal's room, the first time he held a guitar in his hands. He recalled running his fingers over the acoustic instrument and feeling its mahogany neck and metal strings. And the first time he heard someone he knew referred to as *chikna,* a street slang. Heard it when Danyaal was called an effeminate fag.

Yes, another first.

It was the beginning of the monsoon season, and earlier that day after class, Rami and Danyaal went to Liberty Market, a large shopping center in Gulberg, one of the city's affluent neighborhoods. An outdoor plaza shaped like a horseshoe, Liberty Market had a variety of shops, a vaulted bazaar, and a park in the middle. Street vendors separated the crowded sidewalks from the road and were busy preparing a variety of grub. Rami entered the market with Danyaal and inhaled the mouthwatering aroma of street food wafting through the air. They strolled past the shimmering jewelry stores filled with women trying on gold earrings and passed electronic shops with windows covered with large posters of brand names like Sansui, AKAI, and TDK. Rami could hear the high-pitched bargaining taking place by customers inside. Here were some smiling shopkeepers trying to entice the browsing pedestrians to come in and look at the colorful Persian rugs. There were some busy salesclerks in bustling shoe stores, eagerly trying to find you that perfect pair in the correct size.

Rami poked his head into some of the shops. He ran his hand over various styles of shirts hanging on display at the front of the clothing stores. Mostly, they window-shopped. Danyaal disappeared and reappeared between stores; he even tried on a pair of brown shoes. They then strolled through the adjacent Meena Bazaar before ending up at Bandu Khan, a roadside restaurant famous for its spicy *biryani.*

"Saw something you liked?" Rami said to Danyaal after they had grabbed their trays carrying heaping plates of chicken *biryani* and walked over to an empty table.

"Nothing caught my eye." Danyaal put the tray on the table and pulled a chair.

He then leaned over, positioned his face over the rising steam, and inhaled the flavorful smell of the dish. He rubbed his hand over his belly.

"I'm starving." Rami ran his tongue over his lips. He stirred in the spices resting at the bottom of the plate with a spoon.

"That yellow shirt you looked at earlier, Rami," Danyaal said after a long pause, referring to the double-pocketed shirt Rami had skimmed over earlier. "Nice, na?"

"It was nice," said Rami. "I liked the design."

Danyaal nodded while swallowing chewed food. "Very stylish looking." He squeezed a wedge of lime and squirted the juice onto his plate. "We can go back to that store after eating. You want to try it on?" he asked.

What Rami hadn't mentioned to Danyaal was how he had scurried away after his eyes landed on the price tag of that shirt. That clothing store undoubtedly catered to customers who could afford such luxuries. It was more extravagant than any piece of garment he owned.

Rami's weekly allowance from Papa barely covered lunch and gas money for the motorcycle.

"Na," Rami said nonchalantly, kept his head down. "Another time."

"You're sure?"

"I'm sure."

They ate silently for another few minutes before Rami noticed Danyaal darting glances at him through swirling steam.

"What?"

He could tell Danyaal was struggling to say something.

"Rami?"

Rami looked at him.

"You know," Danyaal said, clearing his throat, "I noticed you liked that shirt a lot. I've some extra cash saved up. I could loan you some money."

Rami flinched. It was as though Danyaal were reading his mind.

Or am I such an open book to Danyaal that he could see right through me? The thought startled Rami.

"Just drop it," he held the spoonful of *biryani* an inch from his mouth and said. "Please."

"I think it'd look good on you."

"Danyaal—"

"All I'm saying is—"

"Stop it, Danyaal. I swear to—"

That was when a vaguely familiar voice calling Rami's name entered his ears. Rami turned his head to the right and saw Abdul strutting over. He was with a group of boys his age.

"Hey there, Rami. How's the raga practice?" Abdul stood next to Rami with his thumbs hooked in his belt loops, his self-satisfying grin looming over Rami's face. Rami inhaled the strong smell of cologne wafting from his tight shirt. It accentuated his arms.

"Are you a certified *Mirasi* yet?"

One of the boys in Abdul's group cackled.

Rami hadn't seen Abdul for a few years. He had grown taller and thicker than he'd remembered.

"Word on the street is you're in college now," Abdul said. "*Wah, wah*, soon to be a suited-booted *gora sahib, na?* Like those British bastards who ruled us for so long?" There was no denying the sarcasm lurking beneath his tone.

Rami kept his head low. From the corner of his eye, he glanced at Danyaal and noticed anxiety sweeping across his face.

"You don't hang out with us at the arcade anymore. You think you're better than us?"

"I've been busy, Abdul!" Rami said sharply. "Now, please mind your own business."

Unencumbered by the curtness in Rami's voice, Abdul's eyes flicked from Rami to Danyaal. "Who's this with you?"

"A friend."

"*A friend.*" Abdul relished the words. "I see," he said.

He placed his palms on the table and leaned forward. "What's your name, *chikna.*"

Rami felt his pulse begin to race. The insulting way he had addressed Danyaal. Abdul, undoubtedly, was looking for trouble. And he will find a way to stir something up; Rami was convinced. Something inside him roiled. He saw the apprehension on Danyaal's face.

Danyaal pulled his chair away from the table and looked at Rami. Rami wondered if that was how Danyaal had felt when the boys at St. Anthony had bullied him.

"Don't be alarmed, pretty boy," said Abdul with an unfaltering smirk plastered on his face. "We're all friends here. Ask Rami if you don't believe me." He flicked his thumb over his shoulder toward Rami. "You look yummy, by the way."

"Leave us alone," Rami said. His voice trembled; he felt his chest tightening. "We're not bothering you."

Abdul swiveled his head toward Rami and threw him a cold glance. "I'm trying to make a new friend," he said. Then his voice turned icy. "Don't interrupt when I'm talking to someone."

What will I do? What will I do? Rami's head rang with that thought. *If Abdul continued harassing Danyaal, how would I react?* He felt his stomach lurch. Rami knew how notorious Abdul was for tormenting other boys. *If things turned physical, they could get ugly. Will I stand up for Danyaal? Or will I run?* Rami was aware of the choices he'd made in the past. A sweat broke into his palms. He sensed a sickness coming on.

"Forget Rami. Come hang out with us," Abdul, wide-eyed, said to Danyaal. "We're fun. We'll show you a good time." His accomplices grinningly nodded. "I bet you'll like it, *chikna.*"

"Stop calling me *chikna!*" Danyaal snapped.

Abdul's eyes narrowed before a crooked smile creased his mouth. "I'm sorry." He straightened himself and crossed his arms over his chest. "You like *gandu* better?" he said.

So, this is how it will go down, Rami thought. Abdul's slur meant submissive, passive giver. It was becoming apparent that Abdul wouldn't be willing to let go that easily. *Soon, he will drag Danyaal to an alley and pummel him for standing up for himself. And he'd likely make me watch.* Rami felt dizzy.

He closed his eyes and muttered a prayer. A prayer for help. A prayer for this feeling in his stomach to go away. Rami prayed he wouldn't have to witness Abdul assaulting Danyaal and that he would be spared having his cowardliness on display again.

Despite not being a firm believer in divine power, Rami's prayers were answered. He heard a booming voice coming from nearby, calling Danyaal's name. Rami cracked his eyelids and saw two men approaching.

One appeared in his fifties and had a full head of snow-white hair, cobalt blue eyes, and a wizened yet charming face. His shoulders seemed muscular for a man his age. It complemented his ample chest. The other man seemed younger, had a fringe of peppered-gray hair, and a thinner body frame.

"What's going on?" the white-haired man said as he approached them. "Are you all right, Danyaal?"

Abdul quickly eyed his accomplices, and they all scurried away. "Another time, *chikna!*" Abdul called out over his shoulder.

The man with silvery hair gave the receding shape of Abdul an admonishing look.

"I'm okay, Father," Danyaal mumbled.

Another first for Rami that day was meeting Danyaal's family member. Danyaal's father inquired about the boys who'd taken off.

"It's nothing. It's fine."

"And who's this with you?" Rami met Danyaal's father's eyes settled on him.

Danyaal introduced Rami as his good friend.

'A good friend. Would he have introduced you this way had he known the thoughts swirling in your head earlier?' the taunting voice of one of his demons echoed in Rami's head.

Danyaal's father extended his hand toward Rami, which he shook with both of his.

"*Salaam,*" Rami said.

Rami wanted to thank him and say he appreciated his showing up to rescue his son from those bullies and prevent his being humiliated in front of his friend. But he mostly listened. Let his head tilt and nod at the banal conversation between a father and son. Danyaal informed his father that Rami had also been a student at Forman Christian College and that they were only window-shopping at the market that afternoon. His father asked how the studies were coming along at the college.

"Fine."

His father asked about what they were learning.

"The usual."

Rami discovered that the news agency Danyaal's father worked for was nearby, and he was there with his colleague for a late lunch. Rami learned that the man with pepper-gray hair was Malik, a journalist. Malik lived in Model Town, a newly developed suburban community just north of Lahore; Rami picked up during the conversation. On any other day, Rami would have found that information meaningless. Boring. But at that moment, he felt grateful for the obligatory questions and perfunctory answers exchanged between them. It beat having to deal with Abdul and his band of aggressors. The thought made his innards roil again. He tasted bile at the back of his throat.

Rami nudged at Danyaal. "Feeling sick," he muttered.

They quickly said their goodbyes, and, within seconds, a few feet from Bandu Khan, Rami lurched to the side and heard Danyaal's worried call from behind. He stooped, placed his hands on his kneecaps, and waited for the bile and retching. What came mainly was dry heaves.

Danyaal placed his hand on Rami's bent back. With his eyes closed Rami stayed hunched until a thick drop of rain splashed on his skull. He turned his face to the gray metal sky and saw a shock of white lightning whip across, followed by a delayed thunderous boom.

Rami straightened himself and turned to Danyaal.

"Are you all right, Rami?" Danyaal asked.

"I don't spend time with those boys, you know?" Rami dragged the back of his hand across his mouth. "They're not my friends," he said.

"One of them knew you, said you hung out with him at the video arcade," Danyaal said.

"A long time ago."

They stood there. Rami felt Danyaal's eyes searching his face. Looking. Like there was something he had noticed beneath Rami's skin.

"All right, fine," was all Danyaal said after moments of silence between them.

"You believe me?"

Danyaal nodded. "I believe you."

Rami began to say something, but another streak of crackles interrupted him. They looked up at the leaden sky.

"Be ready to get wet today," Rami muttered.

Danyaal shrugged. "Won't be the first time." They gave each other a look and laughed.

IT HAD continued raining by the time the motorcycle stopped before Danyaal's house. Sitting on the idle bike, Rami dragged a sleeve across his face and wiped the droplets soaking his eyelashes. His hair had become one with his forehead.

Danyaal got off the motorcycle and started walking toward the gate after they had said their goodbyes. But then he turned and walked back.

"Rami!" he shouted over the hissing noise of the steady water falling.

Rami turned his head and looked at him.

"You want to come inside?" he said, wiping the raindrops from his eyes.

Danyaal's saying made Rami realize he'd never invited Danyaal to his house. He wondered what Danyaal would see had he come for a visit: Jalil's scrutinizing eyes? The hostile silence after a quarrel between Rami's parents? What would he think of the weary looks on Rami's sisters' faces?

"You're drenched," Danyaal was saying. "So am I. We could both use a cup of tea and dry up. Why don't you wait in my room for the rain to end?"

Rami felt his heart begin to drum in his chest suddenly. He had often wondered what Danyaal's house was like behind that black metal gate where Rami often had dropped him off. He imagined the rooms, the walls, and the walkway Danyaal strode through after he closed the gate behind Rami all those times. A hint of anxiety stirred in his chest.

"I'd like that," words barely escaped Rami's dry throat.

Moments later, after crossing the entrance to Danyaal's house, Rami's eyes registered a courtyard in the center of the main floor. In the middle stood a lemon tree, lifting its fruit-filled branches toward the sky. Beyond the tree were vines that clung to the wooden trellises, crawling up the adjacent wall. To the right, next to the front doorway, was a glistening, red-tiled staircase leading up to a corridor.

"Danyaal?" It was a female's voice calling from across the courtyard.

"Yes, Mami," Danyaal answered.

Danyaal's mother emerged from a room on the far right. She was a tall woman with slanted eyes on a confident face. She approached them, and Rami sensed a calm, unhurried manner in her. Danyaal introduced her to Rami as Afrooz.

"You boys are wet like fish," Afrooz laughed softly. There was an air of intelligence in her pleasant personality. "Let me fix something for you and your friend."

Danyaal thanked his mother and motioned Rami to follow him upstairs. Rami climbed a narrow corridor behind Danyaal and noticed a waist-high brick wall running squarely across to the left. The corridor overlooked the courtyard below, onto the lemon tree. Danyaal's room was at the far end of the passageway, where he stood beckoning Rami.

Rami walked up to a black-varnished, double-paneled door that opened onto a large room with white-painted walls. There was a redbrick mantel at the center and a window to the left with floral drapes above the headboard of a twin bed. The window opened onto the side of the house. The curtains were pulled back to let the natural light in. Rami could hear the downpour pelting the roof above them and battering the windowpane. After ushering Rami in, Danyaal left the room, said he'd return soon.

Rami looked around and noticed a nightstand, a four-drawer chest, a wooden chair, and a table lamp atop an adequately placed desk. His eyes caught a natural-colored guitar propped at the foot of the bed. To the right, against the wall, was a metal shelving unit filled with cassette tapes. A silver-colored tape deck with black knobs and red VU meter needles sat on the top shelf. On each side of the shelving unit were a pair of floor speakers. There was a rectangular poster of George Michael posing in his leather jacket taped to the wall to the right of the right speaker.

"You like it?" Danyaal reappeared. "My room?" He was carrying a set of bright-colored towels. Rami noticed tiny droplets dripping down the sleeves of his wet, untucked shirt and through his trouser leg openings. They formed a small pool on the Terrazzo-tiled floor.

He nodded.

Danyaal hurled one of the towels toward Rami and unbuttoned his shirt, which was caked to his skin. Rami caught the towel in the air and began to undress, one button at a time. A gust of damp breeze blew in through the front door. Rami's body shuddered. He saw Danyaal moving toward him. Danyaal took the towel from Rami.

"You're shivering," he muttered, got behind Rami, and began running the dry towel on Rami's naked back. The soft cotton strands dabbed and absorbed the moisture gathered on Rami's neck, shoulders, and lower back. At one point, Danyaal's hand came around and gently rubbed against Rami's bare chest.

With the contact of their flesh, a pleasuring tingle coursed down Rami's spine. His lips curved into a sly grin, eyes crinkled at the edges.

Unaware of Rami's reaction, Danyaal finished drying him and extended his towel to him.

Rami blinked.

"My turn," Danyaal said and turned his back toward Rami. Rami took the towel and wiped Danyaal's wet skin— all the while resisting arousal. When he finished, Danyaal rolled his head toward Rami and glanced in his direction. Rami felt a lump lodged in his throat like a small piece of stone. He waited for Danyaal to say something, but they just stood there quietly. Rami's heartbeat matched the pitter-patter of the rain banging against the window.

Danyaal then smiled at Rami and walked over to the chest of drawers. He fetched a shirt and a pair of blue trousers from the neatly folded laundry from the top drawer.

He walked back toward Rami and placed the shirt on Rami's shoulders over his chest. "This ought to fit you nicely," Danyaal said.

It was a plaid shirt with yellow and green stripes.

Danyaal fished a red polo T-shirt and a pair of denim for himself. They wrapped the towels around their waists before unbuttoning and dropping their wet trousers on the floor to change into drier outfits.

"Do you play guitar?" Rami tipped his chin at the musical instrument leaning against the bed and said after a while, after his heartbeat returned to normal.

Danyaal nodded. "You thought you were the only one into music," he teased while running the towel on his head. "Sometimes," he said, "when I'm alone, the sound of guitar strings producing harmony is the most rewarding feeling."

Rami walked over and picked up the guitar. He clutched it by its neck with his left hand, just below the tuning pegs. With the right hand's thumb and the index finger pressed together and without forming a chord with the left hand, he brushed the metal strings outside the sound hole. The room filled with a shrill, grating sound. Rami winced.

"You're a natural," Danyaal laughed. Rami gave him a *ha ha, very funny* look.

Danyaal then moved and stood behind Rami. He pressed his chest against Rami's back. "Let's try it together."

Danyaal's left arm came from the back and ran along Rami's left arm, his hand on top of Rami's. His right arm also enveloped Rami on the same side. He took Rami's left ring finger in his hand and put it on the fifth string, the third fret of the guitar—middle finger on the fourth string, second fret—and the index finger on the second string, first fret. Rami could feel the puffs of Danyaal's breath fanning the back of his neck. For a moment, he thought Danyaal would lean in and press Rami's earlobe between his lips. But he didn't. Taking Rami's right hand, Danyaal strummed the bottom five strings. This time, the sound was harmonious.

"How does that sound?"

Rami's mouth creased into a smile. "Beautiful."

They'd just played a C major chord, Danyaal informed him.

Rami tried mimicking what Danyaal had shown him by placing his fingers back on the second and third fret of the guitar. Danyaal walked over to the shelving unit and ran his hand over the alphabetically organized cassette tapes.

"What should we listen to?" Rami heard him mumble to himself.

He put the guitar back and sat on the bed sideways, back against the wall, legs splayed before him, feet dangling over the bed. The grim daylight was peering in through the window on his left. Never before had Rami seen such a vast, diverse music collection in one place. Depeche Mode, Bee Gees, The Beatles, Alamgir ... were just a few names he heard Danyaal mutter as he scrolled through the list of music-listening options.

In Rami's household, he recalled, they had an old tape recorder that, on most days, needed a smack in the back to power on. And God forbid if a hint of music-playing entered Jalil's ears. Saifa and Narin only listened to Hindi film songs whenever he wasn't home or seen huffing and snoring while sleeping.

Watching Danyaal have the freedom to enjoy his lifestyle—a furnished room where he could listen to music for hours or satisfy his yearning for playing an instrument—made Rami keenly aware of his inferiorities, his vulnerability, his troubled upbringing.

He felt a tiny, yet noticeable, pang of jealousy sting his chest.

"You know what?" Danyaal gave up searching for music and turned to Rami. "How about we create our own?"

Rami returned from his thoughts and looked at him.

"Music?"

Danyaal Nodded.

"The two of us?"

"Sure. Why not! Choose a song you can sing, and I'll match the chords," Danyaal said.

Rami nodded. He thought about the times he'd stood before the class, next to Miss Kiran, and had belted song after song to win the *Naghmabazi* competition.

Danyaal dragged the chair closer to bed, picked up the guitar, and turned a few pegs to tune it. Rami straightened himself on the bed and cleared his throat.

"Pick a song, Rami."

Rami selected a melody from a Pakistani film he had remembered seeing a while back, *Nahin Abhi Nahin*, a story of misguided love between a young man and an older, married woman.

"And one, two, three, and four," Danyaal stomped his left foot to the beat. Rami began singing. Guitar chords strummed: G major, a minor, e minor, D major. Rami continued, loving this shared experience with Danyaal.

"That was great!" Danyaal said beamingly after they finished. "You sing well."

Rami opened his mouth to say something, but a knock on the door interrupted him. He darted a glance at Danyaal.

"You're staying for tea, aren't you?" Danyaal placed the guitar against the desk and rubbed his palms in anticipation.

Rami nodded. Danyaal answered the door by sticking his head out. A bangles-wearing female hand carrying a tray appeared. The tray held a plate of snacks and two steaming teacups. Rami heard them exchange a few words. Danyaal nodded his head a couple of times. He then took the tray and closed the door behind him.

Danyaal wheeled around to face Rami, paused, and gave him a look before starting to walk toward him. It was as though he'd caught something lingering on Rami's face, perhaps an expression even to which Rami was oblivious.

"I saw that," Rami said, his inquisitive gaze settled on Danyaal's face. "The way you looked at me just now. What was that about?"

Danyaal set the tray on the bed. "That was my sister Saman at the door," he said. "She brought us halva." He pointed at the plate containing the confectionery snack and two metal spoons. Rami lifted the cup and blew into the tea before taking a sip.

"Saman and Mami are happy you've come for a visit, Rami," Danyaal said.

Rami filled one spoon with halva, his head low.

"You're the only friend who's ever been to my house," Danyaal said after a brief pause. "To my room, you know?" He then took a spoonful of halva and put it in his mouth.

"Rami," he said after swallowing. "You can ask me anything." He whirled the spoon on the plate and toyed with food. "Anytime."

Rami lifted his head. His eyes settled on Danyaal's face and lingered a bit. They traded stares.

"I could tell by looking at you what might be on your mind," Danyaal made a sweeping gesture with his hand, capturing the things in the room reflecting his lifestyle. "Am I right?"

He's doing it again, reading my mind, Rami thought.

"I ... I was just—" Rami began to say but couldn't finish the sentence. He allowed the silence to fill the air between them while waiting for his demon, jealousy, to crawl back to the dark hole it'd emerged from.

But Rami couldn't help but wonder how Danyaal knew, so he asked.

"It's your eyes," Danyaal said smilingly. "It's your eyes, Rami, which betray you every time."

"My eyes?"

"Yes."

"That obvious, huh?" Rami groaned.

Danyaal chuckled. "Just a little."

Rami heaved a sigh of mock exasperation. "Whatever. Hand over the halva," he said and yanked the plate from Danyaal.

Danyaal smiled at Rami's playfulness. He then asked if Rami would like to hear a story.

"What story?"

"My story. You once said there were things about you I didn't know."

Rami only looked at him.

"Well. I want to share a part of my past with you," Danyaal pressed on. "I want to tell you about my heritage. I want to tell you everything. It's a long story, however. You want to hear it?"

"Yes," Rami murmured.

Then Danyaal took another bite of the halva, sipped some tea, laced his hands behind his head, and began.

ELEVEN

On Danyaal's account of the story, which he had heard from his parents, there once was a house, a beautiful house, in the Dahanebagh Village in Bamiyan, a central province in Afghanistan. Perched on sandstone cliffs, it overlooked the deep-blue lake Band-e-Amir. When trudging up a jagged mountainous trail, one could see the vast terrain of Hindu Kush to the west of the Himalayas. The lake, created by spring meltwater, was surrounded by cinnamon-colored limestone cliffs towering in the background. Everyone in the village agreed this was the most exquisite house in the area. A proud amalgam of ornate Persian, intricate Turkish, and elaborate Indian architecture, its erect walls stood above all the other residences, flanking the arched entryways with red-tiled verandas and marble floors inside. The house's front entrance opened into well-manicured gardens adorned with neatly trimmed shrubs.

"It was when Afghanistan was gathering its breath from the third Anglo-Afghan war in 1919 between the Afghan forces and the British Indian army exhausted from the First World War," Danyaal explained.

In the fall of that same year, Danyaal continued; a lieutenant in the British Army, Duncan Westow, embarked on an expedition through Bamiyan to explore the enormous figures of Buddha inside hillside niches carved centuries ago with living rock. The farther he traveled through the region, the more the panoramic view of the majestic cliffs captured Duncan's heart, making him forever fall in love with the Bamiyan Valley.

When the lieutenant ventured further into the central part of the province and discovered the house by the lake in Dahanebagh, he was just as impressed with *melmestia*, the hospitality, of the owner of the house, King Abdul Hazara. The king was the last of the elites of Hazaras, the descendants of Genghis Khan, Danyaal said. King Abdul invited the traveling British soldier into his home. Duncan pressed his hand to his chest in humility and accepted his host's gracious offer.

A few days later, on a cold desert night, Duncan was taking a walk in the garden when he heard the sound of a rubab playing somewhere: the Hazaras referred to the rubab as the "lion of all instruments", a double-chambered string musical instrument resembling a lute. Duncan traced the melody's source to an open window. He peeked inside and, through the partly pulled drapes flapping in the nightly breeze, saw Nadia, the narrow-shaped daughter of King Abdul.

Sitting in Danyaal's room, Rami felt as though he were listening to a fairy tale through Danyaal's descriptive narrative. At one point, he even suggested Danyaal consider taking on storytelling as a hobby.

Danyaal continued and said Nadia sat on a velvet cushion on the marble floor, and her fingers glided up and down the instrument skillfully, her eyes closed. Enchanted by the music and captivated by the stunning looks of the rubab player, Duncan stood outside the window that night and listened to Nadia play.

The following morning, Duncan sought King Abdul's permission to learn rubab from Nadia. King Abdul's chest swelled with pride upon discovering that a British countryman was keen on learning the renowned national instrument of Afghanistan. Such a display of appreciation for his nation's cultural heritage was heartening to witness, and he gladly granted permission to Duncan.

As Rami listened to Danyaal narrating the story, he imagined Duncan sitting before Nadia the first night of his music lesson, smitten, with a lingering smile creasing the edges of his lips. He pictured the flame of a dimly lit kerosene lantern dancing across Nadia's face, strands of her black hair stroking her blushed cheeks. He saw Nadia's nervous eyes occasionally stealing glances at her unexpected pupil, her willowy figure cosseted by the silk of her dress.

"He was struck again by the beauty of Bamiyan; this time, it was Nadia who captured his heart," was how Danyaal put it.

Night after night, Duncan sat on the floor next to Nadia. He didn't learn a great deal about the complexities of playing the rubab, but he observed his instructor giving lessons, which was the purpose all along:

Oh, Afghan girl
Thy beauty, oh is refreshing hearts
Why don't you come to me?
You are a betrayer
I am in love with you
Oh, Afghan girl

MONTHS WENT by, and one night after dinner, during one of Duncan's return visits to the house, he and the king retired to the vaulted veranda for some brandy and cinnamon-flavored hookah. It was when Duncan Westow, an Anglican Christian, mustered the courage to ask for Nadia's hand—a Hazara Shi'a Muslim—in matrimony.

When King Abdul heard the proposal, he walked over and sat on a sofa across from Duncan and said nothing initially. King's unblinking eyes pierced deep into his guest's face.

Rami imagined the unnerving stillness falling between Duncan and King Abdul, the glass in King's hand twirling, ice clinking and sinking further into the brandy. He sensed Duncan's feet crossing and uncrossing nervously.

No one in King's family history had ever married someone from outside the Hazaras, let alone a different religion. That night his guest, a British man from another faith, had asked to marry his daughter.

"King Abdul had to let the proposal sink in for a while," Danyaal said.

Under any other circumstances, for such audacity, Danyaal went on, King Abdul would have soared and killed Duncan, a non-believer of his faith. However, bound by the pledge of Afghan hospitality, he didn't jump to get the sword hanging on the wall behind the sofa. Instead, King Abdul remained seated, and pondered.

The truth was, Danyaal explained, things were shifting rapidly for Hazaras, a minority group in Afghanistan, since the 1893 genocide by the Pashtun, a Sunni majority. The systemic displacement of Hazaras to neighboring Baluchistan in British India and Iran had further exacerbated the situation. In King's mind, it was only a matter of time before one of the nearby Pashtun tribes attacked and took hold of Bamiyan, which would result in Nadia being captured by one of the tribesmen after the king's imminent death by beheading. Duncan's proposal was nothing short of a miracle, a promise of safety and security for his daughter by the British Empire. King Abdul rose from the sofa and hugged Duncan, his future son-in-law.

THE WEDDING took place a few months later. Undoubtedly it was a simple and private ceremony—aside from close family and a few friends from both the bride's and the groom's side—much of the village did not receive an invitation. King Abdul wanted to keep his daughter's marrying a Christian a secret.

Danyaal paused. He wrapped his fingers around the teacup and sipped some tea. He then asked if Rami was finding the story interesting.

Rami nodded.

Duncan remained in active military service after the wedding, Danyaal resumed. He would travel between Bamiyan and the bordering Durma Kor in British India while his wife stayed at the cliff house with her father. King Abdul didn't live to see any grandchildren, and a couple of years after his death, Nadia gave birth to a boy. They called a midwife from an adjacent town, Band-e-Haybat, to oversee the delivery.

On the day Nadia gave birth, Duncan paced the room outside, and the midwife squeezed Nadia's hand. She would drench the cotton cloth in cold water and wipe Nadia's forehead as she groaned through gritted teeth.

When a newborn crying echoed in the house, Duncan hurried into the room and found the midwife holding the baby in a wool blanket. She was staring at the infant's face.

That wasn't the face of a Hazara. The boy's facial features barely captured hints of his mother's ancestral heritage: the bone structure of Central Asian Turks or the narrow, bamboo-leaf eyes of the Mongolians. Instead, the child's eyes were deep cyan with downturned edges, had a long instead of a round face, a pointy instead of a flat nose, and a fuller rather than pursed pair of lips.

After momentary confusion, the midwife clutched the baby in her arms beamingly and called him *kho-shagal*. Beautiful in Farsi. She suggested the boy be named Gibril, an archangel, to which both parents agreed.

Gibril soon became the center of Nadia's existence. She sang to him, sewed clothes for him, played with toys Duncan would bring from Durma Kor. If the baby got sick, Nadia would sit by her son's side all night, awake, and blow prayers into the boy's ear to ward off the evil eye.

When Duncan returned home from the Durma Kor military base, he would set his luggage down, drop his hat on top, and stretch out his arms. Gibril would come running, slow at first, then fast. Duncan would grab Gibril under his arms and pitch him high, making the young boy squeal.

From above, Gibril's gaze would follow his father's upturned smiling face below. At times, Gibril tried to peek ahead. He hoped that during one of those throws, he'd be able to see what lay beyond the foreboding house walls. Nadia would hear father and son laughing and come out, fretting that one of these days Gibril might slip from his father's hands and fall.

Visitors were rare, but there had been some exceptions. Gibril's favorite, aside from Duncan of course, was Father Patrick. Father Patrick had a wizened face with round wired-rim reading glasses and a stooped—slightly hunched—back. He groaned and placed his hands on his hips when lowering himself to sit on the chair pulled out for him. Father Patrick, a British missionary accompanied by members of the British battalion, would arrive in a jeep from Kabul once a week to homeschool Gibril and tutor the boy in—among other subjects—the teachings of Christ.

Of course, the members of the household and the hired help were obliged to pledge a solemn oath of confidentiality. A whiff of that to the outer world could unequivocally label the family as apostate.

FOR YOUNG Gibril, the house was his only world. The arched entryways were his hide-and-seek; the marble floors were the soccer field where he ran kicking a black-and-white ball. The house servants were the boy's playmates. Kaka, a thin, nearly bald man, oversaw the maintenance of the house. He had a round stomach resting on tall legs and a hoarse voice as though he'd come down with a cold. Kaka conducted day-to-day dealings with the gardener to care for the lawn, with *dhobi*, the washerman, to pick up laundry, and with the local merchant pushing the wheelbarrow filled with soap, oil, sugar, tea, flour, rice, and lentils. Masi, a middle-aged, short-statured woman, worked in the kitchen and cooked for the family. She would huff and puff after Gibril whenever the boy refused to eat and ran amok around the house, letting out a defiant cackle.

ON GIBRIL's ninth birthday in 1937, his mother could no longer bear to keep her only child confined in the house. And on one overcast winter day, Nadia decided to take Gibril to the village bazaar. With wondrous joy, Gibril ran behind his mother in bouncy strides amid shops and tightly packed stalls selling colorful spices, glass and bead-embroidered clothing, and shoes. There were communal clay ovens, *tandoors*, scattered across the bazaar baking fresh *naans*. Butchers plucked the feathers off the slaughtered chickens in poultry farms. Vendors gazed impassively from behind pyramids of apples, oranges, and apricots. Nadia called for Gibril whenever he'd stay behind and play with one of the dogs, whose tail wouldn't stop wagging at the sight of the boy.

One day, during one of the visits to the bazaar, Danyaal said, Gibril met a *faqir*. Nadia was busy picking out fresh vegetables at a produce stall when Gibril wandered off and came face to face with the ascetic dervish.

Danyaal described him as a man with a withered look and wrinkles that sunk deep into the skin. He said the fringes of the dervish's silvery hair matched the color of his tangled beard. Gibril walked up to the *faqir* and looked into his listless eyes. The *faqir* let out a pained sigh and took one step toward the boy, his aged bones creaking. He hunched over and met Gibril's curious gaze. He held Gibril by the shoulders—his toothless mouth opened—and a twinkle appeared in his otherwise jaded sight.

The old man muttered something and asked where Gibril had come from. Gibril turned his head to the side and pointed at his mother. The *faqir*'s hand, corded with blue veins underneath his paper-thin skin, took hold of Gibril's. His lanky fingers ran along the lines etched onto the boy's palm. Stopped. Moved in a circle for a while. Lingered.

Back at the produce stall, when Nadia realized Gibril was missing, she hurriedly scanned the surrounding area to catch sight of her son. Her heartbeat quickened when she saw Gibril's forearm in the hand of an elderly dervish in tatters. Nadia raced toward Gibril. By the time she got close, the *faqir*, near tears, was hugging the boy.

Nadia moved in and quickly pulled Gibril away from him. The *fakir* straightened his lowered back, grabbed the corner of Nadia's shawl, and dragged her to the side.

Danyaal said the dervish told Nadia he'd noticed something in the boy's palm that terrified him. In a low voice, he stated that through the simian line—the line that fuses the head and the heart in a palm reading—he saw a single transverse crease emerging in Gibril's right hand. It was a sign of a bad omen, the *fakir* said. In a cautionary tone, he said a cloud of misfortune loomed over the boy. When Nadia tried to pry the shawl off the deranged dervish's grip, he told her—loudly—that Gibril was cursed.

Nadia clutched her son's hand and offered the *fakir* a quick apology. She straightened the shawl on her head and requested to be left alone.

But the ascetic dervish pressed on. There was something about Gibril that wasn't right, he said. And that a cloud of misfortune loomed over the young boy's head.

By now, a few shopkeepers had emerged from their stalls, their curious hums buzzing against the vaulted ceiling. Nadia gripped Gibril's forearm, fixed the *faqir* with a glare, and staggered away.

The *faqir* hobbled behind the mother and son for a while. He kept shouting behind her, kept stating that a curse would follow Gibril for generations to come.

Just before turning a corner, Nadia heard echoes of the *faqir*'s incoherent shouting, now engaged in a whirling trance.

Danyaal stopped telling the story and sat across from Rami quietly for a while. Outside, the rain had let up, and late afternoon sunrays were peeking through the window.

Rami laced his fingers around the cup and sipped the tea that had turned cold.

"A curse?"

As a child, Rami had heard of bad omens from his grandmother. She used to say that certain actions or sightings were signs of bad luck. Hearing a raven cawing meant Daadi would offer long-winded prayers followed by blown kisses on her grandchildren to ward off bad karma. A bat circling the house was a sure sign of the devil taking hold of the household and could only be chased away by reciting verses from the Quran. Rami remembered how Daadi once scolded Narin when she, Narin, swept the house after sunset because it was bad luck to clean the floors at dusk. Doing so would toss prosperity and happiness out of the house; she scowled at her granddaughter. And aside from knowing other ancient adages to tell spooky stories, Rami hadn't heard of or experienced a curse himself. Certainly not one that was believed to follow souls.

He asked if Danyaal believed in such things. Danyaal told him he'd read cases where negative energy could attach itself to someone. There was a Kennedy family in America, he said, who seemed to have a curse hanging over it.

"I personally don't believe that." Danyaal shrugged. "But I know there are some who believe curses exist. They are mentioned extensively in Indian mythology. There are equally those who think kismet and bad karma are made up. People create energy with their attitude toward others and life in general. What you believe depends on your thoughts and disposition in life, you know?" he said.

"If someone doesn't believe in a curse, does it mean they also don't believe in a blessing?"

Danyaal shrugged again. "God knows."

He then fed Rami a spoonful of halva. "There's more to the story. I hope I'm not boring you."

"Tell me," Rami said.

TWO YEARS later, one day on a warm summer morning in 1939, Gibril, eleven then, overheard a few children at the bazaar boisterously discussing a yearly village fair in a town called Foladi. He insisted on going. He was with his mother and Kaka, who'd accompanied them everywhere since the incident with the *fakir*.

Later, Gibril followed Nadia around the house as she trimmed rosebushes; he called out from the window when she was kneeling with Masi picking carrots from the vegetable garden, seeking permission.

Nadia kept her eyes on the sweater she was knitting for the cold season and told the boy he wasn't old enough to attend the festival alone. But despite the doleful looks from his mother, who was annoyed with her misbehaving child, Gibril persisted.

When Duncan heard about Gibril's pouting, he exchanged looks with his wife. After some deliberation, they both gave in. Gibril could go to the festival if, and only if, Kaka accompanied him.

On the day of the fair that morning, Gibril wore his favorite green vest on top of an orange tunic, a *kameez*, and a pair of white trousers. On his way out with Kaka, Nadia called out his name. Gibril turned and found his mother standing beside one of the arched pillars on the veranda. He scuttled over and curled his arms around Nadia. Nadia crouched in front of the boy, cupped one palm around each of Gibril's shoulders, and planted a single kiss on Gibril's brow, worrying, knowing it was the first time in eleven years of Gibril's life that he had been allowed to go somewhere without either of his parents present.

She held her son in a tight clasp but didn't feel the metal of a necklace tucked inside Gibril's undershirt—a gift from Father Patrick. Nadia had missed noticing the crucifix Gibril was wearing that morning.

It was a ninety-minute journey that Gibril traveled on Kaka's motorcycle to Foladi. The paved road ended shortly after Shahidan, a town west of Bamiyan City, and then the vehicle bounced on a rocky, pebbled pass traveling through a mountainous path to the fairground. A few minutes before arriving, a red-colored triangular flag perched on top of a tented dome rose into Gabriel's view. Soon after, the red-and-white stripes of the dome became visible. Gibril's and Kaka's ears perked up to the high-pitched sounds of the flute and rubab-playing, faint at first, then gradually rising as they got closer.

Danyaal described how Gibril excitedly tugged at the corner of Kaka's shirt and asked him to hurry. In front of them, a cheery crowd inched toward the makeshift tent entrance. Gibril quickly scampered over to the spiraling voices of giggling and squealing children. Never before had he seen anything like it. He stopped after crossing the entrance, surrounded by jugglers, magicians, and vendors selling various foods. There were balloons tied everywhere, and the mass of people was milling about inside the colossal tent.

Kaka followed Gibril. He attempted to keep up with the boy hopping between food stalls and the carnival rides. Gibril barely got off the wooden Ferris wheels before running toward the swings, then to the Merry-go-round, only to get back in line for the Ferris wheel ride and start all over. He ate candies, licked fast-melting ice cream running down his fingers, and shared laughs with the other children.

Later in the afternoon, when Gibril lost steam, he approached a bench to rest. Kaka bought lunch for the boy, *kofta* wrapped in a *naan*. He then instructed Gibril to stay put while he used a nearby makeshift lavatory.

Upon his return, after grabbing a snack from a nearby vendor, Kaka caught the shape of a man with a bronze face, broad shoulders, and a thick chest looming over Gibril. The man, Danyaal said, appeared unruly, with sunbaked leathery skin and a black beard down to his neck just above the collarbone.

Kaka inched closer and heard the man asking Gibril who the boy was with. The man, Kaka soon found out, was a Pashtun warlord from Foladi.

The warlord's unblinking gaze was settled on the frightened boy. The warlord knelt, lifted Gibril's chin with his curved index finger, and continued addressing him.

Kaka was now close enough to hear the crouching warlord introducing himself to the young boy, praising his looks, and asking where Gibril lived. The warlord expressed his desire to meet Gibril's father to request Gibril accompany him on a rite of passage toward adulthood. This tradition was similar to the ancient Greek custom, where young boys were expected to have mentoring relationships with adult males. Historians have often compared such relationships—known as *Bacha Bazi* in Afghanistan—to pederasty.

With a heightened sense of alarm, when Kaka sensed Gibril might blurt out his father's name, he threw the bag of steaming corn to the side and bolted toward them. He hurriedly forced himself between Gibril and the warlord and proclaimed Gibril was with him.

Kaka, an emaciated Hazara, was standing up to the giant of a Pashtun man who was nearly twice his girth, Danyaal said. When the warlord stood to his feet, Kaka's neck craned following the rising tower of the man before him.

A frightened Gibril retreated behind Kaka's tunic. In a low, reasoning voice, Kaka told the warlord that he served at the house of the late King Abdul of Lake Band-e-Amir and that the boy was his master's son.

The warlord's face tightened when he learned Kaka was a Hazara servant of another Hazara. Displeasure sweeping across his face, he asked Kaka to get out of his way. He kept demanding to see Gibril's father to seek pederasty.

Danyaal took another pause from telling the story and explained that *Bacha Bazi* had been prevalent in Central Asia since antiquity. He said that, in Afghanistan, it was common for warlords to take in young boys for service and pleasure.

Rami shifted his weight nervously, making the bed creak.

"Are you all right?" Danyaal asked.

Rami gave him a slow nod.

"Should I continue?"

"Yes."

Kaka draped his right arm over the shaking Gibril behind him and refused, Danyaal went on. Incensed by such disobedience, the warlord gave a final warning and asked Kaka to leave immediately and return with Gibril's father while the boy remained in the warlord's custody.

"Kaka was hyperventilating now, knowing the warlord wouldn't have it any other way," Danyaal said.

The warlord then reached over, grabbed Gibril by the collar, and hauled him from behind Kaka. Gibril shrieked. He tried to break free. He barely had time to swipe the warlord's hand off his collar before the crucifix chain broke and got tangled in the warlord's fingers.

The warlord's head cocked. He stared at the shimmering object and demanded an explanation.

A crowd started gathering. Heads turned. Gazes locked, hands cupped around mouths. Soon, almost everyone was watching the exchange between the warlord and Kaka. The warlord asked Kaka to declare if Gibril came from a Muslim father. When Kaka remained silent in response to the warlords shouting, the warlord wagged a finger before Kaka's face and accused him of protecting a *kafir*. How dare he stand up for an infidel? A low buzzing murmur rose in the air.

The warlord's hands again reached to snatch Gibril. With this, a whirlwind of activities occurred: a fist thrust in the air, a leg kicked, the chain flew from the warlord's fingers that Kaka snatched midair. Kaka then stooped and picked up a piece of rock big enough to fit in his palm entirely. Next, Kaka pushed Gibril to the side, away from the ensuing melee. He firmed his grip on the rock and hurled it at the warlord. The rock slammed against the warlord's forehead. The warlord grunted before slumping to the ground with a thud. The crowd gasped and took several steps back in unison.

Kaka's bewildered look darted from the warlord to the crowd, to Gibril. Without wasting time, he lifted Gibril and pushed through the crowd, climbing over the collapsed warlord and bolting toward the exit.

"Kaka ran," Danyaal said, "muttering prayers like high-pitched squeals."

He pressed Gibril's tear-soaked cheek onto his shoulder and continued to run; he even tripped at times, Danyaal said. "Behind them, the crowd was screaming. The warlord was rising to his feet, groaning infuriatingly."

Gibril bounced up and down in Kaka's arms as Kaka sprinted toward the motorcycle. He mumbled through frantic breaths and asked Gibril to keep his head down. He lowered Gibril on the motorcycle's fuel tank and mounted right behind. After several kicks, the engine sputtered to life and the vehicle sped off, leaving behind a billowing cloud of dust.

Within minutes, a reflection of a military-green Willys Jeep appeared on the left-view mirror of the motorcycle. Its blaring horn echoed against the adjacent cliffs. Kaka draped one arm over Gibril and turned the throttle down with the hand of his other arm.

They were on the outskirts of Shahidan now, an hour or so away from home. Kaka wound through sharp corners to create a diversion for the warlord on his tail, bouncing up and down a few low cliffs.

Then, something other than the sound of engines thundered in the air. The smell of gunpowder followed a loud boom of gunfire. From around the corner of one of the limestone cliffs, Duncan and his battalion emerged in a black jeep. Duncan was returning from the military base when he caught a green vehicle in pursuit of Kaka's motorcycle. Outnumbered by the army men carrying ammunition, the warlord conceded and fled.

LATER THAT day, the sky dimmed when Kaka finished describing what had happened at the fair. Nadia covered badly shaken Gibril in a blanket. She then stepped toward her husband and placed her hand on his shoulder.

With a worried look, Duncan sat beside his son; his military hat dangled from his fingers. Afghanistan, the country he loved, was no longer a safe place for his family. The warlord knew who they were and where they lived. In Duncan's mind, he was undoubtedly arming his men with rifles and gearing up to head toward Lake Band-e-Mir. Staying and confronting him would only mean bloodshed.

"The time had come for him to decide," Danyaal said.

When Duncan took Nadia's hand and shared his concerns with her she agreed, albeit reluctantly. They could no longer stay in that house, in Bamiyan or Afghanistan even, Danyaal said. It was now a matter of time before they would be asked to recant a faith not tolerated in that land. And the refusal would mean facing expulsion—or even death.

Duncan and Nadia gathered a few things and decided to travel to Durma Kor's military base overnight. From there, the following day, a team of British soldiers would accompany them further into British-ruled India, their new homeland.

They said their farewells to Kaka and Masi. Duncan urged them to abandon the house for their safety. Nadia took one last walk through every room with sadness pressing down at her chest. Duncan consoled her as he followed her. He even offered her false hope that one day they might return. They stood holding each other for a long while in the eerie silence of that night, before leaving Afghanistan forever.

DANYAAL GREW quiet and allowed silence to shroud the room. The half-eaten plate of halva rested between them. Rami looked over and realized the night had fallen. A sliver of moonlight glinted through the window, casting a dim glow akin to a feeble beam of a flashlight.

Danyaal reached into the desk drawer and took out a framed picture. It was wrinkled and grainy. In it, a man in an army uniform sits on a sofa next to a hoarier-looking male, wearing a silk, collarless *sherwani*, a knee-high, buttoned-down outer coat. He has a thick pair of eyes above his dense pepper-gray mustache covering the upper lip. They are both smiling for the camera, holding drinks. A sword is hanging behind them on a wall.

"An old photograph of my grandfather and great-grandfather." Danyaal ran his finger over the images of Duncan Westow and King Abdul Hazara. "And you met Gibril today," he said.

Rami gave Danyaal a flat look.

"You met my father this afternoon at Liberty Market." Danyaal then fished something else from the drawer. He opened his fist, and Rami saw a crucifix cross resting in his palm. Their eyes met and stayed on each other for a while.

"Is this—?"

Danyaal nodded.

"The same necklace. Once belonged to my father, now passed down to me—just like his creed—and I embrace them both equally."

Rami squeezed Danyaal's hand and mouthed a *thank you*.

"No one I'd rather share this with than you." Danyaal placed his other hand on top of Rami's. "No secrets between us," he said. Smiled.

"No secrets."

Rami was left fascinated by the meticulous preservation of Danyaal's ancestral past and the manner in which it had been handed down to the younger generation. He glanced at Danyaal's moonlit profile admiringly. It was this feeling of honor and privilege, another first for Rami. Danyaal had placed faith in him and opened up an intensely personal part of his life. No one had confided in him this way before. He felt a new sense of self-worth.

Danyaal continued and said that his grandparents, along with their son, had moved to Baluchistan in 1939, some eight years before it became one of the four provinces of Pakistan in 1947.

Duncan Westow retired from British military duty after the division of the Indian subcontinent. He died peacefully in his sleep one year later. Gibril graduated with a degree in Political Science and married Afrooz. Shortly after their marriage, they moved to Lahore, where a local newspaper company hired Gibril as an assistant editor. Danyaal's grandmother, Nadia, lived to see her granddaughter Saman turn four, but she died before witnessing the birth of her grandson five years later in April of 1970.

Danyaal's parents told him the day he was born, Afrooz, lying on the hospital bed watching Gibril cradling his son, commented that the newborn had the color of his father's eyes.

Gibril corrected Afrooz. Danyaal had taken the color from his grandfather's eyes; he kissed Danyaal's forehead and said.

THAT DAY, in Danyaal's room, Rami came to learn many things. He learned about Danyaal's linear descendants, found out how his demon, jealousy, could stir things up. Rami discovered he and Danyaal were born to two different faiths.

But despite it being a day of "firsts" for Rami, it was also a day of living in the unknown for them.

Neither Danyaal nor he had any notion that Danyaal's family genes weren't the only thing passed onto the next generation—that learning of the differences between them had planted a seed of *otherness*—that the angst of watching Danyaal being harassed had only just begun.

TWELVE

One day in late summer of that year, while Saifa and Narin were visiting relatives in Karachi, Rami returned from college to find Amma had come down with pneumonia. He climbed the stairs of the house and walked through the front door. Inside, he saw Papa grappling to get her off the bed.

"Come, Rami," Papa said, out of breath. "We need to take your mother to the doctor."

At the clinic, Rami waited amid other patients in the hallway across from the doctor's office, which smelled of ether and iodine. He could hear Amma describing her symptoms to a tall, white coat-clad doctor: high temperature, chills, coughing. On the way back, Rami carried the brown paper bag full of medicines for Amma. When she mumbled weakly that she ought to get some rest, he and Papa helped her lie down.

Not long after Amma had taken to bed, the family began to suffer from Papa's terrible cooking and tidying skills.

Papa would cook for the boys. He'd bring *roti* that had burnt in the middle to the table and catch Rami and Jalil trading looks. They would stare and wrinkle their noses at the lentils their father had made floating in the liquid-filled bowl. Rami saw Jalil sifting through unwashed laundry one morning. He smelled a shirt and made a face before putting it on for another day. By the end of the week, after enduring disapproving looks and condemning silences from his sons, Papa threw up his hands and decided to hire help to take care of things until his wife recovered.

Rami had seen families in Lahore, particularly ones with upper or middle-class socioeconomic statuses, employ a variety of help. One of his classmates, Baber, once invited him to a party. Rami saw house staff going in and out of his house all afternoon: Gardeners, security guards, drivers, cooks, and sanitary cleaners were all readily available. However, owing to their lower-middle-class status, Rami's family could settle for hiring only one temporary domestic help.

Rami decided to accompany Papa and Jalil the day they visited a neighborhood that had an unsanctioned settlement of servant quarters with colorful tin roofs. The area was known for its compact dwellings, barely large enough to accommodate families that resided in them. Rami strode down the main road with them bustling with rickshaws, colorfully decorated lorries, and buses before veering off onto a shaded, uneven, brick street winding up to the servant quarters, away from the city's hustle.

Rami walked past houses that were crammed together with shared common walls. Gutters separated the street from the sidewalk on each side. He surveyed the area and noticed small piles of garbage littered across the front of some of the houses. He slowed his pace and watched barefoot boys run past him, rolling used bicycle tires with wooden sticks.

Jalil was leading the way. In his hand was a piece of paper with written requirements for a maid. Rami overheard him saying they were nearing an address he had obtained from the *madrasa*. The referral had come from none other than Mullah Hafiz himself; he'd informed them before leaving the house.

"Keep up the pace," Jalil whirled his head sideways and said. "Stay close."

Papa tugged on Rami's sleeve, and he hurriedly followed.

They eventually stopped in front of a tiny shack with a blue, made out of burlap sack curtain in place of a front door. Jalil made a sound by clearing his throat and rapped his hand on the right side of the front mud wall. They waited close to a minute.

"Anyone home?" Jalil then called out.

With this, Rami heard the sound of a few hurried movements: someone shushed giggling children, a metal pot banged, and a pair of fast-approaching footwear screeched against the floor. Moments later, the curtain parted, and a man and a woman emerged. Within a handful of seconds, while the burlap sack lifted, Rami caught a glimpse of a small yard separating the house from the street. His gaze quickly skimmed over a *surahi* on a wooden stand, a clay pot with an elongated neck used to keep drinking water cold.

There was a cot, a set of shelves on the far-right wall lined with spice canisters, and an old bicycle leaning against the left wall.

The man who appeared from behind the curtain was tall, lean, and had the darkest shade of brown skin Rami had seen before. He had flushed cheeks and thick black hair above a pair of narrow eyes. The woman, looking younger, had her face covered with a *dupatta* below the beaky nose. Her amber-colored eyes briefly met Rami's before darting away. Her name was Rizwana Gulnaz, and the man beside her was her husband, Suleman. The father and sons were there to meet Rizwana, Rami had learned.

From the rapidly blinking eyelids and eager looks on the couple's faces, it seemed apparent to Rami that they were expecting company. Jalil referred to Mullah Hafiz's recommendation, asked some questions, and proceeded to review the document's contents. Rizwana and her husband nodded their heads obligingly to the listed duties: Caring for an ill woman, doing dishes starting with the pile already in the kitchen sink, doing laundry, ironing, and performing other sanitary tasks in exchange for a wage and two meals a day.

Then Jalil said something else—more like confirming a point—to which the couple's heads started bobbing and nodding quickly.

"Yes, *sahib*, of course," Rizwana's husband said reassuringly. "Nothing to worry about."

"You're okay with that?" Jalil said.

"Yes, yes, of course, *sahib*. Non-Muslim only, we know. I can get you references from my church. They know me."

Rami caught Jalil looking at Rizwana as though also seeking her consent.

"Yes, okay," she mumbled through her *dupatta*-covered mouth.

No one talked about this, but Rami had seen job postings like street sweepers calling for non-Muslims only. He was aware that the segregation of people based on their caste and religion in his homeland was blatantly present and part of their daily existence.

Historians argued that it was notably rooted in Hinduism. Rami read once that in the early 1900s, many lower caste Hindus who occupied the sanitary workers' jobs converted to Christianity to escape the constrictions of the religion they were born into.

Not much changed in their status in society as a result, sadly, and the divide continued to be reinforced living in a predominantly Muslim nation after the 1947 partition of the subcontinent into India and Pakistan.

Papa hired Rizwana as a maid that day.

Amma could not have been happier with the help. Rizwana was efficient, detailed, and a quick learner. Aside from performing her duties on time, Rami would return from college and find Rizwana in a chair beside Amma's bed, reading her stories from the newspaper or articles from an Urdu magazine since Amma couldn't read or write. In return, Amma would give her gently used clothes for her children and invite her to have lunch together occasionally.

But oddly enough, Amma's attitude toward Rizwana would change whenever Bibi Jaan or other guests came for a visit, Rami noticed. The pleasant smile on Amma's face would morph into a frown; the stern employer-employee relationship would replace the kind demeanor. He remembered how Amma brusquely summoned Rizwana once to serve refreshments to the visitors, even allowed them to make snide remarks toward her ill-fitting attire when she left the room.

Rami knew Amma felt guilty later and would offer more clothes, more food, more toys for Rizwana to take home.

Her way of penance.

But she didn't stand up for her, didn't confront her guests for their insulting retorts toward Rizwana. The visiting women, with an air of self-importance, would engage in boisterous chatter, and Amma would fill their plates with snacks Rizwana brought, condoning their behavior with a thin, albeit reluctant, smile.

Perhaps Amma's actions were motivated by the pressure of maintaining the socially acceptable persona of holding the hired help at arm's length, Rami thought. It could be that she had to reinforce the notion of *otherness* between a master and their servant, between a follower of Islam and an individual of a dissimilar religious belief.

Curiously, Rami wondered if it had also led to him keeping his relationship with Danyaal at arm's length. Perhaps not in a usual sense. But did he—*truly*—think of Danyaal as his equal? He wondered.

Rami was keenly aware of the blood thudding in his ear, of his heart somersaulting many times when sitting next to Danyaal. In the middle of watching a movie one time, when a kiss between a hero and the heroin dragged on, he noticed Danyaal observing him, one eye on the lips locked on the screen, the other on him. The secret, unspoken yearning for each other, the shared intimate glances, and the indisputable physical attraction amid the cultural taboos—were the things that held them together like the tightly woven strands of a rope. A bond too strong for the most formidable barriers of the religious or social divide to unravel.

Rami remembered sneaking out with Danyaal at nights and going for ice cream at the spur-of-the-moment, picking up the phone and talking for hours, playing cards, lying on the grass by the canal, Rami's head resting on Danyaal's chest, caught in a hopeless spell of laughter over a joke Danyaal had told.

Rami eagerly anticipated his mornings as he would ride his motorcycle to Danyaal's house to pick him up for college. And unless one of them had other commitments later in the day, Rami equally anticipated returning home together.

One afternoon, they strolled through the musty-smelling Landa Bazaar, a local market for low-priced second-hand goods, and whiled away hours going over piles of jeans, good-as-new sneakers, and winter jackets.

The narrow brick-paved streets surrounding the bazaar were packed with rows of compact stalls, bustling with haggling merchants shouting for business, promising the best bargain possible.

They stopped in front of a store with a mound of denim stacked outside. The merchant, a portly-looking man with puffy cheeks and a black goatee, smiled over-politely. His eyes twinkled every time Rami would place a pair against his hips and seek his companion's opinion—and dimmed with Danyaal wrinkling his nose with a half-grinning look of distaste that would result in Rami hurling it back into the pile. Rami must have gone through at least a dozen pairs of jeans that day. Halfway through, he'd lost interest and was simply enjoying the merchant's reaction to the selection process, winking at Danyaal. And when, toward the end, Rami told the shopkeeper he wasn't interested and turned to walk away, the merchant cursed and chased after the giggling boys through tight alleys for wasting his time.

They saw *Ferris Bueller's Day Off* at least half a dozen times, and every time, Danyaal burst out laughing at the comical scenes where Matthew Broderick's character fakes his sickness to skip school and when he prank-calls to get his girlfriend out of school, too. And then, of course, when the Ferrari goes airborne. Rami would reach across and swing his arms around Danyaal in awe when the car slides off a cliff behind the house into the trees below. Danyaal would stoop over and clutch Rami's thigh, barely containing the giggle. One would snort while laughing hysterically, and another round of laughter would ensue.

On their way back from the movie, they talked about the film. Danyaal imitated Ben Stein's character's famous saying, '*Bueller? Bueller?*' and sang "Twist and Shout" The Beatles' rendition.

But never mind aimlessly riding the motorcycle across the streets of Lahore or wincing their noses watching other students dissecting a frog in a lab for biology class. Never mind stopping at a food stall and stuffing mouths with *samosas* and *pakoras* or setting sail to paper ships into the canal. Never mind the fingers touching, the hearts quickening, the pulses racing.

Despite all those things, the question remained: Had Rami considered Danyaal his equal? Like Amma's interaction with Rizwana, had he had an air of *otherness* toward Danyaal, when he was around a different group of friends?

Because, in the end, wasn't Rami a Pakistani and Danyaal, well, a *firangi*? Wasn't he a Muslim majority and his non-Muslim companion a minority in the country? Wasn't Danyaal the boy, comfortable being himself, and Rami—on the other hand—lurking behind a mask atop a mask?

ONE DAY around Eid-Ul-Adha in late August, Rami was chatting with Tariq, Amir, and Noor, his classmates, perched on a low-rising set of cement stairs near the college parking when he saw Danyaal approaching. Eid-Ul-Adha is the second of the two prominent Muslim holidays that honors Abraham's commitment to sacrifice his son, Ismail, an act of obedience to God's command.

And August in Lahore meant monsoon: days of watching the slithering downpour from the blurry rain-soaked windows. But it was brilliantly bright that morning. Danyaal was donned in a pair of purple-colored plaid trousers and a gray Henley T-shirt. Rami recalled Danyaal purchasing the pants when they had visited Landa Bazaar a few days ago. Danyaal meandered toward them. Rami sensed his classmates' eyes keenly observing Danyaal's walk. Through the corner of his eye, he caught Tariq nudge Noor with his elbow. A smile appeared on Noor's face, and he quipped something into Amir's ear.

"There he comes," Noor whispered to Amir. "He's the one I was telling you about." Noor was a raven-haired teenager with a narrow face and hooded eyes beneath thin eyelashes.

Amir, a stout-bodied boy with a shaved head, looked ahead at Danyaal, who was now only a few feet away. "Could be fun, boys," he muttered with a smirk on his face, his voice filled with mischief.

Rami wished Danyaal would change the course and head in a different direction. He imagined Danyaal realizing he'd forgotten something back at the class and backpedaling. Away from the torment his classmates were probably plotting against him. But Danyaal continued to move forward, and Rami's heart continued to drum with Danyaal's every stride.

"I heard him talk the other day," Tariq was saying. He then propped off his parked motorcycle and imitated Danyaal's walk, his hips jerking outward with each step like a fashion model walking down a catwalk. He had a symmetrical body shape: muscular arms, a V-shaped torso, and thick legs. Rami internally remarked that Tariq could pose like a model with a physique like his.

"His voice is just as squishy as his hip sway," Tariq taunted. Laughter erupted.

They've been noticing him; the thought of eyes at the campus observing Danyaal and mouths gossiping behind his back made Rami's stomach churn.

"You're quiet." Noor eyed Rami. "I've heard he lives near you. You must've seen him around," he said.

Rami mumbled something.

Noor arched his palm behind his left ear and leaned closer. "I didn't hear you."

Rami coughed. "I said it's getting late," he said after clearing his throat. He then glanced at his watch and stood up, said it was time to go. But Amir pulled him back. "Come on, Rami, stay for a while. Have some fun."

Amir then cupped both hands around the corners of his mouth and shouted, "Let's hear what this *thuka* is looking for!" More laughter spiraled at Danyaal being called a faggot.

Rami saw Danyaal's facial expression change when he heard Amir's insult: twitching with confusion at first, then frown lines gradually appearing. Rami realized Danyaal's sight had remained focused only on him while walking. He wasn't even aware of the other three until he nearly came face-to-face with the four of them. The smile playing on Danyaal's lips vanished. He stopped.

"Well hello there, delicate flower," Noor teased. He placed his hands on his midriff and swished his hips from side to side. Rami could see his hairy forearms through his rolled-up sleeves. "Can we help you?"

Rami wondered what was more surprising to Danyaal: a group of bullies teasing him or Rami associating with his alleged tormentors.

"Nice outfit, nice and tight. Why don't you turn around? Let us see how it fits from behind." Tariq sneered, winked at others.

Danyaal's puzzled eyes darted from Tariq to Noor, to Amir—then to Rami—clearly seeking his companion.

Rami would stand up and tell these up-to-no-good hoodlums to quit harassing Danyaal. Tell them to mind their own business.

Any second now.

Rami could sense a look of reassurance on Danyaal's face, barely clinging to the hope that Rami had his back. The two of them could confront these bullies, couldn't they?

"We can take care of whatever you're looking for," Tariq said before nudging Rami with his elbow.

Rami crossed and uncrossed his arms. A soccer ball came rolling in from the adjacent field, where a match was in progress. Rami turned his face and looked impassively at the ball, appreciating the interruption, before casting a sidelong glance in Danyaal's direction. Danyaal's mouth had parted as though readying to call out Rami's name, then closed.

Rami kept his gaze on the ground, on his feet. But he was aware of the broken smile crinkling the corner of Danyaal's mouth, of the squinting looks in Danyaal's eyes recognizing Rami was avoiding eye contact, and of the dying hope in Danyaal's heart that his friend would stand up for him. With a wounded look, Danyaal turned to walk away.

"Hey, come back!" Noor shouted. "Hey, you! Where're you going?" He shoved one hand into his pants pocket, fetched some cash, and waved it at Danyaal. "Look."

He then rolled one hand into a fist, brought it closer to his mouth like holding an ice cream cone, pulled it away a few inches. Repeated. He poked his tongue into his cheek, bulging it in and out every time he brought the clenched fist closer to his mouth, repeatedly.

"Me and my friends, one at a time, behind that tree over there, and the money is yours." Noor let out a sadistic cackle.

Danyaal turned to face Noor's shouting. Rami sensed Danyaal's weary and grim gaze again settled on his face. But he wouldn't look at Danyaal. He kept chewing the corner of his lower lip, kept his stare fixed on the soccer ball. He wished for it to be over soon.

Amir was saying that his brother, who studied in London, England, had told him they called people like Danyaal shirt-lifter in that country. Tariq and Noor nodded in agreement, giggled—added that another fun slang would be the *semen gurgler* for a boy like him. Rami kept his silence. His face twitched with half-hearted, close-lipped smiles at each verbal abuse aimed at Danyaal.

Rami agonized over Tariq, Noor, and Amir's pathetic cruelty toward a fellow student. But he knew he was just as complicit. His silence condoned his lack of courage to stand up for Danyaal, which only emboldened others to continue their behavior. He knew.

Rami thought of Amma and wondered if she felt the same way, disgusted with herself and cowardly, as she watched her visitors treat Rizwana poorly. Did she feel sick to her stomach, too, like he did now, for demonstrating the notion of *otherness*? Rami wondered as he watched Danyaal's receding figure—dejected and slumped—trudging away.

EID CAME, and Papa bought a lamb for *Qurbani*, the sacrificial ceremony of slaughtering an animal to symbolize Abraham and Ismail's story from the Old Testament. The night before Eid, Rami was aimlessly flipping the pages of a book while lying in bed when Jalil entered the room.

Since the incident at the college, Rami hadn't seen Danyaal for a week leading up to Eid. He didn't show up at the end of that day to ride home with Rami. Then, in the mornings, when Rami would arrive at Danyaal's house, Saman would come to the gate and inform him that Danyaal had already left. In the afternoons, Rami lingered in the hallways, hoping to catch Danyaal leaving one of his classes, only to discover he had exited a few minutes before the lecture ended.

Rami wished Danyaal would burst in through a door and scream at him. Grab him by his shoulders, shake him. Slap him even. It would've made things much easier if Danyaal had looked Rami in the eye and asked why he'd allowed those bullies to torment him. Why hadn't Rami separated himself from them and stood beside him in solidarity?

But Danyaal didn't.

Sullen-faced, Rami glanced at Jalil, who was saying something about tomorrow.

"Remember what I said. You know now how to handle a knife?" Jalil said.

Rami cringed. "A knife?" *What was Jalil talking about?* "What for?"

"For *Qurbani*, of course. What else?" Jalil responded irritatingly and gave his brother a curt look.

Rami had forgotten all about it. As it turned out, he had reached the age where, as part of the sacred tradition, he was to perform the slaughtering by slicing the animal's vein by the neck. Papa or Jalil made the first cut in previous Eids before the hired butcher would take over. The time had come for Rami to get in line with the rest of the males in the family and draw blood from the lamb grazing on a pile of hay outside. Rami had nightmares that night.

The following morning, dressed in newly tailored, starch-stiffened dresses, Jalil, Papa, and Rami went to the mosque for Eid prayers. At the same time, Amma got started in the kitchen preparing *Sheer Khurma*, a sweet dish made with heavy cream and vermicelli noodles. Afterward, after *namaz*, Rami dreaded going home, picturing the weight of watchful eyes on him. Walking back from the mosque, he mumbled that he felt a sickness coming on, said it best he skipped *qurbani* and slept it off.

Jalil placed the back of his left hand on Rami's forehead. "You're fine." He shot Rami an admonishing glare.

The butcher was waiting for them outside the house. In his hand was a rolled-up leather case containing knives of various sizes. He was a pear-shaped, middle-aged man with a curled handlebar mustache and a toothless smile.

He untied the lamb and brought it to the far end of the street in front of the house.

Rami could swear that day that animals have a sense of knowing what's about to happen to them. When the butcher produced a large knife from his sachet, and its razor-sharp blade gleamed in the sunlight, Rami saw the lamb quickly stepping back. The apprehension in its solemn black eyes was unquestionable.

"Don't be nervous." The butcher placed the knife in the palm of Rami's right hand and gently squeezed his fingers around the base with his. "The first time's always the toughest," he said.

Rami barely understood the quick instructions the butcher provided. Caught only snippets of it: *Would help with grabbing the lamb's legs ... flip it over, you see ... pin it down with the knee ... Jalil would grab its head, stretch its neck ... would guide you to the one nerve ... a quick slice ... watch your clothes for blood ... won't feel any pain ...*

Within seconds, Rami watched the butcher grab the lamb's legs with his hands and slam it to the ground on its side. The animal baa'd. It struggled to get back up; its legs fluttered helplessly to break free from the butcher's grip. Jalil had its head pulled up. He pointed at the exposed lower neck below the fur where the cut had to be made.

The butcher tipped his chin to Rami and motioned him to engage. It was time for Rami to claim his place in the male family hierarchy. Rami lowered himself, felt the knife shaking in his unsteady hand. His eyes peeled away from the butcher's face and wandered to the pinned lamb. He looked into its eyes. They were looking back at him, begging, pleading for mercy.

Then he thought of Danyaal and how he had stood there in the campus parking lot, looking, pleading for Rami to save him from being sacrificed to the conceited egos of those three picking at him, laughing at his expense, subjecting him to verbal assault.

"Pay attention!" Jalil barked.

Rami flinched. His trembling hands gripped the base of the knife. He placed the blade on the animal's neck where he was to slice the vein and ran the sharp edge back and forth on the skin.

But nothing happened.

It was like there was no strength left in his arm. Aware of the collective stares pressing down on him, Rami made another attempt. He dragged the knife back and forth over the lamb's warm fur.

Nothing.

No blood came out. The lamb let out a cry like an animal trying to pry its mangled leg free from a trap. It kept kicking, kept trying to break free, kept looking at Rami.

Rami's hand couldn't bear the weight of the knife. The knife dropped to the ground.

"Rami—" Jalil grimaced.

Water pooled in Rami's eyes; he began sobbing. He slumped down next to the lamb, head buried in his lap, arms rested on his raised knees.

Jalil lunged and picked up the blade. He clutched the wooden base, clutched and unclutched. Rami looked up and saw Jalil fixing him with a hard glare, making no effort to conceal the look of disgust toward his younger brother. It sent shivers down Rami's core. Jalil then reached across and slit the animal's throat in one swipe. A stream of warm blood shot up and sprayed on Rami's face. Rami screamed.

LATER THAT day, Rami passed by the kitchen where Amma and his sisters were preparing the *Qurbani* meat and overheard Jalil and Papa talking.

"—is your brother, be kind to him, at least on this joyful day," Papa was saying.

"Well, he made every effort to ruin Eid for us," Jalil said sharply. "If anyone, it should be you talking with him."

"Jalil—"

"Sometimes, I don't know how he'll survive."

"You were a shy and reserved boy once, too, just like him."

"I wasn't like him." Jalil sounded angry. Frustrated.

"You don't remember."

"I wasn't dancing around, listening to vulgar Western music, Papa, or playing with dolls growing up."

"What's that got to do with what happened today?" Papa sounded grim.

There was a pause before Jalil spoke again. "And therein lies the problem, doesn't it?" He snickered. "You can't see what fuels his behavior, what weakens him."

"With time, he'll come around, son, you'll see. Please let Rami be for a little while," Papa offered his usual consoling tone. "It's a phase. He'll grow out of it."

Rami heard a loud sound of a metal pot dropping into the sink. He inched closer and pressed his ear against the door, listened.

"I'm telling you if he doesn't get out of this—whatever you call this—*a phase* ... soon, he'll be picked on by other boys, shoved around, smacked, laughed at. Like a weakling. And he won't be able to fight back."

"Why is retaliation the answer to everything with you?" Papa's voice raised a notch.

"That's not what I mean, and you know it," Jalil said curtly. "I'm talking about his being able to defend himself—

it has nothing to do with being mean or violent. It's about time he starts acting like a boy entering adulthood."

Papa let out a sigh. "But he is, Jalil. He is."

"Then may God Almighty strike me blind because I don't see it."

"You can't expect everyone to be shaped into your mold. You're still young to understand this. Be patient."

From the edge of the door, Rami peeked into the kitchen and saw Jalil washing the blood off the knife he'd used to slaughter the lamb.

"Sometimes," Jalil said with his back toward Rami, "I wish we were a family of five. Not six."

AFTER THREE days of Eid celebration, Rami awoke to the sound of chirping birds, sipped tea for breakfast, and left for college without Danyaal. He hadn't seen or heard from him for over a week now.

Later that afternoon, after finishing the Economics class, Rami was walking past the Clock Tower when he noticed Amir and Tariq huddled together, talking to someone. Rami moved closer and saw Danyaal standing in front of them with an apprehensive look. Amir was standing to Danyaal's left and Tariq to his right. Rami crept up to a nearby shrub, peered around it—held his breath. Then he heard Amir's spiraling laughter. He noticed Danyaal was avoiding eye contact with them while trying to walk around. But Amir and Tariq wouldn't let him pass.

Tariq would maliciously bump into Danyaal and push him back each time Danyaal took a step forward. Danyaal's books were scattered on the grass.

With his right hand, Amir—grinning—made a circle with the thumb and the index finger. He then poked the middle finger of his left hand through it. Poked it in and out, in and out.

"Come on. I know you're dying for some," Amir said to Danyaal with an arched eyebrow above an unfaltering smirk on his face, poking the finger in and out.

Tariq laughed, which sounded more like a squeal.

"Let me feel your—" Tariq couldn't finish his sentence.

Rami's fist slammed into Tariq's jaw like a hammer and sent him flying to the ground. Rami flung himself at him, landing on top. Tariq grunted. Amir's eyes bulged, nearing the size of a couple of billiard balls ready to pop out of his sockets.

"Rami!" Danyaal shouted. "Please stop!"

It all happened too fast. Rami didn't know what'd come over him. Maybe it was Amma's *jinn* that used to come at night. Or perhaps it was what Jalil had said to Papa that'd been simmering in his chest. That thing about him wishing Rami hadn't been born.

But before he knew it, Rami was sitting on Tariq's chest and punching him in the face. His knuckles turned red, soaked in the warm blood from Tariq's nose.

"Say it now!" Rami's shouting bounced against the Clock Tower. "Say it to me, *harami*. Say what you were going to say to Danyaal. What're you waiting for? Say it!" He kept repeating, kept jabbing Tariq.

Amir and Danyaal moved in. They quickly grabbed Rami from under the armpits and dragged him away from Tariq, who was barely conscious on the grass.

Jalil was wrong about the weakling thing. There were many things he got wrong about Rami. Rami wished Jalil had been there to see what he was capable of, what he had done.

What he'd started.

Part Two

Osman

THIRTEEN

Something boomed like a roaring thunder. The tables and chairs shook in the classroom and jolted everyone. It was early spring of 1987, a few weeks before the beginning of Ramadan. Rami was in the middle of the Sociology class when, within seconds, he heard another rapid sound like a firecracker pop. An alarm bell went off at a distance. There was a sound of glass shattering somewhere. Seated by a window, Rami heard shouting from outside and rushed to take a peek. Behind him, the chairs' legs dragged against the floor. Other students hurriedly got up and made their way in the same direction. Rami heard Professor Hamid, a cantaloupe-faced man with bushy eyebrows and a balding scalp, calling for everyone to stay calm.

Rami placed his palms against the glass and pushed open the panels of the frosted-glass window. He leaned forward. With that came the weight of his curious classmates leaning on him. Everyone was trying to peek outside. An acrid smell of gunpowder, like burning charcoal, swirled toward Rami's nostrils. Rami filled his lungs with the noxious scent through a slow, steady inhale. He grimaced before exhaling a long, deliberate breath.

"Someone call the police!" a man shouted as he ran past the front of the window.

Inside the classroom, a sense of commotion had ensued. Rami felt a flurry of activities behind him. He sensed the weight of the pressing bodies lightening up. Rami turned and saw a classmate bent in pain, having hit his knee on the edge of a table; another was frantically stuffing books in his bag, rushing to get out of the room—and the professor— with a concerned look, had been hunched over trying to comfort a boy who was hyperventilating.

Then, suddenly, the classroom door slammed open with a resounding boom. Everyone froze. The door's panels were thrust open with such a burst of energy that the resulting wind fluttered the opened books on the professor's podium. One even knocked to the floor with a loud thud. Yet another reverberating sound bounced off the high ceiling. All heads turned in the direction of the entrance. A young man, who'd only recently lost the traces of boyhood, emerged from the hallway. He was wearing faded jeans and a white polo T-shirt.

The professor's eyes widened when he saw a handgun dangling from the unexpected visitor's right hand.

"You can't be in here," he said shakily. "What is this?" Professor Hamid revealed a frightened look in his eyes through his wire-rimmed glasses.

The armed intruder ignored the professor. He walked up to the middle of the room and stood facing the students. He was tall and scrawny, with hunched shoulders, dark eyes, and exposed cheekbones. Rami saw hints of a patchy beard growing around his lower jaw and chin on a pimpled face. His rapidly blinking eyes were moving from side to side. He tossed the gun between his hands and shifted nervously on his feet.

In an instant, the air in the classroom filled with the sound of panicked buzz and nervous chatter.

"Quiet!" the young intruder shouted.

He raised the gun above his head toward the ceiling. "No one make a sound."

With this, a hush fell over. Mouths stopped midsentence. Rami saw deep fear and fretfulness in the eyes of many around him. Out of the corner of his eye, he looked out the window and saw Danyaal standing across from him with a similar expression.

"Listen up," the gunman spoke again, "evacuate this room in an orderly fashion and gather outside at the cricket field." He gestured with the clutched gun.

"Cricket field?" Some traded worried looks.

"*Chup karo!* Shut up!" the intruder shouted. "Do as I say, or else." His voice splintered a bit as though he had a sore throat.

He grabbed a student standing in the front row from the back of his neck and shoved him toward the exit.

"Start moving," he said and began using the held gun to point—as if he were an usher in a theater shining a flashlight up and down in the dark aisles—directing the audience to their assigned seating. He motioned wary-eyed students to hurry up and walk the vertical rows between the furniture toward the exit. Rami was the last to evacuate behind his classmates, who had spilled over to the narrow hallway and were inching toward the exit door.

Rami had to squint his eyes as he emerged from the building. He stood amid the flow of panicked students, his arms bumping against shoulders on each side moving past him, and took in the sun shining across the pure blue sky with clumps of puffy clouds drifting in and out.

This was Rami's favorite time of the year. The city of Lahore came to life in spring with fragrant orange blossoms, purple jacarandas, and cherry trees. There were sounds of songbirds heralding the season outside the Lahore Fort—at times singing with such passion that their flute-like tone overpowered the sound of *azan*. And then there were the roars of victory over the kite-flying competition during the *Basant* season and the cracking sound of the cricket bat striking the solid, red ball on just about every playground. Together it meant springtime to many ears.

Sometimes, Rami mounted his motorcycle, shifted it into gear, and set out on long rides in and around Lahore, relishing the refreshing spring air after braving through the stiff winter winds.

He rode up west to Badhu next to the Ravi River, down south along the river to Chung, then east to Nishtar, later named Valencia, and back. He'd ride through the grids of jacaranda-lined streets in the Bukanpura neighborhood, glowing with purple flowers swaying on the branches, some falling to the ground next to the trunks forming purple beds. Rami would ride at a low speed and take the world around him with uninhibited peripheral vision. He would feel the crispness of the spring breeze and inhale the tangy smell of citrus leaves wet in the morning dew.

Occasionally, he stopped at a farmer's stand propped on a dirt road outside the strawberry field in Korotana and enjoyed freshly picked strawberries. Some Fridays, he would rise early and ride to the Race Course Park to watch it being prepared for the Spring Flower Festival. He rode through the tree-shaded streets of Jubilee Town and Shadman neighborhoods that smelled like bark and had cherry blossoms amid the manicured walkways with trimmed shrubs. At times, he would idle before the large houses. More like mansions with bending driveways and intimidating black wrought-iron gates with spikes on top that would open electronically from the inside. Homes that sprawled on vast acres of land and kept going beyond Rami's line of sight from the street. Homes with servant quarters bigger than his house.

But, of all the places to visit where spring bloomed in Lahore, there was one that undoubtedly was Rami's favorite. Once, during one of the random motorcycle rides, he came across a field of marigolds right outside the Jhoke Forest Preserve, flanked with pink and white-flowered cherry blossom trees. Astounded, he returned the following morning and, many after that, waited for the sun to rise and watched the fog hovering above the yellow flowers sprung across the mesmerizing landscape.

Before that, Rami had only experienced the beauty of marigold fields in movies, mostly Hindi and Pakistani, where the female actor would leap across the endless bright-yellow land and burst into a musical number. When his eyes saw that majestic sight in real life, it was as shimmering as he had remembered from his childhood sitting in the dark cinema halls.

He would park the motorcycle and step onto the field. He'd surround himself with the flickering gold pouring from the fringes of his vision, stretching as far as his gaze would follow, making him small amidst the vastness of it all. He would spread his arms with palms facing outward and caress the softness of the delicate flowers. He filled his lungs with fresh air and took in the sweet scent, mixed with the earthy smell of soil soaked from the morning dew. Rami would lie down and gaze at the blue of the sky above, at the hues of yellow swaying to his left and right. He would stare until his heavy-lidded eyes would close, and he would doze off to the muffled stillness broken only by the occasional chirping of birds perched on the outstretched branches of one of the cherry blossom trees.

The quiet around him was comforting, and Rami appreciated the calm of those glorious mornings. But it also made him yearn to share it with someone, share the serenity of these moments with another being. He longed for someone else's hands to stroke the softness of the marigolds, as he did, and inhale the pureness in the air in unison.

NEEDLESS TO say, the rattling sound of gunfire was not Rami's idea of greeting spring that year.

He was adjusting his eyesight to the daylight, standing outside the building, when Danyaal hurriedly approached him.

"Rami," he called out his name, "what's going on?"

Rami told him about the intruder and the class evacuation.

"Well, what did he want?"

"He didn't say," Rami muttered before returning Danyaal's worrisome gaze.

"Are you all right?"

Rami said he was.

"They've guns, Rami."

"Yes."

"Who are these people? What're they doing here?"

Rami placed his hand on Danyaal's shoulder. "We'll find out soon enough what this is all about." He offered Danyaal a strained smile.

"My heart's hammering in my chest," Danyaal said.

Rami opened his mouth to say something but caught a glimpse of Tariq scurrying out of the Science Building. He was glancing nervously from side to side, seemingly looking for a way to sneak out ahead of the trouble brewing at the campus. Then Rami heard one of the intruders who had been guarding the building yell at Tariq to get to the cricket field immediately. Reluctantly, Tariq joined the crowd and started walking in the same direction as everyone else.

Tariq's head turned toward Rami as he strode past him like he wanted to say something, but he didn't. Rami met Tariq's stare that stopped at Danyaal and him for a moment before quickly flying away. For days after his altercation,

Rami was sure that those three would ambush them sometime soon. But they hadn't.

Since the incident, Rami had noticed an air of respect toward him from other students. Never before had he felt so many admiring eyes lingering on his face in a classroom, experienced nodding heads in his direction walking down the hallway, or sensed affirming smiles thrown his way sitting in the canteen. Neither Tariq nor Amir or Noor—nor anyone else—had bothered Danyaal or Rami after that.

Rami also took note of the fact that his companionship with Danyaal was no longer a secret to anyone at the college. Even that day at the canal, Rami hadn't cared when Danyaal spotted Tariq idling past on a motorcycle and eyeing them sitting next to each other and listening to music through Danyaal's Walkman.

Unencumbered by who was watching or gossiping, Rami had a sense of rebelliousness in him. He and Danyaal saw each other freely. Eyes noticing them arriving and leaving together, sharing a canteen table enjoying snacks together— or watching a cricket match perched on one of the low-rise bleachers together didn't bother Rami.

"Hey, you two!" The intruder with clumps of facial hair on his face, the one who had stormed into Rami's Sociology class, turned and saw Rami and Danyaal standing behind him. "Hurry along. We don't have all day." he called out.

They scuttled over to the field where a large group of students was already gathered. Toward the front were a few others, like the young man from the classroom, Rami noticed. They stood with their backs toward the black scoreboard next to a handful of worry-stricken faculty members.

Then, Rami observed the contours of another man appearing to be in his late twenties: big hands, muscular chest, broad shoulders. A towering, rowdy-looking specimen with a thick black beard and a wayward demeanor. He had strands of bristly hair, like cat whiskers, that protruded from a mole the size of a blueberry below his right cheekbone. He was standing in the middle, facing the students.

But what Rami noticed the most about that man was his penetrating stare through his narrow, rigid eyes looking ahead. Eyes reflecting the hue of gray as if they were pencil drawn. His gaze so intense it was like fire smoke whirling from the ashes, ready to engulf everything in its path. It made Rami cringe.

"*Jeeay*, IJT!" someone shouted. "Long live IJT." Another mimicked the same two words. A chant that seemed to be made up of the letters of an organization unknown to Rami. Next, he knew, their fists clutching the guns thrust in the air, and, except for that man, they all erupted in a chanting frenzy.

Another firecracker popping sound was followed by the fearful screams of many students. Some stooped to the ground. To Rami's surprise, it wasn't someone lighting up fireworks to celebrate the beginning of the new season, but rather gunshots fired on the college campus, the latest round by someone toward the front who had gotten too excited chanting *Jeeay* IJT.

Badly frightened, some of the students ducked. Many hadn't heard the sound of shooting in real life before. Rami realized he had been holding his breath for the past several seconds. He exhaled, slowly, and draped his arms over Danyaal. He whispered to him to stay down with him.

Many among the huddled students had also not seen an actual firearm before. The only time Rami had caught a glimpse of one had been on his ninth birthday when Jalil had shown up at the canal with his entourage. Today was undoubtedly the first time most had seen a weapon fired on a college campus.

As history unfolds, the generation younger than Rami would have its ears accustomed to the deafening sounds of explosions and gunfire across academic institutions nationwide.

Its future would be marred by the direct actions of unions like Islami Jamiat Taleba—a student-based Islamic evangelical organization—for engaging in the practices of receiving ammunition from Afghan gun traders arriving in NWFP province near the border.

With a heightened sense of uncertainty, Rami and others around him did not have any notion that it was the beginning of the end of a way of life for them. And for the generation growing up after—too young to comprehend the severity of the hostile shift in the landscape of student unions in colleges and universities across Pakistan.

The chanting subsided. Rami craned his neck and saw the man now standing with his right arm raised from the elbow pointing up, beckoning his followers to end the incantation. One of the young men holding the gun walked over and handed him a megaphone. The man wrapped the black strap dangling from the base of its pistol grip around his wrist and brought the narrow end of the megaphone close to his mouth. Rami heard him say something into it, but all that came out was a high-pitched static noise. Many students grimaced at the shrieking sound and put their fingers in their ears.

The man cleared his throat and tried again. Through the crackling sound coming from the loudspeaker, he introduced himself as the *emir* of Jamiat Ulema-e-Islam, Osman Mahawi, a pupil of Abul Ala Maududi and a believer of *Qutbism*, a claim to the religious moral superiority over the West.

To combat the evil of nationalism, all humans must live under the sovereignty of God and his laws, he stated. IJT and its followers, who believed in its figurehead, Maududi, sought to alter the world's social order through *jihad*, the revolutionary struggle, and utmost exertion; Rami heard him go on.

"Long before the NSF or the Democratic Student Federation, there was IJT," Osman's static voice echoed.

"Sharia would eradicate the state of ignorance that has plagued the world in the form of secularism and liberal democracy," he said in a reassuring tone. And the way to combat such ignorance was by introducing religious regulations into politics and economy within a society, he added.

"We're against everything NSF stands for, and its *darling*, Bhutto!" Osman pumped his fist in the air. He then paused and allowed his followers to chant once more.

"*Jeeay*, IJT! *Jeeay*, Maududi!"

Osman's demeanor had an air of arrogance and self-importance: pacing back and forth between sentences with ranging strides, hands clasped behind his back, clutching the megaphone handle, keenly staring at the ground before lifting his head and speaking.

Osman once again brought the megaphone closer to his mouth. "We're the followers of Abul Ala Maududi, the scholar and the believer in assimilating the true religion into politics to preserve the culture and sharia," he said, his left hand's index finger raised in the air. His followers standing next to him nodded in agreement.

Rami and Danyaal, with their hunched heads, exchanged blank looks. They shook their heads in disbelief, listening to Osman go on making claims about how IJT was superior to NSF. Rami heard him promise that IJT would offer curriculum books to underprivileged students and open their eyes to the religious influence on politics. He heard Osman calling NSF propaganda communist, Maoist, and Marxist.

Rami glanced at Danyaal, who was hyperventilating, and moved his mouth in a silent request for him to stay calm. Then, at a distance, a police siren began to echo. Many students could hear its low pitch increasing in intensity with rapidly approaching law enforcement vehicles. Rami recalled the man running past the classroom window who'd screamed for police. Heads raised, and eyes turned. Hoping safety was on its way, some students steadied on their feet. Two more shots were fired before Osman and the others jumped to their feet and scurried away, bellowing slogans over their shoulders, vowing to return. Startled, Rami and Danyaal dispersed with the crowd of students running in different directions. After the police arrived, the faculty canceled all classes for the day and sent everyone home.

"OF COURSE, he offered books to unsuspecting students so IJT could slip in its propaganda writings of Abul Ala Maududi!" Jalil spat when Rami described to him later in the afternoon what had happened at the college. They were in the room adjacent to the second-floor veranda. "Such a conniving way of promoting the mixing religion with politics," he added. Rami did a double-take at this.

"You've heard of IJT?" Rami asked.

"Heard of it." Jalil smiled demurely at his brother for having the audacity even to ask such a question. "I know it from inside out," he said. He was listening to the radio while cracking peanuts and hurling the shells to the floor.

"Well, what does it want?"

Jalil tossed a handful of peanuts into his mouth and gave Rami a look. "Same as everyone—power and control—what else?" he said. His temples worked as he chewed.

"I heard its leader say it wants to institute sharia law in colleges and universities across the country." Rami hoped to invoke a response from Jalil by referring to what Osman had said.

"Such corrupt lies. Advocating politics in the name of religion," Jalil said and shook his head, simmering. "What could he know about sharia?"

Jalil's stance against IJT took Rami aback. He thought Jalil, of all people, would appreciate an organization trying to bring back the ways of traditional Islamic teachings to the younger generation. But clearly, Jalil had a different point of view when it came to leveraging religion to gain political power.

"Tell me his name again," Jalil said, "the one you said was speaking through the bullhorn. You remember?"

"Osman Mohawi," Rami said. He told Jalil that Osman had referred to himself as a person of a higher rank. An *emir*.

Jalil rubbed his forehead wearily. "What did he look like?"

Rami described Osman to Jalil as much as he could remember: gray eyes, protruding cheekbones, the mole, tan skin.

"Hmm," Jalil grunted.

"What?"

Jalil then went on and described IJT as the byproduct of the students being trained in the madrassas at the Afghan refugee camps, who would later become known as the Taliban. He called them part of a systemic process to infiltrate Pakistan's student politics.

"He could be a Pashtun jihadist who managed to sneak out of the Afghan refugee camp and is now living in Lahore without papers," Jalil said.

"You mean he's an Afghani."

"It's possible."

Rami told Jalil how the gunfire at the campus had startled everyone. To which Jalil said IJT was known to have been in cahoots with the Afghan jihadists living in Peshawar and that he had heard reports of IJT leaders in talks with the Afghan warlord, Gulbuddin Hekmatyar, to obtain AK-47 assault rifles.

"Rumor has it IJT has also secured a couple of rocket launchers from Hekmatyar that it's storing at one of the rooms in Karachi University student housing," Jalil muttered as if talking to himself.

Rami experienced a rare moment where he felt a hint of admiration toward Jalil. How did a high school dropout know so much about the country's student politics and what could be happening in Peshawar, the city bordering Afghanistan? And just as rare was his feeling of kinship toward his sibling at that moment. He felt he could turn to Jalil for advice, connect with him since he already seemed to know these things. Things to which Rami was oblivious.

Over the years, Jalil and he had danced around the periphery of each other's lives. Rami made every effort to ensure their paths crossed as little as possible. The dynamic between him and Jalil had progressed from being borderline hostile to the occasional passing of snide comments to now barely acknowledging each other's presence.

"Best you stay away from all this," Jalil said. "They're dangerous people who want nothing but to monopolize young minds for their gains. You must steer clear of their activities and mind your business."

Rami said he would and turned to walk away.

"Not that I expect you to be involved in any of this," Jalil's cold voice entered Rami's ears. Rami wheeled around and found Jalil cracking another shell and popping the peanut into his mouth. "These are things for boys who take an active role in real-world problems, manly boys. Boys who'd one day hold high positions in society. Not someone wasting time studying Arts, *phhht*." He waved a dismissive hand in the air with a facetious sound. "Wasting Papa's money on a subject with no value, no potential to earn much money." Jalil shot Rami a sidelong glance. He then turned his back to him and fidgeted with the scratchy sound of the transistor radio, trying to fine-tune a frequency.

With that, whatever brotherly affiliation Rami felt toward Jalil dissipated. He cursed under his breath for engaging with him in the first place and stomped downstairs.

LATER THAT moonlit night, Rami phoned Danyaal. Everyone, except for Jalil, had gathered around the television in the living room after dinner to watch the highly acclaimed soap *Dhoop Kinarey*, the story of the frantic lives of a group of doctors working in a hospital in Karachi. Jalil had left the house earlier without saying where he was going or when he would return. Rami told Papa that, after the incident at the college, Rami ought to get some rest. Papa nodded. Rami picked up the green rotary phone propped on its metal stand and dragged the cord behind him. Papa caught him struggling to shove the line through the bottom opening of the Farmica wall into the room on the other side.

"I thought you were going to rest," Papa said. He was looking at Rami in a simultaneously inquisitive and playful way.

Rami started to make something up, but Papa waved his hand. "Don't stay up too late," he said. "Come watch the show with us if you can't sleep."

Rami gave him a nod and entered the room. The blue-white television light peering through the bottom opening flickered across the right wall, dimly highlighting a quiet corner. He slipped into his sleep bottoms, lifted the blanket, and crawled into bed. After settling under the covers, propped comfortably against the pillows, Rami placed the phone on his stomach and picked up the receiver. Dialed.

A female voice answered the phone after a couple of rings. It was Saman. "Hold on. He's in his room," she said. Rami heard her calling out for her brother. He could make out her voice echoing in the background. He pictured her standing on the veranda, looking up at Danyaal's room.

Moments later, with a clicking sound, Danyaal came on. "Hello."

"*Salaam*," Rami wrapped the coiled phone cord around his index finger and said. He could hear the soap's theme song coming from the living room.

"I hear music in the background," Danyaal said. Rami told him about the members of his household watching *Dhoop Kinare*.

"And you?"

"In the other room," Rami spoke into the mouthpiece, asked if he was keeping Danyaal from watching the show.

"No. Not really," said Danyaal. "I like it, though."

"Yes. But not in the mood tonight."

"It's more fun talking to you," Danyaal said. Rami imagined a smile playing on Danyaal's lips. "I like hearing your voice."

Rami wished he could say something appropriate in response, something profoundly romantic like '*I count the hours until I hear your voice again—or that it always brings a smile to my face feeling your presence, even through telephone lines*' ... But words eluded him.

"I'd rather we talk than sit in front of the television set," was Rami's response to Danyaal. "Especially after what happened today."

He heard Danyaal take a deep breath. "What an exhausting day. I was scared, you know?"

Rami sank further against the pillow placed behind him. "Me too."

"Thankfully, you were there with me," Danyaal said, "I don't know what I would've done otherwise."

"I'm glad we were together."

Rami then let the following few seconds pass in silence to compose himself. He used that pause to muster up the courage for what he was about to ask Danyaal.

"Hey," he said.

It wasn't that they didn't do activities together. But those things would typically entail spur-of-the-moment planning and last-minute inquiry to ascertain if one of them was in the mood for something.

This was different.

Rami had been contemplating for quite some time now to ask Danyaal out. He wanted to take Danyaal to the marigold field outside Jhoke Forest Preserve. He pictured Danyaal lying next to him, looking above at the sky. He practiced in his head, many times, how he'd propose: Mention nonchalantly or surprise him. Ride around pretending to be lost and end up there and act amazed. With each idea, Rami scratched his head and dismissed each scenario as more absurd than the previous one.

Now sitting in the passive, lambent white light emitting from the television screen in the living room, Rami gathered his courage and allowed the words forming on his lips to roll. "Um ... I've been meaning to ask you something," he muttered, his heart doing pirouettes in his chest.

"Yes?"

"I'm a little embarrassed about it."

"Why embarrassed?"

"I don't know."

"Tell me," Danyaal said.

"It's kind of silly."

"Rami, please."

Rami then came right out and said it.

"Would you like to go out with me sometime?"

He paused for a second. Switched hands.

"There's a field of marigolds I visit every spring. It's my favorite place to go this time of the year. I'm wondering if you would like to come with me."

There was a silence on the other line. Rami felt his heart pounding in his chest. It had only been a handful of seconds during which Danyaal had remained quiet, but it was enough for Rami's demon, insecurity, to stir in his chest. *'You're an idiot. Why did you do that? He won't like it; just wait a second; here he comes laughing at you for suggesting such a thing. Who goes to a remote field to look at a bunch of flowers? Nice try being a romantic. He is going to hang up. That's what you get for being so forward?'*

A feeling of dread pressed down on Rami's chest, noticing with each ticking second that Danyaal hadn't said anything. He was nearly certain he would be brushed away like a spider's web. Turned down.

"You're asking me out on a date?" Danyaal finally spoke.

"I … I thought … maybe … it's okay if you've other plans or something … or if it's not your thing … forget I said anything …" Rami talked rapidly without pausing between sentences. "I know you're busy… I've lots of homework to do, too ... told you this was a foolish idea ..." he rambled. He heard Saifa laughing from the other side.

"Slow down, Rami."

Rami took a deep breath. "Sorry."

"I don't know what to say," Danyaal spoke.

"I know... I shouldn't have ..."

"Rami?"

"Yes, Danyaal."

"I didn't think you'd ask me out like this," Danyaal said.

Rami allowed a few moments for Danyaal's words to sink in. He cleared his throat, "So, does that mean ...?"

"I would love to go out with you," Danyaal said. Rami heard him cackling with delight. "On a date."

A puff of breath exhaled from Rami's mouth. The tense muscles in his body relaxed. "You will?"

"Of course."

Rami suddenly felt as though he were floating in the air like an autumn leaf. It was like gravity released him, and now he was ascending like a bunch of balloons on a string.

Danyaal had said yes to his proposal!

"You're in bed now?" Danyaal was asking.

"Yes," Rami murmured. "In my pajamas."

Another long pause on the other end of the line.

"Me too, in bed."

Those words ... when Danyaal said it—the way he had said it—what was in them? An invitation, an insinuation?

Or was the adrenalin from the earlier incident at the college gradually releasing from Rami's body, leaving behind a pleasurable sensation?

Rami felt a desire rising in his chest like heat turning on and increasing in intensity. He could feel his pulse quickening.

Danyaal was in bed just like him.

A sense of arousal washed over him.

"Danyaal," Rami's voice was hoarse.

Danyaal didn't say anything. Rami could hear him breathing deeply on the other side.

Did Danyaal feel the same burning desire?

Rami tilted his head sideways and placed the receiver between the right cheek and the shoulder. His hand slid down. It crept lower, lower under the trousers.

"Tell me what you're doing now," Danyaal spoke, his voice barely above a whisper.

"I ... I ..." Rami's chest rose and fell with rapid breathing. "I've my hand ..." he croaked. "I'm ... Danyaal, I am—"

He heard Danyaal's breath puffing into the mouthpiece. "I'm naked," Danyaal murmured. "I wish you were here with me."

There was a tickle in Rami's groin. He coiled his fingers around the blood vessels, felt them pulsate trapped inside the palm of his hand.

He heard Danyaal groan. "God—"

"Stay with me ... until ...?" Rami trailed off.

A silence. Then Danyaal whispered he would.

Rami retrieved the left palm closer to his mouth, spat on it, and slid it back inside. He closed his eyes and imagined Danyaal in the room with him, pictured his warm flesh pressing against Rami under the covers. His body clenched, toes curled up, the palm of his hand rubbed against the taut muscular tissues.

His breathing became heavier. At one point, it sounded in harmony with Danyaal's deep breaths on the other line.

"I'm close," Rami muttered into the mouthpiece, receiver barely wedged between his cheek and the shoulder.

Danyaal, also busy, let out a grunt. "I want you to," his voice said. "I want you to."

Rami's heart banged against his ribcage; muscles tensed; he felt rapid contractions in his groin.

Then, a chair scraped against the floor in the other room. There was an alarming squeak of the rattan seat. Rami heard Papa cough, get up, and walk toward the kitchen.

"Someone's coming," Rami whispered into the phone.

"Please don't stop," Danyaal moaned.

Rami's hand slowed. Danyaal's moaning pierced his eardrums over the phone. Rami, ragged-breathed, remained motionless and listened to the footfall dragging until he saw Papa's silhouette returning to the living room.

Rami waited to hear the legs of the chair scrape once more against the floor before slowly regaining momentum, feeling the rapid-fire contractions again. Danyaal gasped over the phone. He'd finished. Rami's body quivered. He let out a breath he didn't know he was holding. Immediately following was the sweet feeling of ecstasy blanketing him. His body jerked with each pulsation; his cheek dug further into the receiver like it was Danyaal's shoulder he was leaning against, and Danyaal was holding him. Watching him. A few seconds passed. They didn't say much of anything to each other—only the sound of their heavy breathing.

Rami lay there, panting, listening to Danyaal's voice doing the same. "It was—" Rami ran his tongue over the dry lips and finally began to say.

"—amazing!" Danyaal's exhausted voice finished Rami's sentence.

FOURTEEN

It was the *kuukukuuku* sound of a rooster that awoke Rami the following Saturday. He looked at the green-colored hands and markers of an old, hand-wound clock glowing against the dark. Rami rubbed his sleep-clogged eyes and, half-lidded, saw the minute hand was on '4', and the hour hand had slightly edged from '5'. He had a little over an hour before dawn, which, according to the weather report on the television last night, was set for a little past six o'clock.

Like most mornings, Rami rose from the bed, thought of Danyaal, and eagerly anticipated the day ahead. On his way to the bathroom, he glanced at Jalil in the bed across from his, snoring like a herd of cattle running past. In the other rooms, he could hear the rest of the household sighing and grunting in their sleep.

He took his time showering, even hummed a little as he was lathering. After drying, Rami stole a few drops of the

English Leather Papa wore occasionally and rubbed it on his neck.

He'd already picked an outfit the previous night: A blue-checkered shirt paired with a black pair of jeans. Even after getting dressed, Rami lingered before the mirror and deliberated whether he'd chosen the right color pattern. He fretted that perhaps black and blue were too strong of contrast against his olive skin tone.

Eventually, he rolled up his sleeves an inch or two above the cuffs, ran his fingers through his hair, gave his reflection a parting glance, and left.

The blended tones of rosy pinks and peachy yellows were bursting across the sky, merging into the softening blue as Rami made his way to meet Danyaal. He rode past houses, the sharp outlines of which, along with the vibrant greenery surrounding them, became increasingly evident.

Danyaal was standing outside waiting for him. He had the brown picnic backpack on his shoulders.

"You look handsome," Danyaal's lips touched Rami's earlobe shortly after he had had gotten on the bike behind him. "Is that English Leather I smell on you?"

Rami rode along the Ravi River. They zigzagged on 100 Feet Road that bent along the river amid the broken blackness, gradually conceding to a silvery mist. Trees in the backdrop were silhouettes; they looked like still objects in an oil painting. There was a shift in the way Danyaal held on to Rami. More firmly. Rami appreciated the intensity and warmth of Danyaal's forearms chained across his belly.

The sun had been rising ambitiously by the time they arrived at the Jhoke Forest Preserve.

"We need to hurry!" Rami quickly tilted the motorcycle to park on its stand. "Come on. Don't want to miss this," the excitement in his voice was revealing.

At a distance, a flock of sparrows burst into a background melody. Rami wondered if they were the same birds who would sing to him when he had come here in the past. He imagined them happy to see him with someone.

Rami entered the field and did what he had done other times: spread his palms forward and let his fingers caress the yellow flowers kissed recently by the orange sun rays. He turned to his side and glanced at Danyaal standing next to him.

"Beautiful," Danyaal murmured. He was looking ahead at the shimmering gold landscape. His silvery voice carried the element of captivation. Like Rami, his hands also moved back and forth in a gentle dance and stroked the softness of the blossoms. His fingers met Rami's. Danyaal took Rami's hand, shifted his smiling eyes to him, and moved his mouth in a *thank you*.

"You like it?" Rami's eyes gleamed.

Danyaal nodded, subtly running his fingers over the bumps of Rami's knuckles. "It's beautiful."

Hearing Danyaal say that made Rami's heart swell. Felt it swell and wash away the loneliness, the self-effacement he'd felt for so long. The brightness in Danyaal's affirming eyes elated him. It was one of those moments in his life with Danyaal, the memory of which would stay with him for the rest of his days. They walked toward the center of the field and allowed swirling fog below their waist to surround them.

Danyaal fetched a powder blue square blanket from the picnic bag. Rami helped him empty the contents: plastic plates and cups, a thermos filled with Kashmiri tea, containers with boiled eggs, paper-wrapped buttered toast, and fruit.

They poured tea into cups, sat across from each other, and enjoyed breakfast. Later, after clearing the blanket, Rami lay down on his back, his right hand laced behind his head. Danyaal slid down lengthwise to Rami's left and propped his head on Rami's stomach, making the long end of the letter T. Rami could see Danyaal's head raising and lowering with Rami's inflating and deflating stomach. He closed his eyes.

A few minutes passed.

"You're awake?" Danyaal eventually broke the silence.

"Hmm." Rami let out a soft grunt.

"I'm thinking—"

Rami's eyelids half opened.

"It's silly, really."

"What is?"

Danyaal turned to his side and looked at Rami. "Having a password between us."

"A what?"

"You know, like a code or a word, only the two of us would know the meaning of."

"And what would we do with this *secret word*?" Rami propped himself on his elbows. He gave Danyaal a playful frown with an arched eyebrow and noticed Danyaal's smiling eyes were lingering on his face.

"A secret word to describe something, avoid an embarrassing situation, or even warn each other of any trouble ahead," Danyaal said. "Wouldn't it be fun?"

"You're right about one thing."

"What's that?"

"That it is a silly idea." Rami rolled his eyes.

The flora around them rustled with a gust of breeze sweeping across. "Oh, come on! You can be no fun sometimes." After making a face, Danyaal turned on his back and returned his gaze to the sky.

Rami stared at Danyaal's side face for a moment. "Really? Is that all?"

"What do you mean?"

"You're sure you only want this because it would be fun? Or you're still thinking about the shooting at the campus?"

Danyaal returned to his side and met Rami's eyes. "Partially," he said. "But also, because it would remind us of each other, especially if we're ever separated."

Hearing Danyaal say that made Rami feel caught in a net of sadness. Sad for the distinct possibility he hadn't considered before. It wasn't improbable that their life plans could drive them apart. He lowered his head to the ground.

"We're not going anywhere," he said with a sense of certainty as if he knew it to be a fact. "You and I. Not going anywhere."

"I'm not saying it'll happen," Danyaal spoke in a low voice. "I thought it'd be something that would bind us wherever life takes us."

It got quiet. No words were exchanged between them for a while. There was a moment of contemplation before Danyaal spoke again, "I wouldn't wish us to be apart; you know that. Ever."

Rami draped his left arm over Danyaal's chest and kept his gaze toward the sky.

"What's on your mind?" he spoke after moments of silence. "You have any suggestions?"

"All right, here's one," Danyaal said. "We take some letters from our first names and combine them into a word. Say your name out loud."

"Rami," Rami called out.

"Danyaal," Danyaal followed and said his. Then he mumbled something under his breath for a dozen or so seconds, shifting the letters around.

"How about *yaarana*?"

"*Yaarana*?"

"Yes, friendship," Danyaal said. "We take the letters *y and a* from my name, letters *r and a* from your name—and switch the letters *a* and *n* from my name to *n and a*."

"It's like a riddle."

"It is."

"You've been thinking about this for a while, haven't you?"

"Me? No. Never."

"You're so lame." Rami laughed.

"And you're jealous."

"Of what?"

"My smarts."

"*Yaarana!*" Rami shouted the Urdu word. His voice echoed across the wide-open field, jolting a few birds perched on branches to flutter away.

Danyaal followed suit and repeated the word in the open air.

"It's settled, then," he said.

"Fine, whatever," Rami said. "Any buttered toast left?"

LATER, RAMI asked if they should stop at Korotana for strawberries on the way back, to which Danyaal said he'd love some. Rami steered the motorcycle toward Bohewal, down Tariddewala road, and onto the gravel pathway leading to the strawberry stand.

The stand owner, a farmer, was a tall man with legs longer than his torso and a nose that appeared to have been broken and reset several times. He was kneeling beside the crates of luscious strawberries and arranging them neatly. The farmer's eyes registered recognition, and the two-day stubble decorating his jaws flexed in a smile when he saw Rami approaching.

"Welcome, *sahib*. Back for some fresh fruit?" The farmer greeted Rami with a nod and a handshake, his blue veins bulging under his paper-thin skin. "And you brought a friend, how wonderful!" Danyaal offered him *salaam*.

Rami fished into his pockets for cash while the farmer wiped a plate with the corner of the shawl hanging from his shoulders and filled it with strawberries.

"Freshly picked. Enjoy." He handed the plate to Danyaal. "Come back for more when you finish," he said.

Rami found a small wooden table to the left of the stand and sat across from Danyaal. They took bites.

Danyaal gathered a deep breath as if gulping air. "So fresh," he said. "There's something magical about spring air, isn't it?"

Rami nodded and stuffed his mouth with another whole strawberry.

"Such a beautiful morning, Rami."

"The company isn't half bad, either." Rami pretended to show off, loving how well their date was going.

"And cute, too."

Rami fought back a smile. "Really?"

"Really," Danyaal said. He was staring at him coyly.

"More strawberries?" Rami said. He pointed at the plate that had only one piece of fruit left. Danyaal nodded.

Rami grabbed the plate. He was half-hunched, raising himself off the chair, when he noticed Danyaal's smile suddenly disappeared.

"What's the matter?"

Danyaal stayed quiet. The color drained from his face; his eyes were settled on something behind Rami.

Rami turned around. It was Osman, the thick, broad-shouldered man who'd interrupted classes at the campus a few days ago. He was standing next to a beige-colored Suzuki hatchback sedan. The vehicle was old and had rusted dents along the passenger door.

Rami's heart jumped.

Lingering next to Osman was another familiar figure Rami noticed. It was Amir, one of his classmates from last year. Rami caught him balancing his weight nervously. His eyes, fixed on Rami, were looking simultaneously unsure and excited. He leaned into Osman's right ear and whispered something. His sidelong glance stayed on Rami.

Osman listened. Nodded. His mouth creased into a smile.

"You must be Rami. The fearless *talib*!" Osman's deep voice bludgeoned Rami's eardrums when he called him the Arabic word for student or knowledge seeker, which was followed by a short burst of laughter. Rami could detect a hint of Pashto dialect in him when speaking Urdu. There were traces of '*sh*' and '*ksh*' below the surface of Osman's spoken words.

Rami had a good idea what Amir might have muttered to Osman: His altercation, of course, with Tariq the previous year after Eid-Ul-Adha. And now his not-so-secret relationship with Danyaal. He glanced over his shoulder at Danyaal standing a few feet from the table.

Osman walked past Rami toward the stand, turned, and grabbed the last strawberry. The plate shook in Rami's hand. "Such sweet fruit from God's bounty, wouldn't you agree?"

Rami didn't say anything; he only looked at him.

Standing this close to Osman, he realized he had never seen a pair of hands this large. Osman's bulky profile, bulging biceps, thick belly—the sheer size of it all made Rami gasp.

"It's you, isn't it? Rami, is it?" Osman lowered himself onto the chair Danyaal was in moments ago. He planted his feet on the table and crossed his ankles.

"Yes." Rami's lips felt heavy speaking.

"It's nice to meet you, Rami. How fortunate are we to hear a wonderful name like yours on a glorious day like today?"

Osman's eyes then flitted from Rami to Danyaal and back again. "And him?"

Rami's mind raced back to earlier when Danyaal had lain with his head resting on Rami's belly and Rami's arm flung over Danyaal's chest.

"Who's he?"

"A friend," Rami said.

Osman raised both eyebrows, snorted. "Just a *friend*?"

Rami looked in Danyaal's direction.

"Just a friend."

Osman got up and moved toward Rami. He slung his arms around his shoulders. "Walk with me, boy."

They took steps together toward the other side of the car. The weight of Osman's arm pressed down on Rami's shoulder. "You know, I like what I've heard about you. It was brave of you to do what you did to that boy at the college," Osman said. Rami's suspicion about Amir filling Osman's ear was confirmed. "I like boys with the courage to stand up for themselves, their friends, and those in need. You know what I mean?"

Rami said he did despite remembering his past choices—recalling the boy Rayan, Abdul, and his accomplices had beaten—and how shamefully he'd allowed it to happen. He felt a wave of sickness rushing through his stomach.

"But I also hear things that concern me," Osman flicked his thumb over his shoulder and pointed at Danyaal standing behind them. "Like what I've heard about you two. Tell me his name."

"Danyaal."

"Danyaal, yes. Where's Danyaal from?"

"What?"

"Where has he come from?"

"He's from here," Rami said and felt the weight of Osman's stony eyes on him. "He's a Pakistani, like me."

Rami's mind raced to the day Danyaal was called a *firangi*.

"What I mean is, where did his forefathers come from, Rami?" Osman's voice tensed.

Rami hesitated. There was a pause. He felt Osman's grip tightening on his shoulder.

"Afghanis," he blurted out through scrunched teeth in pain. "They were Afghanis."

"Pashtun?"

Rami gave Osman a puzzled look.

Osman leaned on Rami's collarbone. "I need an answer."

"To my knowledge, they were Hazaras!" Rami nearly screamed.

Osman gave out a thick grunt; his grip loosened. Rami felt something cold drip down his spine.

"That wasn't so bad, was it?"

Rami looked at his feet.

"You and I will be good friends, I tell you," Osman smiled.

Rami kept his gaze low.

"And there's something else I must tell you. Rami, look at me."

Reluctantly, Rami did.

Osman's cold stare bore into Rami. "You need to be careful who you're friends with," he said. "You seem to be a decent boy from a noble, God-loving Sunni family. Am I right? I must remind you to stay away from sinful, *haram* tendencies."

Rami blinked.

"A Hazara," Osman said in a displeased tone. "Here's another thing you should know about Hazaras. They're Shi'a, the worst of Muslims. Did you know that?"

Rami was aware of the sectarian violence against Shi'a people by Sunnis and the bitter split between the two main sects over who should succeed Prophet Muhammad as the leader of the Islamic faith fourteen centuries ago.

Rami stayed quiet. He didn't mention to Osman that Danyaal was neither a Sunni nor Shi'a Muslim.

"You see, these people are not worthy of your friendship, these Shi'a Muslims. Their role is to serve as servants and laborers, not be friends, not someone you associate with. I'm aware of your *friend*'s type."

This time, Osman flicked his chin toward Danyaal with a look as though Danyaal were a piece of cellophane discarded on the side of the road.

"His type?"

"People like him are smooth talkers, notorious for corrupting boys like you. The land where I come from, a place I doubt you've ever been to, boys like him are ..." A sadistic grin appeared on Osman's face. "We don't need to go much into detail." He waved a hand in the air. "But understand this. You'll find nothing of value by hanging out with this boy. You hear me?"

Rami wanted to ask Osman what he meant to mention but stopped. *What business is it of his whom I see and with whom I spend time? What other rumors Osman had heard about them? How did he know they would be here? Wait, what was Amir doing with Osman? How did Amir ...?*

Amir.

The whirlwind of thoughts in Rami's head came to a screeching halt. His stomach fell. Tariq, Noor, and Amir weren't done with him, he realized; they were holding a grudge.

"No need to explain much else," Osman said, removing his hand from Rami's shoulder. "You're a smart boy. We understand each other." Rami stood there rubbing his sore shoulder. "Enjoy this beautiful day, child," Osman winked and returned to his car.

Seconds later, Rami's hands were shaking, inserting the ignition key to start the motorcycle. Danyaal was standing beside him with a flaccid smile. He got behind Rami and inquired several times what Osman had said. But Rami didn't reveal much. He didn't have the stomach to describe the exchange between him and Osman. He didn't have the heart.

"It's getting late," Rami uttered. He didn't meet Danyaal's eyes on him. "We should get home."

RAMI INVITED Danyaal to spend *Chand Raat* with him. *Chand Raat*, the night of the moon, which fell on the last Friday of May that year, was the night before Eid-Ul-Fitr, marking the end of Ramadan. According to the Islamic months that follow the lunar calendar year, the beginning of Ramadan rotates and starts several days early every year. A few years back, when Ramadan fell in July, Jalil took several showers daily throughout the month and draped himself with a wet cotton shawl to stay cool in the stifling heat while fasting.

Now, shortly after breaking the fast with dates and lemonade, Jalil climbed to the rooftop with hopes of a moon sighting, a significant affair determining if the days of fasting were over, followed by the Eid celebration the following day. The sighting of the lunar crescent also declares the beginning of Shawwal, the month after Ramadan in the Islamic calendar.

"Anything?" It was Amma who called out from downstairs.

"Nothing, yet!" Jalil hollered back.

Rami glanced at Papa and noticed him stir in his chair. "You'd think these two would wait a bit to hear the announcement on the television," Papa grunted at Amma annoyingly.

For Rami's father, Ramadan meant a lazy hush taking over Lahore, lower-than-usual traffic volumes, and irregular business hours. Shops would close early to participate in the fast-breaking festivities, which he called slacking the population's work ethics, and then blaming the lack of efficiency on hunger and thirst. Then there was the disappearance of the tea stands from street corners and—worst of all—many closed restaurants during the day, leaving Papa, a non-observant of Ramadan, with limited lunch options and a sour mood.

"We go through this every year," Papa was saying irritatingly. "Both you and your son know those up-to-no-good clerics will soon announce it on the television." He was referring to the Ruet-e-Hilal Committee, known for trying to locate the moon, perched on the minaret of a mosque peeking through a large telescope.

Amma gave Papa a stricken look while clearing the dishes and getting the table ready for dinner. "What can one expect from a *munafiq* like you?" she said scornfully. Called him a hypocrite non-practicing Muslim.

"I see it!" Jalil's jubilant voice blared from upstairs. "I see the moon. It'll be Eid tomorrow!"

"Eid *Mubarak, Eid Mubarak!*" Happy Eid! The ceremonious voices of Amma and Rami's sisters filled the air. They hugged each other. Jalil scuttled out of the house to see his friends. And Papa, sitting on a chair holding the latest copy of the *Reader's Digest,* offered pleasureless, half-hearted nods.

Rami retreated to a corner and phoned Danyaal. He proposed going out when Danyaal answered.

"Good idea," Danyaal said on the other line.

Then, it dawned on Rami that asking Danyaal out on *Chand Raat* might be inappropriate. He heard Danyaal asking to decide on a location.

Rami hesitated. "I ... I should've confirmed first," he trailed off.

"Confirm what?"

"Well, it's *Chand Raat.* Not sure if it's your thing," Rami mumbled.

"You mean because I practice a different faith?"

Rami paused. "We don't have to go out," he eventually said. "I'll understand."

"But seeing you would be like seeing the crescent moon, my dear Rami." Danyaal always had a way with words. "That's my thing. Worth celebrating."

They agreed to meet at their favorite fruit *chaat* stand near Danyaal's house. On his way out, Narin asked Rami if he could bring *henna* for her and Saifa for tomorrow.

The bazaar across the street from Danyaal's house was lit with hundreds of little blinking lights looping around poles and trees. Shops and restaurants in the area had planned to stay open late to sell clothing, jewelry, and food to an eager crowd. Such liveliness had taken over the streets filled with people everywhere. Rami could hear the air buzz with a high-spirited public, offering season's greetings to each other. He walked past women haggling over last-minute shopping for glass bangles. Children tugged at their fathers' shirts before food stalls and pleaded for a snack.

"Eid *Mubarak!*" Rami said as he approached Danyaal, who stood by the fruit *chaat* stand. Danyaal smiled, opened his arms.

Rami met him under the pool of a street lamplight and, without hesitation, walked right into Danyaal's warm embrace, holding him tight for a bit longer than usual.

"Eid *Mubarak!*"

It was one of those rare occasions when they could be wrapped in each other's arms in public without worrying about stares locking in.

They grabbed two bowls from the street vendor, filled with heaps of mixed fruit seasoned with tangy *chaat masala*, and ambled along the bright-eyed people milling about. Danyaal asked if Rami was looking forward to the Eid prayer tomorrow.

"More excited about the delicious food we get to eat on Eid than the *namaz*," Rami said.

Danyaal smiled and gave Rami a mock rueful look.

"When it comes to religion in my household, we're split between Papa and me on one side and the rest of the family on the other." Rami let out a chortle before putting a spoonful of fruit in his mouth.

"Your father is not religious?" said Danyaal.

"Far from it," Rami told Danyaal what Papa used to call Mullah Hafiz, a self-righteous hypocritical donkey, and they both chuckled.

Rami then asked about the traditions in Danyaal's household.

"Well, there's Easter that commemorates the resurrection of Jesus," said Danyaal.

"Jesus, as in Prophet Isaah."

"Yes. Him," Danyaal said. "Then there's Christmas, which, in many ways, is the same as Eid."

Rami stopped at a storefront to look for *henna* for Narin, but the hordes of giggling women crowding in front, trying different designs, made him think otherwise. They resumed walking.

"While Eid teaches the virtues of serenity and sacrifice, Christmas delivers the importance of sharing and giving," Danyaal twirled his spoon into the bowl and said. "Just like *Chand Raat*, there're Christmas bazaars," he added. Rami nodded. Listened.

"My family goes to St. Andrew's church for Sunday worship," Danyaal said. "Similar to the members of your family going to a mosque for Friday prayers."

"The church on Nabha Road by GPO?" Rami called out. They were walking past a store that had music blaring from loudspeakers.

"That's the one. Immediately south of the General Post Office."

Rami told Danyaal he had ridden past it many times. "Didn't know you went there."

Danyaal smiled. "Well, religion hasn't been our favorite topic to discuss."

Rami thought about Rizwana and wondered what church she went to worship.

"Danyaal?"

"Yes, Rami."

"I would like to visit your church sometime," he said.

Danyaal stopped and turned to look at Rami. "You want to come to St. Andrew's?"

Rami nodded, wondering why he was struck with a sudden urge to seek Isaah's forgiveness. Was it on his mother's behalf for mistreating Rizwana? Or was it his deep-seated guilt over his past transgressions that Rami couldn't shake off?

"The doors are open to anyone. You're welcome to visit anytime," Danyaal said as they approached the bazaar's end. "Can I ask why?"

But instead of responding, Rami suddenly felt his legs weakening, feet leaden like someone had chained them to a pair of cinder blocks. Up ahead, his eyes were fixed on two shapes that made his stomach churn. A sinking feeling washed over him.

A few feet away, Jalil and Osman were standing facing each other. Their mouths moved over words Rami couldn't hear. Jalil's arms jerked, and Osman had his hands placed on the hips.

"Is something wrong?" Danyaal, a step behind Rami, placed his hand on Rami's shoulder.

Then he said, "That's Osman. He ... he's—"

"—talking to my brother, Jalil," Rami said in a hollow voice.

The tense facial muscles on both Jalil's and Osman's faces indicated that their exchange was not cordial.

"We should head back," Rami had barely said to Danyaal before Jalil spotted him and motioned him over. Reluctantly, Rami moved forward. Danyaal followed. With each step, the muffled voices of Jalil and Osman talking became clearer, heightening the alarm in Rami. Behind him, he heard someone offer an Eid greeting to a loved one.

"—you're a *mehman* in this country." "A guest." Rami could make out Jalil's tightened lips saying. "Show a little respect."

"The generosity of the people of this country hasn't gone unnoticed, brother. The way it has offered refuge to my people, the Afghans; my countrymen and I forever remain in its debt for such kindness." Osman tilted his head sideways and pressed his hand to his chest in humility. But the insincerity lurking beneath his smirk, Rami sensed, made what he was saying sound unconvincing.

"So we're clear?" Jalil said. "We understand each other?"

"I understand that you and I are on the same side of things. That's what I understand."

Jalil turned his head to the side, his right hand raised and pointed in Rami's direction. "That, over there, is my brother," he said.

Rami caught the pupils in Jalil's eyes flick from him to Danyaal.

"He's told me the stunt you pulled at his college." Jalil returned his gaze to Osman.

Osman's smirk broadened. "Rami's your brother? *Wah, wah!*"

Rami felt his chest tightening.

"And as for the incident at F.C. College, it merely reminded this generation that the sovereignty of God and his laws are the only ways to squelch the evil of nationalism in the world. I'm sure you'd agree."

"You go home now, Rami," Jalil said to Rami without looking at him.

"That's not your call to make," he then said curtly to Osman. "Neither is this your place to intervene with our ... my country's matters!"

"But it is, my comrade. But it is," Osman said it twice, speaking in a condescending tone. "You see, both you and I are doing the same God's work. And as you may already know, Allah's work knows no boundaries. I hope you enlighten Rami with similar teachings."

"I don't recall mentioning my brother's name to you." From the corner of his eye, Rami saw Jalil's fist clenching. "How do you know him?"

"Oh, well, we've met before. Your brother and I, I mean. I've gotten quite fond of Rami," Osman tilted his chin and barked a laugh. He then leaned forward and placed a hand on Jalil's shoulder as if confiding in him. "You said it was Rami who told you about what happened at the college?"

Silence lingered between them for a handful of seconds.

"What else has he told you?" Osman snickered. "Has he mentioned what others are saying about him at the college? I must ask. How well do you know your brother's whereabouts and the boy he's with?"

Rami felt a stone lodged in his throat.

A look of confusion drifted past Jalil's eyes before Rami noticed his face reddening. "Rami, go home," Jalil growled.

"Lahore can't be much different from Kabul, my friend," Osman pressed on. "When it comes to gossip, that is. A quip here, a whisper there, some uninvited insinuation, and, before you know it, you're the talk of the town."

Under the thin light of the moon, the moon that had announced a celebratory day tomorrow, Osman's profile looked like a wide-eyed animal, a hyena, antagonizing its opponent, tearing at the skin with small bites.

"I know my brother better than anyone else," Jalil said.

Rami wondered about his statement. He pondered over what Jalil had said. Did Jalil really know him the way he said he did? If he did, then why were they living like two strangers under one roof? Why did eyes avoid contact when sitting at the dinner table? And was it this strained relationship between the two brothers that had prevented Rami from inviting Danyaal to his house? That thought also brought Rami to the following realization: Jalil had ignored Osman's mentioning of Danyaal. He, undoubtedly, had disregarded the way Osman associated Danyaal with him.

But despite questioning the validity of Jalil's claim, Rami didn't mind. He didn't mind even if Jalil was exaggerating in front of Osman. He felt flattered by his standing up for his younger brother.

"Of course," Osman was saying. "I would never question the bond between brothers of the same blood."

"I want you to stay away from him," Jalil raised a finger before Osman's face. "Rami. Go. Home," Jalil's tense voice entered Rami's ear. His stare remained on Osman.

"I don't want you to ever come near him! You hear me?" The edge of Jalil's upper lip curled when he spoke.

Osman raised his arms in a gesture of surrender. "I'm just looking out for him, that's all."

"I think you're doing more than that," Jalil sneered. "Just like the ones before you, I think Kabul is still working toward a separatist movement to divide Pakistani Baluchi and Pashtun citizens to create 'Pashtunistan.' By infiltrating our colleges and universities in the name of our sacred religion, you're working to promote your agenda. Afghanistan opposed Pakistan's existence once to the United Nations. It chose not to recognize this country as a legitimate successor of the territorial agreements reached with those *firangis* that colonized us for so long, the British Empire," Jalil went on spewing, his tone blunt, his mouth frothing a little around the edges.

Once again, Rami found himself admiring Jalil. He admired him for having such knowledge of what mattered to him, without holding a textbook or any book for that matter, let alone reading it, in the past ten years or so.

Jalil then turned to Rami. "I asked you to go home." His glaring eyes fixed on Rami's face, again no acknowledgment of Danyaal's presence. "What're you still doing here?"

"Be careful, brother." Rami heard Osman say before he turned to walk. Osman had his thumb curved on the right pocket of his bright green vest. "You make some serious allegations. But I wish you a happy Eid despite your impression of me. And I pray our paths cross again under better circumstances."

Rami and Danyaal trotted in the opposite direction and quickly mingled into the hordes of people. Rami's heart was spinning in his chest. Closer to Danyaal's house, he stopped, turned, and faced Danyaal.

"I don't want to leave," Rami, nearly out of breath, croaked.

"Rami—"

"Not yet. I want to stay with you. A while longer."

Standing in the middle of the shoulder-bumping crowd, cramped like lentils in a bag, Danyaal reached over and wrapped his arms around Rami. "You don't have to go," Danyaal whispered in Rami's ear. "I don't want you to."

THE NEXT morning, after the Eid prayer, they hugged three times each the family members and those to your immediate left and right according to the tradition. Jalil was walking beside Rami amid the mass of people exiting the mosque when he brought up Danyaal.

Rami replied with the same answer he'd given to Osman. Danyaal was a friend, he told Jalil.

"Then what was he saying about you and that boy?"

"Who?"

"Don't play stupid with me. You know I'm talking about Osman."

Rami shrugged. "I don't know."

"Obviously, he knows something about that boy that I don't."

Rami picked up the pace.

"Well." Jalil snickered. "Knowing you and the type of company you keep, I don't know why I even bother to ask," he said.

Rami rolled his head toward Jalil and fixed him with a hard glare. Said nothing.

"I want you to end whatever you've got with that boy. I can't shake the feeling something isn't right with him."

Rami stopped in the middle of the sea of people passing by and gave Jalil a contemptuous look.

"You know what I want?" Jalil turned to face him. "I want you to mind your damn business! That's what I want," Rami said sharply, startling his brother.

This was the first time Rami had snapped at Jalil this way. "And one more thing. That boy has a name. It's Danyaal. Next time you want to address him, call him by his name," Rami said testily before bolting past Jalil.

Stunned, Jalil stood there for a few seconds, unsure how to react, before trudging behind Rami.

"Why were you returning so late last night after I'd told you to go home right away?" Rami heard Jalil speak irritatingly behind him.

Rami didn't say to him that he'd visited Danyaal's room, where they held each other for a long while. Didn't mention that Danyaal then shoved a VHS tape into the VCR, and they watched *My Beautiful Launderette* with lights switched off, sitting side-by-side on the bed.

Rami didn't disclose to Jalil that several minutes into the film when Daniel Day-Lewis's character had said, '*Just to get us through, Omo. We're going to go on. You want that, don't you?*', Danyaal had set his heart racing by placing his hand on Rami's thigh, and how there was the sound of the bed's springs creaking when Rami had shifted his weight, and how the belt of his trousers had loosened, and how there was the *zziippp* of a zipper lowering, and how there was the movement of hands sliding inside and out.

Rami didn't say anything. He kept walking. In his mind, it was evident that despite their contrasting personalities and viewpoints, Osman and Jalil shared a common sentiment: their disdain for Danyaal. It was also clear to him that his affection for Danyaal was unwavering, impervious to the opinions of others.

Rami didn't say to Jalil why he'd gotten home late last night and why he had forgotten to get *henna* for Narin. Jalil followed him through the streets. And Rami stalked on ahead of him, taking long strides.

FIFTEEN

December 8, 1987, was the last time Rami saw Danyaal in his room.

A couple of months earlier, one late afternoon in October, Danyaal had asked what Rami wished for his birthday. They were strolling through Doongi Ground, a picturesque park in the Samanabad neighborhood. The winding concrete path meandered amidst an array of trees and verdant bushes, guiding them through the lush green grass.

"Soon, you'll be eighteen. We should celebrate," Danyaal had said.

The autumn breeze had a coolness to it. Rami had donned a denim jacket that had white-fur lining inside and a Dallas Cowboys emblem on the left breast pocket, a great find at the Landa Bazaar. Danyaal, ambling beside him, was sporting a black sweater and a rustic-colored scarf wrapped around his neck like a fat necktie knot.

The grass was still green but strewn with brown and gold foliage. It lent a rustic charm to the autumn scenery. The air had a charcoal-burning smell to it. A man and a woman, possibly a couple, walked past them. The woman had a shawl wrapped around her. She tipped her head at Rami and smiled before adjusting it against the chill in the air.

Rami and Danyaal shared a bag of roasted peanuts purchased from a street vendor.

"We don't need to do anything," Rami said.

For almost a decade, Rami's family hadn't been keen on commemorating birthdays ever since he'd turned nine.

And Rami had learned a fundamental truth about managing expectations associated with celebratory events: Like a teeter-totter in a children's playground, lowering the hopes on one side of the lever board meant higher happiness on the other end. Rami knew that his sanity, like a pivot point, hung in that balance.

"Why not?"

Rami grabbed a handful of peanuts and popped them in his mouth. "Celebrating birthdays hasn't been high on my list for a long time." He gave Danyaal a weak smile. Danyaal stopped.

"Is it because——?"

"——What I shared with you happened at the canal. Yes."

"It's in the past," Danyaal said.

"I don't know, Danyaal," Rami said.

"It's the same as last year when I asked you." Danyaal made a face, bumping his shoulder with Rami's teasingly.

"We barely knew each other then."

"Really?" Danyaal was looking at him seriously and playfully at the same time. "You didn't know me enough to celebrate?"

"Danyaal, please."

Danyaal smiled.

"And why didn't you tell me until a week later, last April, that your seventeenth had already passed?" Rami fixed his eyes on Danyaal and looked at him coyly.

The coldness around them was deepening. Rami shuddered.

Danyaal hugged his arms against the chill. "I'm sorry," he said.

They resumed walking. "Here's my promise to you," Danyaal said after a pause. "I promise always to be there for you to celebrate anything worth celebrating. Even when no one else does."

Always.

And just like that, Danyaal had perturbed the balance between Rami's expectations and contentment. Rami couldn't help but feel his hope slowly rising on the teeter-totter.

And the way Danyaal had said it, the way the warmth of his gaze was hugging Rami's face, Rami felt a lump rising in his throat. His eyes teared up; he looked the other way. He knew he didn't deserve the purity of Danyaal's friendship. Despite Rami's shortcomings and the many times he'd let Danyaal down, Danyaal, walking next to him, made a promise no one had before. And the sincerity in his voice made Rami believe he meant it. People like Danyaal meant what they said, and it left Rami speechless.

Danyaal grabbed Rami's hand and stopped him from walking. He reached over with his right thumb and rubbed the water away from the corners of Rami's eyes that were ready to leak down his cheeks.

"I Promise," he murmured.

At that moment, Rami felt nothing but love for Danyaal. He loved him more than anyone in the world.

They stood there, two boys surrounded by the nearly naked trees in the muffled silence of the early fall, broken only by the hissing sound of the wind carrying leaves falling from the branches above, bidding farewell to summer.

"I don't deserve you," Rami croaked.

LATER THAT night, Rami was walking up to the house's front steps when a shape slammed into him as he opened the wooden door to enter. Rami's startled shriek and the creaking sound of the door opening filled the narrow cul-de-sac. Someone jumped out from the bottom stair-landing and dashed off. Had that person not grabbed Rami's shoulders, the impact force would have hurled him to the brick wall behind him.

Panicked, he tried to take a closer look at the quickly receding shadow but couldn't make it out in the shrouded darkness.

ON THE eve of Thursday, December 7, Danyaal celebrated Rami's birthday by taking him to Lung Fung, a Chinese restaurant on Kashmir Road north of Alhamra Art Center. He hadn't revealed where they were going. Danyaal sat behind Rami on the motorcycle and guided him with directions to a specific destination until they arrived. Inside the restaurant, Rami saw customers scattered across a large room that had a lingering salt and vinegar smell. They were seated at one of the corner tables draped with white linen tablecloth. Atop, sets of neatly arranged knives, forks, and spoons were placed beside the beige cloth napkins. Rami surveyed the area and noticed red Chinese lanterns hanging from the ceiling. Paintings of dragons and Buddha figures decorated the wall to the right. He could hear the traditional Chinese music playing in the background.

Danyaal skimmed over the laminated menu and selected a few dishes: a bowl of Hot and Sour soup, vegetarian fried rice, and a tray of Szechuan grilled meat.

"Here's to you turning eighteen," Danyaal raised the Pepsi glass bottle after the waiter had taken the order and left. In the diffuse lighting, Rami noticed Danyaal's eyes looked more sage-gray than emerald.

He smilingly raised his and reciprocated with the clinking sound of the glass. "What a surprise!"

"Don't settle in just yet," Danyaal said, glowing. "This is only a part of it. There's more."

Rami blinked. "There's more?"

"It'll have to be a secret for now." A perpetual smile lingered on Danyaal's lips.

After they both enjoyed a delicious Chinese meal, Danyaal asked if they could take a ride to Shimla Hill.

"What's in Shimla Hill?"

"Next surprise," Danyaal hopped behind Rami and said. "Now, hurry."

They rode from Kashmir Road to Egerton Boulevard, down Davis Road, and up the steep slope to Shimla Hill. The area was a posh mix of residential and commercial buildings. On the hill were rows of high-end hotels overlooking the sprawling metropolis below. There was a lookout at the barricaded edge of the hill. From that vantage point, one could gaze ahead and behold Lahore in all its glory: the dome and the minarets of Badshahi Mosque to the west, the tip of the national monument, Minar-e-Pakistan, to the north, and Jinnah Garden to the front. Even the outlines of the Lahore Fort were visible on a bright day.

It was past dusk, and the city splayed before them like the millions of twinkling stars in the galaxy.

"You're going to tell me what we're doing here?" Rami asked.

"Not yet."

"Danyaal—"

"Not yet."

Danyaal got off the bike and walked over to the lookout. He placed his hands on the metal post of the barricade and rolled his head in Rami's direction. "Come join me, Rami," he said with an air of exultation. "Please be patient a little longer."

Rami stepped forward and stood beside Danyaal. He looked ahead and let the December breeze stroke his face.

"Beautiful, isn't it?" Danyaal muttered. A puff of steam blew from his mouth. "This view?"

"It is," said Rami.

"I love this city."

"It's home."

"Our home," Danyaal added.

"Yours and mine."

Danyaal glanced at his watch. "Get ready," he said. "Any second now."

"Stop teasing me, Danyaal, I—" Rami stopped in midsentence. A loud boom interrupted him.

He looked up.

In a sudden display, like a flower blossoming, a radiant burst of light illuminated the darkened expanse of the sky. Rami held his breath.

"Fireworks!"

As it turned out, Danyaal had planned this moment for Rami, knowing a group of Hindus would gather at Jinnah Garden to mark the beginning of the Diwali Festival with fireworks. For the next several minutes, with every whizz and crackle, the sky filled with glimmering sparks of red and orange. Rami's elation was palpable with each dazzling explosion, evoking boisterous cheers. Between one of those bursts, with an awe-stricken sparkle in his eye, Rami lowered his gaze to Danyaal. The brilliant colors of the fireworks were splashing across Danyaal's face amid the hiss and whoosh of the bouquet of fire thundering above. Danyaal returned Rami's stare. The corners of his mouth creased in a smile. Rami drew closer. He wrapped his arms around Danyaal's belly and melted away in his affectionate embrace.

As if showered by a thousand twinkling sparks falling from the sky, they stood and held each other for a long while. Unaware that from a window of one of the tall-storied hotel buildings behind them, Osman's narrowed eyes were fixed on them. With keen interest, Osman watched the two boys lost in each other's arms.

COMING HOME later that night, Rami was whistling and humming a tune stuck in his head. Killing the motorcycle's engine, he smilingly reflected on the day he'd had with Danyaal. Then, he noticed something rather odd up ahead. Muhammed Khan was shifting on his feet, standing at the front of the house with a horror-stricken look. He quickly moved forward to meet Rami.

"Rami, son, don't go up!" he cried.

"What's going on?"

Muhammed Khan stood before him and blocked the house entrance. "It's Jalil. You don't want to be near him right now," he said in a panicked voice. "Go back. Now is not a good time to go up." He thrust Rami away. "Go back!" he pleaded.

"Why won't you tell me?"

"No, no. Listen to me," Muhammed Khan attempted to grab Rami just as a female scream came from upstairs. He threw his arms around Rami, but he wasn't fast enough. Rami dodged him on the left and ran up to the house.

He stopped at the top landing. In front of him, a cooking pot turned to its side on the floor, the curry splattered on the kitchen wall, slowly slithering down; Saifa curled into a ball and sobbed. There was no sign of Papa. He looked across and saw Amma slapping her chest. Next to her was Bibi Jaan. She had one hand clamped on her mouth, and her wide eyes bounced from Jalil to Narin. Rami followed her gaze and noticed a kitchen knife held in Jalil's hand. Across from him, Narin was on the floor. She was crawling away on her elbows and heels, a look of terror plastered on her face.

There wasn't much time to think of anything. Inexplicably, Jalil, with a smoldering look, was inching toward his sister.

"Jalil!" Rami yelled and lunged at him. "Stop it." He chained his arms around Jalil's stomach and landed on the floor with him. The knife slipped off Jalil's hand. "What's the matter with you?"

"Let go of me!" Jalil bellowed. Rami's body quivered the way Jalil's bloodshot eyes gave him a hard glare. "This *chinaar*, this uncaring *harlot*, will not live to see the sunrise." Jalil struggled to break free from Rami's grip, but Rami's arms remained clamped around Jalil's torso. "I said let go of me!"

"For God's sake, Jalil, calm down! What has Narin done?" Rami said through labored breaths.

"Why don't you ask her yourself?" Jalil's upper lip curled in a sneer. "Ask her how she's dragged the family name in the mud under our noses, under the roof of this house! Ask her how long she's been seeing that *harami*, Kamran, having an affair."

Rami shifted his eyes to Narin's tear-stained face, and then it occurred to him who had jumped out of the front stairs and slammed into him back in October. It had been Kamran, one of Jalil's friends.

He recalled Kamran having a lean physique and a striking head of pepper-gray hair from an early age. He had deep-set brown eyes and a straight nose that complemented his olive-toned complexion. The demanding labor of hauling weighty building material had helped sculpt his physique, which had left an impression on many. Kamran was well-known in the neighborhood for his handy skills: installing fixtures in residential buildings, repairing water pumps and other large-scale machinery across businesses in the area. He and Jalil met when Mullah Hafiz hired Kamran to replace an old electrical circuit board at the mosque. They forged a close friendship soon after. Rami recalled Kamran visiting the house and spending time with Jalil flying kites.

"Kamran?"

"I caught her alone with him on the roof tonight!" A spurt of Jalil's spittle sprayed Rami's face. "He dashed off by jumping over to Mohammed Khan's roof when he saw me approaching." Jalil was running out of breath. "Explains where this *randi* had been disappearing to at nights, climbing in the dark and throwing herself at her *lover*." Jalil's cheeks quivered when he called Narin a slut.

So, as it turned out, Kamran and Narin had been secretly seeing each other for a while. On the nights of their planned, secretive meetings, Narin would tiptoe her way down and unlock the front door. Kamran would quietly enter the house and climb to the roof without anyone noticing. There, he waited for Narin to arrive.

As Rami thought back now, Narin made up some excuse while watching the television with the rest of the family and would disappear. It became clear she'd gone up to see Kamran. And Kamran was scurrying out that night after seeing Narin when he bumped into Rami. Earlier that evening, Rami learned, Jalil had gone up to the veranda to fetch blankets from the metal trunk Amma used to store winter covers, when he heard hushed giggles from the roof. He followed the voices and found Narin and Kamran in each other's arms.

"Right now, only Bibi Jaan and her husband know about this." Jalil skirmished to get out from under Rami. "By dawn, the entire neighborhood will know how she's stained the family name. Good thing Papa isn't home. God knows he would've died of heart attack if he had seen what his daughter's been up to behind his back, behind all our backs," he said. "We must act fast."

"Stop being ridiculous, Jalil. That's our sister you're talking about," Rami said. "Calm down."

"'Calm down,'" Jalil seethed in Rami's grip and stared at Narin sitting with her back against the table in the living room, sobbing.

"I'll calm down when I slay her for defiling the family's honor," he flicked his chin toward her and said through gritted teeth. "After that, I'll take care of Kamran for betraying me and bringing such shame to us. Rami, let go of me."

Somewhere, a child started crying, a gust of wintry wind whistled. Inside the house, the air was stagnant. It permeated the room with the layered smell of sweat, dry curry dotted on the wall, and unwashed clothes. Rami felt drops of moisture forming on his forehead as he held Jalil and waited for his brother's irregular breathing to subside. Bibi Jaan took Narin to her house for the night.

Rattled by these unexpected turns of events, Rami lay awake that night, his mind consumed by thoughts of all that had transpired on his eighteenth birthday, unsure whether to laugh or cry: dinner with Danyaal, fireworks at Shimla Hill, learning about Narin having an affair with Kamran, and Jalil thirsty for blood in the name of honor killing.

WHEN RAMI glanced at his reflection in the bathroom mirror the following day, he saw heavy-lidded, red eyes and an exhausted appearance. He splashed water on his face and finger-combed hair. Then he turned, stood in the eerie, unsettling silence, and surveyed the rooms covered in lifeless gray light as if death had brushed past them. It seemed as though everyone in the house had vanished overnight: dishes in the kitchen sink smeared with food turning crusty, dirty socks piled on each other, bed unmade, linen unwashed.

But Rami knew they were all there, except for Narin. He looked at the unmoving blanket mound that was Jalil. The rustle of another covering in another room with Saifa's hand sticking out and the shut door of his parents' room indicated they were sequestered behind it. He didn't know when Papa had come home last night. But Rami was certain Amma had brought him up to speed.

He crossed into the living room, picked up the phone, and lowered himself onto one of the rattan chairs, heard it creak under his weight. He dialed Danyaal's number. The faint sound of the wall clock ticking played while the phone rang.

"Hello."

"It's me," Rami cleared his throat, "Something happened at the house last night," he said in a raspy voice, sensing tears pooling in his eyes. "I'm okay. Thanks." Pause. "Can I come over?"

He listened briefly, played a withered smile, and nodded. "Yes, *yaarana*. Okay. I'll walk. Leaving now. See you soon."

DANYAAL WAS standing in the corridor looking down when Rami entered through the gate into the courtyard of his house.

"Who is it?" Afrooz called from the room on the far end.

"Rami." Danyaal motioned him to come upstairs. Rami hopped on the red-tiled staircase and met Danyaal's warm embrace.

"Let's go in," Danyaal curled his left arm around Rami's shoulder and guided him to his room.

Rami crossed the doorway and glanced at the daily clutter of Danyaal's life: books, notepads, pens, empty cassette covers littering the desk, a pair of jeans hanging from the back of the chair, the guitar and magazines lying sideways on the bed.

Danyaal pulled the chair for him. "Sit. Tell me everything." He took Rami's hand.

Rami, through ragged breathing and a choked voice, recounted to Danyaal the events of last night after returning home: Finding Jalil reaching over to stab Narin with a knife, falling to the floor gripping his brother, hearing him take a vow to end Narin's life.

Rami cupped his face in his hands after finishing.

Danyaal let out a sound that was between a shriek and a gasp. "God, Rami. I'm so sorry," his voice was barely above a whisper. He raised Rami's elbow and examined the purple bruise on his forearm.

"Must have been from the fall."

"You look tired."

Rami leaned forward on the chair and rubbed his temples. "No sleep last night," he muttered.

"Lie down. Close your eyes," Danyaal said in a kind voice.

But instead, Rami rose from the chair and began pacing back and forth. "I'll need to go home soon," he said in a hushed voice. "Before long, Jalil will be up in a sour mood."

He paced Danyaal's room, restless. Ten paces long. Eight paces wide, fingers running through his disheveled hair.

"Bibi Jaan will be bringing Narin back from her house," his risen voice reverberated. "And—upon laying eyes on her, who knows what Jalil would do?" Nine and a half paces wide.

Then Rami stopped. Something had caught his eye. In front of him, lying on the desk, was a cassette cover with a picture of Liza Minnelli wearing a bowler hat and fishnet stocking, staring at him.

"Rami?"

Rami looked from the cover to Danyaal. "This ... this picture. The music—" his voice broke.

"What about it?"

Rami returned to the chair and lowered himself. "I never told you this."

Danyaal Blinked.

Rami disclosed to Danyaal how, after watching the movie commercial, he had developed a childhood crush on the lead actress.

"You did?"

Rami nodded.

"It's a famous musical film," said Danyaal.

Rami gently traced his fingertips along the surface of the plastic cover. A rush of memories washed over him as he described that crisp December evening in 1979, sitting in the dark cinema hall. And the many times he had spent on the veranda, lost to the music playing in his head.

"Oh, Rami," Danyaal said. He took hold of Rami's hand once more. Pressed on it.

Rami pursed his lips, closed his eyes, and hummed. The corner of his mouth creased slightly. He then leaned back and laced his hands behind his head. "I thought maybe one day I could be a dancer."

"Who said you still can't?"

Rami's eyelids lifted. "With the type of dysfunctional family I've got, it could never be possible." He snapped his eyes at Danyaal. "Haven't you been listening?"

"Anything's possible." Danyaal pressed on. "You just have to believe."

"Not anything," Rami said. "Not this."

"I can play the song for you," Danyaal said.

Rami turned his head toward Danyaal.

"If you would like, I mean."

Danyaal was doing it again, knowing when to say the right thing to cheer Rami up.

"You know what would be even better?" Danyaal went on.

Rami gave him a curious look.

"You dancing to the tune just as you did when you were a little boy." Danyaal smiled.

Rami bit into his fingernail, suddenly feeling shy. His unsure gaze lingered on Danyaal's face.

"I'd love to see you dance even if no one else does."

Rami hesitated a moment longer. Then nodded. Danyaal's smile broadened.

He approached the cassette player and fetched the tape resting on top. "The floor is yours," Danyaal said after inserting the cassette tape into the player and pressing the Play button.

Rami rose from the chair, draped his eyelids over his eyes, and listened to the sultry sounds of trumpets, trombones, and percussion filling the air in the room. He focused.

How did it go? Rami drummed his fingers on the edge of the desk. His muscles tensed, toes pointed, one leg forward, yes, then a twirl. Now, a twist. Within seconds, he found himself twirling across Danyaal's room, listening to the music pouring into his ears, gliding his body in the air. Once again, it was that familiar sensation he'd nearly forgotten, of weightlessness like the undulation of a garment flapping in the wind on a clothesline.

At that moment, in Danyaal's company, he found immense pleasure in the gentle sway, in this mundane glimmer of joy after the night he'd had.

Then, suddenly, his body bumped into another. Rami uncovered his eyes. Next, he knew, he was in Danyaal's arms, out of breath. The song faded in the background. Danyaal's glance lingered over Rami's face, carrying a benevolent smile. Rami's hands ran up and down Danyaal's arms and shoulders.

"So?" Rami uttered through labored breaths.

Danyaal cradled Rami in his arms; his face came closer.

"I loved it," Danyaal mouthed. "It was beautiful."

It was the tip of their noses that touched first. Then Danyaal's head tilted. Their breaths, deep and heavy, mingled—and Danyaal's lips brushed against Rami's before resting on top.

Rami parted the seam of his lips, allowing Danyaal's tongue to penetrate, letting his mouth lock Rami's lower lip. He gasped at the intensity of Danyaal's lips pressing down on his. Rami's eyelids sealed.

It was their first kiss. Soft and slow.

Then, a thought.

SIXTEEN

Rami's eyes sprang open. "What're you doing?" he said sharply.

Astounded, startled ... panicked, Danyaal looked at Rami. Blinked.

"What're you doing?" Rami repeated, louder this time.

"Rami, I—I—" Danyaal began to say something but trailed off.

Rami felt his body clenching. He forcefully placed his palms against Danyaal's chest, which would have knocked Danyaal to the floor had Rami not stopped him from falling.

What is happening? That tender moment of me in Danyaal's loving embrace, the kiss, where did it all go?

Rami heard the demons stir in his head.

"We can't do that. No. We can't."

"You and I ... I thought," Danyaal spoke in a burdened voice. "I thought—"

"You thought what?"

Rami loosened his grip and let Danyaal slip to the floor.

"What we have between us, Rami, and we both know it," Danyaal's voice was low. "Being in denial won't change how we feel toward each other."

"Did you listen to anything I said earlier?" Rami started pacing Danyaal's room again. Seven paces long. Ten and a half paces wide.

Danyaal drew his knees closer to his chest. "You're upset. It was only a kiss," he said.

"Only a *kiss*." Rami snickered while walking back and forth. "Narin almost got killed for being caught kissing Kamran, for having an affair. And ... and that's a scandal between a man and a woman. Something we hear about often."

'*Tell him. Tell this boy he would get you killed with his enticing insinuations*,' his demon, fear, emitted a low groan.

"If the word got out about you and I—like this. Two boys. What do you think they'd do to us?"

Danyaal placed his palms against the floor to propel himself. "You don't know that." He rose and took a step toward Rami. Rami stepped back.

"Look who's in denial now." He snickered again. "There's no room for the likes of you and I in this world, can't you see? We must come to terms with the lives we're born into," Rami said, his head spinning. "Society will never accept two boys together romantically. I don't want us to raise our hopes that this ... *us* ... will ever be anything more than what it is. What's the point in reaching for unattainable goals?"

"You don't know that," Danyaal said again.

"Na? You think people will let us be? That Osman and others like him will leave us alone?" Rami almost blurted what Osman had said about Danyaal that day outside the strawberry stand.

"There's nothing wrong in what we do."

Rami let out a bitter laugh. "Depends on who you ask," he said. "And when I look around, I can't find a soul who'd agree with you."

"There's value in placing trust in our feelings," Danyaal sounded deflated. "Your sister has followed her heart, don't you see? Despite what happens to her, despite the taboo."

Rami fixed Danyaal with a scornful glare. "Life is crueler than your ambitious dreams," he said, turned to walk out, then whirled around.

"This isn't some movie, Danyaal," he said and shot Danyaal a hollow glance. "We're not destined to find happiness in the end. Not here, not in this city or this country," he said in a dull tone. "I've no choice but to exist among the people and surroundings I grew up with. I have nowhere else to go, Danyaal." Rami darted a parting glance at Danyaal's room, unaware this would be the last time he'd be inside these walls with Danyaal, and left.

RAMI EXITED the house and rambled along unknown turns and corners in the lazy rays of the mid-morning sun. He passed opening bazaars where the merchants readied to tackle the haggling customers. He made his way through the slow-gathering crowd and tightly packed stalls. On one side, he saw vendors arranging freshly caught fish on a bed of ice. A few panhandlers in tattered clothes had their arms stretched for a few *pesas* on the other end.

Rami wasn't sure where he was going, yet he kept wandering. His grief kept coming and going like the waves breaking in the sea, rising and falling. All it took was the thought of him nearly shoving Danyaal to the floor, and the feeling of dread pressed down on his chest.

Then, a sense of rage came over and tossed him upside down like a windswept leaf. He rounded more corners and wondered where the streets would lead him. He knew he was somewhere near Mochi Gate, inside Old Lahore.

Rami walked past Nisar Haveli just as a bus was approaching the stop. He got on, unaware of its particular route or a destination in mind. The bus was half empty. Rami grabbed the metal poles and careened his way down to a nearby seat.

He kept pondering, sulking at times, over the boldness of Danyaal's behavior. And why had this rage and anger taken hold of him in such a crippling manner?

He pondered it some more.

Just then, an explanation presented itself, more like a reckoning with reality he could no longer avoid. It wasn't Danyaal's *audacity* to kiss Rami during his emotional fragility that pushed him to his breaking point; he was incensed because Danyaal had exposed him to the feeling that now could not be undone. Danyaal had unearthed the truth for Rami when he, Rami, had longed for it to remain hidden. Danyaal made him see that no prayer, no penance, no fear of the wrath of others would change how much he cherished the kiss between them. There was no denying it now. The weight of the realization bore down on Rami. He could no longer ignore the echoing voice within him growing louder, revealing that he had been born this way.

A boy drawn to another boy.

He didn't know whether to love Danyaal or hate him for making him see that naked truth. He ran his finger over the lips where Danyaal had planted his minutes ago.

The bus drove over potholes as it rode past the packed Shah Alami Road. Rami propped his chin on the left palm of his leaned elbow and stared through the Plexiglas window at the drab, concrete buildings, the hovering web of black electrical cables above, and the showcased billboards with colorful Urdu calligraphy. There were open storefronts, giggling children, a few men walking with their hands laced behind their backs, and women wearing burqas milling around.

THEN, RAMI's gaze turned to a passenger on the bus. He shifted his head to the right and found a boy darting glances in his direction. He appeared a couple of years younger than Rami, had unkempt dusky hair, eyes the color of honey, and a beak-shaped nose between them.

The boy's stare met Rami's, stayed for a handful of seconds, then flew away. Returned a moment later. Rami noticed he had round shoulders under the yellow shirt he was wearing and a noticeable space between the neck and the collar buttons. The other thing that caught Rami's eye was how his right hand rubbed against his thigh while maintaining his unwavering eye contact with Rami.

Rami heard the bus's brakes shrieking. The vehicle came to a stop. The boy got up. He appeared as if readying to get off at the next stop. Rami watched him sway, grasping the metal pole for support as the bus jerked forward. The boy's head turned, and he gave Rami a look; his mouth creased in a smile. Rami's heart quickened. He fought the urge to disembark with the boy. Rami peeled his eyes away and returned his head toward the window.

The bus idled at the next stop; its door opened. Rami looked again and saw the boy giving him one last glance before exiting. Rami nervously shifted in his seat. Other travelers were beginning to climb aboard. By now, the boy had vanished amid the boarding crowd. Rami got up. He slogged his way against the new riders settling in their seats, tilted his head, mouthing apologies to a few irritated faces, and got off seconds before the bus door closed.

Rami stood on the busy sidewalk amid the cloud of exhaust and dust from the bus pulling away and looked around for the boy. He caught him crossing the road and approaching a thin alley between a motorcycle showroom and a hardware store. The boy looked over his shoulder at Rami standing on the other side and walked into the mouth of the narrow opening.

Rami crossed the road and entered the sun-deprived alley. The outer walls of the adjacent businesses were barely an arm's length apart on each side. Once his eye adjusted to the dark, Rami saw the scrap and rubble littering the ground: old motorcycle tires, empty plastic bottles, torn-up pages from newspapers and magazines, piles of bricks scattered around. Next, Rami registered the boy's profile, sitting on one of the low stacks of bricks facing him. Rami stumbled around the rusted metal parts of an old motorcycle tilted against the left wall and stepped forward.

The boy's face was at the height of Rami's belt in a seated position. Rami got closer and stood an inch or two from the boy, his back against the front of the alley. More buttons in the boy's shirt were undone, Rami noticed, revealing his almond-skin chest. The boy tilted his head up; his yearning eyes suggestively lingered on Rami's face. Rami ran his hand down through the opening in the boy's shirt and returned his obliging gaze.

"You looking?" the boy tipped his chin at Rami and murmured in a raspy voice. Rami's heart somersaulted behind his rib cage; he remained silent. The boy's eyes remained on Rami's face. He asked again.

Rami balanced the weight of his body precariously.

The boy's hands reached and pulled the prong of Rami's buckle, loosening the strap. Next, his fingers undid Rami's trousers top button. Rami turned and nervously looked toward the front to ensure no one could see them from Shah Alami Road.

The boy gave Rami another look.

Standing before the boy, Rami's mind raced back to earlier. The way he had left Danyaal's room. The way things had ended between them that morning. And a pang of grief struck his chest, followed by a burst of anger.

In that rubble-littered, desolate alleyway with his pants unbuckled—in a moment of vulnerability—the memories of his bitter falling out with Danyaal resurfaced. Rami found himself placing the blame on Danyaal for leading him down this path.

Or maybe it's I who's to blame; Rami considered the possibility. *Perhaps I am the one who misguided Danyaal with false optimism,* he thought. Blinded by the relentless longing for Danyaal's companionship, maybe he failed to see how it could draw unwanted attention and scrutiny from others: heads turning, stares narrowing, frowningly sensing the *insufferable* intimacy between two teenage boys.

Rami heard the boy groan.

'*You're pathetic,*' a voice buzzed in Rami's ears. He recognized it; it was his demon, insecurity. '*You have resorted to this. Look at you standing in this bleak, lifeless crawl space and looking to get off. Was ruining your companionship with that boy with your impulsive behavior not enough? The one good thing that ever came your way; destroying it wasn't enough?*'

Besieged with yet another wave of grief, Rami pushed the boy away. Avoiding eye contact, he buttoned the trousers, turned, and exited the alley with the lingering voices swirling in his head.

IN THE days and weeks that followed, Rami and Danyaal barely saw each other. They stopped commuting together to and from the college. Endured wounded glances that were thrown at each other, yet they kept it to themselves. Rami would watch Danyaal exit one building at the end of a lecture and briskly walk across the redbrick walkway to get to the next class. He would meander around the corner behind the Science building and avoid running into Danyaal. Rami knew Danyaal didn't enter the canteen after noticing Rami sitting at one of the tables. Rami would catch Danyaal's reflection peeping through the glass window, hands cupped around his forehead and temples. He would see Danyaal's eyes wander over to him, and Danyaal would turn away.

It was the longest Rami had been away from Danyaal, and he hated it just as much as he hated spending time at home. Everyone in the house had gone quiet. Jalil went looking for Kamran, but Rami heard Kamran's parents got him to board a bus leaving for Multan and disappear for a while. They figured it was better than Jalil and Kamran meeting on the street and lunging at each other.

No one in Rami's house spoke much to one another. They became aware of each other's presence through mere sounds: The key rattling when Jalil would come home, the door creaking when Saifa swept the floor behind it, the rattan seat squeaking, newspaper fluttering with Papa lowering himself to the chair, the muffled shuffling of Narin's bare feet tiptoeing in and out of rooms trying not to draw attention, and the click-clacking of pots and pans in the kitchen Amma preparing food. They carried on with their lives with a lingering dread in every corner, every breathable space of the house.

ONE DAY in late December after Christmas, Rami came home and found Amma, Jalil, and Narin in the living room with two women he hadn't seen before. The women were sitting on the bench with the chenille cushions, their backs against the Formica wall. Between them, placed in the center of the coffee table, was a tray of *samosas* and *gulab jamuns* next to a pitcher of Rooh Afza, a red-colored refreshment beverage, flanked with four glasses.

One of the visitors had thinning brown hair, arms with flabby skin hanging from under the triceps, and a pair of small, deep-set eyes. Her name was Afshan. She wore a red *dupatta* draped on her chest and over her shoulders. The woman sitting next to Afshan, Sangeeta, had her head covered in a blue-and-yellow floral shawl. She had long fingers, a round face, and trimmed eyebrows that met in the middle.

The colorful bangles in Afshan's wrist clinked when she reached for the glass Amma had poured for her. "They say it could snow this winter in Lahore. Have you heard, *hamshira*?" she said, called Amma sister.

Amma slapped her cheek with a mock surprise, "You don't say." Sangeeta gave an affirmative nod.

"We hope it wasn't much trouble finding the house," Amma continued with the token conversation.

Rami had a distinct suspicion these women weren't visiting to discuss the weather or to engage in obligatory idle chatter. He watched one of them compliment Narin's powder-blue dress and the matching *dupatta* on her lowered head. Narin was looking at her hands.

Rami soon discovered these women were from a marriage bureau. Their profession: matchmaking.

"I'm eager to hear the good news you have for us," Amma spoke wistfully.

"Of course. Sorry to keep you waiting." Sangeeta reached under a bag and fetched a black portfolio containing pages filled with scribbled notes and pasted photographs of several men. "We've selected a few suitors for you to choose for Narin."

Rami cast a glance at Narin's chalk-white face. After much persuasion from Papa and Amma, Jalil had relinquished his aggressive stance of honor killing toward Narin—but she looked dead to Rami—from the inside, anyhow. He felt a knot tightening in his stomach, sensing they were planning a more severe punishment for his sister: enslaving her to a stranger through an arranged marriage. He saw Narin's lips quiver in agony.

"And, what's great," Afshan adjusted the *dupatta* on her shoulders, "is that two of them are willing to marry your daughter immediately. It'll lighten the weight off your shoulders sooner than we anticipated."

Rami wondered how Narin was feeling inside. Was the windpipe in her throat tightening? Were the walls in the room suddenly closing in on her?

Sangeeta spread open the portfolio from the middle and placed her finger on a photograph. "This is Shahid," she said. "He's a Mechanical Engineer in Dubai, originally from Karachi. Divorced."

"And here is Ali." Afshan turned the page. She lifted the portfolio to display another picture. "He's from Lahore but now lives in Quetta. He's a doctor."

Rami knew marriage bureaus were notorious for exaggerating the professions of marriage seekers to vulnerable families. A suitor presented as a Mechanical Engineer, chances were, was an auto mechanic in a body shop. A *doctor* was likely an assistant to a doctor or, better yet, a receptionist at a clinic.

"Now, you understand they're a little older than your daughter," Afshan went on. "Say twelve-to-fifteen-year age differences. Am I right, Sangeeta?"

"Right. But we've seen much younger girls given to much older men than these suitors." Sangeeta bobbed her head. "Sadly, we had to disclose why you're looking to marry off your daughter so suddenly," she added. "We couldn't solicit any younger candidates to show much interest, you know? It doesn't take long for stories to float around. People like to quip and gossip about girls," she said, hesitated, "well, girls with a *history*."

"We select him. Shahid," Jalil, slouched in the chair across from Narin, jumped into the conversation. "We select the engineer from Dubai," he said monotonously.

"*Wah, wah!* Great choice!" Afshan beamed. "You want to think this through, brother? We can wait to give the suitor good news if you need more time."

"No need to wait. I want her gone as far away from here as possible." Jalil waved a dismissive hand. "As quickly as possible," he added.

"I don't want this." Narin burst into tears. "Don't make me," she cried. She then looked at Amma. "Do something! For God's sake, Amma, make it stop. I beg you," she pleaded in a sniffling voice. Amma dabbed at her eyes, glanced at her daughter with a look of reluctant forgiveness, and said nothing.

"*Bas!*" Jalil barked, slamming his fist at the table, jolting the pitcher of Rooh Afza, almost knocking it over. "You should've thought about this before disappearing with your *lover* at nights, having no regard for family's respectability."

Rami caught Afshan and Sangeeta exchanging glances. Jalil clenched his teeth and bolted up. "Damnit, Narin, show some gratitude for being wedded off with honor, for having another chance in life. Just not here, not in this city. Not in Pakistan," he said and stormed out of the room.

With this, Amma, Afshan, and Sangeeta quickly gathered around Narin. They talked boisterously about what a wonderful life awaited her in Dubai, offered her a bite of *gulab jamun,* and renewed assurances that it would be okay. In the end, it would all be okay, Rami heard them say.

ANOTHER NIGHT. Another eerie silence, reminiscent of the deathly hush in a graveyard on a moonlit night.

Unable to contain the hauntingly quiet air around him, Rami climbed the stairs to the veranda where Jalil had banished Narin to spend her days: to eat, to sleep, to exist alone, away from everyone else. He had installed doors on the staircase on each floor, securing them with padlocks. No one could go up and down the stairs unnoticed anymore.

Rami walked across the veranda to the room where Narin was hidden from the naked eye, like a castaway. He flicked the switch next to the entrance wall, but no light came on.

And as if the night's darkness weren't enough, a pair of black curtains pulled to make it nearly impossible to see anything.

"Narin," Rami hissed his sister's name. His feet kicked empty plates littering the floor, and he stumbled through articles of clothing strewn across. He allowed his eyes to adjust to the sheer darkness and inhaled the lingering smell of leftover food from the previous day.

"Narin?" Rami called out again. The blanket mound on a twin bed placed on the far side of the room stirred.

"Go away," Narin's thin voice mumbled from behind the covers.

"I just want to talk," Rami said. In response, he heard a groan.

"I get what you might be going through, Narin; please talk to me."

Some time passed.

Then, Narin's hand slowly emerged from underneath the blanket, pulling it off her face, exposing her disheveled hair caked against her cheeks. "Rami ..." she croaked; tears leaked from her eyes. The blanket slid down as she pulled herself up. Rami lowered himself to the foot of the bed and stretched his arms open. Narin reached for Rami's embrace, rested her cheek on his shoulder, and wept. Rami cupped his palm around her right shoulder and let his sister cry. Let her tears drip down his shirt.

"I'm sorry for what's happened," he said after Narin's sniffles subsided.

Narin lifted her head from his shoulder. "It's kismet," she ran a sleeve across her face and said. "It's fate for women like us to suffer and bear the burden of society's accusing fingers. It's the price we pay to exist in this world." She stared into the space, her voice hollow.

Rami didn't mean to tell her. He'd decided not to tell anyone he saw Kamran sneaking out of the house that night. It wouldn't bring any good to anyone hearing about it. But he told Narin. He did not want to say anything about Kamran, but it rolled out of Rami's tongue before he could stop it.

Narin's mouth creased in a wilted smile. "I'd asked him always to be careful. But he said he didn't care."

There was a pause.

"You love him?" Rami allowed a few seconds to linger between words. "Narin, look at me."

Narin's wounded gaze met Rami's.

"Do you love Kamran?"

Narin drew her knees and curled her arms around them. Nodded.

"What does it matter now?" she said, resting her chin on one knee and looking to her side. "Kamran's gone. Soon, I'll be, too. Gone to a foreign land. To be amongst strangers. Forever."

Rami told her he wished there was something he could do to change things—anything to prevent her from being forced into marriage.

Narin reached across and ran her fingers through Rami's hair. "You're a dear boy, my sweet brother. Everyone should experience love at least once in their lifetime. I pray you can fall for someone one day and bask in the enchanting feeling it brings," she said, her eyes tearing again. "Because fortunate are those who can feel the trueness of love, even if it may last for a moment, even if it may leave your heart feeling fulfilled and shattered all at once. There is no greater joy than knowing there's someone out there thinking of you. That your heart is devoted to another soul. No force in the world can strip away this feeling of unshakeable yearning for someone."

Rami listened to Narin go on while thinking about Danyaal. His heart filled with dread; he felt a lump shooting up his throat. "I know what it's like to feel this way," he murmured, trying to hide the quivering. "I understand."

"You do?"

He gave her a slow nod. "My heart aches for someone also."

"Who's *she*? Tell me."

There was a moment of hesitation before Rami came right out and uttered, "Actually, it's a boy. Danyaal."

A hushed silence, as thick as the air in the room, fell. They just sat there. Rami's eyes were downcast, his trembling fingers intertwined; he waited for Narin to say something. She was the first person in the family, in the world, in whom Rami had confided his feelings for Danyaal.

Despite the deepened darkness in the room, despite his lowered gaze, Rami could sense Narin's puzzled stare, searching his face for a long while. Through the corner of his eye, he noticed she had opened her mouth to say something, then closed it as if carefully weighing on the words teetering on her curled lips.

"Then you go to him," Narin finally said.

Rami raised his head. "Narin ..." he gasped.

"You find Danyaal and tell him how you feel about him."

Rami's lips parted, but word evaporated from his tongue. His chest suddenly began feeling as light as a weightless flake of foam after hearing his sister's response.

"It pains me that I never got a chance to tell Kamran how much I loved him, that his memory shall remain etched in my heart forever. I wouldn't wish that on my worst enemy to carry such a burden for all eternity. I implore you not to let a similar regret haunt you. If your bond with Danyaal is as strong as you claim, do not hesitate to express your feelings toward him. Life is unpredictable, and we never know what lies ahead. Seize the opportunity while you can, and do not let anything prevent you from conveying your emotions to him."

THE NEXT morning, shortly before sunrise, Rami rode the motorcycle to Danyaal's house and waited for him outside. He zipped the denim jacket with the Dallas Cowboys imprint, snuggled against the cold December morning, and watched the darkness from the previous night gradually morph into a new dawn.

Danyaal appeared through the gate ten minutes before eight o'clock, wearing a purple sweater under a checkered shirt and a pair of light blue denim. He'd begun walking toward the bus stop when Rami, perched on the motorcycle across the street, waved at him. Danyaal stopped. He hesitated a bit before crossing and approaching Rami.

He stood before Rami, arms crossed.

"Danyaal—"

"Yes?"

Rami could tell the unpleasant taste from the last time they saw each other still lingered in Danyaal's mouth.

"I've come to see you," he said.

Danyaal remained quiet.

"I've always struggled to find the right words, but I'll try," Rami said. He cleared his throat. "I … us … Danyaal, I don't want to be away from you anymore," words stumbled a bit before coming out of Rami's mouth. "My days aren't the same without you; I feel lost when not with you. I apologize."

Danyaal uncrossed his arms.

"I'm sorry for the way I behaved that day in your room," Rami said.

Danyaal looked to his side. Rami saw water appearing in Danyaal's eyes.

"—Can you forgive me?"

There was a long pause.

"I don't want us to end, Danyaal," Rami pressed on, nearly choking on his words.

Danyaal rolled his head to face Rami. "I don't want us to end either. But …" he said.

Rami leaned in.

"Rami—"

"I'm sorry—"

"I know I'm partly to blame, too, for …" Danyaal started, but Rami placed his index finger on Danyaal's lips.

"Don't say that."

Their eyes traded amorous looks. Rami felt the ice melting between them.

"There are many things uncertain in my life," Rami spoke. "But there's one thing I am sure of."

"What's that?"

"I'm certain I don't want us to be apart like this again. Ever," he said.

"I've missed you, you know?"

Rami wrapped his arms around Danyaal's belly. "I missed you, too."

And that, what might seem like a mundane gesture to others, was one of the greatest moments of the eighteen years of Rami's life. Like a downpour, it seemed Danyaal's body had seeped into the depths of his being and drenched Rami's parched soul.

"Come on," Rami said after they separated from a long embrace. "Let's go to the college together."

Danyaal's lips stretched into a smile. "All right, fine."

Rami swung his right leg over the motorcycle. "Hop on!" Rami exclaimed delightedly.

"Wait."

"What for?"

"Just a second." Danyaal opened his bag and sifted through the contents before fetching his Walkman. He then fished a cassette tape from a case with a printed cover of *Roxy Music*. He stretched the wires of his orange earphones. Inserted one earbud in Rami's ear and the other in his.

"Now I'm ready," Danyaal said and pressed Play.

MUSICAL LAYERS of synthesizer and drum began to echo in Rami's ear as he kicked the bike into gear. Danyaal sat behind him like before: arms firmly thrown around Rami's torso, chin resting on his shoulder. They rode through the familiar streets, and the paths they had traversed before seemed to extend a warm embrace, welcoming their blissful reunion. The sun cast a radiant glow on the expansive thoroughfares as it rose behind them to its zenith. It seemed to Rami that the roads had widened to make way for their journey. Sharp corners had bent a bit deeper as though taking a bow.

A prayer of gratitude escaped Rami's lips for the cold wind to surge from behind, carrying the scent of Danyaal's freshly washed hair, for the cassette to roll in the Walkman, and for the melody of the song "More Than This" to flow into his ear.

Four months later, Danyaal vanished.

SEVENTEEN

The first few months of 1988 went by in a haze. Between Narin getting married and leaving for Dubai, Rami saw Danyaal a handful of times only: trips here and there to music shops in Fortress Stadium to find newly released albums, occasional lunches from roadside vendors. They saw one film together during that period, went to a field hockey game held at the college, and once to a squash tournament. But aside from that, they spent their time studying for the final exams. Rami, like Danyaal, had occupied himself with matters of Economics, interlayers of the government through Political Science, and complex formula composition of Mathematics.

But, between breaks from studying, they would phone each other to check in, to express wistful wishes for spring to arrive, and to reiterate how sick they were looking at those damn textbooks.

"I hate algebra," Rami said to Danyaal over the phone one cold February evening, his feet pedaling in the air while lying on his stomach on the bed. "Linear equation this, variable carry that." He heaved a sigh of exasperation. "I'm going to fail mathematics. I tell you."

Danyaal chuckled on the other line. "This is the third time I've heard you mention it in twenty-four hours. If it's any consolation, my distaste for statistics matches your disdain for mathematical formulas," he said.

"I just want the graduation day to arrive." Rami heaved another sigh. "Am I being too impatient?"

"Maybe a little." Danyaal chortled, but it sounded as though a snort burst through his nostrils over the phone. "Not that I'm keeping score, but you said that also earlier."

"And I'll repeat it until that damn day," Rami said. "By the way, did you just snort?"

"I did not," Danyaal said in a mock-surprised tone.

"I heard you make a weird noise."

"I think you're hearing things."

Rami could hear the playfulness in Danyaal's voice.

"Whatever," Rami said. "I'm getting back to these stupid books."

"Me too."

"Okay, goodnight."

"Rami?"

"Yes."

"I miss us spending time together," Danyaal's voice got lower. "I miss seeing you."

"I miss you too," Rami replied without hesitation, pause, or lingering reservation.

"Okay, goodnight."

"Goodnight."

ON THE third Thursday in April of that year, Rami and Danyaal completed their intermediate studies, equivalent to a high school diploma in the United States. Rami arrived at the FC College's cricket field for graduation, wearing a green gown and a mortarboard.

Sitting between Papa and Jalil, he looked at Danyaal three rows ahead of him with his father. Amid cameras clicking, students giggling, and conversations flowing around them, they occasionally stole glances at each other and smiled. Papa was beyond happy that day. One of his sons had finished twelve years of education. He kept holding and releasing Rami's hand, kept telling him how proud he was of him. At one point, he asked Jalil to take a picture with him and Rami. Jalil took the black Nikon camera from Papa and peered through the optical viewfinder with a focused intensity. Rami watched and wondered what thoughts lay hidden behind his stoic façade: regret for not finishing school? A stirred-up envy for Papa's favoritism toward his youngest son, showering Rami with paternal love? Was there any lingering sorrow over Narin? Could Jalil be missing the sister he wedded off to a stranger?

But he simply captured their picture with the Clock Tower in the background, handed the camera back to Papa, and returned to his seat.

After the ceremony, with the air filling with spiraling congratulations, Rami made his way toward Danyaal while Jalil and Papa disappeared and reappeared behind the rows of students milling around.

"*Mubarak!*" Gibril spotted Rami approaching and congratulated him bright-facedly. He patted Rami's shoulder. "Well done, son!"

"Such a handsome boy," Afrooz adjusted the knot on Rami's skewed necktie and said gleamingly. "Look, Danyaal! Rami's here." She tapped Danyaal on the shoulder, who was talking with Saman. Danyaal turned to face Rami, standing beside his parents.

"Hi."

"*Salaam.*"

Out of the corner of his eye, Rami noticed Afrooz nudging at Gibril. "We'll be at the canteen, boys," she said and dragged her husband's arm. "Come now, Saman. Leave your brother alone with Rami."

Rami watched them amble away and waved.

"Here we are," Danyaal said with visible dimples on his cheeks.

"Finally."

"We graduate."

"We do."

Danyaal extended his arms toward Rami.

Rami's fingers slid into Danyaal's. Despite being in plain sight of Jalil and Papa, a smile creased his mouth's edges. "I've been dreaming of this day for a long time."

Up ahead, cameras flashed; someone squealed. A few dancing shapes emerged from around a tree. Behind him, Rami heard Papa's voice calling his name.

"My father. I should go," he said. His fingers untangled from Danyaal's hand.

Danyaal nodded. "Meet up soon?"

"Can't wait."

"Perhaps back to the marigold field," Danyaal suggested. "Like last year?"

Rami heard Papa's voice calling his name again and began to walk toward it.

"Don't forget about the Manga Jungle picnic," Danyaal called over the loud crowd.

Rami turned and gave Danyaal a puzzled look. "A picnic?"

Danyaal extended his left thumb to his ear and his pinky to his mouth as if holding a telephone handset. "I'll call you," he mouthed.

Rami returned and found Papa's stare lingering over his face earnestly and amusingly.

"I thought you'd left us, son," Papa said, a smile stretching his face.

"I'm here, Papa."

"Who's the boy you were with?"

Rami heard Jalil clear his throat and look the other way.

"That's Danyaal," Rami said.

"Your friend?"

"More than a friend."

"'More than a friend,' Mashallah!" Papa beamed. "Best friend. Good friends are hard to come by. Don't you think, Jalil?" Papa said. Rami couldn't tell whether Papa was genuinely asking Jalil's opinion or being sarcastic. Jalil grunted something.

"Well. Go on, then," Papa said to Jalil.

"Huh?"

"Don't you have something to give Rami for his graduation?" Papa lowered his voice and said testily.

Jalil fished into his pocket and fetched a sealed envelope containing cash. "*Mubarak* on completing college." He handed Rami the gift, then twined his arm around Rami's neck. Rami could sense the half-heartedness in Jalil's tight-lipped smile that barely let a congratulation slip through.

Another thing that revealed the contempt congesting Jalil's chest, like a chronic cough, was how Jalil's arm had tightened around Rami and how his muscles clenched against the base of Rami's neck. Jalil was making Rami aware that he'd seen Danyaal and him holding hands.

"SOUNDS LIKE fun," Danyaal said to Rami over the phone later that night, referring to the picnic planned at the Manga Jungle to celebrate the newly graduated 1988 class, a time-honored tradition F.C. College faculty had carried out for years.

"Why did I know nothing about it?" Rami spoke into the receiver. He was lying in bed, his finger twirling around the coiled phone cord.

"God knows," Danyaal sighed.

Rami reminded Danyaal he'd suggested going to the Jhoke Forest Preserve.

"We can go there after the picnic," Danyaal said.

There was a brief silence.

Later, Rami would reflect on this moment and wonder what the outcome would have been if they had decided to skip the college picnic. What if they'd just ridden around town on a sunny spring day? What if they had visited the museum at the Lahore Fort instead? What if Rami had turned down the invitation to the outing at the Manga Jungle with hundreds of other fellow graduates?

"The college picnic it is," Rami said. "We can visit the marigold field later."

THEY ARRIVED separately at the college the following Saturday morning. Rami noticed three blue buses in the parking area. The drivers sat inside the idling vehicles and awaited everyone to board for the trip to the Manga Jungle. The nearby area was quickly filling with people roaming around; the air echoed with boisterous chatter. Some held steaming cups of tea, and a few had cigarettes tucked between their index and middle fingers. Rami had his back against a wall, eyes fixed on the college entrance, waiting for Danyaal to arrive. Gibril had offered to give Danyaal a ride since he was to take Saman to a clinic for a checkup later. Danyaal appeared a few minutes later, and Rami noticed the dusty sliver of sunlight bouncing off the Ray-Ban sunglasses Danyaal was wearing. The father and the son threaded through the crowd toward Rami.

"*Salaam*," Rami said to Gibril and shook his hand.

Gibril flung his arm around Rami's neck. "How are you, son?"

Rami said he was fine.

"I wish I'd gotten a chance to meet your father and brother at the graduation ceremony," Gibril said.

Rami gave him an uneasy smile. "I should've introduced you to them. I'm sorry."

"Perhaps introductions can be made between the two families soon?"

Rami nodded and cast a sidelong glance in Danyaal's direction.

That was when a voice said, "Congratulations, Rami!" Rami turned and saw Tariq standing between Amir and Noor, grinning, his arms resting on their shoulders. "Congratulations on passing the exams," he said.

A surge of dizziness churned through Rami's stomach.

"Well, Danyaal?"

"Yes, Father."

"Aren't you going to introduce me to your friends?" Gibril said in a low voice, the kind one uses when embarrassed in public.

Danyaal looked the other way.

"You boys must be friends with my son, Danyaal," Gibril said to Tariq.

"We go way back." Tariq winked. "Isn't that right, Rami?" It was creepy the way he leaned over and winked. Rami noticed a look of anguish appearing on Danyaal's face.

Gibril nodded, unaware of Tariq's malice-filled tone. "When I was your age, I had friends just like you. It's always nice to be in good company."

"I couldn't agree more," Tariq said. He pressed his palm against his chest and tilted his head, pretending to show humility. Winked again. Gibril winked back.

Danyaal reminded his father that Saman was waiting in the car, and Gibril took his leave.

Tariq's eyes flitted from Rami to Danyaal, "You two fags are looking forward to the picnic?" he asked, laughter skulking beneath the surface, ready to burst.

Rami clenched his fist. "Mind your business, Tariq!"

"Take it easy," Tariq raised his arms, palms forward, and stepped back, "Just wishing you two lovebirds a fun day." Amir and Noor grinned.

"See you at the picnic!"

Rami watched Amir ape Danyaal's walk as he scuttled away with Tariq and Noor. He stood there with Danyaal in uncomfortable silence for a while before his fist slowly unclenched.

Professor Hamid emerged from behind one of the buses and announced it was almost time to board.

"What's in the backpack?" Rami attempted to alleviate the unpleasant encounter with Tariq and pointed at the green-colored bag dangling from Danyaal's right shoulder.

"Just a few things," Danyaal said. He unzipped the bag and let Rami peek: his Walkman, a few cassette tapes, candy bars, a pack of Peek Freans biscuits, and a square metal box. Rami asked what was in it. Danyaal hesitated. Rami then reached within the backpack and fished out the box.

"Hey!"

"I want to know," Rami said smilingly.

He opened the lid and saw a Swiss Army pocketknife, a lighter with an attached butane fluid can, a pack of batteries, a roll of bandages, and a small flashlight.

Rami looked at Danyaal.

"What?"

"You packed like we're going to enlist in the army."

Danyaal rolled his eyes.

"Or going camping," he teased some more and put the box back in the bag.

Danyaal shrugged. "One must always be prepared for an emergency. What if our transportation breaks down? What if there's an injury? Have you ever thought of that?" he said.

The queue of people waiting to board the bus started to inch forward.

"You're weird," Rami said.

"And clearly, you're envious."

"Of what?"

"My witty thinking."

A whistle interrupted the playful banter between them. One of the faculty members was guiding students toward the buses for boarding.

"I was trying to annoy you," Rami said.

"Well, it worked." Danyaal gave Rami a sidelong glance and closed the bag without disclosing one last item in a zippered pocket.

BY THE time they boarded the bus, it was already past eight o'clock. Rami climbed the stairs and followed Danyaal. They made their way down the aisle to the back and took the bench behind Professor Hamid. A band of squealing graduates Rami hadn't seen before got on and sat between Rami and Danyaal, sandwiching them. Engaged in playful banter, their shoulders bumped into Rami and Danyaal every time one would jostle and punch the other light-heartedly sitting on the other end.

The trek to the Manga Jungle is approximately an eighty-kilometer journey southwest of Lahore through N-5 Highway, off Chunian. The jungle, its official name Changa Manga, boasts a fascinating history. It was once considered the oldest hand-planted forest in the world. It is named after two brothers, two bandits, Changa and Manga. The notoriously famous dacoits eluded British peacekeepers for a long time in the nineteenth century while robbing convoys of unsuspecting merchants passing through the area. The jungle currently covers about forty-nine square kilometers and is home to various wildlife animals, including reptiles.

After being on the congested highway for nearly two hours, the bus got off to a shaded, winding road where it rode amid the tall forest trees. Everyone on the bus was talking loudly, nearly shrieking over each other. Toward the front of the bus, someone started playing music through a mini cassette player. And despite Professor Hamid and another faculty member's calls for everyone to behave, a few got up and began dancing.

Then, almost everyone on the bus started clapping and cheering the dancing boys. Someone shouted to have seen a herd of deer on the side of the road.

Rami exchanged looks with Danyaal. "You want to check out some wildlife?" he said.

Danyaal nodded. "Any distraction from the ruckus inside would do," he said, flicking his chin at the hip-twisting ahead. Chuckled.

Rami asked the two boys sitting by the window facing each other if they'd trade seats with Danyaal and him. They hesitated at first but then agreed. No deer were left to see when Danyaal and Rami stuck their heads out the window. In its stead, they saw multi-colored vans and lorries zipping past them in the other direction. Rami kept his head out and counted the trees whipping by. He saw Danyaal leaning out in front of him, his eyes closed. The wind blew against his cheeks, a calm smile playing on his lips. Rami moved his hand in waves against the breeze and also smiled.

They were a few kilometers west of the Manga Jungle when, in the midst of the shudders and jolts of the bus stumbling into a few potholes, amid the semi-trailer trucks lumbering by, Rami noticed a car—a beige Suzuki sedan with a dented passenger door—speeding past the bus.

Rami's heart skipped a beat. He had a distinct suspicion he'd seen that vehicle before.

"WHAT'S WRONG?" Danyaal asked when they got off the bus.

It was late morning by the time the busses pulled into the resort area. Everyone was disembarking and heading toward a pagoda in front of Lunar Lake, a man-made recreational body of water. The designated area served as the gathering ground for the graduates and the staff. According to the instructions at the college, they had to check in at the pagoda upon arrival and report back at the exact location at the end of the day before boarding the buses for the return journey.

Rami and Danyaal moved ahead with the crowd. Around them, a minivan pulled up beside a bus, and Rami watched a few men haul provisions out: a butcher towing large chunks of raw meat to roast on a fire pit, another holding bags of spices to marinate the beef. Someone else emerged from the side of the van carrying crates of Coca-Cola and Fanta bottles. The area was teeming with men setting up folding tables and hammering tent stakes to the ground.

Rami's eyes flicked from side to side with unease as if trying to locate something or someone. He then sensed Danyaal's gaze resting on him.

"What's the matter?" Danyaal asked.

"Nothing."

Danyaal placed his hands on his hips. "I know when you say *nothing*, it usually means it's *something*," he said. "What's bothering you?"

There was a pause.

"I think I might have seen Osman's car on the road," Rami eventually said in an alarming voice and saw a shade of pale drift across Danyaal's face.

"What? When?"

"On the way here, when we were sitting by the window in the bus," Rami said.

"You think he's coming here?"

Rami gave Danyaal a side glance.

"You recognized it as Osman's car?"

Rami took a deep breath and informed Danyaal he'd remembered Osman's vehicle from the day he had shown up at the strawberry stand. The car he saw earlier had similar dents on it, he said.

They were standing in the middle row of the huddled crowd; one ear perked up to the professor's static voice, blaring from a megaphone giving out instructions. Students were to stay off the wild preserve area. They were not to venture toward the abandoned rail tracks of the North-Western Railway from 1864, Rami heard him say.

"Should we inform someone?"

"It'll cause panic."

Danyaal waited for a dozen or so heartbeats. "It could be another car with similar marks on it."

Rami considered this. Nodded.

Students were to avoid the rusted carcass of the wood-burning locomotives, the professor intoned.

"Osman has no reason to be here. He probably doesn't even know about the picnic," Danyaal continued.

The professor finished with one final instruction: no one was to go near the Salvation Army Silk Camp ruins.

Rami turned to Danyaal. "You're right," he said. "It must've been a different car." He squelched the rising lump in his throat by gulping down saliva. "I shouldn't have caused this anxiety." He gave Danyaal a close-lipped smile. "You're right. I'm sorry."

FOR ALL the activities taking place that day at the picnic—badminton, volleyball, hiking, the tour of the jungle—there were a handful of moments Rami would remember in precise detail for years to come.

He walked on one of the cantilevered bridges with Danyaal. It was a modest, pin-jointed wooden plank structure using ropes for tension and support. The early afternoon sun shimmered against the murky body of water below, giving it a rippled, amber glow. Only six people could be on the bridge at any given time. Two local guides stood on each end and supervised the visitors. They shouted and waved at anyone trying to sway or bounce on the bridge. Rami and Danyaal were in the fourth group to walk across. The wooden planks beneath their feet creaked, making some of the graduates shriek.

Rami got on a pedal boat in the Lunar Lake with Danyaal, whose eyes were hidden behind the green of his sunglasses, wearing a hat to protect his face from direct sunlight. A procession of other boats quickly followed, and, within minutes, a crowd of cheering, clapping graduates sitting in pairs filled the lake. At a distance, Rami saw Professor Hamid's shiny, bald scalp. He was also boating with someone. The professor smiled and waved at a group of people, possibly a family, sitting on the opposite side of the lake fringed with a row of *sheesham*, North Indian rosewood trees, having a picnic of its own.

Rami rode a miniature train with Danyaal through the forest around a recreation park, a waterfall, and the Lunar Lake. Danyaal tapped his shoulder as they rode past the wild preserve area and saw a herd of hog deer, peacocks, jackals, and *shutar murgh*, Ostriches. Manga Jungle was also the conservation center for the Gypsy Vultures, dedicated to preserving and managing the population of that endangered species, Danyaal told Rami. He was pointing at a gray-colored bird perched on a tree limb. Rami's gaze followed Danyaal's pointed finger and caught Tariq sitting a few rows ahead. His stare met Rami's but quickly withdrew.

AFTER LUNCH, while most chose to lounge around or nap, Danyaal asked if they could hike. He said there was a trail to the east of the wild preserve area worth checking out.

"I am fatigued," Rami said. "Aren't you? Like the rest?" He raised one eyebrow and flicked his chin at the bodies lying on the grass. Some even snored.

"We haven't had time to spend with just the two of us," Danyaal insisted. "Come on. It won't be crowded."

After some deliberation, Rami agreed. But only after making Danyaal promise they would return well before departure.

"I promise," Danyaal said as he slung the backpack on his shoulder. "Follow me."

THE TWISTED path they took weaved around the trees whose aged roots splayed above ground like the spread tentacles of an octopus. Within minutes of their hiking, the sky almost disappeared, leaving only slivers of blue peeking through the dense canopy of thick foliage overhead. Rami walked next to Danyaal and felt the thin air around him.

Danyaal was saying something about furthering education. Said he would love to attend a music program at a college.

"We could be going to different schools," Rami said.

Danyaal nodded. He said it was possible.

On a branch above, a bird fluttered its wings. A squirrel dashed up a tree trunk in front of them. Danyaal was right about them being the only ones hiking that trail. Rami hadn't noticed anyone else nearby.

"I'm not sure if there's an academy in Lahore that offers a music degree, though," Danyaal went on.

They walked in silence for a while.

"What, then?" Rami asked.

"Travel, I guess," said Danyaal.

Rami shifted his eyes at him. "Another city?"

"Abroad. Could go to London, England, to study."

Rami felt dread filling his chest. Listening to Danyaal mentioning leaving for another country made him feel like he'd been struck blind.

"So far away."

"—Rami."

"Someplace beyond my reach ..." Rami's voice cracked.

"I didn't mean that."

Rami dropped his eyes.

"Look at me."

Rami stayed quiet.

"Rami?"

"You should've said something about this earlier."

Danyaal held Rami's hand and stopped him from walking. "Rami, look at me."

Rami lifted his head. Danyaal snaked his arms around him. "Chances of me leaving Lahore are slim. I was merely expressing my thoughts out loud." Danyaal locked his eyes with Rami. Their bodies rocked in slow motion. "You believe me?"

Rami looked at him.

"I won't leave you. Not like this. Trust me."

"Promise?"

"Cross my heart."

The woods seemed to sway gently back and forth around them. Overhead, the leaves were closing in, shutting out the remaining daylight. Everything appeared a shade darker. Danyaal stayed holding Rami.

There was a long pause.

"Hey," Danyaal finally whispered.

"Yes."

"I like you. You know that, don't you?"

"I like you more," Rami replied with an air of playfulness, his body swinging in Danyaal's arms.

A crow began cawing somewhere. It was soon joined by a crescendo of other chirping birds.

"What I really mean is ..." Danyaal hesitated for a moment.

"Danyaal—"

"I *really* like you." Danyaal pressed his tongue on the hard palate of his mouth when saying.

Rami looked at him with a half-grinning, half-contorted look of confusion. Blinked. He could tell Danyaal's sparkling eyes were tracing the expression on Rami's face.

"I love you, Rami," Danyaal's words entered Rami's ears. "I'm in love with you."

With this, suddenly, the woodland became eerily quiet. A hush fell over the tweeting feathered creatures. All that remained was the susurration of the myriad of leaves forming a living roof above their heads. Their bodies stopped swaying.

No one had confessed his love for Rami like this before.

Was he supposed to say something in return? Reciprocate?

Because, at that moment, Rami was like that infant who had yet to utter their first word to the world.

Am I to reach over, press Danyaal against my chest, and tell him I love him too? If so, then why do I feel as if every bone in my body has solidified into cement? Rami's thoughts drifted.

Seconds ticked in quietude. Danyaal's fingers slid from Rami's torso. They must have stood there for about a minute, but each passing moment seemed a hundred years long to Rami. The air between them was becoming colder, thinner, making Rami shiver.

A few leaves rustled in the wind.

Was that the sound of a tree limb snapping somewhere, or did Rami hear Danyaal's heart break in two?

A sliver of light penetrated from the low-hanging leaves and fell on Danyaal's face. Rami felt indebted to the shadows in the woods concealing his. Standing inches from Danyaal, seeing him in that light, Rami watched the pool of water filling the corner of his eyes, which Danyaal hastily wiped by dragging a sleeve across before they could leak to his cheeks. The contours of Danyaal's face twitched in a wilted smile as he desperately attempted to conceal the pain-stricken look.

"Forget it." Danyaal shrugged. "It was a joke."

"Danyaal—"

"Never mind," he said, faked another smile. "I was only kidding."

"You were?" Rami said, but his eyes wondered.

"Got you for a bit, didn't I?"

Rami stood facing Danyaal in an awkward silence. Danyaal kicked a stone with his foot and avoided meeting Rami's gaze.

"We should head back," the deflated tone in Danyaal's voice was undeniable.

He then turned his back to Rami and began walking away. Rami felt his chest tightening, his heart as if being squeezed by a fist.

He knew his next move would change everything. He could go on pretending as if nothing had happened. Choose to ignore the rasped voice stuck in Danyaal's throat and the tears Danyaal so desperately fought back.

Or, Rami could do what he should have done in the first place. Save this relationship, which would never be the same if he remained silent. He thought about what Narin had said to him that night.

'If your bond with Danyaal is as strong as you claim, do not hesitate to express your feelings ... seize the opportunity ....'

"Danyaal, wait," Rami called out.

Danyaal turned.

Rami moved forward and met him under the swerving branch of a weeping willow.

"That wasn't a joke."

"What?"

"You lied." Rami's hands grabbed Danyaal from the waist. "You weren't kidding."

"Rami."

"You didn't give me a chance," Rami said. His breath fanned Danyaal's face.

"To what?"

"To respond."

Rami then cupped Danyaal's face, leaned over, and placed his lips on his, brushing first, then pressing. He squeezed Danyaal's lower lip between his mouth.

"I love you, too," Rami whispered between breaths. "More than words can say."

"Rami—" Danyaal gasped.

His arms curled back around Rami's shoulder blades. His mouth parted, and Rami's tongue found its way in. Rami continued squeezing Danyaal's lips into his, continued feeling the tingling sensation coursing through his body. His cheeks felt the short bursts of Danyaal's breath, his fingers crawling up the sides of Danyaal's curly hair.

A gust of wind swept across, sending the foliage on the boughs to dance around them. Rami felt hypnotized as if the leaves were eyes staring down. The branches seemed to be drawing closer as though creating a cage around them.

Then, a flurry of movement behind him. From the corner of his eye, while locking lips with Danyaal, Rami caught those leaves blinking. Within seconds, he realized they weren't alone. There were actual human eyes lurking behind the leaves; their stares settled on them.

A blur of something whooshed across. A shape emerged from the shadow, and Rami's heart dropped when he saw Osman's stony eyes unblinkingly fixated on his face.

"Danyaal. Run!" Rami screamed.

HE SLAPPED away a hand fumbling to grip his shoulder and bolted.

Even the birds and critters must have sensed the somersaulting of Rami's heart in his chest. Their shrill sounds formed a symphony all around him. The leaves brushed against him; loose branches slashed his sides while he sprang to his feet. In front of him, the trees, tall as cathedrals, rose into the sky. Densely packed together, they offered little room for someone to maneuver through. Rami pressed his palms against their bark and hopped over twigs, rocks, and other obstacles, felt its splintered edges cut into his skin while running.

He smelled the stench of bodies' odor emitting from those chasing him, making him sprint faster despite exhaustion, despite weakening legs and contracting lungs struggling to draw air. He could hear the running footsteps crunching the dried-up foliage behind him. His ear picked up Osman's infuriated groans coming from the left, yelling at someone to pick up the pace, cautioning them not to let the boy get away. Through the corner of his eye, he saw Osman closing in on him with clenching and unclenching fists. Rami gathered all his strength and dashed faster than he had ever before.

An opening was coming up to his right, a gravel path lined with a row of low hedges, surrounded almost entirely by branches interlocking with its neighbors like giant arms, forming an arched canopy. Rami lurched toward the arched roof, thrust in the air, and threw himself into the opening, hoping to dodge his hunters.

His body flung to the hedge to his left and penetrated it.

That was when a voice echoed in his head: *where is Danyaal?*

Rami emerged from the other side of the hedgerow. Then he was twisting and rotating, continuously changing the view from the sky to the earth. He rolled like a soccer ball down a steep slope, bouncing off the protruding edges. Shooting pains erupted all over his body. After a few seconds of falling and trying to hold on to a shrub or loose branch but coming up empty-handed, he finally landed on the marshy ground. Rami cringed with pain. He rolled on his stomach and took in a body of water up ahead. In the distance, he saw the wooden cantilevered bridge he and Danyaal had walked across earlier. In the passing breeze, besides his ringing ears, he heard a murmur as if someone were calling his name. Then, a whisper, other than the hissing of swinging boughs.

"Rami," a voice was saying his name. Rami rolled his head and saw a pair of blinking eyes staring at him from inside what appeared to be a small cave.

Rami blinked and saw Danyaal's face emerge into the thin light. He held out his hand. "This way," he hushed.

Rami crawled on his elbows toward him, making the slightest of sounds, and slid inside with Danyaal. Once in, he noticed it was mainly a mound of compact mud, probably formed by a mudslide during the rainy season, which gave it a concave-shaped structure with a dome-style roof on top. The opening must have cracked off when the dry, hot weather returned, but the roof remained.

Rami raised himself and sat beside Danyaal with their backs against the mud wall. Outside, above from where he had dropped, he heard faint shouting voices. Someone threw a rock that landed a few feet from the opening. A flashlight flooded the ground in front of the cave where Rami had lain a few seconds ago. Danyaal's hand took Rami's, tightened. Rami held his breath. He covered his mouth with the other hand to keep the wheezing from escaping his lips.

They sat shoulder to shoulder and watched their chests inflate and deflate uncontrollably. Danyaal's backpack rested on his lap, torn from one side. Outside, two voices argued over which way Rami could have gone. A question was answered curtly. Another question followed and was returned with an even curter retort. Things were turning ugly until Rami heard Osman's booming voice yelling at his accomplices, calling them lazy and incompetent.

Rami and Danyaal, barely moving, waited for a long time. Rami had no notion of time, but they forced themselves to remain idle until the echoing voices receded. Rami's ears rang; his body trembled in mortal fear. Then he felt Danyaal's hand tapping his shoulder.

"Are you okay?" Danyaal mouthed. Rami rolled his head toward Danyaal and only looked at him. Shaking. Danyaal pointed at his watch. Rami followed Danyaal's gesture, lifted his head, and fixed him with a puzzled stare.

"The bus, Rami," Danyaal hissed. "We're late to get on the bus to go back."

Rami's eyes widened. "What?"

Danyaal placed his hand on Rami's.

The panic spell returned. Rami's pulse began racing; his heart started juddering again.

"What do we do?" Rami's parched lips parted. He felt a tingling sensation sweeping down his throat. "Osman may still be out there."

Danyaal placed a finger on his lips, gesturing for Rami to be silent, and crawled over him. He stuck his head out the mouth of the cave and listened for any sound that could spell danger. But except for the hooting sound of an owl somewhere, all was quiet around them. He motioned Rami to follow him while dragging himself out.

"If we walk along the pond," Danyaal said in a hushed voice as he helped Rami onto his feet, "we may be able to get to the northern edge of the Lunar Lake. From there, we'll see the pagoda and the buses, which I'm sure are still there. They won't leave without us."

Rami steadied himself. "They won't leave without us," he said. Nodded.

Their feet sank into the soft mud as they inched along the pond. After taking a horseshoe turn flanked with white mulberry shrubs, they came across the area fringed with rows of *sheesham* trees where that family was picnicking earlier; the one Professor Hamid had waved at. The thought of the professor made Rami's eyes moisten. A silent prayer rose to his lips, hoping they would still be there. He pictured them split into groups, looking for him and Danyaal, calling out their names.

He followed Danyaal closely behind. A few times, he saw Danyaal's hand swiping the limp stout branches over to make way for them. Danyaal was saying to watch their steps. Said there might be a swamp nearby. One wrong step, he said, could send them sinking into a bottomless sinkhole. Then Danyaal stopped walking—turned—and threw his arms around Rami.

"What's the matter?"

Danyaal remained quiet. Rami asked again, but he wouldn't say. It wasn't until a breeze blew and parted a few drooping branches of a white mulberry shrub that Rami saw the Lunar Lake, saw the pagoda in the background, skimmed past it, and looked for the idling blue buses in the parking lot. Except, the buses weren't there. The parking lot was empty.

Danyaal was wrong. The buses had left without them.

RAMI HEARD Danyaal's muted voice speaking to him as they careened their way back to the mud cave. No buses ran between Manga Jungle and Lahore, but their parents would soon begin to worry, Danyaal was saying in a consoling tone, and that before long, someone would come looking for them. Rami kept on walking, at times stumbling, tripping almost. Danyaal said if they could somehow make it back to the hiking path, where Osman had come after them, they might be able to catch the attention of a guard or a patrol officer. He didn't say, and Rami didn't ask, how they would climb up that steep, nearly flat cliff wall they'd fallen from earlier.

"Are you crazy?" Rami stopped and turned to face Danyaal.

Danyaal grew quiet. They had crossed the bend and were now back where they had started.

"Go back to the trail where Osman's men may still be looking for us?" Rami began pacing restlessly.

"Catch a breath, Rami. Please." Danyaal stopped Rami from pacing. He placed his hand on Rami's shoulder. "Chances are Osman and his men have determined that we eluded them and returned to the bus," he said. "To them, we're probably already on our way back home. Osman would have no reason to stay behind and continue looking for us."

Feeling drained, Rami leaned forward and took Danyaal's hand in his. Danyaal's saying made him realize Osman must have also noticed the buses gone, thinking they were on board one of them.

"Okay?" Danyaal cupped his palms around Rami's shoulders and looked him in the eyes.

"They left us," Rami nearly choked.

Danyaal caressed the back of Rami's hand. "We'll make it through," he said, "it'll be all right."

Wearily, Rami nodded his head.

"*Inshallah*."

"*Inshallah*," Rami echoed his sentiment. Although, "God willing" sounded more sincere coming from Danyaal's lips.

Rami reached over and hugged Danyaal, fought back tears.

He took solace in that Danyaal had remained the strong one between them, holding it together despite having no idea when they would be rescued. They remained in each other's arms for a while before Rami suggested returning to the cave for safety. Danyaal agreed.

Rami was crouching to get down on his hands and knees to crawl back inside when he heard Danyaal let out a low-octave squeal.

"Back away, Rami," Danyaal hissed. He clutched Rami by the collar and pulled him away from the cave. Rami turned and saw a frightening look sweeping across Danyaal's face; his gaze settled on something on the ground. Rami followed Danyaal's stare and noticed an army of large ants, not the harmless little ones they'd see at home, crawling like flowing water, draping over the roots of an old oak on its way to the cave, entering it. He gasped in terror. They were lucky these ants weren't there when they hid there from Osman. The thought of those ants crawling up their ankles and biting their lips, ears, eyes, especially when they couldn't make a move or sound, made Rami shudder. A single sneeze or twitch of a limb would have led Osman directly to them.

"We can't go inside," Danyaal flicked away a few persistent ants attempting to climb up his shoes and said. "Time to find another place to lay low for a while."

While searching for shelter, Rami noticed that the darkness had drawn closer. Everything around him seemed covered in a deep hue of muted green. Badly shaken, he felt exposed. He kept darting his eyes from side to side nervously, kept looking for anyone watching from behind the myriad of leaves in every direction; he even jumped at the sudden screech of a parrot. A few feet ahead, he saw Danyaal flinch at the hums and chirps of insects also. The thought of them possibly being the only two humans in the Jungle was nerve-wracking to Rami.

Danyaal was keeping it together better than he. But Rami knew Danyaal's mind, like his, was preoccupied with the whirlwind of lingering thoughts about basic survival: What should they do if they were to spend the night in the jungle? Will they starve until help arrives? Where would they find drinking water? Where will they sleep?

Without the protective roof of the mud cave, Rami felt susceptible. And there was the added concern about any rabid animals roaming at night. Were there any flesh eaters they should've been aware of? His mind wandered.

Rami followed Danyaal. They trekked around the horseshoe bend, past the mulberry shrubs, before stopping in front of the cluster of *sheesham* trees.

Danyaal lowered himself and rested his back against one of them. "This spot is as good as any for now," he said. "We can rest here." He patted a patch of grass to his right.

Rami sat next to him at the foot of the wide-trunked tree and watched him unzip the backpack and take out the box of Peek Freans biscuits.

"Hungry?" Danyaal said.

Rami said he was.

But when Danyaal opened the plastic pouch, all that was left were flour-like crumbs. Danyaal said the biscuits must have crushed when he slid off the gravel path while running away from Osman's men.

"It was seconds after I heard the thud of your fall and found you lying on your stomach where I'd landed,"

Danyaal said. He returned the pouch to the backpack and fished a candy bar instead. He broke it in two and shared half of it with Rami.

They nibbled in silence for a while.

"You were right," Danyaal eventually took a deep breath and spoke again.

"About what?"

"About spotting Osman's vehicle earlier," Danyaal said.

"I wish I hadn't been." Rami plucked a handful of grass blades. "I wish it had been someone else," he said.

Danyaal took another bite. "I don't understand how he knew we'd be here."

"I can think of one thing. One person, actually, who might've tipped him off," Rami pressed his back against the tree trunk and said.

Danyaal looked at him. "Tariq?"

"Who else?" Rami snickered. "Running into him and the other two this morning was no coincidence."

Danyaal sighed.

"And what better-secluded area than this remote jungle far from the city for Osman to come after us," Rami said. "He waited patiently, like a predator stalking its prey."

"—Waited for the right moment," Danyaal added.

A pause.

"Rami?"

Rami replied with a soft grunt.

"What you said earlier," Danyaal started, hesitated. "When you and I, you know, on the trail ... what made you say it?"

There had been such an unexpected and tumultuous chain of events following their kiss that it deprived them of the opportunity to ponder and savor that intimate moment.

"I said it because that's the truth," Rami said, squeezing Danyaal's hand. "I couldn't let my insecurities get in the way of you knowing I'm crazy about you. I knew things would change between us if I didn't act." Rami looked him in the eye. "I nearly pushed you away once. I couldn't risk it again." He confessed.

Danyaal threw a smoldering look in Rami's direction.

"Besides, I'm exhausted living under a pretense, Danyaal. Tired of it."

"The kiss." Danyaal smiled.

"The kiss," Rami said and leaned forward. "The kiss." he repeated and locked lips with Danyaal.

"God, Rami."

Rami's hand grabbed Danyaal's head behind his right ear. "I don't want this to end," he murmured before separating, his lips wet from the kiss.

"And for this, someone like Osman hates us." Danyaal heaved another sigh and looked ahead.

"He hates the *idea* of intimacy between two boys," Rami said. "He hates the thought of it more than he hates us."

Danyaal's eyes wandered over to Rami.

Rami reflected on their visit to the strawberry farm, recalling the malevolent expression etched on Osman's face that day, the way he had callously disparaged Danyaal's cultural heritage with a scathing tone. He saw Danyaal's face tightening.

"I'm not surprised. My parents told me many stories about Afghans like him!" Danyaal spat.

"There are people everywhere like him that are threatened by what they don't understand," Rami said. He drew his knees to his chest. "It's exhausting. All this resisting, pretending it would all go away somehow." He ran his fingers through his hair.

"Oh, Rami."

Rami reached for Danyaal's hand once more. "I'm grateful to have found you. I don't know anyone else near me living with these feelings, this relentless desire for … you know …"

They fell silent for a while.

"People like us have been around for centuries; you know that?" Danyaal eventually said. "We just haven't met them yet. Many like us have been subjected to public hostility and legal persecution worldwide."

Rami looked at Danyaal.

"There are more like us than you know, Rami," Danyaal said, taking a deep breath. "In one form or another, we're all fighting the same battle: protection against discrimination. We—you and I—are not alone. I'd like us to start anew tomorrow once we leave here. Begin to heal by embracing reality."

Listening to Danyaal and realizing his struggles were shared gave Rami a sense of emancipation.

There were others like him.

He rested his head on Danyaal's shoulder and inhaled the cotton scent of Danyaal's shirt. "I'm with you," he said. "I don't know where this would lead, but I'd like to find out. I want this, Danyaal."

Above, a tree limb creaked. A shape swung through the branches. A monkey, maybe.

"Yes. But first, we must create a shelter to make it through the night, assuming help won't arrive until the morning," Danyaal said as he looked at his watch.

RAMI AND Danyaal spent the next hour or so collecting tree branches in different lengths and sizes. Danyaal made a tent to sleep in by leaning the longest bough against a tree. He then stacked the shorter spurs against the tall stem and covered it entirely with leaves.

While Rami stooped at the pond's edge and scrubbed off the sweat and dirt, Danyaal ran back to the mud cave. He returned with a chipped piece of clay shaped like a shallow bowl.

"To boil water to drink," he explained. Danyaal emptied his pockets of white mulberries that he'd plucked from the bushes on his way back. Once ripe, they were edible, he said. Otherwise, he added, they could be poisonous.

"Press on them to make sure they are tender before popping in your mouth," he told Rami. Rami nodded. He once again felt impressed with Danyaal's level of knowledge.

They roamed the adjacent area and gathered dry wood by sticking their fingers into the trees with holes in them. Rami jumped and snapped low-hanging branches to make a fire. Then, he made a small circle with a few gathered rocks and placed the dry wood in the middle. Danyaal poured a little butane fluid and lit the dried tree limbs. Rami filled the mud bowl with water by dipping it into the pond. They took turns holding the bowl with wooden sticks above the flames, waited for the water to boil, and ate mulberries.

Later, after eating heaps of crushed biscuits and drinking water, Rami took a quick stroll with Danyaal around the camped area to ensure there were no signs of a predator. The thin moonlight had draped its silver glow onto the vegetation and the rocks. At a distance, the black silhouettes of the towering trees stood against the dark. Puffs of steam blew from Rami's mouth and lingered in the air before dissipating as he walked in a wide circle. It was beginning to feel cold. The beam from Danyaal's flashlight, like a lightsaber, cut through the blackness and shone before them, illuminating the ground ahead. On the way back to the makeshift shelter, Rami stepped on a discarded tarpaulin, possibly from the cab of a truck, and decided it would serve as a blanket for the night.

Then, he spent what would be his only night with Danyaal, huddled inside the leafy tent they had built. The tarp was large enough to spread on the ground and also roll on top as a cover. Despite the exhaustion, they lay awake, robbed of any sleep. Danyaal inserted a cassette into the Walkman and shared one of the earbuds and his body's warmth with Rami. They turned on their sides, facing each other, and listened to a song from a Hindi film.

> *The blue sky has fallen asleep;*
> *the blue sky has fallen asleep ...*

After the song ended, after the Walkman stopped playing, Rami took the earphones out of both of their ears and let a few moments pass in quietude. Felt the stillness around them. He then traced his fingers along Danyaal's chest, down to his torso, and, after a moment of hesitation, crept lower still under his trousers. Danyaal's muscles tensed, and Rami appreciated the welcoming gesture. And when their bodies pressed against each other and they kissed, Rami's thumb gently caressed the hollow in Danyaal's neck above the collarbone seconds before his index finger joined and started unbuttoning Danyaal's shirt. Danyaal's hands were equally busy loosening Rami's belt, lowering his zipper. Rami could hear Danyaal breathing deeply through his nose. He rolled on top of Danyaal and exposed Danyaal's chest by pulling his unbuttoned shirt to its sides. He glanced at his moonlit profile. Danyaal's head lifted—Rami's lowered—their lips reunited and traveled together through earlobes, necks, noses, and back again. Danyaal's tongue found its way down to Rami's chest. Rami's body quivered. Danyaal's hand firmed on Rami's crotch.

Rami buried his face into the back of Danyaal's neck and felt the heat of Danyaal's breath on his shoulder while his hand helped lower Danyaal's trousers. He loved the sensation of Danyaal's earlobe brushing against his cheek. Their clenched bodies moved in a slow, rhythmic motion, pressing against each other.

And when they finished a few minutes later, Rami kept his face pressed against the side of Danyaal's cheek for a bit longer before running his lips over Danyaal's ear and whispering in it, telling him once more that he loved him.

THE SUN was already out when Rami opened his eyes the following day. Danyaal hadn't stirred. Rami crawled out of the canopy of leaves and stretched his aching limbs. The water in the pond was pale in the daylight but still had a hint of green. Rami heard bird noises welcoming a new day, perched high on trees. He glanced at Danyaal sleeping like a log and decided to take a walk. He stopped by the pond to splash water on his face before continuing. A smile appeared on his lips, reminiscing about last night and the closeness they'd shared. He recalled how he had confessed his love for Danyaal, and the corners of his mouth creased further.

He stopped at the white mulberry shrubs and began plucking berries for breakfast, but only the ones that felt and looked ripe. While his fingers worked through the droopy boughs collecting fruit, his mind got busy planning a future for them.

Once we got back to Lahore, he thought, *we'd enroll in colleges. We would finish our education and continue learning music together: We'd form a band; I'd be the lead singer, and Danyaal, the guitarist.* Rami stooped over and picked a few berries that had fallen to the ground.

We would travel to someplace where we could live freely. Perhaps to the United States of America. Didn't they say it was the land of the free? They would accept us, and we'd pursue our goals without fearing retribution from Osman or anyone else. His pockets were becoming full of picked berries. He began walking back to the tent, to Danyaal.

We would live in a modest apartment, maybe in New York, and have jobs while following our dreams of becoming musicians. At the end of every day, we'd return to our compact little place furnished with scattered furniture and a few rugs.

Maybe hang a few framed pictures of Lahore to bring back fond memories.

He trekked his way back and was walking around the pond's edge when he saw a man standing on the other side by the pagoda waving at him. He appeared to be wearing some sort of uniform. A guard or a local police officer, perhaps. He had one hand cupped around his mouth and was saying something Rami couldn't understand. The man kept waving.

We have been rescued, Rami thought and let out a sigh of relief. Certainly, someone from either of their families had called the authorities, and they'd come looking for them. He waved back at the man in uniform. His feet began taking longer strides. He couldn't wait to tell Danyaal that help had arrived. Rami returned to where the leafy tent stood, but no sign of Danyaal was inside.

"Danyaal!" he called.

Silence.

"Danyaal?" he called again, louder this time. Looked around to see if Danyaal was by the pond washing up. Maybe he went further into the woods to release himself.

There was no reason to panic. No reason for Rami's heart to begin pounding uncontrollably.

Then, out of nowhere, he felt fingers crawling up his shoulder. Rami jumped and took off running. In the following few compressed seconds, his eyes registered shapes emerging from the woods. He caught Danyaal's slumped figure in the hands of a man. Someone kicked the tent they had slept in, knocking the tree limbs. Another was holding Danyaal's backpack. Next, Rami knew, a pair of hands slid under his armpits and lifted him off the ground. The berries spilled from his pockets. Rami screamed.

HE COULDN'T see anything. A black scarf draped over his eyes, hands tied behind his back with a woven rope. He knew he was being transported somewhere in the back of a vehicle bouncing side to side, sometimes up and down. His head banged against the metal whenever the driver swirled the wheel as if avoiding a pothole. *Where is Danyaal?* Rami thought.

HIS EXPERIENCE of that ride was comprised of sounds and smell: a male voice speaking in a hushed tone; the jingling of bells and mooing of cows somewhere; the nauseous odor of someone smoking a cigarette inches away; the gravel crushing under the tires.

THE WHEELS of the vehicle came to a halt. A pair of hands gripped Rami and dragged him out. A kick at the back of his right knee sent him kneeling to the ground. Rami grimaced in pain. Someone lowered the scarf. Rami's eyes squinted against the blinding morning light. They were still in Manga Jungle, Rami noticed, surrounded by tall trees. He turned his head and found Danyaal to his left, also on his knees with his hands tied behind his back, his head drooping between his shoulders.

In front of Rami, a few feet away, Osman paced back and forth, his hands placed on his hips. Behind him was a crumbling, dilapidated building with a front opening and no windows. Rami heard Osman telling one of the men about how the dacoit brothers, Changa and Manga, built this structure in the middle of the jungle and used to hide in it from the British police after the robberies.

"Fascinating history about this place, na?" Osman said to the man laughingly. "We've nothing like this in Afghanistan."

Rami recognized the man Osman was speaking to. It was the man who had waved at him from across the pond, clearly the person who led Osman to Danyaal and him.

Osman diverted his attention to the others standing around him.

"The devout followers around the world should never doubt God's will," he spoke loudly as if giving a speech, "not even for a second! We must all know there's great wisdom in what our creator has commanded and what He has forbidden. Corrupt democratic ideas have for so long promoted alcohol, denounced divorce, and mocked taking multiple wives. And we know the consequences of such ideas," he said, waving his finger. "When one rejects divorce, renounces plural marriage, men take mistresses instead. When one allows alcohol, immoral acts become widespread."

Osman then shifted his eyes to Rami.

"This act … this perversion of lusting over same-sex, goes against *fitrah*, which God Almighty has created for mankind whereby the male is inclined toward the female, and vice versa." He began pacing with his hands behind his back. "The spread of this heinous act has caused mankind diseases which neither the East nor the West can deny. Spread by sinners like these two *haramis*." He snickered.

"These boys," he spat, "are shamelessly hell-bent on committing sick and sinful perversions!"

Osman patted the shoulder of the man in uniform. "Thank you for your hospitality, brother. I appreciate you offering us a place to rest last night," he said.

The man nodded, fixed Rami with a quick glance, and took off.

There were others, about six in total, standing in a semi-circle with Danyaal and Rami in the middle. Rami recognized two of them from the previous day. One was younger-looking, slim, and had a square face. The other was older, short, and overweight, with breathing sounds as if he were hacking bile. They were both among the group that chased Rami and Danyaal on the hiking trail. Rami recalled listening to the heavyset man's deep breathing behind him while he ran after Rami.

"Ibn al-Qayyim said, and I refer to Kitab al-Kafi: Homosexuality involves immorality that goes against the wisdom of God's creation and commandment," Osman resumed after the man in the uniform disappeared. "Since it involves innumerable evil and harm, it would be best to kill the one to whom it's done than to watch it being done to him because, after that, he'll become so evil, so corrupt, that there could be no hope left for him," he said, paused, and darted his eyes from one man to another. "He'll no longer feel shame before our Lord."

The air buzzed with unwavering agreement.

Osman flicked a lighter, lit a cigarette, and tucked it between the two fingers of his left hand after taking a puff. "Now, I don't think I've been unreasonable, brothers, have I?" he resumed pacing and said.

"No!" they shouted.

"I've been patient with these two more than usual. I tried advice, offered brotherly guidance, even attempted stern warnings but to no avail." Osman shook his head.

He then stepped toward Rami; his smug face loomed over him. "You thought you'd eluded me, didn't you?" Osman clamped his right hand between Rami's cheeks and hissed.

The hanging fold of the black scarf on Rami's neck fluttered in the wind.

"I knew you didn't board the bus. You were hiding in the jungle. I must say, I admire your resilience."

Osman jerked Rami's face away and looked around at his accomplices standing with intertwined wrists. "These two are a perfect example of what the evil of secularism and liberal ideas can do to our brothers and sons: corrupt their minds, stain their souls," he addressed his accomplices as if he were a college professor standing at a podium lecturing. "Now, more than ever is the time to institute the sharia law and the teachings of Abul Ala Maududi to govern the sovereignty of God and his commands!"

They all chanted something Rami didn't understand.

Despite the steadily rising temperatures, Rami felt his feet turning cold. He felt numb. Then, a blur of something fast came toward him. Osman's hand slapped against Rami's face with great force. Palm, then the back of the hand. Rami's ears rang. He saw black dots covering his vision. His cheek, turning warm, began to sting. He fell to his side, landing on his left shoulder. From that position, Rami saw Osman walk over to Danyaal and repeat: palm, then back of the hand. Back and forth.

"The crime of a man lusting over another is the worst of sins, the most abhorrent of deeds that God punished in a way He didn't other nations." Osman straightened himself after beating Danyaal and said it aloud.

"Verily, you practice your lusts on men instead of women. Nay, but you're a people of Lot transgressing beyond bounds by committing great sins." he recited in Arabic while circling Rami and Danyaal.

"It violates the original disposition and shows a lack of religious commitment," he said sharply. "A sure sign of impending disaster and denial of God's mercy." He paced again from left to right.

Rami caught a few heads nodding.

"My brethren, there's an opportunity to learn a valuable lesson today. This isn't something I invented in my head. It is the guidance and instructions of the *sahabas*, the disciples of many prophets, that we must carry."

Two men moved forward and steadied Rami and Danyaal back on their knees. Rami was feeling nauseated. The gathered tears in his eyes made it difficult to focus. He blinked rapidly to clear his sight, saw Danyaal's head downcast, his shoulders slumped. Rami wished he could untie his hands, run up to him, and tell him it'd be okay—console him—even with false, wishful hope.

In the background, Osman was quoting specific names, specific passages from particular books: al-Tirmidhi (1456), Abu Dawood (4462), and Ibn Maajah (2561).

Osman went on to say that *sahabas* agreed on the execution of homosexuals. They differed, he said, on how to execute them. Some were of the view that they should be set on fire. And others amongst them thought the guilty should be thrown down from a high place and then have stones thrown at them, he added.

"If a man commits the act of sleeping with another man, he, in effect, kills him in such a way that there's no hope of salvation after that." Osman hooked his right thumb into the front pocket of his gray vest.

He paused and allowed a nasal voice to chant something in Arabic. Rami's quivering lips moved in silent prayer.

"Both are to be killed, the active and the passive sinner, you see. Both have to be killed," Osman repeated, his face tightening.

He flicked the unfinished cigarette and dashed toward Rami, grabbed him by the collar, and propelled him to his feet. He shoved Rami and pinned him against a tree behind him.

"These two will be punished the same way as adulterers. Stoned!" His expressionless, stony stare penetrated Rami's bulging eyes.

"Osman, listen to me," Rami made a guttural choking sound. "Have mercy on us, please. Tariq and Amir have misinformed you. Please don't do this."

Rami's shoulders jerked as he struggled against him, but he was powerless. With his hand clamped around Rami's neck, Osman slowly squeezed the air out of his lungs.

"You think I'm here solely because of what others have been saying about you?" Osman's eyes squinted, his upper lip curling into a sneer, revealing nothing but spite. "Na, child. You're mistaken. I've seen it with my own eyes. Seventh of December last year … Shimla Hill … fireworks. Rings a bell?"

Rami's stomach fell. A wave of shock passed through his contorted face.

"I've had doubts about you for quite some time," Osman jeered.

"Leave him alone!" Danyaal yelled, tears leaking out of the corners of his eyes. Osman unclenched his fingers around Rami's neck, let him drop to the ground with a thud, and lunged toward Danyaal. He clutched Danyaal's hair. Pulling his head back, Osman raised him to his feet.

"Such compassion for your *lover*," Osman hissed the word through gritted teeth. Danyaal screamed in pain.

"Osman, stop," Rami pleaded. "Let us go. You'll never see us again." His body shook in sheer terror. "We'll go away."

"Go away? Where? This isn't about making you disappear. Don't you see? This is about making an example out of you so no one else dares to commit such a sin after you."

"Osman, no!"

Osman shot Rami an admonishing glare. "You should've thought about that when I tried to talk some sense into you," he said. He was now hunched over, surveying the ground for small to medium-sized stones. He picked a few and distributed them to the others. "It's too late to beg for your life, Rami. Now it's time to pay for your sins." He collected a few more rocks, examined one for its pointy edges, and tossed it in the air.

"Tie them to a tree."

So this is how it will end, Rami thought. *Soon, they would pelt us with stones until we stopped shrieking. What would others think happened to us when they found our bloodied, lifeless bodies slumped against the tree trunks? I would never get to share with Danyaal what I had dreamed of earlier about our life in New York. He would never find out how happy I was to spend last night with him.*

Rami's head rang with these thoughts.

Then, through his distorted, blurred vision, Rami saw one of the men nervously approaching Osman. He tried to listen but only got snippets: *Sure you want to do this? ... is Jalil's brother ... what if Jalil found out ... things could go bad ... not our country ... warn them ... still young boys.*

Osman waved his hand in dismissal at first. Then the man leaned into Osman's ear and whispered something. Osman listened, nodded, considered what he heard while darting occasional glances toward Rami, his fingers drumming the bark of a tree.

The silence shrouded the woods. All eyes were on Osman's profile, leaning against the tree for support. A pair of crows cawed somewhere. One of the men smacked the back of his neck, squashing a mosquito.

"Mercy. But of course, my brothers, we should also not doubt God's graciousness," Osman eventually turned to face the men and said after a long pause. "There's always room for those who seek His forgiveness and repent."

The air again buzzed with agreeing voices.

Osman sauntered over to Rami and Danyaal.

"Despite your relentless disregard for decency, I have decided to extend forgiveness to you, even though you may perceive my behavior as cruel," he muttered. "You two are free to go."

Rami couldn't believe what he'd heard. Osman was letting them go! He was willing to let them live! Rami felt his breathing begin to regain normalcy.

He and Danyaal exchanged looks. Rami stirred to adjust his hands against the rope cutting through the flesh of his wrist and gave him a strained smile.

"But, as you know, I want to ensure you've learned your lesson." Osman threw Rami a cold glance.

Rami's smile faded. He began to see where Osman was going with this.

"—and promise to stay away from sinful acts in the future—"

"No," a puff of breath escaped Rami's mouth.

"—Repent and state that you no longer possess these deviant tendencies toward other males—"

"No. Please, no."

"—Pledge to never act on such desires. Ever—"

"No ..." Rami met Danyaal's refuting eyes.

Osman asked one of his men to untie Danyaal. But Rami kept shaking his head, "No. No. No." Kept whispering it.

"You first," Osman said and tipped his chin at Danyaal.

Danyaal rubbed his sore wrists.

A few seconds passed.

"I'm not going to waste my breath on you again, boy!" Osman barked. "Speak, or else."

"Danyaal, please," Rami pleaded with him to say what Osman asked.

"Begin!" Osman roared.

Danyaal flinched, almost tumbling. "I ... I," he began.

Come on, Danyaal; please do as he says. They're only words, meaningless. Say what Osman wants to hear, and we could soon be on our way to Lahore, back to our lives.

But his heart dropped when the word Danyaal uttered entered Rami's ears.

"No."

Stares frowned.

"What did you say?"

"I won't say it."

Osman's eyes narrowed. "Perhaps I didn't hear you right."

Danyaal hesitated ... "Because that would be a lie."

"Last chance," Osman hissed.

"I can't deny who I am," Danyaal said, his eyes terrified yet defiant. "These *acts* you speak of are part of my existence. Can't change the way I was born."

Rami saw Osman's fist clenching.

What's happening? Why aren't we heading home already? Suddenly, the trees drew closer, pressing down, suffocating Rami. *What was Danyaal doing? Why couldn't he just lie for once to get out of this dire situation?*

But deep down, Rami knew the answer to his questions. He knew it wasn't in Danyaal to turn away from the truth. It wasn't Danyaal's nature to lie. But the problem was, his *nature* would get them both killed by this homophobic maniac towering in front of them.

Osman's glare lingered on Danyaal's face before shifting to Rami. One of the men approached and untied Rami's hands.

"Your turn." Osman flicked his chin at him. "I'll deal with this boy shortly, but here is your chance, Rami. Say what I've asked loud, and you're free," he said.

Rami rubbed his aching wrist, thinking he wasn't the type of person someone would look at and say, 'You're the reason I didn't give up.' He wasn't the one who motivated others to persevere in the face of adversity. He wished he could be like Danyaal, who possessed the fortitude and conviction to stand up for his beliefs, even if it meant standing alone. He wished he had that type of bravery.

But Rami knew all too well that he was the antithesis of it. He was weak, someone who'd lie to extricate his way out of a bind, someone who'd look the other way and change paths if it came down to fighting for what was right.

"Rami!"

Rami jumped. "I repent," he breathed and blurted out simultaneously.

"And?"

"And … and I vow never to act on these desires again." Rami could feel the weight of Danyaal's wounded gaze on him, searching for something, questioning Rami's conviction when he had said he'd embrace the truth.

Was that simply an addition to his many other lies?

Rami dropped his eyes.

"What kind of desires?" Osman asked.

Rami nervously chewed the corner of his mouth, shifted on his feet.

"Speak!"

"The desire toward other boys, other men. Osman, please—"

Osman gave a self-satisfying nod. "I'm glad you've come to your senses. You can go now."

"Let me speak to Danyaal, Osman. I'm sure we …" Rami began to bargain with him but then, from the corner of his eye, saw the man holding Danyaal's backpack approaching Osman.

Osman took a cursory glance inside the bag before squinting his eyes, his intent gaze lingering on something. He reached in, unzipped a pocket, and fetched an object. He placed it in his palm, curled his fingers around it. He then walked over to Danyaal, smug-faced.

"Explain this," Osman opened his fist and dangled a crucifix-cross necklace tantalizingly before Danyaal.

With this, a hush fell over. The collective eyes shifted to Danyaal. Lips curled. Two shapes moved from behind and grabbed him by his elbows.

The jungle was now swaying side to side, swooping up and down. Rami felt his skin shrinking. Danyaal's face had turned as pale as the bone-colored moon Rami had once compared it with.

"To whom does this necklace belong, boy?" Osman said, his unblinking gaze settled on Danyaal's face.

Danyaal looked at him.

"I need an answer."

"Me … It belongs to me." Once again, despite feeling terror, isolation, and vulnerability, Danyaal chose truth over avoidance, his tone resolute.

Osman slapped his palms together while clutching the crucifix cross.

"I must say, this day can't cease to amaze with its surprises," he barked a bitter laughter. "Not only do we witness deviant sexual behavior, but also a hidden agenda by a non-believer to corrupt an innocent youth."

A low murmur rose through the woods.

"It's clear now who's the culprit and who's the victim," Osman said. He walked over to Rami and placed his hand on Rami's shoulder. "Do not be afraid anymore, young Rami. May God have mercy on your misguided soul." Osman dropped his hand and began walking away. "Get home to your family. I'm sure your parents are worried," he glanced over his shoulder at Rami and said.

The two men holding Danyaal pulled him away toward the enclosed building. Danyaal's heels dragged against the ground, stirring a small burst of dust.

"Rami!" Danyaal shrieked.

Stunned, Rami stood there. Unable to move, unable to stop Osman, unable to save Danyaal. Unable to do anything. Once again, he found himself at the crossroads where he could stand up for what mattered. Or walk away.

"Please don't do this!" Rami cried out.

Osman turned and shot Rami a chiding glare, enough to make Rami's body shudder.

His left leg took a step back. Dried leaves crushed under his feet. Then, his right leg backpedaled. More leaves crunched.

"Walk away before I change my mind!" Osman's voice roared.

Danyaal cried, "Don't leave me!"

Rami wished the ground would open up and swallow him whole. But it didn't. He kept taking small steps backward. "Don't leave me alone with them, Rami!" Danyaal was screaming hysterically.

"Rami … *yaarana! Yaarana!* Help!"

Rami's memory: *He walks through the marigold field where yellow flowers have sprung in a brilliant carpet. His stretched hands touch the flora drenched in orange sun rays. Danyaal walks next to him; beyond him, the pink and white cherry blossom trees sway, and Danyaal looks at him, smiles, and mouths 'Yaarana'.*

Danyaal's screams were fading with his receding figure. Rami kept backpedaling, kept staring at Danyaal's thinning silhouette until it vanished behind the dark opening of the building.

Rami then spun on his heel and ran.

HE RAN but didn't know where he was going. He did a sharp intake of breath and, amid the sobbing spasms and hiccups, dragged a sleeve across his face to wipe the tears to clear his vision. Danyaal's terrified face flashed before Rami's eyes, and the breathing became uneven again.

"I left him!" He cried. "I left Danyaal behind."

'*You betrayed Danyaal.*' one of his demons snickered in Rami's head.

Rami opened his mouth to draw air to his lungs, but nothing seemed to pass through the airways. He opened his mouth wider. Nothing. His hands shook. He felt the cold sweat drenching his body. He wanted to scream but could only feel the tightening of his windpipe.

And then, suddenly, it was as if someone pulled the ground from beneath his feet. He became airborne before stumbling and falling into a ditch face-first. The sharp edge of a broken branch sliced just below his right eye upon landing. An intense pain shot up his ankle. Blood mixed in with tears and stung raw flesh. Rami grabbed his bloody face and rolled onto his back.

Silence all around; his blank stare unseeingly fixed at the canopy of leaves swaying in the high boughs above.

He felt lightheadedness coming on, heard himself muttering long-winded prayers with dizziness growing. Lying in that ditch as if it were a grave, his mind wandered. Rami reminisced.

It is a Monday afternoon in July. He is in Danyaal's room. They sit cross-legged across from each other on Danyaal's bed. Danyaal has finished telling Rami a story about a nine-year-old boy in Afghanistan. In that story, there is a faqir in a bazaar. The faqir shouts something. Says the boy is cursed.

The boy is now eleven years old. He is at a carnival in the village of Foladi. A warlord is towering over him. The warlord reaches to grab the boy's collar.

Back at the bazaar, the faqir yells. He says that the curse will follow the generations to come.

The memory of Danyaal meeting Daadi: *Rami invites Danyaal to the house with the red-colored facade. Daadi emerges into the room after praying namaz, hunched over. Her hand, covered in a thin layer of skin with protruding blue veins, runs through Rami's lowered head. Rami guides her slightly to her right, and Daadi's fingers trace the shape of Danyaal's face: the broadness of his forehead, the outline of his nose, the outer edges of his lips. Daadi's sightless eyes begin to flick side to side. Her hand comes to a stop. Lingers for a moment. Then, a cloud drifts across her face, and she abruptly removes her hand from Danyaal's face as if the pads of her fingers came in contact with a hot surface.*

A sharp pain interrupted Rami's drifting mind. His vision began fading to black, but then he caught a blurred image of a sparrow flying into view. It perched at the foot of the ditch and broke the silence with incessant chirrup notes.

Beyond the bird, Rami saw a glimpse of an approaching chest, the contour of a shoulder drawing closer, and a silhouette of a head becoming clearer. Through his barely open eyelids, he saw a shape emerge. Heard a voice call his name. Someone tapped on his cheeks. The voice was asking him to wake up. Rami forced his eyelids to lift and saw Jalil's concerned face looming above.

"Wake up, Rami." Jalil shook Rami's shoulders. "What happened?"

Rami opened his mouth but could only let out a strangled moan.

"I'm going to lift you," Jalil said. He held out his hand. "Hold on tight."

Rami grabbed Jalil's fingers. He raised himself and screamed when applying pressure on his sprained ankle,

Tears began to pool around his irises. Feeling a sense of safety in Jalil's presence, Rami wanted to break down in his brother's arms.

Jalil flung Rami's arm around his shoulder and carried him off the ditch. "Looks like you broke your foot," he said. Rami grimaced in pain through pursed lips and held Jalil for support.

"I've been looking all over for you. Amma and Papa are worried sick," Jalil said. "Let's go home." He supported Rami, leaning on him, and stepped forward.

"Wait." Rami hobbled a few steps, then stopped.

"Danyaal's here, too."

"What?"

"He's missing."

Jalil looked at him.

"Osman and his men have taken him," Rami said, taking rapid breaths. He sensed Jalil's facial expression tightening.

"What're you talking about?"

Rami recounted Osman's pursuit of them. Bit by bit, he told him about yesterday's misfortunes that resulted in Danyaal and him missing the bus. Told Jalil they spent the night in the Manga jungle instead of returning home.

"—knew we were hiding in the woods. A man helped him track us down."

Rami finished and grew quiet; his panting remained.

"And he let you go but not Danyaal?" Jalil sounded doubtful.

Rami stood leaning on Jalil; silence lingered between them.

"Rami—"

"We need to find Danyaal," Rami said between anxiety-ridden breaths. "You must help him."

"You can't be serious."

"His life is under threat, Jalil! Don't you see? You could be his only hope," Rami pleaded.

"All right, fine." Jalil waved a hand. "Once we get to Lahore, we can notify the police and his parents," he said.

"No!"

"What do you mean, *no*?" Jalil's frown creased his split brow.

"We cannot wait that long. We must look for Danyaal now."

Rami uncurled his arm from around Jalil's neck. He hobbled over to a tree and leaned against it. "I won't leave without him." He buried his fists under the armpits.

"Don't be an idiot."

"Leave me here if you want," Rami said.

"Rami ..." Jalil gritted his teeth.

Rami remained quiet.

After a moment of silence, Jalil sighed irritably and asked if Rami recalled where Osman might have taken Danyaal. Rami steadied himself and described the square building in the middle of the jungle as much as possible. When he finished, he found Jalil intently looking at him.

"Why does this boy mean so much to you?" Jalil asked. "Who's he to you?"

If it were any other day, Rami knew he would've evaded the questions. But today was unlike any other day. Today, he had walked away from nearly losing his life. Today, Danyaal was in grave danger. Today, he'd witnessed the sheer intensity of hatred firsthand. The time had come to confront the hidden truth, to let the light get in through the cracked corners of his soul, to let the secrets reveal themselves. The mask he'd concealed behind all his life, Rami realized, needed to be removed.

"Everything. He's everything to me," Rami said, looking Jalil in the eyes, feeling the weight of his chest lessening with words rising to his lips. "Danyaal is my true love. I'm nothing without him."

Another hush enshrouded the dense air. He expected Jalil's face to turn red and his fist to clench.

Any moment, Rami thought, *Jalil would begin shouting.*

Instead, after staring at Rami for some time, Jalil walked up and slung Rami's arm back around his neck.

"Describe to me again the building Osman took Danyaal to," he said.

There were two men already in the Jeep Jalil had driven in. They had accompanied him to search for Rami when he hadn't returned home last night. One of them, a tall, longhaired man with a thick beard, stated he was familiar with the building Rami had described to Jalil. He helped Rami climb in the back, where Rami sat with the other, thick-bodied man. He smiled at Rami while twisting the long whiskers of his English mustache.

Rami clutched the metal bar of the bouncing vehicle. His heart pounding in his chest, he felt disoriented. He was unsure of the lapsed time since he'd tumbled into the ditch. He couldn't shake the thought of what condition he would find Danyaal if he were still there. A prayer for Danyaal's safety rose to Rami's lips.

A few minutes later, the square building came into view. Rami's chest tightened, recalling he and Danyaal were kneeling before Osman a few feet from it, certain they would be stoned to death.

The Jeep came to a rest a few feet from the entrance. Jalil asked Rami to stay in the vehicle and left with the other two. The man with the long hair opened the glove compartment and slid something under his shirt before leaving. Rami watched them cautiously approach the shadowy entrance of the building.

Then, a sudden burst of shouts.

There was a bang of a metal.

Jalil said something loudly, to which Osman's voice shot back. Rami jumped. He heard more words curtly exchanged, followed by an eerie silence.

He tumbled out of the jeep. Fell. Shooting pain invaded Rami like daggers jabbing into his flesh. He raised himself on one leg and hopped forward.

"Jalil?" Rami yelled. "Danyaal?"

He could hear the murmurs of a few voices talking in a hushed tone. He got closer. Called again.

"Stay outside!" Jalil's voice boomed from behind the walls. Rami hobbled over and stood at the side of the entrance, his heart racing. He waited.

In the following handful of seconds, Rami witnessed something that would haunt him for the rest of his days: A man scurried out while fumbling with his unbuttoned trousers, one hand cupped against his bloodied forehead. Osman followed behind, grimacing, finger combing his hair. He caught Rami standing at the side and threw him a glare. Said something in Pashto, spitting almost on Rami's face. Two other men hurriedly emerged. Behind them, Jalil walked out holding a pistol, his face red, his cheeks quivering. Jalil's companions followed closely.

Then, Rami saw Danyaal's pale face emerge. His hollow stare bore into Rami's face but didn't seem to register a sign of recognition.

"Danyaal," Rami murmured. He raised his arms.

Danyaal staggered past him. Rami's gaze lowered and settled on the tiny drops of blood that spilled from the right leg opening of Danyaal's trousers.

Rami's head spun. He dropped to the ground with a thud.

And the blackness came. Finally. Thankfully.

EIGHTEEN

There is a room, dark as though coated with charcoal. Rami has his arms outstretched to his sides as he inches through the solidness of the black before him. The air is dense, and it is hard to breathe. Like walking through a mass of Styrofoam, suffocating. He looks for someone but can't seem to know who. His hand touches a wall. He steadies himself and takes cautious, small steps. Outside, a vehicle is idling. There is a human hand; it's moving. Rami feels its fingers, the knuckles, the heel. The hand is unattached to the body. It's fixed to a wall. Then, another sprouts through the concrete like a bud shooting off a tree. It takes hold of Rami's forearm; its fingers clamp on Rami's flesh. Panic strikes. More hands emerge, like tree branches growing, snaking around his feet, thighs, and chest, grabbing him, pinning him to the wall. Jalil is outside. He calls his name and asks him to return. Rami realizes he's inside the windowless structure in the Manga Jungle. He hears a faint hissing. A word. He focuses, tries to listen. The voices grow.

They chant in a chorus, Yaarana. He opens his mouth to scream, but hands on the wall coil around his neck.

Rami's eyes sprang open. His heart pounded from the nightmare, his mouth loose as if to scream, but only a high-pitched wheezing came out of his throat.

THEY TOLD him he'd been in and out of consciousness for a couple of days after returning to Lahore. His fever hovered between 38.8 and 39.4 centigrade until one day it broke. Jalil said he took him straight to the hospital after Rami had collapsed in the Manga Jungle. Danyaal's parents were arriving with the police when he drove past the parking lot across from the pagoda; he informed Rami.

"Osman escaped while I carried you back to the jeep," Jalil said. "Police went in to look for him and the others, but I doubt they found them."

"Danyaal," half-lidded Rami whispered through parched lips.

"I helped him. His parents took him, but I helped Danyaal get in the car with his parents," Jalil, sitting at the foot of Rami's bed, said in a consoling tone.

What did he witness inside that building that made his admonishing glares dim and his accusing insinuations soften? When Jalil spoke, Rami didn't trace the usual dismissive look on his face or the suppressed hostility in his demeanor. He was sure Jalil had ample time to think about what Rami had said while standing against the tree. It was no small feat for Rami to confess his love for Danyaal to Jalil.

After he finished, Jalil patted Rami's leg, wished him a speedy recovery, and left the room. He didn't say how he found Danyaal when he crossed into the dark opening of the building. And Rami didn't ask. He didn't need to. Rami closed his eyes and clutched the sheets of his bed by the fistfuls every time the image of the blood trickling down Danyaal's pants flashed before his eyes.

THE SWELLING in Rami's ankle reduced after a couple of weeks. But his joints were still tender and needed rest, so the doctor prescribed him crutches. Rami hobbled around the house for days and couldn't go out alone.

Most mornings, he rose from the bed, put on a clean shirt and fresh pair of pants after cleaning himself, ate breakfast, and yearned to see Danyaal. And during that period, he experienced a moment of striking realization. Rami came to learn the concept of time's harsh and unforgiving nature. How it shrunk and expanded when he was and wasn't in Danyaal's company. It flew by like pouring rain when they were together. But now, being away from him, it felt as if the black hands of the old wall clock had never moved. The seconds, the minutes, the hours ... all seemed stuck in the same position for the longest time.

One evening, a few days into the house rest, Rami found the courage to dial Danyaal's phone number. Saman answered.

"He's sleeping," she said.

"I'll call back."

There was a pause on the other end of the line.

"He seems to be sleeping a lot lately," Saman's voice carried a concerned tone. "He doesn't eat with us, takes his meals into his room, doesn't even play the guitar. He closes the door behind him and disappears."

Another pause. Rami sensed a hesitation.

"Can I ask you something?"

"Yes?"

"Did something happen to my brother at the Manga Jungle? Baba and Mami said they had to take him to the clinic immediately."

Rami chewed the corner of his mouth in angst, didn't say anything.

"All I know is that a few men came after you two but not much else. No one tells me anything. You were with him. What happened to my brother?"

"I don't know, Saman," Rami's voice was broken. "We were separated."

"But you would tell me, right? Rami. If something had happened to Danyaal, you'd tell me?"

Blood thudded in Rami's temples; he felt a headache coming on. "I wish I could," he said, sounding deflated, "I don't know what happened to Danyaal. I'm sorry." He hung up and crawled under the blanket.

TIME. CRAWLING again. Like a lazy sloth climbing up a tree, it passed slowly. To fill it, Rami cleaned the house for visitors coming to meet Saifa for a marriage proposal. He read and re-read the letters to Amma, which Narin had written from Dubai. He rearranged the checkered square box where he kept his novels. Once done, Rami climbed on a chair and went through the *Reader's Digests* on the high bookcase shelf, found the 1978 edition with the rainbow-colored lotus flower, and stared at it for a long while.

THAT OVERCAST day he could walk without the crutches, Rami hopped on the motorcycle and rode to Danyaal's house. He parked the bike from across the street and knocked on the gate. While waiting for someone to answer, he leaned to his right and saw through the upstairs window that the light in Danyaal's room was on. Rami knocked again.

A rickshaw puttered by, leaving behind a small cloud of dust. Giggling children in gray-and-white uniforms stepped off a school bus.

Rami returned his gaze to the window in Danyaal's room and noticed a silhouette standing against the yellow glow of the light. It was there for a moment before it disappeared in a flash. A pair of hands appeared and quickly pulled the curtains. A second later, the light switched off, and Danyaal's room went dark.

Moments later, Afrooz appeared at the door with a woebegone look and told Rami Danyaal wasn't home.

Rami waited a few more days before returning.

"How are you, son?" Gibril appeared from the gate this time. Rami was grateful to Gibril for offering him something he had longed for weeks: a warm smile.

"*Salaam*," Rami said, shook Gibril's hand, and noticed the single transverse crease emerging through a simian line in his palm.

"Is Danyaal home?" Rami asked. Internally, he expected Gibril to offer another pre-mediated excuse and say Danyaal was sleeping, busy, or not home.

But Rami was determined to keep trying. He needed to see Danyaal; he needed to talk to him. He had to explain. He had to apologize. He had to.

"Why don't you come inside?" Gibril said instead. "Come."

With his palm cupped around Rami's left shoulder, Gibril guided him through the gate into the veranda. Right away, Rami's eyes darted at the corridor upstairs, wishing to see Danyaal's face looking down, except he wasn't there. He found Afrooz by the lemon tree. She stepped closer. She and Gibril stood next to Rami on each side.

"I hope you're recovering well, Rami," she said.

Rami said he was.

"What an ordeal. How are your parents? I'm sure they've been just as worried about you."

"They're fine. Thanks for asking," he said.

Gibril caught Rami throwing glances upstairs toward Danyaal's room. He cleared his throat. "Danyaal isn't here, son," he said.

Rami said to convey the message that he'd come by for a visit and opened the gate to walk out.

"Listen. What I mean to say is that Danyaal *no* longer lives here."

Rami turned. His face flushed; a wave of dizziness coursed through him.

"What?"

"We decided it was best for Danyaal to continue his education abroad. He left for London, England, two days ago," Afrooz said in a low voice. "Even though he never told us what happened at the picnic in the Manga Jungle, we met with the doctor privately after Danyaal's medical examination and—" Afrooz dropped her gaze and dabbed at her eyes. "He's our only son, you know? We didn't feel it was safe for him here any longer."

Rami felt a lump, like a piece of stone, lodged in his throat.

"He left without saying anything?" his voice croaked. The shapes of Danyaal's parents were becoming blurry with the rapid pooling of moisture in his eyes. "He left without saying goodbye?"

Gibril's palms re-cupped Rami's shoulder. "You two were close. It all happened quickly. His visa papers arrived. I'm sure he meant to contact you but couldn't find the time."

"When will he be back?"

Gibril paused for a brief while. "I'm sorry, Rami. London is Danyaal's new home now. He won't be returning to Lahore anytime soon."

And just like that, Danyaal disappeared from Rami's life—until the phone rang twenty-six years later.

Part Three

Finding Danyaal

Nineteen

October 19th, 2014

Who was on the phone earlier?" Brian called out from the other room.

Rami was standing by a dusty sliver of early morning light piercing through a dingy opening, illuminating the apartment's floorboards.

Beneath his feet, the old wooden planks creaked in a ghostly echo as his legs tried precariously to balance the weight of his body. Rami found it comforting to see traces of dawn peeking through. He stepped forward toward the dappled sunlight filtering through the front window in the living room and let it spill on his face like liquid gold on that crisp Sunday morning in Chicago. He closed his eyes, took a deep breath, and embraced the warmth of the golden rays on his skin, recalling the phone conversation from a few hours ago.

"*Salaam.* Long time no talk!" the raspy male voice on the other end of the line had said after confirming that Rami was the person it needed to speak to twice.

Rami had just returned from a tiring performance. His droopy eyelids flew open. "Who's this?"

"Oh, I think you know who I am," the voice cackled with delight.

There was a silence. Rami heard a throat clearing. "Guess what?" the unknown caller spoke again, "I have a surprise for you. The name Danyaal rings a bell?"

With this, Rami's mind raced through time that had stood between his past and the present like an immovable object.

Hearing that man's voice was like waking up from a nightmare and realizing it hadn't ended. The fear of many years pressing down on his chest that the people he once ran from would find him one day had resurfaced.

"Did you say *Danyaal*?"

It had been over two decades since Rami had heard that name. But not because his memory had failed him or a lack of effort. Many times, over the years, he'd attempted writing, calling, talking, and explaining. In the end, he concluded, when his inquiries were met with sheer silence, that Danyaal no longer wished to rekindle what they once had. Rami was no longer a part of Danyaal's existence. There was simply no more room for Rami.

But, hoping time could heal the deepest of wounds, he kept writing to Danyaal, kept calling. He willed himself to dream that one day, Danyaal would write back, maybe just a sentence—stating how he despised Rami for what he'd done.

But Danyaal didn't.

"You're older now. And it was a long time ago," the voice on the phone was saying. "Memories get rusty with time, but wait for what I'll let you hear. It'll bring it all back." It was jarring the way that male voice bludgeoned Rami's eardrum.

At forty-five, the images of that inconceivable journey of over ten thousand kilometers between Lahore and Chicago flashed before Rami's eyes: a plane ride to Istanbul, Turkey ... being at the mercy of strangers ... an exchange of some money ... setting out on yet another journey across the Atlantic Ocean on a large oil vessel, destined for the shores of the United States of America ... declaring refugee status upon arrival. All to escape the ongoing harassment inflicted by one man. The dull clouds from his memories began to shift.

Rami recalled the insurmountable task of arriving in a foreign land over two decades ago, where he had to learn to live among strangers, concede to new customs, survive frigid winters, and grasp the meaning of homesickness.

There was no doubt in Rami's mind that he was speaking with Osman on the phone.

"How did you—" Rami paused. "What am I about to hear?"

"Patience, Rami." Osman snickered. "Here we go." Rami heard him take a deep breath. "You're ready?" he said.

Clicking sounds followed. There was a muted exchange of words between Osman and someone at the other end. The phone line was static.

A moment later, someone else came on.

"Hello."

Also, a male, carrying a tremulous voice.

Rami felt disoriented. He clutched the phone and pressed it hard against his ears.

"Danyaal?" Rami whispered.

A muffled silence followed his question. There was a pause, some hesitation as if that voice were contemplating what to say next.

"Rami?" The voice eventually said shakily.

In front of Rami, Danyaal's face appeared through a haze, stayed, faded away. Suddenly, he was in the canteen of Forman Christian College, looking at himself at a table, staring at the entrance. There was a boy with sparkling green eyes, a broad nose, and rosy lips—standing nervously at the door against the flickering sunlight from the salt cedar tree leaves.

"You remember me, Rami?" the male voice was saying.

An eerie silence, like a thick fog, swept across the room, broken only by Rami's deep breathing.

"It's me. Danyaal." the voice spoke again, timidly.

How did Osman know where I lived? Did he have someone follow me? What was Danyaal doing with Osman? Rami's mind rang with these thoughts.

"Is that you, Rami? Are you there?" Danyaal asked.

Rami tried to say something. His mouth opened, but the words cracked through his parched throat and choked before they could even reach his lips.

"Danyaal."

On the one hand, hearing from Danyaal made Rami want to jump with joy—but the suspicious circumstances by which he had reappeared in Rami's life, on the other hand—were bone-chilling.

Then, trying to absorb the immensity of what had just happened in the past few minutes, it occurred to Rami that it could all be a sick joke. What if it was some prank caller pretending to be Osman? Maybe Osman, or someone claiming to be him, had made it up that Danyaal was with him. How could Rami be sure it was Danyaal talking to him over the phone?

Rami gathered his strength, reclaimed his tattered breath, and asked.

"If you're him, then tell me. What's the one *word* only you and I would know?"

Another pause. Rami knew it wasn't because of Danyaal searching for an answer. If it were indeed him, he would know what to say. The recollection of it, however, would inevitably evoke melancholic feelings to revisit, Rami thought.

Then he heard Danyaal breathe heavily over the phone before saying, "*Yaarana*."

LATER THAT day, Rami sat across from Brian, his fiancé, on the sofa. Between them, in the center of the coffee table, lay a manila envelope with Rami's name hand-written.

After being together for nearly fourteen years, Rami and Brian had gotten engaged in August of that same year, two months after marriage equality officially became the law in Illinois in June 2014, granting same-sex couples equal rights as others.

Rami's languished stare lingered on the envelope briefly before darting away. Brian extended his left arm across the table and offered him a warm, caring gaze. Rami leaned forward and took Brian's hand in his.

Earlier, Brian had found the envelope lying on the floor outside the apartment's front door when he'd returned from the gym. Rami was sitting by the living room window; his undiscerning look stared through the windowpane at nothing.

"This came for you," he said, holding the envelope and a bouquet carrying a card congratulating Rami on last night's performance.

Rami placed the bouquet on the coffee table. Then, his eyes shifted to the envelope dangling from Brian's hand.

"Someone left it at the door."

Rami took it and ran his fingers nervously over his name. His heart pulsated behind the rib cage.

Shakily, he tore open the envelope and took out a folded piece of paper. Rami's unblinking eyes flicked side to side as he read the brief message written in Urdu. The phone conversation with Osman from that morning echoed in his head.

I want you to listen carefully! I have gone to great lengths to find you. You thought time would take away and make me forget what you did? You must come, and come alone ... must come to your lover, he awaits you ... don't need to tell you what I would do to Danyaal if you tried anything funny! You know that well. Don't bother calling the police or talking to the FBI! You understand? Do as asked or Danyaal dies.

The letter slid from Rami's hand and glided down to the floor.

"What's the matter?"

Rami lifted his head to meet Brian's curious gaze.

"Rami?"

There was a silence.

Rami rose from the chair. Water pooling around his eyes, he curled his arms around Brian's neck and melted in his embrace.

Brian laced his hands around Rami's back. "Say something," he said.

But Rami said nothing. He only wept. He held Brian long before pulling away and dragging a sleeve across his face. He wiped the tears and muttered while sniffling, "You'd asked earlier who called last night."

Then Rami sat in front of Brian on the sofa, and, through labored breaths, recounted the events from earlier: the phone call, hearing from Danyaal after all these years, the grave threats from Osman. Now, this hand-written message on a piece of paper resting on the coffee table was overwhelming proof that it was Osman who had sent it.

"Osman knows where I live," Rami said.

Brian sat across from Rami with an unwavering morose look and listened. While describing to Brian what'd happened, Rami caught an expression of incredulity drifting across Brian's face.

Over the years, he had mentioned Danyaal fondly to Brian as a friend from college, someone from his past whom he admired, someone who had taught Rami many things.

But Rami hadn't told Brian everything. Brian didn't know what had happened at the Manga Jungle and why Osman was after them. Now Rami told Brian everything. Everything that had inevitably led to Danyaal and his nearly losing their lives that day in April of 1988, months after Rami turned eighteen. He clung to Brian's hand and confided in him how, for years, he had occupied himself with the life he had built with Brian instead of dwelling on the memories of Danyaal or what had transpired that spring.

Brian got up to fetch Rami a glass of water after he had finished.

When Brian returned, he sat beside Rami. Rami took the glass from him and took several sips. Then he told Brian that despite trying everything to forget the misfortunes from his tragic past, every nightmare that jolted him from sleep in the middle of the night had Danyaal's fear-filled eyes, his screams, and the image of his profile receding into the windowless structure in it.

"Oh, Rami." Brian shifted in his seat, gasping as if to draw enough air to his lungs.

Rami glanced at Brian under the soft, yellow light of a lamp on an end table: his ruffled blonde hair graying around the sideburns, his eyes shimmering with the shade of green that always reminded Rami of Danyaal. Like Rami, there were traces of crow's-feet etched around the corner of his eyes. Rami loved holding Brian's hands. The softness of his palm gave Rami a sense of comfort, as if all were well in the world. He knew Brian's presence in his life was akin to stumbling upon a beam of sunlight piercing through the dreary downpour. Brian was the family that Rami thought he would never have in this lifetime.

Rami also recalled the heartache over Danyaal that had plagued him. The pain struck him sharply at first and then gradually dissipated into a dull sensation that ebbed and flowed over the years. During his early years in America, the mere thought of missing Danyaal triggered strong emotions, leaving Rami utterly bereft.

"I thought it was behind me." Rami heaved a sigh and gave Brian a burdened smile. "I thought it was over. And now this," he said.

Brian took the note from the envelope and asked Rami to reread it.

"This is absurd," Brian said after Rami had translated it from the Urdu for the second time. "You can't be considering this."

Rami looked at him.

"It sounds fake, Rami. Made up." Brian waved the paper before tossing it back to the table. "It has to be," he said.

"What if it isn't? What if Osman has taken Danyaal? What if the only thing keeping him alive is Osman expecting me to arrive at the address in this note?"

Rami leaned against the back of the sofa and crossed his arms. They sat in wary silence; their unspoken incongruity lingered in the air.

Rami opened his mouth to speak again and hesitated for a moment. "I have betrayed Danyaal before. This could be my only chance at redemption." His breathing got ragged. "What would you do, Brian? If you were in my shoes, what would you do?"

Brian looked at him. Rami noticed the hint of doubt reappearing on Brian's face, now staying.

"You're holding on to something that happened over twenty-six years ago," Brian said.

"And?"

"So much could've changed between then and now."

"I know, but there're—" Rami cleared his throat, "somethings don't change."

More silence.

"You're sure that was Danyaal on the phone?" Brian said after a long pause in an uncertain voice.

"Look. I understand if this is too much for you to grasp. I sense you're having difficulty believing me even after I've told you everything," Rami said.

"You don't know that."

"I do," Rami said.

"And how do you know it?"

"I can see it in your eyes," Rami said with a thin smile, recalling what Danyaal had said to him once. "It's your eyes, Brian, that have betrayed you."

"I want to believe you," Brian said.

"Then, believe me."

"I can't fathom what it must've been like to face what you and Danyaal endured. But that was long ago, Rami. I want you not to be afraid and know you have protection from such evil in this country. You're not in Lahore anymore, and this isn't the eighties. There are laws here to protect citizens from such unimaginable deeds and threats."

Rami said nothing; he just looked at him. He didn't expect Brian to comprehend the situation entirely. Perhaps that was why Rami hadn't disclosed it earlier, thinking Brian wouldn't grasp the gravity of it.

You must live through the experience of being hunted to understand the fear it can evoke.

Rami's mind raced back to when he had been in a room without windows on the third floor of the foreboding United States Immigration and Naturalization Service building on Wells Street in downtown Chicago. There was a table filled with disorganized clutter across from the chair where Rami sat; his eyes fixed on the stack of paperwork flattened under a dolphin-shaped paperweight and mounds of files teetering at the table's edge. With a vacant expression, he glanced at the paperclips, the pens stuffed in a square tin holder, and several staplers scattered across. The air had a smell of mustiness in it, like old books in a library. On the other side of the table sat an immigration officer in white, wearing the agency patch on the breast pocket of his shirt. He drank coffee from a ceramic mug with a Bart Simpson imprint.

Between sips of the steaming beverage, the officer placed the mug next to a miniature, table-sized American flag. He was a large-headed man with square shoulders, thick arms, and a dimpled chin on an expressionless face.

His penetrating blue eyes remained settled on Rami's face while interviewing him for the asylum application. The officer required him to disclose everything, demanded that Rami verbally declare he was a homosexual who escaped persecution in his native country. Rami recalled how daunting he had found it to utter the word for the first time in his life in front of someone else.

During the hour-long interview, Rami remembered grimacing whenever the officer asked about Rami's sexuality.

"How did you discover you were gay?"

"How long did it take?"

"Do you have a boyfriend?"

"What was the acceptance of your sexuality like?"

The INS officer inquired how it had affected his friends and family—and the images of Jalil and Danyaal flashed through Rami's mind.

Rami broke out in a sweat during the brutal interrogation. And with each question, it felt like a small piece of rock had gotten stuck in his throat, making it nearly impossible to speak.

Internally, Rami snickered at the irony, however. He had spent most of his life concealing his identity from others. And now, this man was coercing him to reveal everything to the world—to prove that Rami wasn't fabricating.

When the officer didn't comprehend why Rami found it so taxing to disclose his sexuality, Rami felt empathy toward him, just as he did now for Brian. Unlike him, Rami imagined, the officer hadn't had to spend his life hiding from the truth or worrying about not having a voice or someone to turn to for support. Rami justified the officer's lack of understanding as the explanation presented itself.

Like Brian, the officer found it perplexing that Rami couldn't overcome his fears now that he was in America, thousands of miles away from anyone looking to inflict bodily or mental harm.

Rami had struggled to articulate it back then, and—while sitting next to Brian—he was agonizing over it now.

Words eluded him when he attempted to describe that people such as himself never cease to feel the horror—people broken by life, living with a scarred soul, driven out of their homeland for fear of persecution.

For years living in Chicago, Rami looked over his shoulder walking down the street. He jumped at the snap of a tree limb in Foster Avenue Park by the lake. Once, he was startled at the screeching sound of car brakes while turning a corner onto Thorndale Avenue, fretting Osman might jump out and come after him.

He spent his days in perpetual fear that Osman and his people would track him down wherever he went. Rami clicked out of online chat rooms when someone showed the slightest interest in him and asked a personal question. He used fake names on social media to conceal his identity, worried that one of Osman's men might be lurking behind the computer screen and recognize him.

It was his hell, Rami realized, his purgatory that he had to live through. He did not expect the immigration officer or Brian to acknowledge it. Sitting to his right, Rami gave Brian a side glance and took in the questions with which Brian had pelted him in an anxiety-ridden voice.

"You're assuming based on a random phone call. Have you considered that this hand-written note could be a hoax?"

"You haven't seen Danyaal for over twenty-six years. How can you predict who he might've become?"

"Why do you think contacting the police is a bad idea?"

"What does this mean for me? Rami. What does this mean for us?"

"I don't know." Rami rubbed his temples. "I don't know what any of this means, Brian," he whispered.

Despite the overwhelming sense of isolation during the early years of living in this country and enduring the perpetual scrutiny as he established his identity as a gay man, the truth was America was that vast, blue sky Rami had once longed to fly on like a bird. That one clumsy bird flapping its wings, trailing behind the others.

To him, the United States was that flock that had carried him through his struggles, his grief, his loneliness, his self-disparagement.

Standing at the airport in Lahore in May of 1988, Rami had mourned the death of his life as he knew it. He hugged Papa, soaked his shirt sleeve with his tears, and swore never to return. Ever. It was here in this new land where Rami buried the corpse of his previous life with the ghosts of his past, sought atonement for his sins—sought a new beginning.

A DREAM. *Danyaal is standing on the summit of a hill, overlooking the surrounding terrain. He finds Rami standing below, looking up. Danyaal smiles and motions for him to come to him. Rami ascends the jagged, rocky path toward Danyaal. But, as he gets near, someone thrusts him off the hill's edge. And the ground beneath him disappears.*

He's free-falling; gravity is pulling him with no end in sight. He plunges into a large body of water, a lake perhaps.

Someone's screaming, 'Get out! Get out!' There are other voices warning him to watch out for something lurking beneath.

Rami's eyes strain to see through the murkiness. He senses a shape stir at the bottom. It swims toward him. Rami shudders with terror. He paddles his limbs up to get to the surface, but the surface gets farther with each attempt. Helpless, he's sucked into the mouth of the beast lurking below.

Rami bolted up in bed, covered in sweat.

Moments later, he pushed back the blanket, careful not to disturb Brian's sleeping. He swung his legs off the bed, got up, and tiptoed to the closet. He opened the closet door and heard their hinges creak. Rami reached for the overhead shelf and pulled out a travel-size duffle bag. He then walked over to the chest of drawers, fetched a few pieces of undergarments, shirts, and pairs of slacks, and threw them in the bag before stepping into the living room.

Rami placed the bag on the table, picked up the manila envelope beside it, and removed its contents. The note made a crumpling sound against the midnight's stillness as he unfolded it.

Danyaal is with me. You have two days to come to this address or else. Don't play smart. Come alone. You have been warned.

1958 Finch Avenue, Toronto, Ontario

Rami stepped toward the living room window and glanced at the quiet street below, lit in the tarnished silver of the thin moonlight. He shut his eyes and took a deep breath.

From behind the sealed lids, his pupils moved in a flittering manner, picturing Osman's leering face just as he had remembered it all these years: his stony eyes piercing into Rami's, his cheeks quivering with rage, the edge of his upper lip curling in spite, the gust of his breath slamming against Rami's face.

Rami snapped his eyes open, fished his passport from the desk drawer, and exited the apartment on his way to find Danyaal.

TWENTY

October 20, 2014

It was early evening the following day when the Greyhound bus got off the Gardner Expressway, and Rami arrived in downtown Toronto, Canada. Brian was sleeping soundly back in Chicago when Rami left the apartment to catch the subway to the bus station. He had left Brian a note before leaving, knowing if they spoke again, Brian would try to talk Rami into not going or insist on coming with him.

He was afraid that the more he listened to Brian's point of view, the more he'd be prone to rationalize, deliberate, and end up not going.

Rami was concerned that the appeal of his life in America could hold him back. He fretted internally that the allure of the comfort and security he now felt in his adult years might render Danyaal a faded memory. It would be like remembering the receding figure of someone on the platform left behind when a train pulls away. Rami cogitated that it could entice him to turn away from the past that had reappeared—and make him forego the unexpected chance, possibly the only one, at finding Danyaal.

Twenty-six years is a long time to let go of the past. But for Rami, the opportunity to see Danyaal again, despite the unusual circumstances, was not something to let go of. To forget.

He hated leaving this way. Without saying goodbye to Brian, without a kiss, communicating through a note left on Brian's side of the bed, assuring him he'd be back soon—a promise Rami wasn't convinced he'd be able to keep. He knew Brian would be upset. But that was the only option Rami felt he had if he wished not to further agonize and ruminate over the letter and his conversation with Osman.

He purchased a one-way ticket to Toronto at the Greyhound terminal on Harrison Street and boarded the 6:00 a.m. bus. During one of the rest stops in London, Ontario, Rami checked his phone; there were nine missed calls from Brian and four voice messages.

Rami wrapped a scarf around his neck against the chill when he climbed off the bus stairs and heard the hydraulic doors closing. He stood at the corner of Bay and Dundas Avenue and, up ahead, saw a sizeable digital thermometer flashing a temperature of eight degrees Celsius, or approximately forty-six degrees Fahrenheit. Rami fetched the letter from the manila envelope and approached an orange taxi parked outside the bus terminal.

"Can you take me to this address?" he leaned over the driver's side window and addressed the cab driver.

Appearing to be in his mid-thirties and holding a cigarette tucked between his index and middle finger, the driver took the paper from Rami and read it out loud. "1958 Finch Avenue," he muttered. His fingers drummed the outside of the taxi door. "It's by Jane and Finch Mall."

"Is there a hotel closer to this address?"

The driver paused and glanced at Rami before answering. "There are a couple," he said. "Mostly motels."

"That'd be fine. How much?"

The driver raised an eyebrow and eyed Rami up and down. "What's a man like you doing looking for a place in an area like that?" he said. His curious gaze skimmed through Rami's designer scarf, cashmere sweater, and fitted denim.

"How much?"

Another sidelong glance. "Get in." The driver shrugged, flicking his thumb over his shoulder to the backseat. "Standard fare," he grunted.

Moments later, Rami was back on Gardner Expressway, in a taxi this time, on his way to the address on a note that had mysteriously appeared at his apartment's front door. The driver, a man with a straight neck and a protruding Adam's apple, flicked the ash off his cigarette through the slightly cracked window and continued to smoke. "Where're you from, my friend?" He glanced at Rami through the rearview mirror and attempted to engage in conversation. He had a thick, presumably Eastern European accent.

"Chicago."

"The Windy City!" he exclaimed.

Rami rolled down the window to ventilate the smoke swirling inside the car and said nothing.

"First time in Canada?" the driver continued.

"Yes."

The driver snickered. "Hmm."

Rami turned his head to meet the driver's gaze in the rearview mirror, "Why did you do that?"

"Never mind."

"No, I want to know. Why did you do that?"

"It's none of my business, really," he caught Rami's unblinking stare on him through the mirror and said. "It's just that an American, for the first time in Canada, going directly to the surrounding inner slums of Jane and Finch instead of visiting the beautiful places in this city sounds a little odd, that's all."

"What's wrong with where we're going?"

The driver snickered. "Nothing if you're looking for drugs or interested in witnessing crime and ethnic gang violence. Typical tourists aren't even aware of that neighborhood, let alone go there the moment they arrive," he said.

Rami's heart began racing. The way the taxi driver described it, it appeared Rami was headed to an area similar to Cabrini-Green in Chicago, a public housing project riddled with crime and gang violence over the years that resulted in the city shutting it down in 2011. He noticed his phone vibrate. He took it out of the bag and saw Brian's number on the screen. Rami felt his stomach churning.

"I'm going there to meet someone," Rami croaked, doing his best to keep his eyes focused on the morning traffic outside. They were getting off the highway now. He put the phone back into the bag and let the call go to voicemail.

"Going there to *meet* someone?"

Rami felt a wave of nausea rushing through him. "I don't mean to be rude, but can we not talk anymore?"

The driver shrugged. "Suit yourself." He threw a cold glance at Rami. "A friend, I hope," he said.

With this, Rami attempted to steel himself against his innards roiling, against what he sensed might be coming. But the severity of the circumstances hit him. He closed his eyes, turned his face toward the open window, and felt the cold breeze. A sense of regret drenched his entire being.

A *friend*? No. He wasn't going to see a friend. He was going to face Osman, his greatest adversary.

What was I thinking? I lacked the courage to stand up to that homophobic bully before. How could I have forgotten all my nightmares about him, about what he'd done to Danyaal and me? What makes things different now?

Rami broke into a sweat, realizing the gravity of the situation, not having thought this through thoroughly.

"Pull over," he muttered.

"What?"

"Pull Over, damn it! I am going to be sick." Rami cried, sensing bile rising at the back of his throat.

"Hold on!" The driver yelled, quickly pulling the taxi over to a curb.

Rami had already opened the door before the vehicle could ease up to the side of the road. He stooped forward, held his stomach, and retched.

HE CALLED Brian from the hotel room. The driver had dropped him off in front of a flickering neon-lit sign, True North Inn. He informed Rami this motel was a few blocks from the address Rami had provided. Situated between warehouses, auto-repair shops, and drab-looking high-rise apartment buildings, the motel was a modest structure with powder-blue wall siding and matching rows of doors. The pungent smell of tobacco and female perfume bludgeoned Rami's nostrils the moment he opened the door to the front lobby. He took the key to his room from a woman behind the receptionist's desk, wearing a bouffant-style blonde hairdo. The wooden stairs outside the front entrance led to a corridor with a row of doors on the right. His room was third down the hallway. Rami closed the curtains, sat on top of a floral comforter on the bed, and held the phone to his ears. He let Brian's angry voice yell for a full minute at the other end, knowing he'd deserved it.

"—I know … I shouldn't have; I'm sorry," Rami finally said during one of Brian's pauses, listened.

"—Well, I'm not sure," Rami replied to a question, his head downcast. "Honestly, I don't know what I'm doing." He listened in silence, nodded, hesitated a little, shifted his eyes to his reflection in the mirror, and heard Brian asking him to return home.

"Soon … What? No. I'm here now," Rami's voice bounced from the receiver. He held the phone tightly in his hand. "Best I see this through. Yes, I know. All this could be for nothing."

Another pause.

"I'll catch the next bus back to Chicago. I love you, too."

AN HOUR later, after assuring Brian he'd call the police if there was any danger, Rami stepped outside the room and stood in the silver dull of the moon for a while. He then descended the wooden stairs and began walking toward 1958 Finch Avenue. The night had fallen, and the air buzzed with critters' chirping noises. He must have walked five or so blocks to a high-rise apartment building with the address matching the writing in the letter that was folded in the left pocket of his pants. He crossed the road and entered a park across from the building. Rami located a nearby bench and lowered himself onto it. He breathed in the brisk air and stared at the tall highrise in front. If there was any truth to Osman's claim, Danyaal awaited him somewhere in that concrete and glass structure. Sitting in the park, Rami's thoughts drifted to the day he had stood in the courtyard of Danyaal's house after discovering he'd left for England. Gone. Vanished. Not to be seen or heard from for a very long time.

HE REMEMBERED that the lemon tree looked lean as though it had been pruned for the season. Or was it the pooled water in Rami's eyes creating an illusion? He had stood there, unaware if he would ever heal from losing Danyaal like this, how he would manage to go on with life without him, or whether he would ever be able to fill the emptiness in his heart. Enduring the silent ache of missing

Danyaal for the first time, the pain that would linger and become permanent, Rami had just stood there.

"Did he leave anything for me?" he eventually mumbled in a barely audible voice, breaking the hushed silence that had fallen over. "A message, perhaps?"

Gibril had exchanged looks with Afrooz before pursing his lips and shaking his head remorsefully. Rami had lowered his gaze, his shoulders slumped. He'd struggled to come up with anything else to say. But no words came. Danyaal was gone from his life, someplace Rami wouldn't be able to reach him. Leaving without a hug, not even a goodbye. Rami had managed a broken smile, pressed his hand against his chest in respect for the elders standing before him, and turned to walk out the open gate.

"Wait, Rami!" Afrooz called out behind him.

Rami turned and met her consoling eyes. Afrooz was looking at him as if she could see through him and sense the air of defeat that had besieged Rami.

"Maybe he did ... maybe Danyaal left something for you and didn't tell us," she said.

Gibril cocked his head and gave her a *what are you doing* look.

"Everything is where it used to be in Danyaal's room; we haven't moved anything. You can go upstairs and look for yourself," Afrooz ignored her husband's strained stare and went on. "If it makes you feel any better."

Rami's burdened stare flitted from her to Gibril, looking to validate the invitation.

"You two were close. We understand what you must be going through, son. Go on. Go to his room." Afrooz ran a hand over Rami's head. "Take all the time you need."

With his lips, Rami formed a soundless *"thank you"* and climbed the stairs. Layer upon layer of sadness grew inside him, thickening with each step landing. With every heartbeat came a sharp longing for Danyaal. He paused after reaching the corridor and looked ahead at the door on the right that led to Danyaal's room. Many times, he had found Danyaal standing there smiling, holding out his hand, ushering him in.

'Come, Rami. Come along, now' Danyaal's voice echoed in Rami's head. Through slow, crippling steps, Rami moved along the corridor. His eyes roamed as he crossed the doorway into the room: the bed, the nightstand, the chest of drawers, the wooden chair, the desk, the lamp. He looked to his right and saw the shelving unit with cassette tapes, the tape deck, and the speakers. Everything familiar was in its place like it used to be, except for the guitar. Rami didn't see Danyaal's guitar.

It was as if Danyaal had stepped away momentarily and would be walking through that door any second. Rami lowered himself to the foot of the bed and choked back the urge to cry.

In this room he thought, with a quivering chin, they had made so many memories. Here, they had lain on their stomachs, feet pedaling in the air, and listened to The Mamas & the Papas. There, they fought over an algebra equation when Danyaal tried to make Rami learn the difference between a quadratic and a second-degree equation.

Rami could hear the echoes of the songs they sang together. It was in this room that their lips touched for the first time. Rami squeezed the inner corner of his eyes with his thumb and forefinger and rose from the bed. He opened the desk drawers and looked for anything that might come across as a note from Danyaal, but he saw nothing. The drawers were empty. He plodded across the room, running his fingers over the furniture's edges, corners, and curved shapes once touched by Danyaal's hands. Opened and closed the empty chest drawers. Then, something caught Rami's eye. He noticed the bottom chest drawer was slightly ajar. He stooped and discovered that, unlike the top drawers, it had something in it. He grabbed the handle and pulled it open. Lying in it, neatly folded, was a plaid, yellow, and green long-sleeved shirt on top of a pair of blue trousers. It jogged yet another memory of Danyaal and this room for Rami.

Why did Danyaal pack every other article of clothing to take with him except for these two items? The ones he'd lent Rami to wear the day Rami had visited this room for the first time.

Rami removed the shirt, drew it closer to his chest, and returned to the bed. He sat back down. Then, an explanation presented itself. The only explanation that made sense: This was the message Danyaal had left for him, Rami realized. Danyaal anticipated the conversation Rami would have with his parents; he knew Rami would be allowed to return to his room after his departure. Danyaal left these garments behind to convey to Rami the intensity of his repulsion for his once lover. He detested Rami so much that he chose not to take anything that had Rami's memory associated with it.

This was Danyaal's message to him, Rami reckoned. He was gone, shedding any thought or remembrance of Rami's existence.

With this, the tears came. Rami clutched Danyaal's shirt in his hand and broke down. His final recollection of this room was his weeping, utterly bereft, and calling Danyaal's name amidst the sobbing spasms.

BACK IN Toronto, it was beginning to feel cold. A gust of wind wafted through the trees. It invoked for Rami the familiar smell of burning coal in the fall. He looked at his watch and saw it was close to ten; he realized he had been sitting at that bench for nearly two hours. The night's stillness was shattered by a gasoline-fuel-carrying semi-trailer rattling by. Rami exited the park and waited for the traffic light to change at Finch Avenue before crossing the road. He patted the pocket containing the instructions. He'd read it enough times to know the steps he had to take: enter the building, press #, then 018 at the intercom. Wait for more instructions.

The traffic light turned green. He moved forward on the crosswalk toward the building's entrance. He couldn't shake the thought that he was at this particular junction solely because of a strange phone call and a short, hand-written paragraph, unaware who'd answer—if anyone—uncertain how he would react seeing Osman, all the while wondering with a fluttering heart if Danyaal would be there.

Then, moments before his hand could reach the entrance door handle, Rami heard the shrieking brakes of a fast-approaching vehicle behind him. He turned. Saw a black sports utility truck with tinted windows approaching the curb. Two shapes emerged from the vehicle. Rami jumped. Before he could say or do anything, two men in black grabbed him by the back of his arms and shoved him into the truck's back seat. The entire episode couldn't have lasted more than ten seconds. The vehicle sped off, slamming Rami's body against the backseat.

AFTER TRAVELING a short distance, the black truck turned the corner into a narrow street with no outlet. Speechless and startled by this new development, Rami's heart writhed in his ribcage. When the vehicle came to a rest, along with Rami's swiveling body, the man sitting on the passenger side escorted him out and into the rear compartment of an unmarked armored truck parked at the far end of the street. Rami stumbled inside; his gaze skimmed over the closed-circuit monitor screens, signal interception equipment, audio recorders, cameras, and detection devices—the kind he had seen used at airports by transportation security. It was just like what one would see in a spy movie. Rami felt his knees would give out. He grabbed his shaking hand with the other, spotted a bench on the right side of the compartment, and lurched toward it.

He slumped on the bench and took deep breaths to draw air to his lungs, hyperventilating.

A man and a woman, sitting in rotating chairs closer to the truck's cab, wheeled to face him. The woman rose from her seat and extended her arm in which she held a red paper cup with the Tim Hortons logo.

"Hello, Rami," she said. Rami gave her a blank stare. She had a round face, a pink, buttoned nose, and a rosy tint to her cheeks. Her blue eyes were lively and warm. She had her blonde hair tied behind her back in a ponytail. "I hope you don't mind me addressing you by your first name."

Rami didn't say anything.

"My name is Deidre Ralston. I'm with the Federal Bureau of Investigations." She handed Rami the coffee and flashed her credentials. Rami threw a cursory look at her ID and smelled the aroma of freshly ground coffee beans.

"What's all this?" he mumbled in a terrified voice. "What's going on?"

Holding a gray folder, the man wheeled his chair over Rami's way. There were solid, dominant surfaces on his face and square eyebrows above his heavy eyelids. He had a full head of pepper-gray hair and appeared in his mid-fifties. "This is agent Steve Kaufman," Deidre introduced the man. "He's with the Canadian Security Intelligence Service."

Rami squirmed and pressed further into the back of the bench.

"Why don't you begin by telling us what you're doing here?" Steve said, skipping the pleasantries and getting right to business.

Rami's bewildered look drifted between him and Deidre, then back to him. "I was brought here in a vehicle," he said through parched lips. "Against my will."

"What I mean is what you are doing in Canada. What is your business here?"

There was a silence, a pause, before Steve opened the folder. He took out a photograph. "Do you recognize this individual?" He handed Rami the picture. Rami caught the two federal agents trading looks.

His heart fell the instant he glanced at the image. In the picture Osman, appearing old and clean-shaven, is staring at the camera with a keen smile. There are deep wrinkles on his face and grey in sideburns, but Rami would've identified him even if he was a hundred years old. He recognized the mole below his right cheekbone. The intensity in Osman's eyes made Rami cringe.

"Can you identify him?"

Rami raised his slumped body. Deidre placed her hand on Steve's shoulder to ease up on the interrogation. She then took a seat next to Steve.

"We're here to help. You're safe with us," she said. She then tapped her finger on Osman's photo. "This man's name is Osman Mohawi. He lives in Syria. We have credible intelligence that he's an Islamic State operative in Iraq and Syria. We have been monitoring his activities closely. He was last seen going into the building you were about to enter. He arrived in Canada through Buffalo, New York. We suspect he might be engaged in organizing a sleeper cell for ISIS. We intercepted a call he made yesterday and traced it to the phone number registered to your apartment in Chicago, where you live with Brian Cullen. We're trying to establish the nature of your involvement with this man," Deidre said without trying to conceal that Big Brother keeps a tab on everyone. "I would like you to share with us why you tried to enter that building."

"Osman didn't live in Syria back when I knew him," Rami uttered, frowning internally at how these two seemed to know every detail about Osman's life yet weren't aware that Osman migrated to Pakistan as an Afghan refugee in the eighties.

"Go on," Steve said. "What else can you tell us about this man?"

"Where is Osman now?"

Deidre and Steve exchanged glances.

"Is he in that building on Finch Avenue?"

"According to our sources, yes," Deidre said.

Rami then straightened himself on the bench and recounted his phone conversation with Osman, his claim that Danyaal was in his custody, his demand for Rami to come to him. Rami also took the two federal agents on a brief journey into his past life. He described who Danyaal was to him and how Osman once persecuted them in Lahore.

When he finished, Steve rose from the chair and walked up to the workstation by the truck's cab. He returned with a piece of paper in his hand.

"Could this be Danyaal?" he said and handed it to Rami.

It was a blurry facsimile. Rami's eyes landed on a grayscale image of a man. He wasn't like the man Rami had imagined him to be over the years: a thin mustache, wire-rimmed glasses resting at the tip of his nose, timid demeanor. But he was still tall, still had a full head of curly hair, still exuded a sense of self-confidence, smiling at the camera. It sure was a fuzzy image of him, Rami's Danyaal. The air inside the armored truck got too hot suddenly. Rami handed the facsimile back to Steve. Nodded. He wondered if they could see the moisture gathering in his eyes.

"Are you positive?"

"It's him," Rami croaked. "I know. It's Danyaal!"

Steve slid the photograph into the gray folder. "A missing person's report was filed this morning for this individual," he said. "We know him as a British national who entered Toronto four days ago. When his friends back home didn't hear from him directly or through social media for several days, they contacted the authorities. We obtained a copy of Danyaal's photograph from Toronto Police, who are looking for him," Steve went on.

Rami asked how Osman could have gotten hold of Danyaal.

"We haven't determined it yet," Deidre said. "But we do know that Osman came to Buffalo and visited the cemetery where Abul Ala Maududi is buried. Do you know who Abu Ala Maududi is?"

Why did this name sound familiar? Rami wondered.

Steve said that Maududi was the founder of Jamaat-e-Islami in India, a scholar and a theologian whose ideologies helped shape extremist groups like Al-Qaeda and ISIS. Maududi denigrated nationalism in the 1930s, he added.

Steve's comment took Rami back to when he'd first come across Osman at the F.C. College campus. That's where he had first heard Osman mentioning Abul Ala Maududi, he recalled now.

Maududi moved to Pakistan after the 1947 partition of the Indian subcontinent; Deidre took over from Steve and continued. The Pakistani authorities imprisoned him between 1948 and 1950 for civil disobedience, during which time he wrote several books. In 1979, Maududi migrated to the United States, received medical care from his physician son, and died in Buffalo on September 22 of that year.

"We believe Osman, now affiliated with ISIS, regards Maududi as his spiritual leader. He arrived in Buffalo to pay homage to Maududi by visiting his place of death. While there, he somehow got wind of Danyaal's visit to Canada and allegedly plotted to settle an old score," Deidre explained. "Osman and his kind can be very resourceful in tracking people when they want to."

Deidre's comment made Rami cringe.

"What happens now?" Rami asked after listening to Steve and Deidre explain based on gathered intelligence.

"Now, we prepare you to visit Osman since he expects you," Steve said. "Can I borrow your watch?"

TWENTY-ONE

October 21, 2014

Rami emerged into the early morning crimson light across the sky, awash with streaks of pink, and began trudging toward 1958 Finch Avenue. Never in a million years could he have imagined that the FBI and CSIS would use him as bait to entrap an alleged terrorist. He thought Deidre and Steve would send him back to the motel or, better yet, force him to board the bus back to Chicago, telling him to stay out of their investigation. But Deidre made the point that if Danyaal were in Osman's custody, which the evidence suggested he was, Rami's not appearing before Osman could spook him and jeopardize Danyaal's safety.

"What do I need to do?" Rami had asked.

HE FELT jittery as he listened to the Canadian and American federal agents giving him specific instructions for the next hour or so. Before that, he'd even dozed on the narrow truck bench for a couple of hours, during which he had nightmares. Steve and the driver of the black vehicle took Rami's watch apart while he slept. When they returned it, Steve said it had now been equipped with a location tracker chip and a microphone.

"Chances are you'll be frisked as soon as you enter the building for a firearm or wiretap," Steve had said. "But with the tracking devices installed in your watch, it would be unlikely for Osman to know we're monitoring you."

Rami removed his mobile phone from his pants pocket. "This?"

"You leave this with us."

RAMI TURNED a corner and saw the park across the road from the address where he had sat last night. Somewhere beyond it, a pair of eyes and ears inside the metal compartment of an armored truck was tracking Rami's moves. Rami ran his finger over the watch and felt a sense of calm.

Based on the plan laid out to him by the authorities, Rami would appear before Osman, maintaining the facade of following the instructions received in the letter and pretending the whole episode with the feds hadn't happened. He would locate Danyaal or try to get as much information about his whereabouts as possible, along with Osman's real intentions for being in Canada. The agents would listen and record the conversation through the tiny microphone chip in Rami's watch. A SWAT team would surround the building, ready to act immediately. Deidre said the FBI would be prepared to intervene if they sensed his or Danyaal's life were in danger—if Danyaal were, in fact, in Osman's custody.

Rami met her assuring gazes with nervous nods.

Now, he stepped through the front door and entered a dimly lit, unkempt foyer littered with old newspaper inserts scattered across the floor and a graffiti-filled wall on the left. He made his way toward the intercom to his right and pressed #, then the numeric 018. A dial tone came on, followed by a phone ringing. Someone answered with a click.

"Hello," Rami leaned forward and spoke into the intercom in a hollow voice. But no one answered. A second later, the entry door buzzed. Rami quickly pulled it open and walked inside. Unaware of where to go, he stood there and waited for instructions. A couple of minutes passed. Rami was nervously balancing his body weight on his feet when a boy, appearing ten or so years old and wearing a white skullcap and a loose tunic, peered from around the corner where the elevators were.

"Third floor," the boy whispered and retreated as quickly as he had appeared.

Rami's heart somersaulted in his chest; his feet felt as if they were tied to a stack of bricks. He entered the elevator and took it to the third floor. After exiting, he found himself in a grim, long hallway lined with closed doors on both sides.

Again, he waited for the next set of instructions. Moments later, he heard the faint creak of a door swinging open at the far end of the hallway. Another boy, similar to the one on the main floor, emerged and beckoned Rami to come toward him. Perplexed by the young boys appearing and giving instructions, Rami looked to his left, then to his right, before taking small, cautious steps and moving forward. As he neared, he noticed this boy, also wearing a skullcap, looked even younger than the previous one. Then, it occurred to Rami that Osman was using these boys as shields to deter a possible ambush from the police or FBI. A sniper from the SWAT team was less likely to shoot a ten-year-old than an adult.

"*Salaam,*" Rami said. The boy blinked. His eyes lowered, and he ushered Rami in by moving to the side. Rami crossed the door and entered an apartment. After shutting the door behind him, the boy turned off the entrance ceiling light. In the smudged darkness, two shapes emerged from an adjacent room and began frisking Rami: his legs, his crotch, his chest, just as Steve had indicated might happen. One of them took out the folded letter from Rami's pants pocket.

"I'm here to see Osman Mohawi!" Rami called out. He grabbed one of the men by his waist. "He's expec ..." the man swiped Rami's hand off him and stopped him midsentence by placing the index finger on his lips. He unstrapped Rami's watch, flipped it several times, brought it closer to his ear, and put it on a table behind him.

Rami's heart dropped.

Both men clutched Rami by the elbows on each side and began escorting him toward the back of the apartment.

"Wait!" Rami cried. "My watch, please let me have my watch." But to no avail.

His toes dragged against the floor. Through the corner of his eye, Rami saw the young boy in the skullcap standing on the side and watching him being hauled out of the apartment. Rami felt disoriented. Next, he knew, he was exiting the apartment with them and climbing down the back stairs.

"Where're you taking me?" he said shakily, marveling inside at the precautions these men had taken. But neither of the men said anything in response; they kept stepping down, kept pulling Rami along with them.

They descended to a shared courtyard between the building Rami had entered and an adjacent highrise. Rami walked with them across a narrow walkway in the middle and entered the second building. This time, the elevator took Rami to the eighth floor. He ran his hand over his left wrist, where his watch had been a few minutes ago, and muttered a silent prayer for help.

He entered another sparingly-decorated apartment after walking through the layered smell of stale carpet permeating a hallway similar to the other building. Beyond the foyer, his eyes squinted against the mint green walls with high-gloss sheen under the tubular fluorescent lights. A beige, wall-to-wall carpet with splotches of stains covered the floor. A large, flat-screen television sat on an entertainment center in the far corner of the living room, across from a set of a black leather sofa and a glass coffee table. To the right was a window draped with a pink floral bedsheet. The shorter of the two men nudged Rami at the elbow and nodded toward the loveseat. He dropped Osman's letter on the coffee table. Rami staggered forward and collapsed onto the sofa. He tried to avoid looking nervous by crossing and uncrossing his arms on his chest. Repeated. He turned his hands and stared at his sweaty palms. He raised his left hand and ran his fingers across his chin and cheekbones.

There was a room, slightly angled to his right, where Rami's eyes wandered and noticed the frayed edges of a prayer rug on the carpet. On it were visible tips of bent toes in a prostrate position. It appeared as though someone was praying the morning *namaz*.

The man who'd nudged Rami to sit handed him a handkerchief, which Rami took and dragged across his sweat-drenched face. Then the two men stood behind the sofa while Rami decided precariously on a seating posture: back straight or slightly hunched, legs parallel—feet grounded or one leg propped over the other, demonstrating dominance. He contemplated whether to let hands rest on the lap, fingers intertwined, or arms crossed on the chest again. Blood pulsated on the sides of his head, and he felt a headache coming on.

What have I gotten myself into? Where is Danyaal? This isn't me. This has never been me. Why did I have to be a hero? Where is Danyaal? Thoughts swirled around Rami's head.

The realization, like an unstoppable wave gathering strength and speed, came crashing in. He was in a different country, hundreds of miles away, in a depressing room resembling a prison, and in the company of suspected terrorists. Rami thought of Deidre and Steve out there, and, at that moment, a feeling of utter loneliness washed over him.

Don't think of them. They weren't part of your insane scheme to show up here. Find a way to get yourself out of this situation. But can you? Have you forgotten what a coward you have been most of your life? Rami's mind rang and rang with these thoughts.

A fit of remorse claimed Rami. He thought about Brian, his fiancé, his love, and how irresponsible it was for Rami to have departed the way he did.

There is a good chance Brian would be mourning my death in a few hours. And where is Danyaal? Rami was sitting in this life-threatening situation fueled by his desperation to find him. *Where was he?*

Rami wanted to grab his temples and curl into a ball on the sofa to stop the whirlwind of these thoughts.

Just then, his gaze returned to the adjacent room, and he saw a pair of hands lifting the prayer rug from the floor and folding it.

Then, Rami's eyes stopped blinking as he glanced at the thick-shouldered figure of Osman dressed in white and emerging from the door. Rami's complexion suddenly turned a shade paler as if the color had been drained out of his face. His legs went numb. Despite prominent dark circles under his eyes and strands of silver in his hair, Osman was still a towering specimen with a solid chest and intimidating personality. The image of him looming over Rami in Lahore flashed before Rami's eyes, which he quickly shook off. He didn't want to think about that. Not at that moment. He had to focus.

Osman took a seat across from Rami, his fingers drumming the armrest. The same fingers that once choked Rami two and a half decades ago. For a long while, Osman didn't say anything. He just sat there and watched Rami with those same stony eyes. Rami felt more beads of sweat erupting across his forehead. After realizing he'd stopped breathing, he gasped for air and inhaled the layered stench of mold and food on unwashed dishes. Rami breathed out, slowly, through his mouth.

"You came," Osman's coarse voice battered Rami's eardrums. Rami jolted as though he had woken up from sleep. He saw Osman's eyes darting at the letter on the coffee table between them.

Rami ran his tongue over his dried lips and wiped the sweat off his forehead with the already wet handkerchief. "Where's Danyaal?" the words barely squeezed through his parched throat.

"From America. Alone. Knowing too well who I am." A hint of admiration drifted across Osman's face as quickly as it vanished. "Did you make sure he's here alone, Sadiq?" Osman snapped his gaze toward the guards who stood behind Rami.

"Yes, Agha. We checked," Sadiq, the older of the two guards, spoke, "he's clean."

"Check again."

"Agha?"

"Check again, damn it!" Osman's voice thundered.

The guards jumped. They quickly moved to lift Rami and frisk him again. Sadiq shook his head a minute later at Osman, affirming. "Nothing."

"No cell phone?"

"No cell phone, Agha."

Osman looked at Rami.

"Left it at the motel," Rami lied.

Osman nodded; his fingers resumed drumming the sofa. "Good. So where were we?"

Rami stood across from him.

"You can sit now," Osman said.

Rami returned to the sofa.

"Comfortable?"

Rami remained silent.

"I wonder, though," Osman spoke. "I wonder, Rami. Does it make you afraid?"

"What?"

"Being here alone, does it make you scared?"

"Where is Danyaal?"

"Answer the question."

"Forget how I feel." Rami ran his tongue over his lips again. "I'm here as you asked. Isn't that what you'd wanted?"

Osman waved a hand to one of the guards, and he fetched Rami a glass of water.

"Drink."

Rami emptied half of the glass in one gulp.

"And you always thought I was unreasonable," Osman smirked. He then leaned toward Rami as if he were about to share a secret with him. "It's humane to squelch the animal's thirst before slaughtering it for *qurbani* on Eid. You know that, don't you?" he said in a lowered voice with one eyebrow raised. Rami tried to blink, but his eyelids were too heavy to move. The mint green walls appeared to be pressing in. He was sure he would see a bloodless face had he glanced at his reflection in the mirror.

"It was a joke," Osman twirled his fingers in the air and snapped them, grinning, looking at Rami.

Rami thought about Brian, and it calmed him. He pictured Brian's face inches from his every night in bed, the caress of his hands, the warmth of his luminous, green eyes. The kiss they exchanged before turning off the lights and saying goodnight. Rami thought of the day they had met at a neighborhood bar and winked at each other. He thought about the marches they had joined and their fight for equal rights for their community. He remembered the overwhelming exhilaration the day marriage equality became federal law in the United States, jumping with joy in the apartment, holding each other, dancing.

There is a good chance I wouldn't leave this room alive, Rami thought. He forced his legs to stop shaking and fought the rush of terror throughout his physical and emotional state.

"Was that what it was?" he swallowed hard and said. "A joke?"

"You didn't think it was funny?"

Rami looked at Osman.

"What did you two think?" Osman asked the guards without peeling his eyes away from Rami. "Funny, na?"

They giggled.

"What're you doing here, Osman?" Rami's voice sounded distant and muffled to him as if he were speaking from inside a cave.

"What am I doing here? Umm, let's see." The horizontal lines on Osman's forehead became prominent. "Doing the God Almighty's work. What does it look like?"

"Where's Danyaal?"

The silence that ensued seemed to last an eternity.

Osman tightly crossed his arms, his left hand's thumb and index finger resting on his chin over the short gray beard with neatly trimmed sides. "I'll ask you something: You have any inkling of the effort and dedication it takes to scour the world and seek virtuous boys and men willing to answer the call of duty? Can you conceive through your weakling brain the commitment required to dedicate one's life to fulfilling God's will?" he spat.

"People like you can never understand what it's like to fight for one's faith, to save misguided souls, and to bring them back to the righteous way, the true way." He snickered. "Likes of you, who abandon their homes, their roots, and sink into the filth of unimaginable sins, can never comprehend." Osman uncrossed his arms. His left hand returned to the armrest, now curled into a fist. "With your stained heart and blackened soul, I'm not surprised you're unable to see the hole you have dug for yourself to burn for eternity on the Day of Judgment."

"So that's what this is all about," Rami said. "Punishment."

Osman let out a harsh laughter. "Punishment? You really think that?"

"What else could it be?" Rami attempted to compose his quivering tone. "Why else would you travel from Pakistan? Ask me to come to Canada, claiming Danyaal is with you."

Osman's eyes narrowed. A look of surprise passed through his face.

"I left Pakistan a long time ago," he said. "I spat on that nation that's become a cheap whore to the country you now call home. Like a prostitute, it bends over and takes it from behind whenever America tells it to."

Osman tilted his head, smirked. "You know how to bend and take it from behind, don't you?" He winked.

"If not Pakistan, then where?" Rami ignored the insult.

"You pathetic fool. If you must know, I now live in Syria and fulfill my duty as a servant of the Islamic State."

"Islamic State?"

"ISIS, you imbecile," Osman grunted and shot Rami an admonishing glare. "And as for seeking revenge or punishment, don't flatter yourself. I wouldn't go this far out of my way to waste my time on you and your likes." He snickered again. "As chance would have it, an opportunity unexpectedly presented itself, and God paved the way for me to pursue the path of justice. It is worth the effort to seek the rightful evenhandedness," he said.

"Justice?"

"Justice for the many virtuous men and women who've been wronged by people like you, inflicting this deviant act on them, a deed that's such an affront to the sharia law!" Osman gritted his teeth.

He stood up, walked behind the sofa, leaned over, and spread his arms on its arched back.

"There's a city called Mosul in Iraq where I lived for a few years before moving to Syria." He looked into space as if mumbling to himself. "Big city, beautiful city, by the Tigris River, once ruled by the Ottoman Empire. Rich with history and culture. Many from around the world traveled to Mosul for education and trade of oil and marble. I and many other Sunnis lived in peace with Arabs, Turks, Kurds, non-believers even, you know?

"And then the call came some time ago. And we went whenever we heard the news. We called on the men and the boys and informed them what their neighbors, their friends, and their wives had accused them of. We warned them to give up such devious deeds and repent. And when they didn't stop, we arrived at night and broke down their doors. We went into their rooms and caught them. Door-to-Door. We dragged them in front of their mothers, wives, and children into the streets," Osman spoke rapidly. "And there were dozens of them. We amputated limbs, whipped them, even crucified some."

Rami caught Osman's fingers clamping on the sofa.

"We gave them the punishment they deserved for violating sharia." He paced around the back of the sofa a couple of times. "But of all the decent, God's work we did, there is one that I remember clearly." Osman returned to his seat and got quiet.

"His name was Nashid," he started again after a brief pause, "a sixteen-year-old with striking Assyrian looks: tall, slender, piercing blue eyes. I have to admit, he was a handsome young man with a promising future. His father was a shoemaker. Not a street-side kind, no. He had his shop in the bazaar next to a garment merchant who traded in cotton and silk. Nashid's father, Ashur, made shoes for the rich and influential class of people, you see, the aristocrats. Modern people. It was only natural that I befriended him. I became one of his customers. He made a pair of custom-made loafers for me. *Wah, wah* ... what craftsmanship of that *mochi*!" Osman again twirled his fingers in the air and snapped them. "I used to watch Nashid at the shop assisting his father; he was learning the craft from one of the best in business. I even got invited to their house for dinner. Saeeda, Ashur's wife and Nashid's mother, God bless her, made lamb *kipteh* and *Boushala* soup. To this day, my mouth water thinking about how delicious the food was." Osman planted a *chef's kiss* in the air.

"Anyway, one afternoon, I was visiting Ashur at the shop when I noticed Nashid and the garment merchant exchanging looks and smiling at each other but not saying anything." Osman glanced to the ceiling and sighed. "Soon, my suspicions about them were confirmed. That boy got caught in the misguided deed of lusting over another man, inspired by the rotten sexual revolution of Western civilization. He was sleeping with a man much older than he, the garment merchant, a man with a wife and three children. Nashid was sleeping with a married man, you see. And by doing so, he robbed a woman of a husband and young children of a father." Osman was speaking through deep breaths, panting almost. "We then did what needed to be done to a robber," he bragged, "and made the entire city watch the punishment for a thief like him who stole so much from those innocent people. The city had never before witnessed the implementation of such a decree. Let me tell you, the simultaneous delivery of public justice and mass education was a remarkable feat!" He clapped. "It set the precedence for carrying out similar future punishments across the region.

"I digress. My caliphates and I blindfolded them both, took them to the tallest minaret in the city center, and shoved them off the minaret to fall hundreds of feet down with an eager crowd looking up, yearning for the noble judgment."

Rami's face twitched in agony.

Osman then leaned forward with an astonished look. "I watched them both fall, flailing, plunging to their deaths. But you know what? Nashid survived the fall. He didn't die," Osman said. He pushed himself back against the sofa. "I couldn't believe it! But then, you know what we did to him when he kept breathing, despite broken limbs and a fractured skull?"

Rami closed his eyes. He knew what Osman was getting at.

"The crowd gathered stones and hurled them at him until that thief stopped crawling." Osman tilted his head. "You know what it's like, Rami, don't you?" he said, smug-faced.

Rami shuddered.

"Of course you do," Osman went on. "You came this close once yourself to getting what you deserved," he said delightedly, as though he were telling of a time when he'd had a wonderful picnic in the park. "It was a mistake to let you go. I should've finished you and your *lover* when I had the chance."

Rami felt anger rising in him.

"Anyway. Guess who led me to Nashid."

"I don't want to know," Rami said through scrunched teeth. "I don't want to hear it."

"But you must, Rami," Osman slammed his palms together. "That's the best part of the story!"

There was a silence.

"It was his mother; may God bless her brave soul; it was Saeeda. She told on her son when she found him naked in bed with another man, stealing from his wife and children what wasn't rightfully his!" Osman barked. "After stoning him to death, we left their corpses on the street for days for dogs to feast on spilled guts and rotting flesh, you know, left the animals for the animals." Osman let out a cynical laugh, arms crossed. "Tell me you don't think it's funny," he said in a cheery voice.

Osman then leaned forward. "That's how justice is served."

"Stoning people to death, burning women and children alive, enforcing your beliefs onto others: that's what you call God's work?" Rami snapped. "Who are you kidding? You're the thief; you're the criminal. You're the one who's taken from people what did not belong to you: their lives, their happiness, all in the name of your beliefs. Yours. You don't speak for me or any other Muslim in the world. You're not doing anyone any favors! You've committed crimes against humanity, and nothing will change that!" the words spilled from his mouth like blood gushing through an open wound. He wished he could snatch them before they reached Osman's ears and shove them back down his throat. But it was too late. Undoubtedly, any possibility of his seeing the rising sun was now gone. Rami was certain he'd signed his death warrant with this outburst.

Osman's mouth creased in a smile. "You still have that spark in you. I always liked that about you." A chortle burst through Osman's nostrils and sounded as if he'd snorted. "Wait, I'm forgetting something," he said, slapping his cheeks in mock amazement. Then he flicked his chin at one of the guards who scuttled into the other room where Osman had prayed a few minutes ago.

Moments later, Sadiq returned with someone.

Rami's eyes fell on the person standing next to Sadiq, stayed.

His mouth slowly opened, recognizing the curly hair despite the gray, the broad nose, heavy-lidded and sleep-deprived green eyes. Rami suddenly became aware of the time that had passed between the moment he had stood at the entrance of that crumbling cement building in the Manga Jungle, watching Danyaal emerge behind his assailants and now.

It felt surreal. Somewhat strange. Like the entire world had come to a standstill. The things Rami had longed to say to Danyaal all these years were again bubbling in his chest. He made a wheezing sound and realized he had neglected once again to take a breath. He felt his face getting warm, burning almost.

Osman was saying something. Rami turned to look at him.

"I said you thought I'd made it up to lure you here," Osman repeated. "Go on." His upper lip curled in a sneer. "Go on, Rami. Say hello to your *lover*," Osman pressed his lower lip with his upper teeth when he said the last word as if relishing it.

Rami arose from the sofa. He walked up to Danyaal, who was standing looking down at his naked feet. Rami approached him and cast a strained look in his direction. Danyaal lifted his head, a hint of recognition appeared in Danyaal's irises.

"Danyaal. It's me."

"Rami," Danyaal mouthed.

Rami's fingers laced his.

"I'm here."

Rami could tell Danyaal hadn't washed or had a change of clothes in a while. He stared at Danyaal's face, and nostalgia washed over him. The way they once were, young and carefree. In the handful of moments that just passed, Rami went back in time and recalled the wideness of the roads when they rode on his motorcycle, the wetness of Lahore Canal when they dipped their toes in the water, and the scent of grass on warm summer evenings when they lay next to each other holding hands. Standing before Danyaal at that moment, Rami felt heartache and a profound longing for the life he'd left behind in Lahore.

The air inside the room grew increasingly dense, almost suffocating, saturated with sweat, a palpable sense of fear, and overwhelming sadness.

And then Danyaal said something that nearly floored Rami.

"There's a field of marigolds in the countryside near me where I go every year in spring and think of you, Rami," Danyaal murmured with a slow, tired smile.

Rami flinched, jumped almost. Danyaal had remembered him all these years. Rami had lived most of his adult life, assuming Danyaal had removed him from his memory. But he hadn't. It was quite the opposite. Danyaal hadn't stopped loving Rami or stopped thinking about him. He had remembered Rami last year, the year before, and the years prior. Danyaal might not have extended forgiveness toward Rami. But he also hadn't allowed himself to forget about him.

"Danyaal—" Rami croaked.

And before the tears could leak, out of the corner of his eye, Rami noticed Osman tipping his chin at the guards. Osman's gesture of dragging his left thumb across Adam's apple sent shivers down Rami's body. Then, a flurry of activities around him: through the swaying makeshift curtain, a sliver of the window became exposed, and Rami caught a glimpse of a blonde ponytail in the courtyard below. He yanked the pink bedsheet off the window. And just then, a round, metallic object gleaming in the morning sun shot up.

Someone shouted.

A bullet hit the TV and shattered the screen.

Rami screamed at Danyaal to get down.

One of the guards reached for something from under his shirt. The window smashed, and the cylindrical object flew in, releasing white smoke.

Rami heard Osman yelling something.

He took Danyaal's hand into his, squeezed. The front door slammed open with a loud bang, and a team of masked men carrying weapons stormed in.

Lying on the floor with his hands above his head, Rami felt nothing but gratitude for Steve's sharp thinking: a risky move that possibly saved their lives. Before leaving the armored vehicle, Steve had given Rami a second tracking chip. He had asked him to find an opportunity to slide it into the pocket of one of the men with whom Rami would come into contact. Possibly the one who would frisk him. That way, the FBI and CSIS would continue to track Rami's movement and record the conversation even if Rami were no longer in possession of the watch. Because of that—because of the chip Rami had slipped into Sadiq's pocket when he patted Rami down the first time—it led the authorities to zero in to their location and rescue them.

The last thing Rami remembered before losing consciousness in the hovering white smoke was Osman's figure backpedaling with an astonished look plastered on his face and Danyaal's hand reaching for his.

TWENTY-TWO

December 06, 2014

St. Mary's Church in Crawley, a town in West Sussex County, is located about forty-five kilometers south of London, England. After arriving at Heathrow, Rami took the express train to Paddington Station. It was a chilly afternoon. The rain had begun falling by the time the train pulled away from the airport station. He sat by the window and looked through the blurry glass, listening to the murmuring of the raindrops sounding like musical chimes. According to the directions Danyaal had provided, he would transfer to another train after arriving at the station.

Rami felt the damp yet invigorating breeze on his face when he exited the platform and noticed that the rain had let up. He fished a pair of leather gloves from his coat pocket and put them on before clutching the luggage and raising his collar against the brisk wind. After some contemplation, he decided to take a lengthy walk around town to London Bridge. From there, he would catch the Thameslink train for another hour-long ride to Crawley. Rami ambled along Hyde Park Square, slight right onto Oxford Street, along the British Museum toward St. Paul Cathedral, and down Cannon Street before turning right onto King William Street.

St. Mary's was on Southgate Drive, several blocks from Rami's hotel. The spire became visible as he walked toward the church through the town decked for the holiday season. The building that came into view was a gray stone Victorian with high-arched stained-glass windows flanked by a wrought-iron fence. Rami heard the bells ring from the tower as he grabbed and opened the heavy wooden door.

Entering the nave, the air felt still, infused with the lingering scent of incense, candles, and musty prayer books. There was a glimmer of afternoon sun peeking through the stained glass, their spectral hues splashing against the white walls before spilling onto the tiled floor.

The church appeared empty. Rami gazed toward the elevated chancel, beyond the flowers and freshly polished candlesticks, and observed someone sitting on a bench facing away from him. He stepped forward and noticed they were at an organ console beneath a facade of tall metal pipes. The organist turned slightly to their left. Rami's heart quickened. He took in the side profile of Danyaal. Dappled lighting at the corner of the nave had partially shadowed his face. Rami looked on as Danyaal adjusted his navy blazer. He watched Danyaal placing his hands over the keys and beginning to play. The organ came to life.

Deep musical notes filled the vaulted ceiling like sunlight awakening the dawn, rubbing its sleep-clogged eyes. Danyaal continued, and Rami marveled at how he—Danyaal—had embraced his love of music through all these years. The way his limbs glided across that seemingly complicated instrument, Rami felt his heart swell with admiration for his companion—for his once lover—separated by time and distance.

He lowered himself onto an old oak pew to the right. Waited. When Danyaal finished a few minutes later, silence descended the nave until Rami interrupted the quietude with applause.

Startled, Danyaal flinched and turned toward him. Rami's thought wandered over to the day they had first met at the college canteen and how Danyaal had jumped when Rami, inches away from Danyaal's ears, had said hello.

Danyaal spotted Rami. A smile appeared on his lips.

"Welcome to Crawley," Danyaal said, approaching Rami. "You made it."

Rami took his hand.

"Let me show you around."

Danyaal took Rami on a brief tour of the church. He showed Rami the small vestry room on the right, the prayer room, his office, the kitchen. Walking down the hallway toward the back of the building, Rami realized Danyaal was saying something.

"What?"

"Where did you go?"

"I'm here."

"Rami—"

"I was just thinking."

"Yes?"

"—That I never made it to St. Andrew's church on Nabha Road," Rami said.

"Oh." Danyaal stopped and gave Rami a timid, close-lipped smile. He then asked if Rami was hungry.

"Starving," Rami said.

THE SKY was dimming and quickly spreading the wintry darkness by the time they walked out of the church and made their way to a nearby café with salmon-colored walls and a glass storefront. Danyaal, wearing a pair of gray slacks and a maroon turtleneck under the blazer, sat across from Rami in a leather booth with red and beige stripes. Rami glanced at this grown man whose head had rested on Rami's stomach many times.

"I'm glad you came," Danyaal said.

Rami nodded. "Thanks for agreeing to see me."

"Under better circumstances this time." Danyaal smiled.

"Yes."

Rami paused for a moment. "And after so long."

Danyaal sighed.

They sat in silence, stealing uneasy glances at each other.

Rami did his best to hold back the deluge of questions percolating in his chest: *why did you leave Lahore without seeing me? Why did you go away without saying goodbye? Why wouldn't you return my messages? Did you know what I had planned for us after the night we spent in the Manga Jungle? Did you know how painful it'd been for me to live with the things left unsaid for so long?* Instead, he mindlessly nudged at the silver fork and the knife placed atop the red-checkered tablecloth.

They hadn't had the opportunity to see or talk much to each other after the authorities arrested Osman in Toronto. Shortly after receiving medical care and having given a statement, Danyaal took the next flight back to England. Earlier, Deidre had told Rami that the FBI had contacted Brian and that he was on his way from Chicago.

"I'm sorry I won't be able to meet Brian," Danyaal lifted the oxygen mask and said. They were sitting at the foot of the cab of an ambulance, ready to transport them to the hospital for medical treatment.

"He's very understanding," Rami said.

The paramedics began escorting them into separate ambulances.

"Thank you, Rami," Danyaal said. "If there's anything I can do for you ..."

Rami hesitated. "There is one thing," he said after a brief silence.

"Yes?"

"I would like to visit you in England."

The ambulance doors were closing, and Rami couldn't help but notice a look of reluctant forgiveness on Danyaal's face.

"Danyaal?"

"Yes, of course. I'd like that," Danyaal's voice entered Rami's ears seconds before the ambulance's siren came on.

"How're things back home?" Rami asked now after a tall server with a pale, freckled face brought them drinks and sandwiches. "Lahore, I mean. How are your parents?"

Danyaal informed Rami that Gibril died in the year 2000 from a heart attack. He said his mother moved in with him for a few years after that.

"She passed away in a hospital in London in 2005," Danyaal said.

"And your sister? How is she?"

"Saman married a man from the States and now lives in New York. Has three children."

Rami toyed with his glass of whiskey before taking a bite out of the triangle-shaped chicken salad sandwich.

"You and Brian." Danyaal tipped his chin at Rami's ring.

"Engaged," Rami said. He thought of his fiancé back in Chicago, worrying about him. Despite how foolishly Rami had handled the whole episode in Toronto, Brian graciously had given him the time and the space to travel to London and reconnect with Danyaal.

"After fourteen or so years of being together, we finally decided to go for it in August of this year," Rami said. He cleared his throat. "Someone special in your life, too, Danyaal?"

Danyaal took a sip from his drink, a gin and tonic, and flipped the back of his left hand before Rami. "No engagement ring on my index finger," he said. A gentle snort burst through Danyaal's nostrils.

Rami lowered his gaze.

Danyaal then inquired about Rami's family in Pakistan. "Have you been back?"

Rami told him that Papa and Amma died the same year, 1998, due to health complications. He told Danyaal he hadn't returned to Lahore or seen anyone from there since he had come to America.

"That was the condition, you know? That once I left, I wouldn't return."

"Oh," Danyaal said, wrapped his fingers around the drink, and didn't ask any more questions. Rami had known Danyaal to be instinctive when they were teenagers. He had a feeling that hadn't changed about him now as a grown man.

They carried on the perfunctory conversation for the rest of their meal.

"Let's go for a walk," Danyaal said after they finished.

"Where to?"

"There's a cemetery behind the church. It's quiet. I go there periodically to clear my head. We can go there."

Rami nodded. "Lead the way."

They walked south for a few blocks before turning onto a narrow, cobblestone street. The night had fallen. Rami could see the feeble glow of a lamplight up ahead, shining on the gated cemetery entrance. They crossed the gate, and the outlines of several tombstones became visible. There was a cool breeze sweeping through under the cloudless sky. Rami hugged his arms against the wind.

"There's a chill in the air," Danyaal said, eyeing Rami.

"A little."

They took small steps.

"When did you leave Lahore?" Danyaal asked.

Rami recalled the day at the airport when he had stood before Papa and hugged him for the last time before boarding the flight to Turkey.

"Lots happened since you left," he said.

"You can tell me."

Walking beside Danyaal, Rami recounted how, for weeks after Danyaal's departure, he continued to receive threats from Osman's men. He shared with him the memory of Jalil coming home one day in May of 1988 in a state of panic.

"God," Danyaal whispered. He gave Rami a sober look.

"Jalil had learned from some in the *madrasa* that Osman was desperately seeking revenge after being humiliated at the Manga Jungle," Rami said, noticing Danyaal's face twitching a little at the mention of that day.

He shared with Danyaal that Jalil had bribed someone to get Rami an expedited passport so that he could flee the country.

"Jalil arranged through a man for me to travel to Europe. After arriving, I stayed in Istanbul for several months before another man contacted me and slipped me onto a freight ship transporting oil to the United States. I spent twelve days crossing the Atlantic Ocean, hiding at the pitch-black bottom of the fuel-carrying vessel. I only went up to the main deck once the kitchen closed and the crew slept. I'd take whatever uneaten food I could find and scurry back below deck for fear of being caught for being trafficked to America."

"Rami." Danyaal held his breath.

"I spent twelve unforgettable nights surrounded by the stench of gasoline. Sometimes, I would pass out from inhaling fumes and have nightmares. And when I got to the United States, I did what the man in Istanbul had instructed. Before encountering an immigration officer, I disposed of the passport in the Men's Room and requested refugee asylum when prompted for identification."

"Twelve days?" Danyaal covered his mouth with his hand.

At a distance, some mourners loomed over a few gravestones. A puff of air swept across, carrying the scent of pine needles. Rami could hear the sniffles of a woman visiting nearby.

"Twelve days."

They were now toward the back of the cemetery.

"Rami?"

"Yes, Danyaal."

"You remember the times we waited for *amawas*?" Danyaal pointed at the thin crescent of the moon appearing in the dark sky.

"*Amawas*," Rami said and let out a soft grunt.

"The sighting of the new moon. How we waited for it."

The seams of Rami's lips parted in a slight smile. "I remember," he said.

"Us singing songs those few days of every month during *amawas*."

Rami stopped. He closed his eyes, remembering.

"We eagerly waited for the dark moon to disappear and the new moon to arrive," Danyaal reminisced. "How happy we felt. You remember that?"

Rami could sense Danyaal smiling, his eyes on the moon.

"Except this time, *amawas* took twenty-six years before the new moon appeared," Rami said, his voice breaking. He opened his eyes and looked the other way, fought back the tears.

"The dark moon lasted longer than either of us anticipated," Danyaal's voice was weak. "So much slipped away in the wait this time."

"Our youth."

"Us."

A moonlit hush fell over them. They resumed walking past more graves: some new and taken care of, others looking old and crumbling.

"It's somewhat strange to see you as a grown man," Rami said.

Danyaal smiled and shoved his hands in his pants pockets. "And you."

"Danyaal?"

"Yes."

"Are you happy?" Rami asked.

"Happy?"

Rami looked at Danyaal with curiosity and concern. "I mean, the path life has taken you on so far. Are you satisfied with the outcome?"

With this, Rami saw Danyaal's chest inflating. Danyaal took a deep breath and looked down at his feet.

"I came to your house in Lahore, you know?" Rami stopped and turned to face Danyaal. Danyaal lifted his eyes to Rami. "I came by your house many times after—" the words got stuck in Rami's throat, "—after what'd happened that day."

"I know you did," said Danyaal. His face carried an indecipherable look. Rami couldn't tell whether the slow-appearing lines on his forehead were due to the recollection of the trauma he endured or the rising anger. "My parents informed me."

"I wish you had let me see you. I wish I'd gotten a chance to speak to you, Danyaal," Rami said through labored breaths.

Danyaal placed his hand on Rami's shoulder. "What's the point in dwelling on it now? It's in the past," he said. Even the dull moonlight and night shadows couldn't conceal the teardrops on the verge of leaking from his eyes.

"I wish I didn't, but I still think about it. And now, seeing you again, I would do anything to get past this," Rami said. "For so long, I have been holding on to this apolo ..."

Danyaal placed his finger on Rami's lips. "There's no need for that."

"Danyaal."

"You asked if I was happy."

Rami gave him a slow nod.

"I've made peace with things, with life. I've no complaints from anyone, Rami. I'm glad Osman is behind bars, content that I get to practice my beliefs and live in a community that has embraced me and my values." Danyaal breathed deeply.

"But if you're wondering if I've gotten over you not being in my life ..." he stopped, paused, "... then the answer is *no*. I've simply grown accustomed to existing without your presence. That's the beauty of us humans. We have the remarkable ability to continue through life, carrying our broken hearts and embracing our grief.

"We can't reconstruct the past, Rami. We'd never know what might have happened had we stayed together." His breathing became uneven. "We can merely concede to unyielding truths of existence and learn to live with what happened to us. I'm afraid we can't get past this," Danyaal said.

Rami felt warm tears spilling onto his cold cheeks. "I know we can't change the past. But I wish there was something I could do to ease this burden!" His voice quivered.

Danyaal reached across and draped his arms around Rami. "There is one thing you can do," he said. "You can let go of the past."

They stood holding each other that frosty night for a while.

For over two decades, Rami had thought countless times about how he would convey his regrets to Danyaal that day when he finally saw him. He practiced in front of a mirror, spoke out loud while driving on Lake Shore Drive, trying to come up with the right words to say that not a day went by when he didn't wish he could go back in time and change things.

But now, in Danyaal's presence, there was no need for words. The healing had begun; he could sense. A flicker of hope appeared in Rami's heart that Danyaal might forgive him. Even if not in the present moment.

"There's something else," Rami said after he cleared his vision by squeezing the inner corners of his eyes with his thumb and forefinger.

Danyaal's eyes drifted toward Rami's face. "Yes?"

"Come to Chicago."

"To visit?"

"Yes. And for another thing," Rami said coyly.

"What thing?"

"I'd rather you come and experience it," Rami said. "Will you come?"

Danyaal looked at him for a few moments. Blinked.

"—It would mean the world to me."

"Rami—"

"Will you, Danyaal?"

There was a pause. Another undecipherable look on Danyaal's face: curiosity at odds with hesitation.

"Please—"

"—All right," Danyaal said after a few seconds of deliberation. "Fine."

TWENTY-THREE

March 27, 2015

Someone knocked on the door. Rami averted his eyes from the mirror and glanced at the clock on the wall. It was an old hand-wound clock with green numbers on a beige face; the hour hand was reaching 'seven'. He heard the knuckles of a hand rapping on the door again and arose from the bench.

"Just a minute," Rami grunted as he dragged his slippers against the floor. He answered the door, and there was a man in the doorway, wearing a yellow and red uniform and a baseball hat holding a bouquet. He appeared in his mid-twenties and had hairy forearms and deep-set black eyes.

"Delivery for you." He handed Rami the flowers.

Rami took the wrapped package from him and ran his fingers over the bouquet.

As the deliveryman fished for an electronic signature pad, something caught Rami's eye.

"How did that happen?" Rami signed the electronic signature pad and gave him a sidelong glance, remarking at the scar that split his right eyebrow.

The man in uniform ran his finger over the scar. "Oh, this?"

Rami nodded.

"I tripped and fell down the stairs at school when I was ten. Ended up hitting the edge of the bottom landing," he said. "I got lucky. Thank God it didn't pop my eyeball out."

"Very lucky."

The young man paused. His left eyebrow arched. "What made you ask?"

Rami offered him a thin smile. "It reminded me of someone," he said. "Someone I knew a long time ago."

The deliveryman tipped his hat at Rami. "All right, then …" he glanced at the signature on the pad and gave Rami a look, "… have a good evening."

Rami waved and watched the deliveryman walk down the backstage corridor, past the other two dressing rooms, before closing the door behind him.

He read the card that came with the bouquet. It had come from his friend Susan. 'Break a leg today, Rami!' It read.

Rami placed the flowers to his right on the dresser, sat back down on the bench in front of the lighted mirror, and began the preparation.

Shortly after, Rami's gaze shifted to the bouquet to his right. It made him think of the scar running down the eyebrow of the deliveryman and the person it'd reminded him of.

'Listen, boy. I hope there's still a chance of you growing up to be a man one day' Jalil's voice echoed in Rami's head.

He recalled the times Jalil had thrown him scrutinizing glares with his arched, split brow.

Rami's eyes returned to the mirror. He heard Jalil's accusing shouts receding behind the billowing cloud of his faded past.

He applied the lip liner.

Another knock on the door, and Rami saw Brian come in.

"Hey," Brian greeted Rami with a bright smile.

Rami took Brian's hand in his.

"Ready for tonight?"

Rami sat still and glanced at Brian's reflection in the mirror behind him. "As ready as I'll be."

Brian squeezed Rami's hand before asking who'd sent the flowers. Rami told him.

"Hmm," Brian grunted.

Rami fixed him with a curious stare. "What was that for?"

"Nothing," he said. "I thought these might be from Danyaal." Brian leaned over and smelled the bouquet.

Rami heaved a sigh, said nothing.

"No word?"

"No," Rami said, trying to hide the disappointment. Danyaal hadn't messaged back after he'd sent him the date of the show. Standing behind Rami, Brian cupped his palms around Rami's shoulders.

"I love you," he uttered smilingly.

IT WAS time to head to the stage. His performance at a local venue on the north side of Chicago was about to begin.

While waiting at the backstage stairs, Rami adjusted the scoop neckline of his gold gown and listened for the announcement.

Near the end of the introduction, when he heard, *'Please welcome to the stage, the one, the only, Sassy L'Hore!'* Rami took a deep breath and climbed the stairs. He entered the stage through black curtains.

With an engaging, ready-to-entertain smile, Rami let his eyes roam, admiring the packed hall before him. Amidst thunderous applause and excited whistles, he stood still and took it all in. He patiently waited for the wave of excitement to fade away gradually. His calm demeanor was a stark contrast to the fervor around him. His gaze swept over the seas of faces. They were cheering for him.

Then, Rami's glance skimmed past a face.

Returned.

Lingered.

In the third row, center aisle, a man wearing blue trousers, a white button-down shirt, and a plaid blazer was in the audience, clapping. Rami's heart skipped a beat following that man's profile: curly, salt-and-pepper hair, green eyes, dimpled cheeks.

Rami's mouth creased in a smile. No matter how crowded the hall, no matter how low the lighting, he would've had no problem recognizing Danyaal's face.

Rami's gleaming gaze caught Danyaal staring back.

Rami's lips moved, "*Yaarana.*"

"*Yaarana,*" Danyaal mouthed back.

It was a simple word for companionship, but what Rami understood was redemption. Salvation. Forgiveness.

His entire being became as buoyant as the swaying rainbow feathers on the boa curled around his neck.

He had finally found Danyaal.

Before the tears could spill, Rami pulled his head back, arms extended. The lights dimmed. The sound of musical notes reverberated through the packed venue.

The performance began.

AFTERWORD

A good part of Rami's journey into adulthood resonates with my own experiences concerning family, friendships, bullying, and accepting my sexuality. Like many others, I struggled to come to terms with my emotions until I was able to discover and embrace my true self. I view my writing of this love story as a form of catharsis, a letter to my younger self, and a way to convey my experiences to others who may be going through similar challenges.

Rami and Danyaal's struggle with bullying bears a striking resemblance to what many modern-day households encounter. Especially within the LGBTQ+ community, the battle for equal rights and to overcome the fear of being persecuted at home and abroad continues. From the brutal hurling of gay men from rooftops by

ISIS in Syria in 2015 to the senseless mass shooting at the Pulse nightclub in the United States in 2016 to the smug denial of the LGBTQ+ presence in Chechnya by the country's leader in 2017—the struggle for freedom from retribution goes on.

Organizations like Rainbow Railroad, a Canadian-based not-for-profit, helps lesbian, gay, bisexual, transgender, queer, and intersex individuals escape violence in their home countries.

To help or to learn more about its work, please visit www.rainbowrailroad.org.

Thank you.

Zia Ahmad
December 31, 2023